THE WHITE LADY

THE WHITE LADY

A Novel

JACQUELINE WINSPEAR

HARPER
An Imprint of HarperCollins*Publishers*

THE WHITE LADY. Copyright © 2023 by Jacqueline Winspear. All rights reserved. Printed in the United States of America. No part of this book may be used or reproduced in any manner whatsoever without written permission except in the case of brief quotations embodied in critical articles and reviews. For information, address HarperCollins Publishers, 195 Broadway, New York, NY 10007.

HarperCollins books may be purchased for educational, business, or sales promotional use. For information, please email the Special Markets Department at SPsales@harpercollins.com.

FIRST EDITION

Designed by Kyle O'Brien

Library of Congress Cataloging-in-Publication Data has been applied for.

ISBN 978-0-06-286798-8

23 24 25 26 27 LBC 5 4 3 2 1

In memory of the wonderful writer and teacher, Barbara Abercrombie, who died in 2022. Barbara was a UCLA Writers' Program Distinguished Instructor, and my dear friend.

And remember, where you have a concentration of power in a few hands, all too frequently men with the mentality of gangsters get control. History has proven that.

—John Dalberg-Acton, Lord Acton
(1834–1902)

Society prepares the crime; the criminal commits it.

—Vittori Alfieri (1749–1803)

War is a thug's game. The thug strikes first and harder. He doesn't go by rules and he isn't afraid of hurting people.

—Anne Morrow Lindbergh,
The War Within & Without

THE WHITE LADY

CHAPTER 1

Kent, England
1947

E very morning as Rose Mackie leaned over the bars of the wooden cot and picked up her three-year-old daughter, she gave thanks for the cottage. She gave thanks for the roof over her head, and she gave thanks for the fact that she wasn't putting up with Jim's mum and dad, and she wasn't living in a London prefab set among the thousands of other London prefabs built in haste to accommodate families left homeless during six years of war. She gave thanks because her little Susie could run across fields in fresh country air, and the child didn't have to wear a scarf over her nose to protect her tiny lungs from the lumpy yellow-green London smog that looked like something nasty the dog had brought up. Just the thought of those pea-soupers made Rose feel queasy.

A lot of things made Rose feel sick about living in London, the city its dwellers called "the Smoke." There was Jim's family, for a start—in fact, his family alone amounted to a good reason not to feel very well at all. But here, now, Jim, Rose and their precious child were safe. Or as safe as they could be. They'd managed to get out of London, exchanging the Smoke for the quiet of the country. In the past year, since they had altered the course of their lives—forever, they hoped—Jim had lost that sunken look in his cheeks and those lines of worry that no young man of five and twenty should feel every time he ran his hand across his forehead. There were no longer dark circles under his pale-blue eyes, and he didn't startle every time wind rattled the windowpanes. They had escaped London. They had run as far as they could from the bomb sites—and more than anything, they had dragged themselves out from under the fingernails of the Mackie family.

It had been a miracle, the way things had fallen into place. Rose even thought her mum, dad and brothers must all be helping from what her aunt called "the other side." Without doubt, luck had been with Rose, Jim and their little girl when they stepped off the Victoria to Hastings motor coach in the small village of Shacklehurst, on the winding rural route some sixty-five miles from London. They had gone only as far as their fare budget would take them. Not knowing quite what to do next, they walked into a teashop across the street from the bus stop to ask if there was somewhere in the village they could stay for a night or two. In truth, they knew it didn't look as if they were there for just a night or two, what with a couple of suitcases, the child on Rose's hip wearing half the clothes she had to her name, and a tension in their voices that might as well have announced to everyone in the teashop that they were not, in fact, on a bit of a holiday. The proprietor gave them a broad smile when they entered her establishment, which was a good start, Rose thought. She had noticed the spotless shop and that the woman was wearing a clean, starched pinny, with the only indication that she was rushed off her feet being a single errant curler left in her hair. And people weren't always welcoming in the country when they heard an accent or turn of phrase that screamed "We're Londoners!" Still smiling, the woman looked them up and down and nodded, beckoning them aside and adding that by chance she had a spare room she could let them have for a few nights, and could put out a breakfast for them into the bargain, perhaps even a supper, though she'd need their ration books. They had to be off the premises during the day because there were customers to consider and she didn't want anyone hearing heavy feet or a baby screaming above their heads while they were enjoying a cup of tea and a cream bun. That was alright with Jim and Rose; after all, they had a good few things to accomplish during the course of their country sojourn. Finding work was at the top of the list, and a place to live came next—very much next.

Lady Luck remained at their side. In short order their new landlady, Mrs. Butler, told them a local farmer had just lost a worker, the silly old whatsit having ruptured himself so he couldn't do the job anymore. The absent worker was getting on in years anyway, so the farmer knew it was coming, and what with first losing men to the army and then the land girls demobilized, she said it looked like Jim had turned up in Shackle-hurst at the right time because the farmer needed a hand with the cattle and sheep, and had let the word out that he was looking for a strong bloke who would put his back into anything asked of him. Mind you, the gossip was that every last job on the farm would be asked of him.

The family walked a mile and a half along the road and then on a woodland path through a few acres of pine forest to find Mr. Wicks, the farmer. He was a plain-talking man who took Jim inside the farmhouse and made it clear he would brook no shirking, adding, with a shake of the head, that an aversion to hard work was half the trouble with Fred, the worker who had ruptured himself. Old Fred had forgotten how to lift something heavy because every day of his working life he had done his best to avoid it. "No muscle, that was his problem," said Wicks, reaching across the table to feel Jim's bicep. He nodded approval. Jim swore he was as strong as an ox, that he knew cattle and sheep inside and out and could drive a tractor—driving being his specialty. Oh yes, driving was definitely Jim's specialty. An awful lot of blokes from his part of London thought well of his skill behind the wheel.

Jim landed the job. A tied cottage went with it, though the two-bedroom accommodation needed a coat or three of paint, and there were vermin to be evicted. That was nothing to Jim—he'd come face-to-face with pests who were a lot more trouble than a few rats or mice. As he emerged from the farmhouse, having shaken hands with the farmer, adding that yes, he'd be ready to start work at six the following morning, Jim opened his arms, ready to embrace his wife and daughter. "Nice work if you can get it, Rosie, and I've got it! And guess what? The missus in there needs a hand with a bit of cleaning a couple of mornings a week. You up for it?"

Of course she was up for it. So there they were, settled, with no furniture, no pots and pans and no crockery. Then Mrs. Butler said she had some old china she could let them have, and by the way, could Rose help her out on Saturday afternoons, because it was when day trippers came out to the country and rolled in for a cup of tea and a cream bun or scones after they'd had a walk through the forest, which meant she was run off her feet and could hardly keep up. Jim worked Saturday mornings, so it all fell into place—he'd look after Susie when he returned to the cottage at one o'clock, while Rose brought home some pin money in the evening. Every little bit helped. Now they had a roof over their heads, they had work and they would get the other bits and bobs to make their house a home as they went along.

That was over a year ago now, and they hadn't seen any family since—which was alright with Rose. Not that she had much in the way of family. She had been evacuated to Sussex at the end of August 1939, just before war was declared, and was living with her foster family when everything in her world changed. The billeting officer came to the door to tell her that her mum, dad and two brothers—who were fifteen and sixteen, old enough to remain in London and work, but with not enough years on them for the army—had perished when a bomb came down on the house while they were halfway through dinner. There they were, Mum, Dad, Andy and Bill, minding their own business, eating sausages with mashed-up turnips and a few peas, when, boom! Now they were on the other side.

She'd gone to live with a maiden aunt as soon as she turned fourteen—working age—just a few months later. Rose, Andy and Bill had been close in years. Her dad always joked that her mum hadn't seen her feet for a good while, what with those babies coming one after the other. Her brother Bill earned himself a clip around the ear when he grinned and said, "And whose fault was that, Dad?" Rose missed her family, truth be told.

At eighteen Rose was employed on the sweet counter at Woolworths, and one evening met Jim at a dance in Camberwell. Jim took to Rose from the minute they began talking. She was a down-to-earth girl, with no side to her. She wasn't mouthy—not like some when a soldier chatted them up—and she wasn't a wallflower either. Solid, that was Rose, an honest sort, and it didn't take long for Jim to love her for it. In fact, Jim adored his Rose. He was with the Royal Electrical and Mechanical Engineers—REME—where his ability to remain calm under pressure led to training in bomb disposal before being stationed in London, where his skills were needed most. Experience had taught him how to keep breathing and retain a steady hand while executing the precise movements required to remove the detonator from one of those great big UXBs—unexploded bombs. He explained to Rose that the Germans deliberately made a lot of bombs so they didn't explode when they landed, because they knew the strain of having a UXB in the street, its menacing tail fins sticking out of the tarmac, would cause the British people to get nervy. It was all to undermine morale. Rose remembered those words when she met Jim's family. It seemed to her that Jim's dad was like that, and so were his brothers; they had dodgy detonators that scared the you-know-what out of people and undermined their morale.

Jim's family, all still very much alive, lived south of the river in Walworth. John Mackie—Jim's dad—was angry when Jim told the family he and Rose were planning to move to the country. He told them Jim was mad to leave the manor —that's what he called it, his "manor," as if he owned the streets, which really, Rose supposed he did. The old man disowned Jim after the young couple added that they were going anyway because they wanted to bring up Susie in fresh country air, away from bomb sites. John Mackie got up from the table, took an ornate china bowl and ewer from a marble-topped sideboard, poured water from the ewer into the bowl and began scrubbing his hands. He made a show of shaking out the water and taking a towel to dry himself. "I wash my hands of you—but you will be back. You wait and see. Even if you leave her and the girl behind, you will be back. You belong in this family, Jim Mackie, and don't ever think otherwise—you're nothing, nothing at all without us, and let's see the look on your yellow face when you come crawling home."

"That was horrible," said Rose later.

"We both know what he's like," said Jim. "He's a hotheaded, miserable old sod."

In those early weeks, every day without word from the Mackie family was a relief, and now Rose had begun to believe she would never see them again. As far as she and Jim were concerned, his people could languish away in his father's so-called manor for a long time. They'd had enough of their London lives to last them all the way to the other side, wherever it was. To be fair, Jim's mum had cried when they walked away, but she was no angel either.

Rose popped Susie into her pushchair, tucked a blanket around her chubby little legs, handed her Teddy One Eye and locked the door, pressing hard against it to make sure the lock held. It was always important to make sure. She stopped for a moment as she maneuvered the pushchair along the path, turning to glance back at the dwelling. It wouldn't have been much to most; a sixteenth-century weatherboard cottage with only cold running water—and yes, it could do with a drop of paint, some new flashing around the base of the chimney, and that outside toilet was bitterly cold in winter—but it had become her beloved home. She tucked a strand of coppery hair behind her ear, smiled and said aloud, "Thank you, my lovely house." Then she went on her way, wondering if she'd see the quiet woman this morning, the one who walked along the road every single day. That's what they called her in the village—"the quiet woman"—and Rose could understand why, though she was also known as "the White lady" on account of her surname and the fact that she seemed like, well, a lady.

Although Rose had never heard a word pass the woman's lips, she must have said something to someone, because she went into the village every few days. Rose noticed that as soon as the woman saw her emerging from the cottage or walking along the road toward her, she would adjust her hat as if to hide her face under the wide brim, then pull up the collar of her dark-grey mackintosh and walk on, for all the world as if Rose were invisible. But Rose persisted because she wanted to greet her neighbors; after all, for a London girl it could be lonely in the country if you didn't know people.

"Good morning," she would say, hoping the woman would look up.

Nothing. Never a reply. Never a smile, though once or twice there was a nod on those days when it appeared as if the woman had seen Rose. And perhaps that was it—she was so deep in thought, she hadn't heard a thing.

Then one day, as the White lady approached, little Susie took the initiative. Rose thanked the house, as usual, and as she turned around to open the gate and step out onto the road, she saw the woman just a few steps away. Susie beamed a smile, waving Teddy One Eye as if determined to gain the White lady's attention.

"Hello quiet lady," Susie had said, before Rose could even open her mouth, then threw Teddy One Eye in the woman's direction. Susie's babyish effort at communication came out as "Hayo kite yadey."

The woman stopped, picked up the toy and looked down at Susie as if she were taking in her blond curls, scarlet rosebud lips and that little nub of a nose with its liberal smattering of freckles. Susie reached forward, fists opening and closing in anticipation of Teddy's return.

"Well, good morning to you, Miss Susan Mackie," said the woman as she brushed a few fallen leaves from Teddy One Eye before handing him back to the child.

She smiled and nodded, bidding Rose a good morning before continuing on her way.

Rose watched her walk away until she turned right to step over the stile that gave way to a narrow path leading into the densest part of Denbury Forest. Rose was perplexed. The woman knew Susie's name.

can't say I know much about the woman," said Mrs. Wicks, sitting at the farmhouse kitchen table with Susie on her knee while Rose finished mopping the floor.

"She lives along the road, doesn't she?"

"Hmmm, yes—in a 'grace-and-favor' house. There's a few around here, though that's a nice one. Big garden, and apparently she does it all herself. She doesn't have a daily going in to clean either, and that's unusual for a woman of her sort."

"Grace-and-favor?" Rose squeezed out the mop.

"You know—belongs to the crown, just like the forest here. They give these estate houses to people highly thought of, people who've done something for the country—a sort of favor granted by the grace of the monarch, or something like that. It's a bit like you having a tied cottage because Jim works here on the farm—mind you, your little cottage isn't like her nice big one. A person with a grace-and-favor home can live in the house until their life's end, because they served the crown."

"Did she work for the government?"

Mrs. Wicks shrugged. "She was probably a lady-in-waiting, or a private secretary to the king. Mind you, she's a clever one, is Miss White."

"That's really her name then—Miss White?"

"Miss Elinor White. And like I said, very acute she is. Mrs. Marchant told me that a couple of weeks ago, there she was at the back of the queue at the butcher shop, and Mr. Hatcher, the butcher, was weighing up some bacon for Mrs. Larch. Well, he does his usual, you know, puts the bacon on the scale, then does his little flourish with another rasher, winks and says, 'A bit over for you, Mrs. Larch.' He does that for everybody, so we think he's generous going over on the ration, but of course we still have to pay for it."

The farmer's wife took a sip of tea, her captive audience now leaning on the mop handle. "Well, everyone got what they came in for, but Mrs. Larch had forgotten something, so she was about to walk back into the shop when she heard Miss White, who had finally reached the counter. No one else was in the shop. Mrs. Larch told me that Miss White leaned toward old Hatcher and said, 'Mr. Hatcher, I am sure you don't realize this—or perhaps you do—but your scales are off, so when your customer thinks you're giving them a bit extra, you're still not handing them the weight they're paying for. You're shorting your customers and you're charging them the full whack. I would imagine that rather mounts up in your coffers, over the days.' Mrs. Larch said he flushed beetroot, mumbled something about his scales, then said he'd check the weights directly." Wicks nodded. "She caught him out, did Miss White, and more power to her."

"I don't see her around the village much," said Rose.

Wicks shook her head. "No, you wouldn't. Apparently a van from London comes to the house once a week, sometimes once a fortnight, and she walks out to collect a box of groceries, all sent down from up there. She's looked after, make no mistake. Mind you, she has a motor car herself, but she only takes it out every now and again on account of the government limits on petrol—you know, if you've a motor you can't go more than ninety miles distant in a month, so it's not as if she can wander far from home, is it? Anyway, the royals look after these ladies-in-waiting when they've stopped working—though I would have thought she was a bit young for being retired."

"How old is she, do you reckon?" asked Rose.

"I would put her at about forty-two, forty-three, something of that order. Bit more, perhaps, but not less. Anyway, none of our business, is it? Now—do you think you could go over that bit of floor again, there, in the corner?"

Rose pushed the mop into the bucket of water and scrubbed away at the heavy red tiles in the corner of the kitchen. There was no mark left after the first mopping, but she knew Mrs. Wicks liked to find fault by way of keeping her on her toes.

"Mind you, one thing I know," continued Wicks. "She's handy with a gun. Saw her early one morning, just past dawn it was, when I was out picking mushrooms for Sunday breakfast. Couple of pheasant went up and she had them." The woman snapped her fingers. "Just like that, one after the other, boom-boom. I didn't think she had any idea I was there, because it was all I could do to see the fungi at that time in the morning, but she picks up the birds and calls out, 'Good morning, Mrs. Wicks. I wouldn't touch that clump of mushrooms because they're set among a few Destroying Angels—they're the ones with a bright white cap.' Then she was gone, and I hardly saw her set off on her way. But she had a steady hand, I'll say that for her. And she knows her mushrooms, because when I got back to the kitchen, I looked into the basket and she was right, there were a number of the bad ones she'd told me to look out for. I could have killed me and Mr. Wicks with just one of them if she hadn't warned me." She paused. "Could you do a bit of laundry for me? My smalls, if you don't mind—I like to get them done before Mr. Wicks comes in from the fields. Not right for a man to see his wife's knickers, is it?"

While Rose stood at the sink washing half a dozen heavy-duty bloomers that must have pre-dated the Great War, Mrs. Wicks continued talking about their neighbor.

"And she reminds me of that funny sort of lizard I read about once. You know, the one that changes color to match whatever leaf it's sitting on. Can't say I remember what they're called. Anyway, I was at that kitchen window one morning, wondering if the snow would stop and whether the pipes would freeze—they say last winter was the worst on record for years and years, perhaps even a century. Well, as I said, I was looking out of the window, and I thought I saw something move. I squinted, peeled my eyes to have a good look, and then I saw her—Miss White wearing a white coat, marching across the field, her hunting rifle over her arm. A white coat in the snow!" The farmer's wife shook her head. "It's like she never wants to be seen. Funny, eh?"

"Chameleon," said Rose.

"What, love?"

"The lizard you were talking about—it's called a chameleon."

As time went on, Rose thought the woman was more like a hermit crab, one that Susie had tempted away from its shell house. It seemed the White lady smiled a little more with each encounter, and sometimes even waved when their paths crossed as Rose and Susie were on their way to the farmhouse. She often stopped to talk now, just a few words here and there, though Susie remained the focus of her attention. It occurred to Rose that the woman might have trouble making friends—perhaps she never knew quite what to say. Some people were like that. "Fumblers," her aunt had called them: people who weren't very good at having a chat or passing the time of day with a neighbor. Perhaps Miss White was one of those—more at ease in the company of children, though it had taken a while. Or she could have been widowed and lost a child, because there was a sort of melancholy about her. Rose couldn't help speculating—after all, she was an orphan on account of the war, so anything was possible, and she knew what it was like to lose people you loved.

Rose considered inviting the woman in for a cup of tea, now that they were on friendlier terms. She said as much to Mrs. Wicks, who frowned and tutted, then counseled that it was never a good idea to get too familiar with your betters. They might seem gracious enough, but they were all the same, those sort of people—nice to your face, but the bonds of fellowship were limited to their equals. Rose agreed that Mrs. Wicks probably knew best, but she still thought it would be a good idea, one day, because that White lady seemed a very nice person. And after all, she might be lonely, on her own in that grace-and-favor house along the road. She had probably been used to having lots of people around her when she worked for the king and queen or the government. Indeed, the image of a hermit crab was uppermost in Rose's mind; she remembered learning that they were quite social creatures, down there on the sea bed, though they scurried back to their shelters on account of their outsides being quite fragile. They had to protect their insides, those hermit crabs. Rose had liked nature study—it was her favorite subject when she was a girl in school. That's how she knew about chameleons.

Elinor White stood at her kitchen sink and stared out of the window, across fields where in the distance cattle grazed, flanked by lush woodland. If she turned and walked through the house to the front door, she would view another part of the garden, one that a passing rambler might stop to admire—a very traditional English garden, with a poetic blooming of narcissus, daisies and foxgloves bordered by a goodly planting of heritage roses. The narrow country road was just beyond her white picket fence. The opposite side of the thoroughfare formed the eastern perimeter of Denbury Forest, a mixed woodland of conifer and deciduous trees that extended for miles, dissected by a branch of the South Eastern railway and dotted with farms and cottages.

Elinor's back garden was devoted to the practical, to the growing of vegetables, the mulching of compost and a trellis bearing honeysuckle, chosen with care to provide pollen for the farmer's bees working away in hives on the other side of the fence. Her father had kept bees when she was a child, in Belgium, so nurturing something that gave such sweetness was a thread stretching down through her past. She enjoyed this benign memory; there were other strands of reflection reaching back over the years that were akin to electric cables, able to shock if touched. Those hot wires of remembrance were all around her.

She took up a pair of binoculars and held them to her eyes, scanning the landscape from her window. Dozens of crows, sparrows, blackbirds and starlings swooped down to follow a farmer's plough as it moved across a field, the horses pulling hard, finding balance in the rich clay soil. It was the only sign of life she could ascertain beyond the house, so she put the binoculars aside, pulled on a pair of leather work gloves, and set off into the garden, having pushed her feet into a pair of black rubber boots.

Elinor worked for two hours—a good use of a Sunday morning, she thought. She would down tools at noon, then go into the house for a sandwich and a cup of coffee. Good, strong coffee made with real beans she prepared in a small box grinder. The grinder was another connection to Belgium. Born of a Belgian father—who loved good coffee—and English mother, Elinor had spent her early years living in a small community not far from Antwerp, where her father was a diamond merchant. It was, until 1914, a lovely life. They had been a happy family—her father, mother, and her sister Cecily, who at thirteen was three years older than Elinor. So very happy.

Elinor changed her mind. She couldn't be bothered to make a sandwich, but she craved the coffee—it would set her up for her walk. Every day she walked in the forest, and every day she found or created another path. She couldn't say she knew the forest like the back of her hand— after all, she had only moved in to the house some eighteen months earlier—but she was at home among the conifers, the oaks, hornbeam and hazel. Sometimes she stood in one place for so long, she wondered if her feet might sprout roots reaching down into the soil, anchoring her to this new life. Then she would move on into deeper, darker parts of the forest that offered her a quiet, lonely place to polish, perfect and retain skills that had stood her in good stead over the years. She had yet to feel safe enough to relinquish them.

Elinor put on a light jacket and hat, both in a pale green reflecting the colors of late spring, and stepped out of the cottage. She checked the locked door once before taking a sliver of tape from underneath a window ledge and rubbing it with a firm hand across the top of the door where it met the frame. It would not fall away of its own accord.

Sunday was her favorite day to walk. There was less chance of an encounter with another human being. It was not a well-traveled route anyway, which was another reason to be grateful for the home provided for her after the war, as if it were another medal bestowed in exchange for services rendered. But there again, she had worked hard for every brick, every peg tile on the roof, every door and every stick of furniture already in place. Yes, she had earned it, she thought, stepping out along the road. The day was fine, though brisk—early June was not quite flaming yet, though it was warming up and July promised more sunshine. Elinor looked forward to summer, not for the pleasure of discarding a cardigan or because there would no longer be a need to chop firewood, but for the light and those late evenings when the sun seemed as if it would never go down. She remembered staying at the manor house in Scotland, during the war, when on a midsummer's eve nighttime was but a flash of darkness before dawn.

Her chosen route was to clamber over the stile just past the Mackie cottage. She hoped she could pass without seeing the child and her mother again. She thought it best because she didn't want close associations, not anymore, and as much as the little girl enchanted her, she was afraid another "Hello, how are you?" could fast become an invitation to tea, and an invitation to tea heralded idle chatter, and idle chatter might segue into the sharing of secrets. She was not in the business of sharing secrets.

These considerations were running through Elinor's mind—sometimes she wanted to stop her mind wheeling around and around dissecting the machinations of every thought—when she saw the motor car. It was a black vehicle, and it was outside the Mackies' cottage. It was a strange addition to her Sunday walk, and anything unexpected in her daily round was a most unwelcome visitor.

She identified the marque even from a distance—it was a Ford Pilot motor car, a new vehicle with a three-liter engine capable of reaching high speed, even while maneuvering around a tight corner. Then, as she approached the cottage, she saw Rose Mackie in the front garden, clutching her child while pacing back and forth. Elinor quickened her pace.

"Rose? Rose, are you alright?"

Rose Mackie looked up, her eyes red-rimmed as she held on to Susie.

"Oh, nothing. It's nothing, Miss White. We're just getting a bit of fresh air out here. To be honest, Jim's older brothers are visiting us, and those boys never saw eye to eye, so I thought us two girls would leave them to it and get a ray or two of sunshine."

Elinor looked up as raised voices came from behind the closed front door, then back at Rose. She could see the reddish outline of a bruise beginning to form along Rose's cheekbone. "What's happening, Rose? What's going on?"

"N-nothing. Nothing at all. As I said, it's just a bit of a family upset, about . . . about Jim's . . . about Jim's granddad." Rose Mackie stalled; Elinor knew another lie would follow. "You know, he's getting on, and the family want to put him in a home, and well . . . there's a bit of a row. And silly me, I picked up Susie and she had her toy train in her hand and bonked me on the nose with it. I'm perfectly alright—but you know how it is if you're hit on the nose, it causes a few drops of water to run." She paused, smiling through tears at her child. "Let's tell the nice lady we're perfectly happy—shall we, Susie?"

The child mimicked her mother, saying only the word "Happy" while waving Teddy One Eye.

Elinor nodded, then smiled at Susie, running her fingers through the child's curls. "Rose, look, if you and Susie—"

"Well, I'd better get going inside," said Rose, interrupting whatever Elinor White planned to say next. "I'll make Jim's brothers a nice cup of tea so they all calm down. I tell you, family! Can't live with them or without them, eh?" Rose Mackie smiled. "Wave to the lady, Susie. Wave goodbye."

Elinor returned Susie's wave, knowing it was time to turn away. She had been dismissed, her concern neither required nor welcome. She nodded to Rose, then began to walk toward the stile—though she did not proceed toward her intended route through the forest. Instead she clambered over a five-bar gate to her left and ran alongside the field toward her home, which she approached from the back garden, then along the gravel path at the side of the house to the front door. She tore off the tape from above the doorjamb, unlocked the door and closed and bolted it after entering. Speed was of the essence, but speed should never compromise diligence—even if she could not help but imagine a livid bruise beginning to flower around Susie's eye, and not her mother's. Elinor knew that if a man hit a woman, then a level of societal restraint had broken down, and in time—even a short time—brutality against a child might not be far behind. Perhaps it had already happened. And if Jim had seen a brother strike his wife and not acted, it meant he had been restrained. There was a visceral feeling deep within Elinor, a sudden internal commitment to protecting her neighbors—one in particular—so the young family would not have to endure another unexpected drop-in from Jim's siblings, who she was sure had no interest in any future arrangements for an aging grandfather.

With haste Elinor changed into a dark-grey skirt and jacket, a silk blouse, silk stockings and a pair of shoes that were both stylish and practical, the heel enough to draw attention to a well-turned ankle, but not so high that she could not run. Or drive. Picking up a black brimmed hat and her shoulder bag, she opened a drawer set underneath her desk and took out cash and a set of motor car keys. She ran down the stairs, out the front door, locked the door, replaced the tape and stepped along the path to a small barn that served as a garage at the side of the house. Selecting a key, she released a padlock securing the double doors, pulled them open and removed the cover from a black and maroon Riley RMB motor car—an automobile that could achieve a speed almost equal to that of the Ford parked outside the Mackie house. She started the motor car, then stepped out—the engine had been dormant for a while, so she had to allow a minute for the oil to get around the engine—and pressed another key into the lock of an adjacent cupboard. She nodded as she chose a silenced 9-millimeter Welrod pistol, a weapon she was well familiar with. They had called it the "bicycle pump" in the war because it could be concealed with ease and was close to silent. She locked the cupboard, took her place in the driver's seat and slipped the pistol into her shoulder bag—if she carried a bag, it would always have enough room to conceal a weapon.

After reversing the motor car out of the garage, she ensured the doors were secured again and drove at a low speed toward the Mackies' cottage. Pulling over to park on the grass verge, where she knew the shadow of a giant conifer would obscure the fact that she was there, she waited.

Her timing was good. Within a few minutes, two men came out of the cottage, one looking back and waving a fist at Jim Mackie, who turned away into his home, an arm around his wife and child. Was it instinct on her part? Foreknowledge? Experience? Whatever the source, Elinor knew the men must in some way be disabused of the notion that they could prevail, for she understood that the only reason for the visit was to bring Jim Mackie back to London, and not because his family missed him.

And how did Elinor know all this? Because she made it her business to know. Just as she knew the butcher was fiddling the books and his customers, just as she knew Mrs. Butler at the tea shop in Shacklehurst was a receiver of black market goods. She also knew that Wicks, the farmer, spent many an evening in Mrs. Butler's company and not walking the perimeter of his land checking fences, which is what he'd told his wife. To be sure, she recognized the Mackie name—anyone who read the newspapers would have seen it on occasion in connection with a police inquiry, though as far as she knew, nothing had ever been pinned on the family. A few days after her first encounter with Rose and Susie, Elinor had taken the train into Tunbridge Wells—just for a change and to visit a shop or two—and used the opportunity to spend a couple of hours in the library, leafing through a clutch of old newspapers. She told the librarian that she was writing a novel, a mystery, and she wanted to find out more about the criminal underworld. The librarian was most enthused—indeed, she was a fan of mysteries—and proved to be a helpful accomplice in the quest. Elinor thought it was enlightening, what she learned about crime and the Mackie family. Of course, there was another source of information she could have approached—a man who had an intimate knowledge of organized crime—but at that point, early in her acquaintance with Rose and Susie, Elinor thought she understood enough about the Mackies to be going on with. And she wasn't ready to consult that particular oracle.

As the Ford accelerated away from the cottage, Elinor released the handbrake, slipped the Riley into gear and kept a discreet distance behind the Ford. She knew they were bound for London; she would follow them all the way to be sure her information regarding their identity was correct. Then she would go to the flat. The flat was her secret. If the house in Shacklehurst had become her retreat, the flat was her safe house. To her knowledge, it was her best-kept secret, and Elinor White knew how to keep secrets.

Tomorrow morning she would go to see Steve. It was time. Her reappearance in his orbit would come as a surprise, might disarm him at first—she knew that much. He would ask why any of this was her business, and he would doubtless lecture her about London's gangs, about the machinations of organized crime. Naming his adversaries, Steve would tell her more than she wanted to know about the Sabatinis, about the likes of the Maltese Alfred Messina, his brothers and their gang, and the types of ne'er-do-wells who toiled for a nasty piece of work known as Jack Spot, and then he would list every other crime lord in London who was giving him and his men a headache. Finally he would tell her to go home. He would insist she return to her safe, quiet and secure house in the country and put all wars behind her. He would tell her the underworld wasn't her battle. In the meantime, she would devise an answer for him, a counter to convince Detective Chief Inspector Stephen Warren that she was serious, that she knew something was going down with the Mackie family, though her motive for taking immediate action would not be the truth. But he might guess. He might well intuit that it was the child. And he would smile at her; the penny would drop, and he would know that for Elinor, Susie Mackie was both the reason and the opportunity. The little girl had triggered something elusive she had yearned for since the war. It was the possibility of atonement.

Yes, she needed Steve's help, even though she was aware that any assistance from him could open a very big bag of worms. But Elinor White—a woman fluent in English, French, Flemish, German and

Italian—was trained for almost any and every eventuality. It was a training that had begun in 1916 when she was just twelve years old, when her name was Elinor De Witt. Her parents had teased Cecily and Elinor that it was a wonder their hair wasn't white, given their mother's maiden name—White—and the meaning of De Witt, their father's name. Perhaps it was ordained from the earliest days of her parents' union that the women of the family would in time be introduced to La Dame Blanche—the White Lady.

CHAPTER 2

August 4, 1914
Belgium

GREAT BRITAIN DECLARES WAR ON GERMANY
DECLARATION LAST NIGHT AFTER KAISER'S UNSATISFACTORY REPLY
TO BRITISH ULTIMATUM: BELGIUM MUST BE KEPT NEUTRAL

—Daily Messenger

They were told to pack one bag each. "Now then, girls—come on, hurry. Your father said we must be quick."

"But Mama, why isn't Papa packing a bag? And where are we going?" Elinor De Witt, ten years of age, pressed her mother.

"Questions, questions, questions—we're in a hurry, Linni." Charlotte De Witt pulled open a drawer and took out a pouch containing identity documents. "I'll hold on to these—we can't lose them."

"But where are we going?" asked Cecily, Elinor's older sister.

"To see Nana in England, and we must get to the port before all the boats go without us."

"Will Papa fight the Germans, Mama?" Elinor dropped her school cardigan into a cloth bag. "And what about Polo?"

"Polo will stay here with Papa as soon as he gets back. Papa says we can't take the dog with us."

"When will we come home?" asked Cecily.

"Cecily De Witt, stop asking questions. Set an example for your sister. When he went out, Papa said we have not twenty minutes to catch a train to the coast, and it might be the last. Those minutes are ticking by, so hurry!"

The two girls followed their mother's instructions, moving closer together as they finished packing their bags. There was one more task. Charlotte came from the bedroom she shared with her husband; she was clutching two cotton petticoats.

"Slip on another petticoat each under your skirts."

"But I already—"

"Ceci, not now. I don't care if you are wearing ten petticoats—please put this one on, and don't take it off until we arrive at Nana's. Now then—pull together. Don't make me wish I had sons."

"Just as well—they'd be at the front by now."

Elinor's eyes widened; in a flash her mother's hand thrashed across Cecily's face. Tears flooded both their cheeks as Charlotte De Witt reached for her daughter, weeping.

"Oh my darling—I am so sorry. So, so sorry. That was unforgiveable. I'm just so . . . so . . . it doesn't matter what I am. That was terrible of me. I'm so sorry—but please, Cecily, do as I say. We must leave now."

The train rumbled at a slow pace, stopping at almost every station and several more unscheduled halts until the locomotive could go no farther. No one knew the reason for the terminated journey, but they walked the final stretch into the port at Ostend. They had no idea how many kilometers they had trudged, as they followed the weary trail of people seeking safe harbor from the Kaiser's invading army. Once at the port, they waited. And waited. Elinor's ankles ached, and she was tired, her legs throbbing because her mother had made her wear thick lace-up boots. They were hard to pack, and no one could afford to leave good leather boots behind—boots that would be needed in winter. She was wearing several petticoats underneath a woolen skirt, and she was tempted to remove one or two and stash them behind a wall, or give them to someone. But she knew the final petticoat was special. She had felt tiny bumps along the seams as she pulled it on, tying the ribbon around her waist to secure it, making sure it would never fall below her skirt. Her mother was adamant about letting no one see the pretty white petticoat. "Don't let snow fall in the south," Charlotte had warned. Elinor knew they were perhaps carrying a few diamonds each, and some folding currency.

They stood in the long line, a queue that moved at a sluggish pace. In time, as fractious children settled and the earlier earnest chatter descended into silence, word ran along the line. No more boats. No more evacuation. No more chance to cross the English Channel to safety. They would have to remain. They would have to return to their homes, to a life changed. As if the footwear worn by each man, woman and child were encased in concrete, they were now prisoners in their own country, unable to escape a land with declared neutrality that was now at war with an occupying army marching into every town, every community.

A few scuffles broke out as the line of desperate humanity snaked back toward their villages, but the skirmishes were soon settled—people, after all, had to stick together. Children were picked up and carried, then when arms wearied, they were passed to rested hands, or set down to stumble along on tired legs, or placed atop push barrows. Cecily and their mother argued. Elinor wished they would both just be quiet. A year earlier she had heard Charlotte telling their father that Cecily was entering "that age," and it wouldn't be long before Elinor was voicing strident opinions and becoming argumentative along with her sister. Their father had laughed. "Give me strong young womenfolk with sharp elbows, Charlotte, my dear, and they will make a good account of themselves in this world." Elinor had wondered then what a woman might need to do to make a good account of herself.

How long did it take to reach the house, the home Elinor thought they would never see again? The De Witt women had lost count of the days, but they were home—yet without Thomas, a forty-two-year-old man who they wanted to believe was now wearing the uniform of the Belgian army somewhere near the front. Even if he had remained at the house, it was known German soldiers would go door-to-door to take males of working age, or boys who were on the cusp of manhood. They always took the men, leaving only the women, children and elderly. Women were considered easy to control. They would do as they were told and not fight back.

Trudging along the path to their house, in a row where each identical three-storey dwelling was joined to the next, Elinor at once dropped her bag and ran ahead.

"Polo! Polo!" She fell to her knees and enveloped the rough-haired hound with her arms. "Polo—you're here!"

An elderly neighbor came to explain that Thomas had left the dog with her, but Polo ran back to the house as soon as she opened the door to let him out, and then sat on the doorstep, waiting. She held out money Thomas had provided for the dog's keep.

After the woman was thanked time and again, Elinor turned to her mother. "I wonder if Papa will come home now."

"Linni, we're tired—let's all go inside the house."

Perhaps it was the look in her mother's eyes or a strange echo that seemed to reverberate through their home, but in that moment, Elinor De Witt knew she would never see her father again, would never hear him call out to his daughters, "Where are my Amazons, where's my Ceci and my little Linni?" She knew her father was dead.

The years of Belgium's occupation would be seared into Elinor's memory as if she had been branded with time's hot iron. They were years of brutality, not just toward individual citizens but whole villages of elderly men, women and children who were gunned to death, or funneled into a church which was then blown into the heavens—in one case all because an old lady had answered back to a German soldier.

The news of such terror traveled, embedding fear in the populace. Elinor would never forget that time of want, of always being hungry, despite sporadic success with vegetables grown in the garden. They were the years of not knowing when it might all end, years when her mother seemed to say time and again, "Well, life has to go on." Yes, life had to go on—there was no other choice. A table with a paltry meal of boiled turnip and perhaps a slice of dry bread had become their staple diet, with meat being the stuff of dreams—dreams where family gathered amid laughter and joy to sup at the table of plenty. Now there was never enough, and as time passed, enough became smaller and smaller, a living nightmare.

Yet life went on. Before the war, the De Witt girls had enjoyed a good education at the British Academy, but with its closure in 1914, they were enrolled at the convent, where the nuns ensured young women were immersed in an education that combined academic excellence with a strong moral and spiritual code. Before he left for the front, Thomas had settled funds with the nuns to ensure the continuation of his daughters' education.

From Monday to Friday Elinor and Cecily walked a mile to the convent, and were directed by their mother to come straight home after classes. They were not to engage in conversation with German soldiers or do anything to attract their attention. If her daily round took her to the market, Charlotte would accompany them to and from school, though as queues at the baker and butcher grew longer with every passing week, she spent more time each day standing in a line. Elinor grew tall; in 1916, when she reached the age of twelve and Cecily fifteen, she was only an inch below her sister in height, though at that point she retained the features of childhood, whereas Cecily had the demeanor of a woman. The family had become a tight trio, looking out for one another, staying home as much as possible. Charlotte knew what happened to young girls when soldiers were in the streets, so she kept her daughters as close as she could. The doors were locked and bolted every night and throughout much of the day. Their only fortune was money Thomas had left in the house, hidden, squirreled away. For their safety, only Charlotte knew where it was, and she never carried any more than a woman should be seen with as she paid for comestibles at the market or the bakery. It was harder to turn diamonds into currency or food for the table.

But later that year, Elinor noticed a change in her mother during the course of just one day. Charlotte returned from a visit to the market, and over a cup of weak tea she told Elinor and Cecily that she had met another woman, someone she had noticed once before as she went about her daily round.

"She seemed very nice, though as I said, I've only once seen her in the market," said Charlotte. "I was quite surprised when she approached me and began to talk about the weather, and asked about my family as if she knew who I was."

"So what did you say?" asked Cecily, lifting the cup to her lips but not taking a sip.

"I told her my daughters were still in school and that you were both doing well. She asked your names and said how lovely it must be to have two almost grown daughters."

"Was that it?" asked Elinor, convinced there must be more. There was something about her mother's demeanor that unsettled Elinor. Charlotte seemed excited, yet she was speaking as if pacing herself, choosing her words with care.

"I told her that, all things considered, I was grateful my girls are still enjoying a good education and keeping up with their studies. Of course, I informed her you'd had to leave the British Academy when it closed due to the German invasion—but I let her know that your father paid the nuns in advance for your lessons. I mean, we can't have people thinking we're accepting charity."

"Oh, Mama, you are so English at times!" observed Cecily. "Did you tell her the nuns are really strict with us, and we get weak potato and leek soup for lunch?"

Elinor stared at her sister—this did not seem the time for more snippy comments.

"Well," said Charlotte, "I told her you did not care for the convent school, but you were learning your subjects well. Mind you, I also told her my eldest daughter would soon complete her studies. She was not sure what kind of work might suit her, yet she would have to earn her keep."

Oh, *here we go*, thought Elinor, glancing at Cecily as her mother made the pointed remark. Fortunately Charlotte did not see her older daughter roll her eyes.

The issue of Cecily taking up employment drew the conversation to a close, but later, over a simple supper of soup and bread, Elinor noticed that her mother appeared distracted, as if every thought were fabric to be turned over and inspected for flaws before purchase. A few minutes later, Charlotte leaned forward and continued recounting the conversation with her new acquaintance.

"Just as I was about to go on my way, she asked me if she could visit us here, you know, at the house, and—"

"Here? She wants to come here?" asked Cecily.

"I haven't finished yet, my dear. I've told you it's rude to interrupt. Anyway, she whispered to me that there were ways of showing the Germans that they made a grave error when they assumed poor little Belgium could not fight back." Charlotte looked around, as if checking they were alone in their own home, then leaned forward to continue the story. "She said to me, right there on the corner of the street, 'Mrs. De Witt, we Belgian women are strong. We prove how resourceful we are every time we put food on the table.' " Charlotte's eyes were wide, as if she were telling a tale of suspense to children. "And she told me there are ways to show that we are a force to be reckoned with."

"That's strange," said Cecily.

Charlotte shrugged. "I thought so too. I said I didn't really understand what she meant."

"And what did she say then?" asked Elinor.

Charlotte's eyes widened. "Well, she said, 'I think you do, Mrs. De Witt.' And then she told me her name was Isabelle."

"Is that all she said? That sounds even more odd," said Cecily.

Charlotte shook her head. "No, there was more. She said, 'We know only too well, don't we, Mrs. De Witt, that womanhood starts when childhood ends. And in wartime childhood ends early.' Then she turned around and nodded toward the line of women outside the bakery. She pointed out that the old ladies elbowing to keep their place in the queue knew perhaps more than any invading army, that when a woman rose up to prove her mettle, she claimed a power that would be hers until her dying day." She paused. "So, what do you think?"

Elinor laughed. "She's right—the old ladies really do elbow everyone out of the way."

Charlotte De Witt glanced from one daughter to the other. "I thought she was interesting, so I invited her to come to the house to talk to us. She said it would be an early visit, but she turned around and went off down the street, so I don't know if she meant soon or early in the morning."

"You invited her here?" said Cecily.

"Yes. We hardly see anyone at home anymore." Charlotte paused. "And I confess, I was also curious. She intrigued me with the prospect of doing something more for our country, though I cannot think what on earth it could be."

Elinor stared at her mother and sister as they sat in silence, and knew that, like her, they were indeed considering what this Isabelle woman might have meant and why she wanted to speak to them.

"Oh, I nearly forgot this part," continued Charlotte. "Before she went on her way, she touched my arm and said, 'Do you know the legend of the fall of the Hohenzollern dynasty in the lands of our invaders?' Of course I shook my head—I hadn't a clue what she was talking about."

Elinor leaned toward her mother. "I know what it is."

"How do you know?" said Cecily.

"Sister Jeanne-Marie told us the story a week ago. It's that the fall of the dynasty would be heralded by the appearance of a woman wearing white. The Hohenzollerns are German. I think the German Kaiser might be related to them—it was something like that."

"Yes, that's about the measure of it," said Charlotte. "Anyway, Isabelle said it was interesting, given our name—which means 'white.' And you know that was my name, before I married your father. She said she would see us soon and I didn't have to tell her where we lived—she knew." She regarded her daughters for a few seconds, and then changed the subject.

C eci, Linni—I want to talk to you."

Charlotte De Witt held an oil lamp to illuminate the way as she entered her daughters' bedroom and sat on Cecily's bed. Before the war Charlotte had often felt as if she were her daughters' contemporary, but now fear had worn her down—fear for her husband and concern for her girls, both terrors compounded by a dread that she might never see her home again. Yes, home was Belgium, but for the Englishwoman, an ache had grown for the land of her birth, and war had rendered it so far away.

Elinor loved to hear the story of how her parents met. Charlotte White was twenty-one years of age when she stepped off the boat in Zeebrugge, excited to take up her new employment as governess to the children of a wealthy British businessman. She met Thomas De Witt in Bruges while walking along the street. Attempting to put up her umbrella in a sudden squall, Charlotte almost poked the gangly Thomas in the eye as he passed. She thought later that he might have stepped into her path on purpose, and even feigned injury as he held his hand to his face. Yet love soon followed the encounter. After several months of walking out together, they traveled to London to meet her family, where Thomas asked Charlotte's father for her hand. Raymond White had one request, informing Thomas that while he would not lay down a condition to his consent, he and his wife would very much like the couple to spend a reasonable period of time in England after their marriage, to see if they might settle.

Two years of residence in the city followed, Thomas having found employment with a diamond merchant in London's Hatton Garden. But home beckoned for the young man, and Charlotte was keen to return to life "on the continent," so they crossed the English Channel and settled in the small town not far from Antwerp. Now, following the departure of her beloved husband and the German invasion of her adopted country, at forty years of age, Charlotte no longer had the abundance of confidence and joy that had been a hallmark of her character. Yet as she sat on the bed framed in low light, Elinor could see that her mother's bearing had changed, as if her old strength of spirit had been rekindled.

"Girls," she whispered. "We have a task."

"Why are you whispering, Mama?" asked Cecily, rubbing her eyes.

"Because walls have ears and we have neighbors, Ceci. We can trust no one."

"Not even—"

"Ceci, dear—do please listen."

Cecily and Elinor were silent while Charlotte reminded them about the meeting with a woman named Isabelle. She had seen her again, and during their conversation, Isabelle had repeated that there was more they could do for their country.

"Why didn't you tell us all this at supper?" asked Cecily.

"Because I had to think about it. I wasn't sure."

"We could be like the three musketeers," offered Elinor.

Charlotte nodded, smiling. "Yes, like the three musketeers." She took a breath. "So, what do you say?"

"Yes!" said Elinor.

"Yes," said Cecily.

"Then when she comes to the house first thing in the morning, I will not turn her away. Your father has been gone for two years now, and I can endure the waiting no longer. We must play a part in Belgium's fortunes, however simple the task set before us."

Charlotte kissed each daughter on the forehead.

"I miss Papa and Polo," said Elinor.

"Yes. Me too," said Charlotte. "Very, very much." She left the room, closing the door without a sound.

"She had to do it, Linni. We couldn't keep Polo—there's no food for us, so she had to take him to Arthur."

"I hope Arthur was kind."

"Polo didn't feel a thing."

"I hope Papa didn't feel a thing."

"Go to sleep, Linni. We have to be downstairs in the kitchen early, and you know how I hate mornings."

Indeed, Elinor understood only too well how much her sister hated mornings—it was a struggle to rouse her in time to walk to the convent for the start of lessons.

"What do you think this Isabelle woman will say? What does she want us to do?"

"Probably steal food from the nuns. Now, go to sleep. I'm tired."

Elinor and her sister sat on either side of their mother at the table and stared at the woman who called herself Isabelle. Elinor would not have been able to offer an explanation for her doubt, but she had a distinct feeling that the woman was not an Isabelle. She couldn't imagine what name might suit her, but it wasn't the one she was using. Elinor judged the woman to be younger than their mother—perhaps she was twenty-five, twenty-six or thereabouts, though it was hard to estimate age anymore, because anyone who wasn't a child seemed old.

Isabelle was of average height, and her clothing was no better or worse than anyone else's. She was thin, though everyone seemed thin since the occupation. When her mother put her arms around Elinor and wished her sweet dreams before she went to bed, Elinor could feel bone against bone, as if her mother's ribs might become entangled with her own and they would never be able to snap apart.

The visitor wore her dark, almost black hair drawn back in a chignon, topped with a brimmed hat that shielded her face. Her skin was clear, but her pallor grey. Her skirt skimmed above her ankles, and her boots were worn but polished. She wore a navy-blue woolen jacket that fell to her thighs, with a cotton blouse revealing a frill at the neck, secured with a nondescript pin. If the woman had ever owned a brooch, it might well have been sold by now. Elinor could see that Isabelle would never stand out in a crowd and could even pass a German soldier without him taking a second glance or asking to see her papers. She would be viewed as a Belgian nobody.

"The tasks you will be assigned at this point are not difficult, though discretion is crucial," explained Isabelle. She took a map from underneath a sheet of newspaper in her shopping bag, on top of which a couple of less than fresh potatoes languished. She spread the map on the table and tapped her forefinger on a place where the women knew the river ran close to the railway line, overlooked by a meadow that rose up to a hill commanding a clear view of the railway line in both directions. Closer to the railway, a path ran alongside, interspersed with stands of deciduous trees, some overhanging the tracks. It was a place where lovers met, where children would play in summer, and which would draw ramblers on a fine day.

"I would suggest a walk along the path here—not the one along by the railway, but this one leading up to the top of the hill. You are taking the fresh air. Bring a blanket and sit for a while. Do the girls have paper and perhaps colored pencils? A set of paints? Draw the trees, the landscape. Stay together. As each train passes along this railway line, count the carriages, count the flat rolling stock if you see anything mounted on top—a gun carriage, for example. Make a note of the time when you observe the train. That is all I need. Go to church tomorrow and afterward for your walk. Return to your home by four o'clock, when I will come to join you for tea." She smiled. "I know—don't worry, I will supply the tea." A few seconds' hiatus followed, as if Isabelle were leaving the air pure for the De Witt women to absorb her instructions. Charlotte opened her mouth to speak, but seemed to think better of it. Isabelle continued, making eye contact with her audience. "Do not tell anyone about this meeting. When I leave, wave to me as if I were your friend. Thank me for the potatoes. Do not keep an account of your task anywhere in this house." She stared at Cecily. "Do not write in your diary, if you have one, and do not tell your friends."

Elinor suspected Isabelle could see into her sister's mind. She glanced at her mother, who had cleared her throat to speak.

"Why us, Isabelle? Why have you come to us?"

"It's not just you, Mrs. De Witt. Women across our country are being asked to serve in this way. Any one of your neighbors along the street might also be assisting, but they will never tell you, nor must you tell them. If your instructions change, it will be me who informs you." She paused, and at that moment young Elinor thought she could see a fire amid the weariness in Isabelle—perhaps it was the same flame that had reignited her mother's confidence. "We have no choice, Mrs. De Witt. The Germans do not suspect women of working against them. They see us standing for hours in long queues to provide for our young and our elders. They see us doing our best to try to live our lives, and they see us withdraw into our lairs while under the threat of their violence." She smiled. "They have no idea what we are capable of inflicting upon them."

Charlotte nodded.

"Will you do what I have asked of you?"

Elinor felt her mother take her hand and saw her reach toward Cecily on her other side. As if by instinct, all three women leaned toward one another and nodded.

"Yes," Charlotte, Cecily and Elinor De Witt replied in unison.

Elinor thought of her father, of the man she had held on to before he left the house, until finally he had to take her arms and pull them away as if releasing himself from the tentacles of an octopus. "Come, Linni. Be brave. We shall all be home together soon. You must be a help to your mother now. You have much to do, and I will see you again soon—I promise." She hoped Papa would be proud of his womenfolk. She hoped this visitor would give her a chance to make a good account of herself.

CHAPTER 3

June 1947

A Sunday journey by motor car was never an arduous drive. There was little traffic, nothing much to distract Elinor White from her quarry—the black Ford Pilot in the near distance. Yet the quiet roads meant Elinor could not fail to be vigilant, aware of any maneuver on the part of the driver ahead to indicate that he was aware of her presence following him.

The Ford proceeded along Old Kent Road—the London end of the original Watling Street, a thoroughfare that had crossed England since the Roman invasion, and was now almost consigned to mythology for its part in bringing news of the city to the county of Kent from ancient times, before London was known as Londinium and did not extend much beyond the banks of its famous river. Now that same road was bringing home the two men who had made life difficult for the young Mackie family.

When the Ford turned to the right onto a street of larger Victorian dwellings that were once the homes of wealthy merchants doing business in the warehouses along the river, Elinor slowed down but did not follow. She watched as the motor car braked, rear lights indicating the men had arrived at their destination. Mickelham Street. Checking the number of the house on the corner to her immediate right—number 1—she estimated the property the men were now entering was number 15. Fifteen Mickelham Street, Camberwell. She had already noted the motor car's number plate, and now she knew the address. Slipping the Riley into gear, she waited for a costermonger's horse and cart to pass, then eased onto the empty road and drove toward Kennington, crossing the Thames via Vauxhall Bridge.

Gaps in rows of houses and piles of rubble where the streets had been bombed during six years of war were still being cleared. Elinor wondered how long it would take to restore the capital again, to repair the devastating damage not only to homes but to the thousands of people caught up in the maelstrom of another world war. She thought she would be an old woman before London ceased to bear the scars of bombs, of firestorms and of the V1 and V2 rockets that slammed into life itself. Those rockets were the most feared messengers of death, almost invisible as they buzzed their approach in the skies above until ready to fall. So quiet was their descent that people looking up, wondering where the rocket might land, would panic and run in all directions as if they were ants avoiding flame to the nest. Only a few souls would escape the explosion that followed.

The bombing of Britain's cities brought death and despair along with a resilience that was already the stuff of proud reminiscence. Everyone had a tale to tell, but there was another side to the story. Wartime conscription had sucked in the bad along with the good, and while the bad could fight with an uncommon ferocity, they had returned battle-hardened and with darker skills in the art of killing learned in the prosecution of war. Demobilization had brought them home to the streets—and with a bounty of weapons that should have been left behind.

Elinor glanced in the rearview mirror before moving off again. There was more traffic now, but she retained awareness of every motor car and bus within a narrow proximity. Stopping along Queen's Gate, lingering to ensure she had not been followed, she turned into a cobbled street of mews houses, the brick and stone lane marked by its shallow V shape, with drains along the center; a mews was where horses had once been stabled, with drainage built to ensure waste could be swept away. She parked the motor car close to one house in particular, stepped out and opened the garage doors. Without losing a half second, she drove into the garage, closed and locked the doors, then made her way up to the first floor by way of an internal staircase. Not one of her fellow residents' curtains had twitched. Elinor White was not aware of an onlooker—and she would have known if someone had observed her returning to the flat. In Belgium during her girlhood she had learned to feel the eyes of nosy neighbors, had learned to deflect their interest by waving or calling out a greeting to the elderly man at the window or the woman in her garden. And if she was staring out of her bedroom window late at night and witnessed a neighbor's return, she would remain silent. It was often best to remain silent. Often, but not always.

The flat comprised a galley kitchen with an extension large enough to accommodate a dining table. The sitting room was situated to the left of the dining table, and from there a hallway gave access to two bedrooms, one of which would accommodate only a narrow single bed.

This was the room Elinor preferred—within the close walls she felt soothed and swaddled.

She turned on the gas fire, taking a match to light the jets; she did this first, not for the heat but the comfort of flames. Later, when darkness descended and it was time to switch on the lights, she would draw the blackout curtains—a leftover from the war—and breathe more easily. While her neighbors were not as a rule inquisitive, by the same token she had no desire to entertain a caller dropping by to say how nice it was to see her again.

Supper would require only the simple task of heating a tin of soup. Elinor had brought bread from the larder at the cottage, along with a small amount of cheese—she looked forward to the end of rationing, because she liked cheese. First, though, there was one more task for Elinor before she settled in for the evening—she had to place a telephone call, and could not do so from the flat because she had never installed a telephone. If she could reach others with ease, it meant others could reach her. And she did not want to be reached.

Elinor left the flat on foot and walked back in the direction of Queen's Gate. Stopping at a nearby telephone kiosk, she lifted the receiver and slipped coins into the slot. She checked her watch, knowing the person she wanted to speak to would be at his desk. He was rarely at home, and Elinor knew this much about him; if he wasn't at work, even on a Sunday—and often especially on a Sunday—then he would be with a woman who was not his wife. But Elinor understood that his wife had entered marriage with her eyes open; she was nobody's fool.

The line was answered on the first ring. Elinor spoke before the male operator could offer the number and location.

"Put me through to Detective Chief Inspector Stephen Warren, please."

"Right you are, madam. May I say who's—"

"No. That won't be necessary."

There was a second's pause. Elinor heard the man clear his throat.

"Of course, madam. Connecting you now."

Elinor glanced right and left before turning to look through the kiosk's narrow panes at her back. "Old habits die hard," she whispered.

"Warren here. Who am I speaking to?"

"Elinor."

She heard papers ruffle and knew that Steve Warren had been leaning back in his chair before allowing it to fall forward, the landing of his elbows on the table causing documents on his desk to concertina and crackle.

"Linni . . . Linni, are you alright?"

"Yes, Steve. I'm well. But I want to see you."

"Well, there's an offer I can't refuse, Miss White. My place or yours—though my guess is you're not shackled in Shacklehurst."

"Tomorrow morning. Kensington Gardens. The Albert Memorial. Let's cross paths there."

"Time?"

"Nine."

"What's it about, Linni? Is it to do with—"

"No, Steve. It's not about the war."

"Will you give me a clue?"

"It's about a family—the Mackies. I believe you may have heard of them."

Another pause. She thought she could almost hear Warren's brain cells jockeying for position in an effort to comprehend her answer. "Bloody hell, Linni, what have you— Oh, never mind. I'll see you at nine. I'm looking forward to it."

Elinor put the receiver down. "Yes, I believe you are," she said aloud.

She left the telephone kiosk and returned to the mews flat she had owned since the war, a property she had bought on a whim because it represented a future she could not imagine.

Detective Chief Inspector Stephen Warren was with the Flying Squad—"the Sweeney," as they were known, Cockney rhyming slang alluding to a department founded to bring the violent perpetrators of organized crime to heel, if not to face justice.

" 'Sweeney Todd—Flying Squad.' Get it, Linni? Get it? You know who Sweeney Todd was, don't you?" Steve had explained, soon after receiving his promotion.

"That was quick, Steve."

"The joke? That's me, always quick."

"No—the nice promotion, that was fast."

He had looked at her, his stare cold, as if he were reading her mind. "It was hard work and results, Linni. I work hard, and hard work with results maketh the man."

She responded with nothing more than a nod.

He went on, defensive now. "They gave you a grace-and-favor house in the country for your trouble."

Her response came with the smile she knew would confuse him. "And they gave you a grace-and-favor job, so we're even—it's all come right, hasn't it, DCI Warren? I'm glad it turned out so well for both of us."

There was nothing Stephen Warren could say. She was right. It wasn't stellar police work that had earned him a promotion almost as soon as he returned to his old prewar place of work—Scotland Yard—but another kind of duty. In truth, the other kind of toil deserved an honorable compensation, just as Elinor deserved the house in Shacklehurst.

E linor did not use the motor car the following morning, so it would remain in the ground floor garage at her mews flat until she was ready to return to Kent, a journey she expected to make within a few days and early on the morning of her departure, before the streets—and anyone who might venture out at that hour—were fully awake. If she were honest with herself, she was not sure exactly how she would accomplish her aim for this sojourn in London, which was to begin to untangle Jim and Rose Mackie from the crosshairs of his family—but she felt compelled to take a chance, to give it her best shot.

Alighting from the bus at the Royal Albert Hall, Elinor crossed the road to enter Kensington Gardens and proceeded to the Albert Memorial. She had always been curious about the many tributes to Albert, Queen Victoria's consort. There was the Royal Albert Hall, which inspired her to wonder how many boys with the surname "Hall" had been burdened with the name "Albert." And there was the Albert Memorial, the Albert Bridge and a goodly number of streets named after Victoria's beloved Albert. Was Albert worthy of these tributes? Elinor thought he probably deserved more recognition than some of the aristocracy.

"Linni!"

Elinor looked around to see a tall man walking in her direction, though he stopped for a few seconds when he saw her, then seemed to regain his lost composure before removing his hat and waving it to gain her attention. He wore a dark-grey suit, white shirt, a silk tie and polished leather shoes. For a copper, Warren was a dapper bloke. The last time she had seen Stephen Warren—in 1945, at the end of the war—grey hair had only infiltrated his temples; now it was more widespread, a salt-and-pepper crown that proved more attractive on a man of his bearing. She knew Steve would view this sign of aging as an affliction, not a natural or elegant testament to time's passing. Yet at least he had not resorted to dye. His gait was that of a younger fellow, so he wore the years with ease—he had retained the muscle and backbone trained into him. As had Elinor White.

"Steve. You're looking well." She smiled, but tensed as he leaned forward to kiss her on both cheeks.

"The continental way, Linni." And there it was, that smile.

"May we walk?"

"You lead on, ma'am."

"Jim Mackie," Elinor began as they strolled away from the memorial. "What do you know about him?"

"Linni—I am floored that you seem to be giving in to this wild curiosity. Are you bored down there in the country? Nothing going on? Nothing to get the old adrenaline rushing around your body? Missing the intrigue? The challenge? Surely there's a wellie-booted young farmer waiting to swoon over you, or a handsome geezer to liven things up a bit for the old girl." He shook his head. "Look, seriously, Linni, don't get involved with the Mackies, even if your neighbor is the youngest son who for some reason fancies himself as a man of the land."

"I know a bit about the family, Steve. I make it my business to know something about everyone I meet even in quiet little Shacklehurst. But you're the person with your finger on the pulse of his sort of people."

Warren shook his head. "His sort of people? Believe me, I wish some of those pulses would stop thrumming away and all those sort of people would just keel over like dominoes or take one another out and be done with it. It'd make my life a bit easier."

"More than that, you would be on the streets jobless, Steve. Those villains give you a purpose, don't they? Then where would *your* dose of adrenaline come from, eh?" Touché, she thought.

"Alright—look, let's sit down over there. I know it goes against the grain for people like us, but we won't die a terrible death in a London park if we stop moving." He pointed to a bench. They walked toward it in silence and sat down.

Warren sighed. "The Mackies. There's history—and do not be distracted by the Gaelic-sounding name. The old granddad—his name's Francisco—came over from Italy when he was young. Started off in the East End, then moved south of the river. He worked on the water; a lighterman—well, that was his aboveboard occupation. He nurtured contacts at the docks, in the warehouses, and before long he was selling all sorts of goods on the side and making a pretty penny. Soon enough he wasn't working on the water anymore—he was king of his manor. Mind you, he retained a partnership with the river—because as we know, where there's water, there's someone floating in it." He gave a half-laugh. "He and his wife—he married a London girl, born and bred—had three sons. The eldest is John Mackie, Jim's father. The old man called him 'Gianni.' And there was Elisa Mackie, a sister—Jim's aunt—but they call her Elsie, and she married a Finch. Abe Finch was a small-time East End spiv, the sort who thought he was a big fish, not a tiny stickleback. The Mackies left him alone as long as their sister was happy and Abe didn't do anything too stupid to damage the Mackie family fingers, which are in a lot of pies. Abe died of a heart attack after a doodlebug came down in the street while he was on his way to exchange knocked-off ration books for folding money. Pity the rocket didn't drop on Mickelham Street."

"Number fifteen?"

"You don't waste any time, do you, Linni?"

"Go on, Steve."

"Anyway, Francisco was nobody's fool, because from the time he got off the boat, he knew that 'When in England' was the key to his intended success, so he gave himself and later baptized his sons with

British names and in short order changed the surname. Francisco has been known as Frank for years, and I hear he can't control his bladder now he's past eighty. But he could always dredge up the eye-tye banter when it suited him to scare the s-h-one-t out of a few people—the sort of people who aren't easily scared. I'll give him this—it was almost as if he could see the war coming long before anyone else. Look at what happened to Italian restaurants and cafés after Mussolini threw in his lot with Hitler. And there were some in the Italian gangs who were taken off the streets and put in detention, whereas none of the Mackie lot were ever packed off to an internment camp, though you could say John's boys did their bit for the country."

Elinor nodded.

"Going back, by the time 1918 rolled around, the Mackie moniker was well established, and when war broke out again, memories of their original name were short. It's Marchetti, by the way. Mackie was a good choice; I've even heard people saying the family originally hailed from north of the border."

"What sort of pies do they have their fingers in?"

"Oh, Linni, what pies aren't they into? They're well-established south-of-the-river people now, as I said, but their rackets extend in every direction. John Mackie's middle brother, Joe, holds court in Liverpool. He married a local girl up there. John has London and his brother Eric—'Rico'—the youngest of Francisco's boys, is in Bristol, though they've all got form here in the Smoke and throughout the south east." He sighed. "So, let's count their ways, shall we? Armed robbery of banks and jewelers. Robbery of racecourse takings, doping of horses and at the dog tracks, and of course fixed races. They have control of drinking clubs and spielers—the gambling clubs. There's a goodly amount of fraud, and let's not forget shoplifting. And we're not talking about someone picking off a few pairs of knickers in the local haberdashery shop—Elsie Finch née Mackie might be small-time compared to her brothers, but she has been running a little gang of women who are in and out of Harrods, Bourne and Hollingsworth, Dickins and Jones, Debenham and Freebody, Fenwicks—you name the shop, and they're pinching from it. Bond Street is a favored place for Elsie's girls to wander in and wander out—that's how easy they make it, though as I said, her game is small fry, nothing as big as her brothers' rackets and hardly worth our bother. John, Joe and Eric consider it Elsie's pin money for doing all the hard work looking after Francisco."

Elinor rubbed her forehead and nodded. "Jim was wise to leave then."

Warren sighed again. "Linni, the kid had a good idea, and he's done his best to shed the family glue, no two ways about it. I take my hat off to him. But the Mackies have just been playing the line out a bit. They won't let him go, and time will tell."

"Italians are big on family."

"Linni, it's more than that. The Mackies are big on family, but not in the way you might imagine. There's no great affection between any of them. I don't think there's a sliver of personal loyalty to speak of either. John, his brothers and even his sister were foot soldiers to be trained up, and that goes for the next generation. It's a business. A cutthroat business." Warren sighed, stared into the distance, then began again. "Every one of them has a role, a specialty, if you like. For his part, Jim Mackie is the best driver in London. He could handle himself and win laurels racing motor cars at Brooklands if he had to. And on top of that, when he was demobbed, he not only came out of the army with a cheap suit but he'd learned a lot more about engines with the Royal Electrical and Mechanical Engineers and perfected his driving skills in very trying situations."

"And he doesn't want to do that for his family—that's the rub?"

"Jim Mackie was detained at a borstal, you know, a prison for younger offenders, down in Kent before the war. The lad was caught red-handed behind the wheel of a stolen motor car. His mistake was that he couldn't resist nicking a Bentley. But if I were to guess, I'd say he's the only one in the family whose heart isn't in it. He did his time at His Majesty's pleasure, and was released straight into REME's arms. God knows why they put a Mackie into the engineers, because with his 'previous' they risked him running off if they put him in the driver's seat of a bloody tank! Mind you, I reckon bomb disposal is enough to calm anyone down. Anyway, I think you know the rest—he met Rosie Phillips, fell in love, and that was it—they got out of the Smoke as soon as they could."

"And now the Mackies want him back."

Warren frowned and was silent for a few seconds. "Linni, if his family came calling, it means they need him, that it's Jim and no one else will do. Next time John Mackie might send all three of his boys and a few cousins down to have a word in his shell-like ear—Jim's older brothers are Bobby, Fred and Sandy, and that Sandy is a pigheaded violent sod with clodhopper feet and massive fists. Jim was persona non grata for a good while, but if they want him home, it's not because his mum misses him. It's because there's a big job in the offing."

"I would say he doesn't want to do it—not from the altercation I witnessed."

"He might have to, Linni. And he owes them."

"Those family ties?"

"You may know irregular war work better than anyone I've ever met, but you don't know organized crime. The Mackies will have threatened their younger brother with the worst-case scenario—which for Jim is losing his wife and child. As the saying goes, Linni, the boy can run, but he can't hide." He rubbed his forehead. "And as I mentioned—he owes them. When Jim and Rose left London, it was in a hurry because he didn't want to do a particular big job. He'd had enough—we know that. Yes, they let him go, mainly because Sandy—who has always had a chip on his shoulder the size of a two-by-four—said he could take his brother's place, that he was as good a driver if not better. But he wasn't. He smashed up the motor car during the getaway, and his face along with it. Yes, the gang escaped and nothing could be pinned on the family—they had solid alibis. Sandy was swept out of the country to a fancy surgeon in America, and that was that, though the clever doctor couldn't erase all the evidence on Sandy's already ugly mug." He shrugged. "Net result—Jim Mackie is in hock to his family up to the eyeballs."

Elinor felt any color in her cheeks fade. Steve Warren turned to her.

"Oh, now it's falling into place." He tapped the side of his head. "How could I have been so bloody dim? It's the child, isn't it? It's Jim's little girl—what's her name? Susie?" He put an arm around her. "Linni, you can't change the past, love. Let it go. It's gone. We're home—and life goes on."

Elinor raised a hand, lifted his arm and pushed it away from her shoulder.

"I can't change the past, Steve. But I will do all I can for Jim, Rose and Susie Mackie."

"Especially the child."

Elinor nodded, and whispered. "Alright, Steve. You're right. Yes—especially the child."

Warren rubbed his forehead again. It was a tic she knew well—a sign of indecision. There was a time when that same rub across the forehead was a warning to keep an eye on the man at her side. Keep an eye on him because any faltering could be the death of them both, and a whole line of comrades into the bargain.

"Alright, Linni. Just this once, for old times' sake. Come to my office. I've some people to talk to, and though this is irregular—to coin a phrase we both know well—we must all be in on whatever is going on. I've got to clear the path for your presence, so to speak, because the information you've brought to my attention suggests that we have to be on our toes."

She consulted her watch. "Will you have cleared the 'irregularity' by one o'clock?"

"Yes," said Warren. "Come at one. You know where to find me."

"I do—and even if I didn't, I would find you." Elinor recognized the look in Warren's eyes. "Forget it, Steve. Not in that way."

He shrugged. "Can't blame a bloke for trying."

M iss White, let me introduce you to Detective Sergeant Robert Mills and Detective Sergeant Charles Kettle. Bob and Charlie." Warren turned to the two men seated before him. Elinor sat to his right. "Lads, this is Miss Elinor White. I will embarrass her in front of you by saying she can go toe-to-toe with either of you when it comes to taking care of herself, so I would advise you not to get near her bare hands if you've annoyed her."

The men smiled, both nodding acknowledgement.

"And to you she is always Miss White. Alright," added Warren.

"Yes sir," said the men, one echoing the other.

"Don't listen to a thing he says," said Elinor, easing the introduction, which she considered unnecessary and inflammatory. Mills and Kettle were not neophytes, but she wondered if they had any idea of their superior's role during the war.

"We'll have your back, Miss White," said Mills.

"Thank you," added Elinor, smiling.

"Right, here we go. Miss White has provided me with firsthand information to suggest that the Mackies are planning a sizable hit. We don't know whether it's a racecourse, a jewelers', bank or even a blimmin' great mansion where some lord is having a party to celebrate the fact that they all got to the end of the war without anyone knowing how much they loved old Hitler." There was a snigger of laughter. Warren continued. "Bob, what's coming up on the racing calendar?"

"The big one came and went in March," said Mills. "The Grand National—the one hundred and first since the race started—and it pulled quite a crowd." He smiled. "Nice little earner—I put a five bob each way on the one-hundred-to-one outsider, that Irish horse, Caughoo."

"Go on, Bob—now we all know you're in the money, let's look at what's on the gee-gees dance card next, shall we?"

"Royal Ascot is coming up—and so's the Derby."

"You're frowning, Bob," said Warren.

"Can't see any of the families taking on one of those. If it's racing, it'll be something else—not one of the big ones."

"Sniff around, Bob—if a horse loses a bloody shoe for no reason, I want to know about it."

"Aye, sir."

"Charlie—what about the banks? Heard of anything in the offing?"

"I've kept my ear to the ground, sir. All the big banks have tightened up security—they don't like spending their own money, but they're sick of being hit by armed gangs and their staff knocked about."

Elinor shifted on her seat and raised her hand.

"You're not in school now, Miss White," said Warren. "You can just dive in with your two penn'orth. No need to raise your hand."

"What if the plan is for something . . . something quieter. Not a raid, not a caper you might see at the pictures in one of those gangster films, but a plan with more stealth. So perhaps this time the need is for a driver who can not only maneuver a vehicle at high speed but can seem like he's a delivery driver going about his business. Or perhaps it's a heavier-duty vehicle, something Jim would have been used to driving in the army. What if—"

Kettle interjected. "These gangs like to get in and get out, and they do it fast."

"But what if they didn't? What if it's time for a change?"

"Sniff around, Charlie," instructed Warren. "See what your informants might know."

Kettle nodded.

"What else?"

"There's Hatton Garden and all them other wholesale jewelers, you know, with big safes underground," said Bob Mills. "What with the weddings and engagements, and a little more formality and romance coming back into the sealing of a union, well, diamond trading is doing very well thank you. Oh, and it's helped that Princess Elizabeth is getting married in November—seems a lot of girls want to tie the knot in the same year."

Elinor nodded. "My father worked in Hatton Garden before I was born. Diamonds were his business. How easy is it to turn the stones into hard cash at the moment?"

"There's always someone looking for diamonds, Miss White," said Warren. "You'd know that if your dad was in the business—they're currency by any other name."

"And these blokes can sit on whatever it is they're after for a long time," added Mills. "They're not desperate for a few readies in their pockets. They can play what they call a 'long game.' "

"The long game? You're another one who's been skiving off to the pictures again, haven't you, Bob?"

"Just making an observation, sir." The detective sergeant shrugged. "If you've got diamonds, you've set yourself up for a while."

Though Elinor continued to pay attention and could have recounted every comment, every opinion voiced, along with plans to find out—and fast—what the Mackie family might be planning, the image that came to mind was her mother opening the seam along her sister's petticoat and removing one single diamond, every facet catching the candlelight. This diamond was food. Sustenance. It was their schoolbooks, cloth for their uniforms. It was a safety net, their parents' gift of foresight, ensuring that together with other tiny gems their mother had sewn into the seams of their petticoats, they would survive what was now called the Great War.

"Miss White . . . Miss White . . . Linni?"

"Sorry, Detective Chief Inspector Warren. You were asking how I could find out what else might be afoot?" She gave a half-laugh. "I didn't expect Scotland Yard's Flying Squad to sound like a Sherlock Holmes mystery!" She paused, meeting the eyes of each man. "I was wondering . . . is there anything you can tell me about Elisa—Elsie Finch?" She shrugged. "Just curious."

"Interesting question, Miss White," said Warren. "I don't think there's much to add there. She's the little sister, though she's no spring chicken." He mirrored her shrug and brought his attention back to the men. "Right, let's meet here tomorrow. We'll pick over what you've come in with. Soon as we're a bit clearer on the intention, we'll bring in more shoe leather and I'll have a word with the guv'nor. Alright?"

"Sir," said Mills and Kettle, acknowledging Warren's instruction as they stood up to leave. They nodded toward Elinor and left Warren's office.

"What do you think, Linni? I know this isn't your bailiwick, but what's your impression after this little meeting?"

"My impression? First off, you've a pair of very good men there. But

Steve, I think there's a bigger game . . . afoot, as you might say. It might be into a new field of endeavor altogether." She was thoughtful. "Yes, my money's on a bigger game."

"They would run the risk of being manor interlopers, then they'd have to deal with the likes of Jack Spot or one of the other gangs." He rubbed his hands. "As I said, my dream is a dustup where they all do away with one another without any civilian or police casualties—and there you have it, my work would be done and I could escape to the South of France, or wherever people escape to. Perhaps Brighton."

"Hmmm, perhaps." She stared out of the window, then brought her attention back to Warren. "Or like a dictatorship, the Mackies could be planning a march into another country because they think they're strong enough and it's time to expand their base of operations."

"Organized crime doesn't operate like that, not now, not in London. They all understand how the status quo works—it's a balance, and there's honor among thieves."

Elinor shook her head. "No, there's not. We both know that. And the higher you go up the totem pole, the more honor ceases to exist." She stared at Warren. "As I said, we both know that, don't we?"

CHAPTER 4

Mrs. Elsie Finch, née Mackie, left her home—also on Mickelham Street in Camberwell—at ten in the morning. The weather was fine and it promised to be a sunny day in London, so residents were hopeful that the smogs of winter would abate, though the factories continued to pump out toxic smoke, stoves would still be lit for cooking and fog lingered along the Thames—a witches' brew that led to the thick green air that for a few more years to come would envelop London, sully human lungs and kill more people than crime.

Elsie was on her way to have her hair done. She'll be having a shampoo, cut and set, thought Elinor White, who guessed the reason for Elsie's expedition because when Jim Mackie's aunt emerged from the house and made her way toward a waiting motor car, this one a Vauxhall, she was in a hurry to tie a scarf around hair that appeared, well, flat, as if she could not be bothered to even run a comb through the thinning strands because someone else would be having a go at it.

Despite what seemed to be a rush—Elsie flapped her hand at the driver, showing her frustration that he had not stepped forward to assist her one second earlier—Elinor noted that the woman seemed to have some difficulty negotiating the umpteen steps down from the front door of the Victorian house. Elsie lived at number 18 on the

same street as her widower father, Francisco, who was—as Steve Warren had pointed out—hanging on to his mantle as the patriarch of
one of London's most feared crime families. In addition, Elsie carried
a fair bit of weight, not helped by wearing a plush pale-brown fur coat
on a warm day. She was holding two bags, yet from a distance, parked
at the end of the street, Elinor could not have identified whether they
were both made of leather, though one was large, suggesting a shopping expedition.

As the motor car moved forward and merged onto the main road,
Elinor slipped the Riley into gear and followed—all the way to Mayfair,
where the Vauxhall came to a halt outside the salon of Raymond Bessone, a hairdresser considered to be on the "up and up." Elsie Finch was
assisted from the car by her driver—no one could have described the
man as a chauffeur, dressed as he was in brown corduroy trousers and a
tweedy woolen jacket topping a shirt with no tie. Elinor could not fail
to notice the way the sun caught the fabric of his jacket as it fell across
his chest, causing the hint of a shadow that suggested he was carrying
a pistol. It led her to wonder if the driver might be a former soldier, perhaps a man one of Jim Mackie's brothers had befriended in the army,
and then on demob put the association to good use.

Elinor considered entering the establishment, but having her
shoulder-length light-brown hair teased and pulled around by a man becoming known for a deft hand with comb and his fingertips was not an
appealing prospect. She waited. And waited, until at last Elsie emerged
with hair that had been rollered, hot-dried, brushed and lacquered into
a pageboy style fashionable with the younger set. Elinor was surprised;
she had once read that Mr. Bessone maintained that only young girls
should wear long hair, as it could age a woman. Perhaps certain clients
were well worth a dose of ego-pampering.

"Mutton dressed up as lamb," whispered Elinor from the relative comfort of her motor car, before once again slipping the Riley into gear and following the Vauxhall to New Bond Street, where the vehicle remained stationary, parked on the street close to Fenwick, another old-established store favored by those for whom rationing had meant little in the way of lack. Elsie Finch did not step out of the Vauxhall, but as Elinor watched, a well-dressed young woman approached from Oxford Street carrying a Selfridges bag. The back door of the motor car opened. The young woman looked both ways, then handed the Selfridges bag to Elsie in the back seat and took the larger bag, which Elinor now suspected was made of good leather—she thought it might even be very good Italian leather, employed to underline the social stature of the shopper. The exchange was complete within two seconds. An onlooker would have been pushed to recall the young woman slowing her step to execute the swap.

Turning toward the famous store, the woman appeared every inch the well-heeled prospective customer. She wore a costume comprising a shell-pink jacket and skirt, the latter with kick pleats tailored just so to accentuate her calves. A silk blouse was worn to emphasize the collar set flat against the jacket's lapels. Shop assistants would take the woman to be the daughter of a wealthy man, perhaps a member of the lower aristocracy, possibly a Member of Parliament or a high-ranking officer in the army. No—if she was the daughter of an officer, it would be the navy, the "Senior Service."

It was time for Elinor to make her move. She was ready. Having dressed with care that morning, she was equally well turned out, though her costume was black and she wore a lavender shawl-collar blouse, so only a hint of silk was visible. As if by habit, she checked her white petticoat to ensure it had not slipped beneath the hem of her skirt, remembering her mother's warning about snow in the south, leveled at her daughters on the day they tried to escape the Kaiser's army. She could hear Charlotte's voice echoing down the years as she walked toward the store entrance.

The young woman proceeded straight to the perfume counter, where she sampled several fragrances, shaking her wrist and then bringing it to her nose, as if to ascertain the impact of air on the scent. Nearby, Elinor studied a lipstick—it seemed the American "Victory Red" was still popular, though she decided against it. At that moment, another young woman approached the counter and began to make almost too much of returning a cologne her husband had apparently bought for her birthday because his mother wore it.

"Oh my dear, can you imagine how that felt?" she said to the assistant. "He wants me to smell to high heaven just like his mother! I *must* change it for something else, something that's more . . . that's more me." Her accent was like cut glass, revealing a provenance within the most upper of classes.

The assistant agreed, but was so distracted by the story and the woman's loud requirements, she failed to notice several bottles of expensive perfume vanishing into the first woman's bag.

"Thank you so much," said the woman in the shell-pink costume. "I'll come back in a little while, after you've helped this lady. I just want to see how the Chanel smells after it's been on for a while."

"Slick," thought Elinor. She followed the woman to the clothing department, where the performance was repeated—only this time a third woman complained that she never knew what on earth to buy her older sister for her birthday. "You'd think she was from the last century—what would you suggest? She's thirty this year—thirty, would you believe?"

And so it went on, while half a dozen silk blouses of various design found their way into the bag with a newspaper laid on top of all but one. Then came what was obviously the pièce de résistance, when the first young woman returned to the counter.

"I'm so sorry, but this blouse really didn't suit me after all—may I return it? It has all the price labels still pinned in place, and—"

"Now that is exactly the sort of blouse I should purchase for my sister," interjected the third woman. "Thank goodness you came along!"

And so the story went on, with the first woman claiming a nice sum in the shape of a refund on a silk blouse she had just lifted from one of London's most revered stores. By the time she left the department, Elinor noticed that the woman with the frumpy sister had changed her mind yet again, saying she despaired of ever finding anything to suit such a difficult woman, and perhaps that blouse was just a little too revealing after all.

Elinor followed the first woman out toward the motor car, whereupon the door opened and Elsie Mackie's ring-heavy hand reached out, her face not visible. She took the bag and handed an envelope to the young woman, who turned and walked away to join the fellow members of Elsie's little gang.

Not bad for fifteen or twenty minutes' worth of work, thought Elinor, though she also wondered if Elsie Finch knew the women had made a bit extra on the side with the refund. She suspected there would be several more shops hit on the same day and by the same women, who would never travel in a chauffeur-driven motor car, or even a taxi— they would be unmemorable passengers on a bus weaving along Oxford Street toward Liberty, that oldest of stores, followed perhaps by a foray into Bourne & Hollingsworth before they called it a day. Elsie would distribute the goods to her "receivers" and collect payment within a few days, the next rung of women having sold the goods while earning a commission from Elsie along the way. Elsie was onto what she probably described as a "nice little earner" with minimum liability, while her brothers were landing bigger fish to fry—a far more ambitious game of risk and chance, but with greater returns for a successful operation.

Elinor wondered what elements would have to be in place if the whole Mackie family were planning a much more substantial and profitable outing than usual. And if there was a more sophisticated operation and Elsie was part of it, which of their many lucrative pies would they concentrate on? She knew there was more to be discovered, because while the income from bags of stolen expensive clothing and perfume was nothing to be sniffed at, it was just another drop of water in the Thames to a Mackie.

B ob, you first." Steve Warren was leaning forward in his chair. "And don't keep anything back—as I said, for the purposes of this little inquiry, Miss White is one of the lads."

Elinor raised an eyebrow as she turned toward Warren. There had been times when she wanted to end his banter, when she would have liked to slice the side of her palm against his throat to shut him up. This was one of them, and he knew it.

"Forget I said that, boys." He blew out his cheeks. "Go on, Bob."

"Not much to report, sir—and I've got to say, that's a report in itself. As far as the Mackies go, it's quiet. Too blimmin' quiet, if you ask me."

"Same here," said Charlie Kettle. "You know, I was a boy soldier in the last war, sir, and it sort of reminds me of the quiet before the big show. I've been thinking about it—there was the cannonade, then there was this sort of silence for a split second, and then the whistle blew and all hell broke loose. Reminds me of it. Except we're in that second when nothing's happened yet and the silence is going on for a bit longer than usual—sir, I can almost feel a sort of ediginess on the street when I talked to my blokes."

Elinor noticed the man's hand shaking. Ah, that explains a lot, she thought. Shell shock. Poor man. Mind you, war was like that, wasn't it? It stayed with you; could leave you with shaking hands or strange tics. An eye that twitched, a smile that couldn't be stopped when bad news came, or laughter in the face of tragedy. Terror still blurring the lines between extremes. Love and hate. Happiness and despair. Joy and anger. Tears and laughter. They were all sitting there, talking about villains in London, but the big villain was in all likelihood already inside every single one of them, under control. To a point.

"I think—" said Elinor. She cleared her throat. "I think Charlie's right, and what Bob has said backs it up. It's harder to pinpoint where to look—which is why I suspect there's a plan to deflect the police with a hit or many smaller hits." She paused. "We all know it was done by the army in the war—send a few troops in on one side to distract the enemy so the whole army can move in on the other. How would it be best to distract the Flying Squad? You've a raft of resources, but like any other department, there are limitations."

"Go on, Miss White," said Warren, his eyes revealing an instant intense focus on Elinor—a focus that disarmed her for a moment.

"Right," she said, composing herself. Warren's reaction had unsettled her. "Some of these questions are probably not important, but I'm shooting from the hip, as they say in those American western pictures." She looked around. "Might be handy to get a blackboard in here—you know, to keep our facts straight and identify any patterns."

"Yes, miss!" said Warren, now smiling as he gave a mock salute.

"I asked for that one, didn't I, lads?" Elinor smiled at the three men, who seemed to be bearing down on the thin layer of ice that had formed. She was an outsider, a woman into the bargain, and she could feel the cold air of prejudice as it wafted toward her. "Let me continue—or is this where I say, 'Pencils down and listen to Miss White'?"

The men laughed again. Ice broken.

"Now, as I said—or was going to say—if there was to be a same-day, same-time hit with minimum interference, I would imagine . . . and correct me if I'm wrong, because this is your business, not mine . . . but I would imagine it would be best to identify banks, shops etc., etc., in towns where a police presence is limited and where the Flying Squad is not likely to be waiting. What if, say, a number of banks around the country were targeted at the same time as jewelers and the pricier shops? And what if you added a few racecourses—not Epsom or Newmarket, but others where the takings are not as big, but nothing to be sniffed at either? Then at the same time add—"

Warren and his two men, Mills and Kettle were shaking their heads.

"Why not?" asked Elinor.

"Too much organization. Apart from the men at the top, you're not dealing with the sharpest knives in the drawer here, Miss White," said Warren. "That sort of 'bigger' is too labor-intensive, increasing the risk of any link in the chain breaking, or an informer coming to us and blowing the whole job—or jobs."

"Hmmm, yes, I can see that," said Elinor. "But, Detective Chief Inspector, what if there is only one man pulling the strings, so each job is encapsulated? That means that if the informer talks, only one job is blown."

"These boys don't like too many strings for someone to pull on. This isn't easy in and easy out," said Warren. "That's why they want Jim—I would put money on the fact that it's one big job and he's the man they want behind the wheel."

Elinor felt frustrated. She could have saved everyone the trouble of thinking about this if she had just walked along to the Mackie house and offered to help the young couple get away, suggesting that they go to a place where the brothers would never find Jim. Across an ocean sprang to mind. No, that wouldn't have worked. Jim's "previous" would make immigration to the lands of opportunity difficult. With the assisted passage scheme, it cost just ten pounds a head to sail to Australia for a new start in life. "Ten Pound Poms" they called the new wave of British entering the country. It was a pity Jim, Rose and Susie couldn't join them.

"I'm sorry, Miss White, but—" said Warren.

"But what if—" she countered. "What if . . . look, from all you've said, the Mackies have done without Jim for well over a year. They haven't needed him because they have other men, men equally talented behind the wheel of a fast motor car—yet might it be the case that they need him now because there's more than one job on the go at the same time?" She paused. There was silence. "It's just a thought—that he's not the main driver, but another body behind the wheel of a fast motor car."

"Remember what I said about the debt? Anyway—" Warren held up his hand to stop the conversation, and picked up the telephone on his desk. "Val, love, I've got a funny old request—could you get a blackboard and some chalk in here?" There was silence while he listened, followed by his reply. "I don't know where to get a blackboard, love. Nip along to Hamleys, the children's toy shop—you're bound to find one in there. Take the money out of petty cash." Silence again. "I know petty cash is for the bloody tea fund, but right now I need a bloody blackboard and some chalk in my office." Warren slammed down the telephone receiver. "Sorry about that. There's a blackboard on the way."

"I'm sure she'll rush down to get it after you've asked so nicely," said Elinor, looking up as Bob Mills chuckled, then leaned forward to speak.

"Miss White, I think you've got a point. There are other drivers, and we know from two big jobs—a bank in Margate and armed robbery of a jewelers in Tunbridge Wells that we're attributing to the Mackie family—that they've been doing well without Jim." He looked to his right and continued when he saw Charlie Kettle nod agreement. "And it's occurred to me that Jim Mackie is out of practice, like you suggested.

You have to keep up your reflexes if you want to be the sort of driver they need—and you don't do that behind the wheel of an old Fordson tractor, and definitely not a pair of Suffolk Punches!"

Warren listened, then raised his eyebrows as he consulted his watch. "Anything else, Miss White? I daresay you've got something more for us, because I know you're not the sort to have been out doing a bit of shopping of a morning!"

She felt the jab but smiled at the two detective sergeants, rolling her eyes in a conspiratorial fashion. She had been in similar situations—she knew how to handle the barb while at the same time ensuring that the man didn't have to reach down to protect his crown jewels in the process.

"Actually, Detective Chief Inspector, that's exactly what I was doing. Let me tell you all about it."

She recounted following Elsie Finch, describing how the woman had spent part of her morning and likely would make the most of the rest of her day.

Warren shook his head. "I don't believe it. Right under the noses of the shop security bods—and we have uniform on the street too. How does anyone miss that kind of operation?"

"It's simple," said Elinor. "People have underestimated poor old Elsie. If they hadn't, someone here at Scotland Yard would be able to identify exactly who was working for her, and there would be no overlooking that level of theft—even if at first blush it doesn't seem worth your while." She sighed, took her shoulder bag from the back of her chair and stood up.

"But Elsie isn't going to go looking for Jim, is she?" countered Warren. "And that's why we're all jawing away here and I've got Bob and Charlie wearing out their shoes—to find out why the Mackie boys want their brother home. Now, that is the concern here."

Elinor turned to Mills, asking a question to which she already knew the answer. "Do you have children, Bob?"

The detective registered surprise at the question. "Two boys and a girl." Then he grinned. "I get it, Miss White. I can see what you're getting at, and I think you might have something there, but like the boss said, not for this job. My little Janet runs around after her brothers all the time, doesn't want to be left out of anything. 'Me too, me too,' she says. And by golly, that girl knows how to play her brothers. I'd put money on her outwitting them every single time."

"Well, on that score, I rest my case," said Elinor, drawing her attention to Warren.

Warren gave a single nod and addressed his men. "You know what to do—start with the drivers."

"Sir," said the two detectives as they stood up, shoved their notebooks into their jacket pockets and left the room.

"Well, you've certainly set the cat among the pigeons, Linni. Mind you, you were always one to think in ways that others didn't, but you're wrong to set any stock by Elsie Finch. She's a chubby little nobody well past her prime. Her brothers and nephews protect her and let her run her little sideline so she doesn't get bored and lonely at home all day—and they applaud her for earning her keep and keeping Francisco happy."

Elinor smiled. "Past her prime? I worked out that she's not much older than me. Watch yourself, Steve. I'm keeping score, you know."

She left the office and walked out past the desks where Mills and Kettle were getting ready to leave, preparing to put their noses to the ground so that with a bit of luck and working the shoe leather, they might return with the information Warren wanted for the blackboard. She stopped when she entered the outer office, where a woman of about twenty-four sat behind a typewriter. A pencil was pushed behind the secretary's ear, held in place by strawberry-blond curls swept back in combs on either side of her head. She was ignoring the two ringing telephones on her desk, though she looked up when she became aware that Elinor was standing in front of her.

"I've got to get this report finished for his nibs in there," she said, inclining her head toward the door. "And both these telephones have been ringing off the hook! I tell you, there's no peace for the wicked!"

"You must be Val," said Elinor.

"That's me, Val of all trades!"

"Val, please don't worry about the blackboard—I'll get one."

"But—"

"It's alright, Val. No need for you to go running all over London looking for his nibs' blackboard." She smiled and was about to leave when she added, "Oh, and Val—don't get in any deeper with the chief inspector. If he told you he'd leave his wife, he lied. He's a first-class detective who deserves your hard work and your respect, but no more than that. I believe I can trust you not to repeat what I've said. But take my advice and extract yourself. Find yourself a nice young man—there are plenty around just waiting to walk out with a lovely girl like you."

Val's eyes widened. "How—"

"Doesn't matter. Now, if Detective Chief Inspector Warren asks for his blackboard, just let him know that Miss White offered to purchase it and will be advancing him the receipt for reimbursement through the appropriate channel. Not petty cash."

Elinor had a little time before making her way to Hamleys in search of the blackboard and chalk, so she stood across the road looking up at the grand buildings known as Scotland Yard. She didn't have to linger for long. Within fifteen minutes, Detective Chief Inspector Stephen Warren had departed the building, pulling on his jacket as he walked along the street. Elinor waited a few seconds before following him, in her heart hoping his destination was benign; perhaps a shop, or a café where he would get a decent cup of coffee to buoy him through the rest of the afternoon. Yes, she hoped it was an innocent port of call.

CHAPTER 5

1916

This is all crucial information." Isabelle took the papers from Charlotte. "You and your daughters are extremely observant, plus your notes are clear. And you seem to have gone beyond the call of duty, giving me more detail than I expected."

"The girls sketched, though they kept those papers tucked under the picnic blanket, and as trains passed they made notes on anything they observed until it was quite late to be sitting on the bank of a meadow overlooking the railway line," said Charlotte. "While they were sketching, I decided to take a short walk along to the point where I could look down and see the tracks diverge—and from that junction I could ascertain the onward direction of certain trains. It's all in our notes."

Isabelle nodded. "Were you seen by the Germans?"

The woman looked from Charlotte, to Cecily, to Elinor. Charlotte cleared her throat.

"A German officer was out for a stroll and stopped to talk to us. I had just returned to the girls and saw him in the distance while I was laying out a picnic, so we were able to conduct ourselves without drawing attention to any ambiguity of purpose—and a German train had already passed."

Isabelle frowned. "Tell me what happened."

"Well, he approached us and seemed to enjoy studying the girls' drawings. He said he had once been an art student and also had daughters who loved drawing. I offered him some water—fortunately he declined and went on his way."

"But, Mama," said Cecily, "he reminded us to be home before curfew."

"And he didn't mention your choice of location to spend a Sunday afternoon?" asked Isabelle.

"Only that it was a perfect sunny spot," said Charlotte.

"And you conversed in which language?" asked Isabelle. "I know all three of you are fluent in German."

"We spoke in French," said Cecily.

Isabelle turned to Elinor. "Did he speak to you?"

"No. And I didn't speak to him."

The woman nodded, addressing all three De Witt women. "Be seen around the town sketching in other locations. I'll tell you when I want you to return to observing the trains."

"Isabelle—" Charlotte leaned across the table toward the visitor. "Who receives the information we're providing? You never told us, specifically."

Isabelle was silent, then pushed back her chair and walked to the kitchen window to stare out at the garden. Charlotte, Elinor and Cecily looked at one another and waited. Elinor thought Isabelle reminded her of her mother. Charlotte would stand by the window, sometimes with her hands steeped in a bowl of hot water, as if she found both the garden and the warmth soothing in some way. A moment later, Isabelle turned around and took her place at the table.

'I am the only person who knows that you three women have assisted me. By the same token, you only know me. However, I am in contact with others, chiefly but not exclusively women and girls who are also gathering information and taking on similar tasks. But they only know me; they do not know one other, and they have no knowledge of your part in any plan to thwart the enemy."

"It's like Chinese whispers," said Elinor.

"A little. But understand this—and you must pay attention to what I am saying—if you are arrested while about this work and interrogated, the risk of you having enough information to reveal a whole web of resistance across our country is diminished. Being in the dark about anyone else—with the exception of me—is a means of employing ignorance to protect the chain of activity. And don't worry, I can look after myself."

Charlotte, Cecily and Elinor offered no response, so Isabelle continued.

"The precaution has been taken ever since one of our founders was arrested and detained by the Germans, and though he did not reveal a thing to the enemy during his interrogation, which was brutal, we realized the risk involved in one person having so much knowledge." She looked at each De Witt in turn. "That man paid with his life, shot by the Germans—they knew he had information, and to be frank, I believe his refusal to speak under the most terrible circumstances undermined them. Make no mistake, you must understand that this is dangerous work. Many are engaged in it, and every single contribution is invaluable. We are at a most crucial juncture in the war."

Elinor looked at her mother and sister. Neither spoke, but she fidgeted in her chair. She raised her hand. "Yes, but, Miss . . . Isabelle, we've given you our pages of observations, but where do they go?"

"You're not in school now, Elinor; you don't need to raise your hand." Isabelle's smile was brief. "To answer your question—the information gathered goes to the people who are furnishing the necessary funds to keep us going, which enables us to continue this vital reconnaissance. They are the ones who are in a position to use any intelligence provided by our resistance work—and they use it well. Everything you do is for Belgium."

"But who are they?" Elinor pressed, despite hearing her mother clear her throat again, a warning to be quiet.

Isabelle smiled. "Good girl—you have a right to ask. If you are risking your life, you should know. The Germans have a broad idea of who is receiving information, but they don't know how we are either obtaining or transferring it. Suffice it to say that it is for Britain and her allies—they are in the midst of a tremendous push against the Germans. And beyond that I will add no more. Remember what happened to Nurse Cavell."

Silence descended once again. Yes, they all knew what had happened to Edith Cavell, the British nurse who had offered a means of escape for lone Allied soldiers separated from their army. She had been assassinated by firing squad, a warning that anyone engaging in resistance against the German military would meet the same fate.

Following Isabelle's departure, Elinor remained at the table with her mother and sister. They were silent until Charlotte spoke.

"I'll put the kettle on for some tea."

"Mama, aren't you always the British lady? You're so British that when you're worried, you make a cup of tea and your accent changes."

Elinor stared at Charlotte, then Cecily, knowing her sister was spoiling for an argument, as if she had a stick in her hand and was tormenting wasps in their nest.

Charlotte had no immediate response, but seemed to take her time placing the kettle on the stove and opening the dampers to boil the water. Satisfied that the water was heating, she turned to her daughter.

"Cecily, it's tea because it's all we have to warm us, and to do the serious thinking needed at this very moment in this household, we need something to do with our hands, and clutching a cup of hot tea is as good an idea as any. And I, for one, am thirsty." Charlotte glared at Cecily. "I might also add that you were born in London, my dear, so you too might as well have a target on your back. Tea will help you bear it."

"Well, that shut her up," thought Elinor, who was soothed by the rhythm of Charlotte's tea-making—the warming of the pot, the single level scoop of tea leaves, the water now boiling poured onto the leaves then stirred. The teapot lid was slotted into place and the padded cotton cosy pulled over the top while the brew grew stronger. The single scoop was not enough for a hearty cup of tea, so Charlotte took her seat once more while she waited until the liquid resembled something she would want to drink—until the color was akin to the tea she would have made at home in England, when she was a girl.

"So, what do we want to do?" asked Charlotte. "Shall we withdraw our assistance or do you wish to continue in full knowledge of the danger?" She sighed. "I don't think we had a complete appreciation of the threat before, but I will tell you now that the appearance of the German officer scared the wits out of me. I thought we would be discovered."

"Oh, he was so involved in talking about his daughters, he wouldn't have guessed," said Cecily.

"He might have," said Elinor. "He might have known all the time—someone on that train might have reported that three people were on the bank overlooking the railway line, sitting there with pencils and paper, so he came out to see for himself."

"Yes, but just him?" countered Cecily. "For goodness' sake, Linni—he would have brought soldiers with him."

"But what if he wants to continue keeping an eye on us, so he can capture us when . . . well, when he can get more than just we three?"

Having delivered her question, Elinor sat back, folding her arms as she watched the color drain from her sister's face. Cecily was beginning to get on her nerves. Charlotte cleared her throat—Elinor noticed she had been doing a lot of throat clearing lately, as if framing her sentences was an act for which she had to brace herself.

"Yes, quite," said Charlotte. She stood up, lifted the cosy from the pot and poured tea into three cups. She added a splash of milk to each cup—just the day before she had swapped green beans with a neighbor for a quarter pint of the precious liquid—and passed a cup of tea to each daughter. She took her seat again, sipped her tea and coughed. "Shall we wait for a week or so? Perhaps at this juncture it's best if we just take each day as it comes, which means school for you, waiting in lines and looking after the house and vegetable garden for me."

"What if we see the German again?" asked Elinor.

Charlotte nodded. "I believe we might. As I said, we simply go about our business. If we do that, no one can fault us."

"He didn't ask for our identity cards, so I think he doesn't know about Isabelle," said Cecily.

Elinor wondered how her sister could be so dense—but perhaps it was her fifteen-year-old brain confusing her. After all, she'd heard her mother call it "that age." Perhaps that's what had happened; her mind had become thick with distraction.

"Ceci," said Elinor, staring at her sister. "I don't for a single minute think her name is Isabelle, and we don't know her surname. I've not seen her before she came to us here, and Mama had only seen her once in passing before they met in the market. And what's more, I wonder if that German didn't ask for our papers because he knows who we are."

"Girls—" Charlotte began.

"Mama," Elinor went on. "I think we have to do what we can to help Isabelle, or whoever she is. I don't want to do nothing when I could be doing something—just like Papa. That's why he's not with us—because he chose to do something, to fight the Germans. If what we do can help the British beat them out of our country, then I'm not going to be scared of them and what they can do to me."

Charlotte raised an eyebrow and looked from Elinor to her older daughter.

"Ceci? What say you?"

There was a pause of several seconds before Cecily replied. "Linni's right." She sighed, then her smile was sudden. "Yes, my little sister is right. Let's see what Isabelle asks us to do next."

Elinor thought that Cecily didn't really want to admit that her little sister was right—but she hated to look fearful in front of their mother.

The sisters continued to attend classes at the convent from Monday to Friday, though now lessons in what were called "Caring" were added to Cecily's timetable. When Cecily described the lessons, Elinor thought it sounded not only boring, but really common sense once you'd sat through a session or two. There was the looking after of children, the dressing of wounds, keeping a clean house, and of course the care and management of the spirit through constant prayer. Elinor wondered if the nuns had grasped that when daughters lived in a house with no servants, they already knew a thing or two about cleaning, about the treatment of white linen before washing, and about the dressing of wounds, though Cecily told her the nuns weren't stopping at a simple cut earned while pruning roses—she now knew how to treat a bullet wound. The revelation spurred Elinor to wonder what else the nuns might be doing when they weren't trying to prepare young girls for womanhood, though Cecily seemed to have a lack of curiosity regarding the lives of nuns.

"So what did they say about a bullet wound—and how would they know?" Elinor sat back against her bed pillows, put her finger on the page she was reading in her book and stared at her sister.

"Oh, it was nothing really. Sister Jeanne-Marie said that because of what's been happening in our country, people can be wounded even by accident, so we should know how to help them."

"But how do they know about bullet wounds?"

Cecily put down her own book. "For goodness' sake, Linni, how do I know? I mean—they're nuns. Nuns are everywhere, aren't they? You know—they treat people's illnesses and then give them a dose of the Bible at the same time."

"Ceci!" It wasn't what her sister said that shocked Elinor, but the insouciant way she expressed herself.

"You ask too many questions, Linni. I—"

"Girls, I want you to come down to the kitchen." Charlotte De Witt poked her head around the bedroom door.

"But it's late," complained Cecily.

"Isabelle is here," said Charlotte. "She wants to see you both."

The sisters looked at each other, scrambled out of bed, put on their dressing gowns and followed their mother downstairs. As before, Isabelle was seated at the kitchen table. The heavy linen curtains were drawn, but to make sure not a sliver of light leached through, Charlotte took clothes-pegs from a drawer and secured the places where one curtain met the other.

As soon as the women were seated, Isabelle began.

"Before I describe the task I must ask of you, I will tell you that I would not be making this request if I had any other choice. However, I believe you can do this, though it is not without danger." She looked at Charlotte, who nodded for her to continue. "Extreme danger," she added.

The assignment described by Isabelle was not one of gathering knowledge, but of sabotage. It demanded swift action and cool heads.

"Charlotte, I think this is one assignment your daughters must complete without you, given their youth and ability to move with speed. I will wait with you until they return."

"But—"

"Mama, we can do it—I know we can," said Elinor. "We're both really good runners—remember when Papa used to race us alongside the river, to see who could get to the bakery first?"

"Time has passed, Linni."

"Exactly," said Elinor. "We're older—and this job must be done." She looked at Isabelle, who was frowning, as if surprised by the younger daughter's willingness to take on the task. Turning to her sister, Elinor reached for Cecily's hand. "We will have a good story—that Cecily . . ." She pulled away her hand and rubbed her temple as if to stimulate her thinking. "Yes, that's it . . . if we're stopped, we'll say . . . we'll say that it's a local custom for a young woman to float a letter down the river to her lover if he's away from home, hoping that the message from her heart reaches him." She grasped Cecily's hand again. "And we'll say that Ceci misses Peter so much, she just had to write the letter and I said I would go to the river with her."

Charlotte seemed perplexed. "Who is Peter?"

"Mama, Peter is nobody. I just made him up," said Elinor. "It's part of the . . . of the story we can tell." She looked at her sister, who appeared to be blushing. "Ceci?"

"Yes, I think Linni is right—it's a good story." She stared at her mother as if to persuade her, then toward Isabelle. "We'll do it."

Isabelle lost no time, at once taking a map from her pocket, which she spread across the table. "You know this point where the train crosses the river—" She tapped the map with her forefinger. "The bridge is not high here, as the river is narrow and shallow at this point. You proceed in this direction, and there are points here where two lines of track meet. Our information indicates that a train carrying significant ordnance and soldiers will cross those points in about one hour and five minutes. Here's what you must do to effect the derailment. It's simple."

"What about the guards—won't they be on the bridge?" Charlotte leaned across the table toward Isabelle.

"That is why this part of the railway line is best—it's away from the bridge, and there is a path here."

"We're familiar with the path—that's where we used to walk with Papa and Polo," said Elinor.

Isabelle nodded. "Yes, I know."

Elinor saw her mother frown, heard her clear her throat to speak, but she was quick to interject with a question. "Where do we find what we need to make the train go off the rails?"

"Elinor, always jumping right in." Isabelle smiled, and pointed to the map again. "There's a very old oak tree right here, and—"

"Where we used to climb," said Elinor.

"Good, you know it. At the base of the tree there is a sort of little cavern where the roots rise up."

"Where Papa said the fairies lived," added Elinor, now barely aware of her mother's growing uneasiness.

"You will find a number of thick metal plates there. They are not light, but they are manageable." She tapped the map. "You take them to this point, and you lay them across the track here, here and here on both sides. Then you leave. You do not wait to watch, you just leave. Is that clear?"

Elinor nodded, looking at Cecily, who stared at Isabelle and said, "Yes. We understand and it's perfectly clear."

"Your mother and I will expect you home in—" She consulted her wristwatch. "About forty-five minutes from now, at half past ten. Now then, Cecily, pen the letter to your boy, just in case you need to use it. Both of you, dress in the darkest clothing you have to hand, and once you reach the path, roll your skirts up from the waist so you can move with speed. Wear your lace-up boots, tie your hair back and you will not need a hat—it can come off and be left behind. Walk close to walls as you make your way along the street, though fortunately you are close to the path."

"Isabelle—Isabelle, wait. Let's stop for a moment. My daughters are not trained for this kind of work—isn't there anyone else?"

"If there were, I would have asked them."

"Mama, do not worry," said Elinor. "Make up the stove, open the dampers and put the kettle on at a quarter past ten—then you'll have a nice cup of tea for us at half past, when we return."

I don't know how you can see in the dark, Linni—you must have been a cat in another lifetime," said Cecily, walking behind her sister along the rough path.

"Shhh, and just follow me, Ceci. Don't say another word, and if you trip, just keep your mouth shut!"

"I just want to remind—"

"Shh!"

Five minutes later, Cecily spoke again. "I'm getting used to the dark now—I can see my way quite well."

"Good. We're almost at the tree."

Elinor turned to Cecily, reaching for her sister's jacket to pull her closer as she whispered in her ear. "Let's stop, I want to listen."

The girls were still and silent. Elinor nodded. "I can't hear anything. Now to the tree."

Elinor had only a vague awareness that her sister was following instructions without dissent, without complaining that she was the eldest. But Elinor wasn't doing this to gain her sister's approval—she was doing it for Papa, so that he could be proud of his daughters. Reaching the tree she touched Cecily's arm, moved around the trunk to the cavernous roots and knelt down. Cecily stooped beside her as she rolled her sleeve and reached into the roots, hoping a rat wasn't inside.

"I'm touching the metal plates, Ceci. I'm going to pass them to you," said Elinor. "But let's not talk again until we've done this."

Despite the darkness, she could feel Cecily nodding accord.

Trying not to rustle fallen leaves as she pulled each metal plate from its hiding place, Elinor handed them one after the other to Cecily, who made a pile just beyond the tree. They were some twenty-five feet from the railway line.

The daughters of Thomas De Witt lifted two plates each at a time and situated them along the railway track, following Isabelle's instructions to the letter. The task complete, Elinor took her sister's arm and they walked back to the path, the river snaking along on the opposite side.

At first they continued on at a slow pace, their steps measured as they removed themselves from the site of their act of sabotage. After another two minutes had passed, without communication, they picked up speed, until they were almost running. In a fingersnap, Elinor stopped and reached for Cecily's arm, pulling her into a ditch.

Cecily was about to complain, perhaps even scream, but Elinor clapped her hand over her sister's mouth.

A group of drunken German soldiers ambled along the path, handing a bottle back and forth to one another as they passed the hiding De Witt sisters. From the ditch, Elinor counted four men.

How long were they in the ditch? Was it five minutes? Ten minutes? Elinor thought about the elasticity of time, that a watched clock never moves, that fear transforms every second into an hour, and that seconds and minutes blend with sound in way that could lead to confusion, to poor judgment. She was afraid of having poor judgment, afraid that she might be the one to make a bad decision.

When the only sound was the rustle of a gentle breeze in the tree fronds overhead, Elinor took Cecily's arm and helped her to her feet. Elinor chose another path to the house, a shortcut her father had shown her in what seemed a lifetime past. The girls fell into their mother's arms only two minutes beyond the anticipated time of their return.

Isabelle's smile was brief. "Tell me everything, from the moment you left the house."

Elinor was alone with Isabelle, her mother having taken Cecily to the washroom to hide her embarrassment at having lost control of her bladder while she was in the ditch watching German soldiers pass, their heavy boot-swaddled feet only inches from her face.

Isabelle nodded as Elinor recounted their progress, and described finding the metal plates and positioning them on the railway line.

"You have both done very well." The woman paused, not taking her eyes off Elinor when Charlotte and Cecily returned to the kitchen. "Were you scared?"

Elinor nodded. "Yes. I was scared we'd make a noise, terrified that we might not hear the soldiers if they came for us, or that we would make too much clanking with the metal plates—they were heavier than we thought they would be."

"Good girl," said Isabelle. "I worry more about people who claim to have no trepidation. A healthy measure of fear will be your greatest protector." She drew her attention away from Elinor to Cecily as she sat down. "And do not be embarrassed, dear Ceci—a physical reaction to fear has happened to the very best of us." She grinned. "I know grown men who will only wear brown trousers when they are on an assignment."

Elinor looked at her mother, at the concern writ large across her face.

"I'll pour us a cup of tea," said Charlotte

Isabelle pushed back her chair. "Not for me, Charlotte. I must go. There will be soldiers on the street soon enough. Have your tea and then brush every last scrap of mud or dust from your boots. Attend to your coats and make sure there is nothing along the hem of your skirt to suggest a recent walk." She glanced at her watch. "In fact, forgo the tea and do it now. Lock the door behind me, and when your tasks are complete, go to your beds."

The house-to-house search began even before dawn, though sunlight was just beginning to break through when Isabelle's words came true, not with a gentle knock at the door, but with a determined banging. Elinor, still in her dressing gown, stood up and held out her hand to stop her mother.

"It's best I go. I'm the youngest. You and Ceci stay with your breakfast."

The German soldiers were not as mature as Elinor imagined they would be. Why had she thought the men who came for her would be her father's age? Before they had a chance to speak, she addressed them in German.

"Why are you here, banging on our door? We've only just got out of our beds."

"We're searching all houses," said the soldier who seemed to be more senior.

Elinor made a point of leaning out of the door to look along the street. Soldiers were everywhere, banging on doors. Neighbors were in their front gardens, some ready for work, others wearing their night clothes, all at gunpoint.

"Why? What do you think we have here?" asked Elinor.

"Will you get out of the way, or do I have to push you?" The first soldier stepped forward.

Elinor held up her hand. "Wait! Let me make sure my sister and mother are clothed—we are three women alone, and we don't receive men in our house as a rule."

She made her way along the narrow hallway toward the kitchen and stood in the doorway. In a loud voice, she spoke in German.

"Put your dressing gowns on—there are a couple of soldiers come to search the house—oh no, Mama, I don't think they have time for tea, but I'll ask them."

She returned to the soldiers and stood aside for them to enter, though she whispered to the first soldier, "Don't accept her tea—it's terrible, very weak."

The search lasted ten minutes. The contents of wardrobes were pulled out and left on the floor, the soles of boots lined up against the back door were checked and clothing hanging from a line in the scullery inspected.

"Would you like tea?" asked Charlotte, as the soldiers passed through the kitchen in the direction of the front door.

The first soldier smiled at Elinor before turning to Charlotte, snapping his heels together and declining the offer, with thanks, yet he lingered in front of Cecily on his way to the door. Looking Cecily up and down, he flicked his finger under her chin and smiled. Elinor thought it more grin than smile, more something a man would do to a woman over whom he had some control. It was not a mark of youthful flirtation, but a show of power. She had not seen this behavior before and feared her own observation at that moment—but it spurred her to make a silent vow that she, her mother and sister would do all they could to arm themselves against their obvious weakness; the vulnerability of being female.

At lunchtime, while Sister Louise was serving a watery potato and leek soup, half-filling bowls to feed the many assembled girls whose stomachs rumbled as they queued in the dining hall, a number of soldiers marched into the convent to shepherd everyone outside into the street at gunpoint. Townsfolk were lined up around a place where two nuns and two old men from the town were standing, hands and feet tied. Soldiers patrolled those gathered, poking women and children with their bayonets—there were no young men in the town, only the elderly, the infirm, women and little boys. As the four prisoners refused a blindfold one by one, Elinor grasped her sister's hand, and then, finding the comfort not sufficient to still her heart, she wrapped her arms around Cecily and felt her need returned as Cecily held her tight.

The firing squad did their work with speed and efficiency. The bodies of Sister Jeanne-Marie and Sister Hildimar fell to the ground, blood oozing across their starched white habits, their dead limbs entangled with those of a man who had once been a teacher of geography at the boys' academy. The remains of another man slumped down across them—from birth he had been unable to hear or speak, but was held in great affection by everyone in the town.

An officer walked across the square to stand before the dead. Lifting a loudhailer to his mouth, he said, "Consider this a warning." He did not need to elaborate, but threw the loudhailer to the ground and walked away. Elinor recognized him as the same officer who had once studied art in Germany, the proud father of two daughters at home, sisters who loved to sketch.

CHAPTER 6

1947

Elinor followed Detective Chief Inspector Stephen Warren until he reached Whitehall Place. She knew her unofficial surveillance came with risk in this area; there were few pedestrians, no shop doorways to step into and at that moment only a smattering of vehicular traffic. At one point when Warren turned around, he might have noticed Elinor had his attention not been on the ankles of a young woman emerging from one of the government offices along the street.

Warren continued walking at a fair clip and did not slow as he approached a black motor car. The door swung open, and without losing momentum, he climbed in. The vehicle pulled out before even a second had elapsed after the passenger door closed—fortunately the motor car proceeded away from Elinor, not toward her.

She slowed her pace, looked both ways and crossed the road. She hoped she appeared suitably nondescript, another civil servant walking between offices, just in case the driver had glanced in his rearview mirror and seen her. Clouds moved in the sky above at an opportune moment, allowing a beam of sunlight to catch the back window, revealing the silhouetted figure Warren had joined. Was Warren keeping to a previously arranged meeting, with no link to Elinor's appearance in London? Or was there a direct relationship? She reminded herself that there were a good number of open cases to keep Warren and his men in the Flying Squad busy for a very long time, and work had become Warren's first love, his first commitment. She was sure that if Steve Warren prayed at all, it would be about his work. But all the same, Elinor would have parted with good money to know who he was joining in the motor car. The chauffeured vehicle suggested official government business, and though communication with those in the higher echelons of the country's security was part of Warren's remit, Elinor knew her curiosity regarding the identity of the other passenger would nag like a stone in her shoe until she had put a name to him. When the car turned left into Whitehall, she doubled back toward Scotland Yard. Deep in thought, she approached the Embankment and stopped to watch the capital's famous river wind its way toward the sea.

The tide was out, providing opportunity for the mudlarks—Londoners who picked over the Thames mud—to appear. Using their fingers or sticks, they came in search of long-lost treasures or anything washed up by the current that could be sold or bartered. She understood that clay pipes from the Middle Ages were still to be found, though since the Blitz part of a downed Spitfire or lumps of shrapnel were not unusual, and scrap metal could always find a buyer. But it was the promise of an ancient gold coin or two that brought in the scavengers at low tide every day.

The Thames was the part of London Elinor felt most drawn to. It was always there, and more often than not it had a way of reflecting her moods. It could seem at rest, moving at a slower pace during times when she felt the need to withdraw, to go into herself. Then it would turn, swollen by grey storms and full tide, a mirror for her frustration or anger. And it would change again, as if meandering with intent to get on with doing the job demanded of it, which for "the Water" was the safe passage of people and goods from far and wide. That's what the local people called it: the Water. *I'm going over the Water. He works on the Water. The Water will flood again, just you wait.*

The Luftwaffe had used the moon's reflection on that precious water, following the glorious silver ribbon to come in time and again to inflict bombing after bombing on warehouses, businesses and houses— back-to-back homes where ordinary working people lived ordinary lives. They were a people who sought refuge as London's lifeblood spilled into the ancient river on the nights they dreaded; a Bombers' Moon illuminating the way for terror. And on one December night, Hermann Göring planned a raid with meticulous detail to coincide with low tide, so as fast as the London fire crews fed hoses into the Thames, expecting to draw water to fight the firestorm razing the city, so those hoses were choked with silt and debris. *London's burning, London's burning. Fetch the engines, fetch the engines. Fire! Fire! Fire! Fire! Pour on water, pour on water.* A children's rhyme coming true again, centuries after that first Great Fire.

True, Elinor had only a few years of knowing London before it was changed forever by war, but this waterway drew her in. It was hard for her to imagine that it began as springs arising from an aquifer at Thames Head in the Cotswolds, and it was only when the German George I—the first Hanoverian monarch in Britain—acceded to the throne and could not pronounce "th" that the name of the river might as well have been spelled "Tems." She remembered asking about it when she visited London as a child, and her English grandmother informed her, "What the king says is what is right. And he said 'Tems.' " Now, standing alongside the river, she knew that within a few miles the very water that was the focus of her attention would join the North Sea, its burgeoning swell rising to be battered by heaving waves rolling in at

Gravesend. *Graves end. The end of graves.* Names of towns along the way marked the river's passage, a waterway used by incomers, welcome and unwelcome since early times, buoying them along to their destination. Londinium. Lunden. Londoun. London. *Home.*

Elinor stood on the Embankment and focused on the entrance to Scotland Yard, waiting. She did not need to linger long before the man she wanted to speak to emerged. She watched him turn to his left. He looked both ways, crossed the road and stepped onto the pavement only a few yards from where she was standing. Sometimes serendipity worked in her favor.

"Oh, Charlie!" She waved to him as he turned. "Mind if I join you? I'm walking that way."

Detective Sergeant Charles Kettle's eyes widened for a second. He had been reaching for a packet of cigarettes when she called out, and now returned them to the inside pocket of his tweed jacket. Elinor noticed two things as he drew back the buttonholed side of the jacket: a grey shirt that should have been white, and was therefore in need of a wash, starch and hot iron, and the weapon he wore to the left against his rib cage. It was a Webley revolver, an armed forces standard issue. Along with the Enfield No. 2 it was the sidearm of choice, though she knew the Smith and Wesson was also being put to good use on both sides of the law. It paid to know the weaponry made and used by friend and foe alike.

"You don't have to put away your cigarettes on my account, Charlie," said Elinor, approaching the policeman. "It was so stuffy in DCI Warren's office, I thought I would go for a walk along the Embankment."

Charlie reached for his packet of cigarettes again and pushed up one to offer Elinor, who shook her head.

"Had to give them up so I could breathe, Charlie. I smoked a few too many during the war."

He nodded. "I should probably do the same." He coughed as he lit the cigarette and drew on it before taking it from his mouth, blowing smoke to the side and studying the glowing end of the cigarette for a second. "I'm going to the Tube. You?"

They fell into step, shafts of sunlight once more breaking through the clouds.

"Bit of shopping," said Elinor. "Anyway, I'll walk with you toward the Tube. Not often we get some clear air here, is it?"

"Not often."

Elinor allowed a step or two in silence before speaking again. "You've got your work cut out for you, haven't you, Charlie? These criminals are like jelly; tricky to round up, and I bet they slip through your fingers as often as not."

"I'll say." He drew on his cigarette again, closing one eye as a breeze blew smoke into his face. "You know what the trouble is—well, there's a good few things causing trouble, but half the trouble is the people who live on the streets around where these villains operate."

"The people—you mean locals not involved in crime?"

Charlie Kettle laughed. "Oh, Miss White, you don't know the streets, do you? Everyone's involved in crime. For a start, them same locals will tell you that it's the likes of the Mackies who keep the streets clean. Any filth comes in—and by 'filth' you know what I mean; your pimps, your prostitutes and your spivs from outside—well, the Mackie family gets rid of them." He held out two fingers, the cigarette clutched between them as he pointed to the river. "And after someone in the Mackies' employ has dealt with a problem they don't want, you'll see the problem floating along, never to be seen walking the streets again. When the river police haul out the body, there's usually only half left. Or they don't float in the first place because they're encased in concrete. We know for a fact that there's a number of small-time bad seeds holding up Rotherhithe Docks, even as you and I stand here."

"A charming thought," said Elinor.

Kettle gave a half-laugh. "Ask anyone who lives within a mile of Mickleham Street what they think of Francisco's boys, and you'll hear them say, 'He loved his old mum though, and they keep the streets clean around here.' Then they'll say, 'Which is more than can be said for the police—coppers can't even keep their shoes clean.' And they would be right. We can't be everywhere. And if we're everywhere, then we're nowhere when there's trouble, so we have to pick our battles. Sometimes I wonder if it's all worth it, but the pay packet keeps a roof over my family's head. My army pension doesn't give me a pot to—"

"Yes, I see," said Elinor, not waiting for him to finish the phrase.

"And of course the bad boys look after people," continued the detective. "The housewives think they're getting something free when they're offered a pound or two of sugar on the side, so they pay up and say 'Thank you very much, nice of you to think of us.' But the Mackies are offering sugar because they're making a tidy profit from a job over at the sugar factory that the company didn't report. And why don't they report it? Because they don't want trouble either. They say south of the river is London's breadbasket for all the food factories over there—but it's nice pickings for the Mackies." Kettle drew on his cigarette again. "And for all the talk about keeping the streets clean, don't think for a minute that they're not into running their own ladies of the night. The Mackie family keeps their manor boundaries sparkling while they make sure the money comes from a clientele who can pay more for a bit of posh, instead of a quick one round the back of a garage with an underage girl run by a pimp."

"You can't stop that?"

He shook his head. "Hardly worth trying—and that's not a job for us anyway. We'd pass it on to 'Clubs and Vice' over in Soho. Mind you, they've got the Chinese gangs operating over there, so we have the odd parley about that lot. To be honest, it's the bane of our job, because most of the time we've all got our heads down sorting out what we can get done, rather than what we definitely can't, which means half the time the right hand hasn't a clue about the pudding the left hand's stirring."

"Hmmm," said Elinor. "Charlie, do you think there could be something bigger than usual on the cards concerning the Mackie family?"

Kettle stopped and turned to Elinor. He took a deep draw on the remaining inch of his cigarette and dropped the end onto the pavement, grinding it with his foot as he blew smoke through his nostrils.

"Miss White, there's something big, as you put it, going down with the Mackie family—you can bet on it because there's always something big on the cards, though most of the time they're a canny lot. They plan it like they're going into battle. If they find holes and it's too risky, they chuck out the plan and think again. That's why they're successful—though let's be fair, they have a higher tolerance for risk than the average man on the street, and that's why crime is their business. Old Francisco trained his family well—he always told them to answer the why and the how of the job before they even started it, so there's not a second or a person unaccounted for. It's like school—you know, do your homework and check it before handing it in. Now then, I know this much. There's the old geezer's way of doing things and then there's his sons—Jim's dad is more or less at the top of the pile. But now, what with the old boy getting on, there's Jim Mackie's brothers and their cousins coming up, and they aren't as patient. They're starting to push against the old guard a bit because they want it all now and John's generation are saying, 'Why not?' The younger ones have got the money from their grandfather and fathers—oh, and perhaps a bit from Elsie too. But they want to be top dogs, and they know any family power comes from the next big job, not all these smaller jobs. It could be their downfall though, because keeping their manor safe and how it all looks to any rivals is as important as what a job brings in." He sighed, squinting as he stared at the water. "So yes, Miss White, of course I think something big is on the cards. Trouble is, where will the big happen and exactly how big is it? They've had a flawless innings for a good while, and it's well past time for them to dive in with something even more . . . even more . . . let's say even more 'ambitious.' "

Charlie Kettle paused again, as if wondering whether he should go on. Elinor did not interrupt, but allowed him to consider and then voice his thoughts.

Kettle pressed his lips together, was silent for another second, then began again. "You know, my eldest boy came home with his homework yesterday—geography, it was, all about earthquakes. Not often I'm around to talk to him about it, but he loves all that stuff—mountains and rivers, countries, studying maps. Anyway, he was telling me about it, and you know, it was more interesting than I thought it would be. And it got me to thinking about all them earthquakes and how it's like London right now. You see, Miss White, my feeling is that there's an earthquake on the way, and what we have to do is find out where the rumbling's coming from and the—what did my lad call it? Yes, the epicenter." He stopped and looked out at the water. "We have got to find the epicenter, the job at the top of the pyramid—or the bottom, or the middle, depending upon how you look at it. I reckon my boy must have lost me after we got to the epicenter bit because I can't remember where it is in relation to all the rumbling."

"Do you think Jim Mackie will falter—will he get involved?"

Kettle shrugged. "He's family and family is hard to break up—especially that lot, where every cog has its place in a well-oiled wheel.

But he's got that wife of his and the little one, and now he's out on a limb. Cut himself off. The old boy won't have liked that and neither will his father. There again, we have to assume that Jim and Rose Mackie could do with a tidy influx of cash. Working on a farm doesn't pay much, and neither does a tea shop." He shrugged. "Jim Mackie might cave, or he might not. That's down to Rose, I would imagine—and how much pressure she can take. She's a good, respectable sort of girl, is Rose. But everyone has their limit." He turned to Elinor, staring at her. "I'm not one to speak without thinking. I watch. I listen. And out there when I'm wearing down my shoe leather, I ask questions. I don't know what you being in on this is all about—apart from the fact that you know the boss and you've brought in some information for him. But as I said, I watch and I listen—and I reckon you know that just because little Susan Mackie is a child, it doesn't mean she's safe. If the old boy or Johnny Mackie gave the word to do away with the three of them, it would happen just like that." He snapped his fingers. "And it would be fast. Jim knows it, but I'm not sure Rose does."

Elinor nodded. "Yes, I thought as much, Charlie."

"There's one more thing—and this is just what my nose tells me." He tapped his nose with his right forefinger. "They want Jim back in the fold, with or without the girl. Him leaving the Mackie manor is seen as a slight against everything Francisco has built up. DCI Warren told you what they were like, I'm sure. And what with Jim down there in the country now, working on a farm, well, him and Rose might as well have taken up residence in a sewer as far as the family is concerned. Now, Jim being that far away—does it make a difference to the Mackie family's line of work, in the grand scheme of things?" He shook his head. "Nah, not really. But it's like losing a tile off the roof. There's no big difference to the whole house, but if you know the tile's not there, it'll annoy you until that roof is mended." He lifted his hat. "Nice talking to you, Miss

White. I reckon you'd better be off to sort out that blackboard if DCI Warren is going to stand a chance of spotting any links between what they're all up to."

Interesting, thought Elinor as she made her way across the street toward Trafalgar Square. Her conversation with Val about the blackboard had been in private, so it was clear she had to remember that even within Scotland Yard there were few secrets. She had been trained to act as if walls were thin everywhere, so she should have known better. Yet there were elements of greater importance to ponder. If she was not mistaken, Detective Sergeant Kettle had just made a comment revealing a level of doubt regarding his superior. Or was he joking about Warren standing a chance of spotting any links? Was Warren losing his touch, not accepting the evidence his men brought to him? Perhaps. It could have been a joke, but on the other hand, Elinor was well aware that the British often served up a hot and sizzling slight with a flourish of humor.

Despite rationing, despite the bleak aura left by five years of war, Hamleys was always a joyous place. The world's largest toy store had been bombed five times during the war, and every single time it carried on doing business, opening again even as the building was being made safe, with staff wearing protective helmets as they brought joy to children waiting outside for a toy to be wrapped and handed to them.

Navigating the store with the help of an assistant, Elinor found a suitable blackboard. She purchased the largest one available and said yes, colored chalks as well as plain white would be best, thank you very much. She paid cash for the purchase, received a receipt and asked for the blackboard to be delivered soonest to Detective Chief Inspector

Warren at Scotland Yard. Indeed, she added, his boy would be delighted with the gift.

As she made her way toward the door, a display of the new "Rosebud" dolls caught Elinor's eye. She picked up one of the baby dolls, dressed in a little white bonnet with a ribbon tied under her chin and a matching broderie anglaise dress. Her lashes were long and her tiny vermilion lips were set in the sort of sweet, gentle pout Elinor had only ever seen once on a living, breathing child—but real children weren't made of plastic, and that little girl had been wearing lipstick. She stared, mesmerized by the doll, but as she moved to return it to the place on display, a crying sound came from inside the body. It was a tinny wail of a cry that caused Elinor to hold the doll to her chest. She looked around, embarrassed in case anyone had seen her, and once again reached forward to set the doll back on the display.

"All the little girls love those. They're new—we've not long had them in, and they're going quite quickly," said an assistant now at Elinor's side. She reached for the doll. "She has sleeping eyes—see, they close when you lay her down, and of course she cries. Would you like that one, madam?"

Elinor looked down at the doll, at the innocent face and broderie anglaise dress. "Um, yes." She smiled, imagining handing the doll to Susie Mackie and seeing her smile. "Yes, I would like it. Could you put it in a box and wrap it for me? It's a present for a little girl."

"Right you are, madam." The assistant grinned. "And yes, for a little girl—after all, they're not usually for little boys."

"Of course—silly me," said Elinor, now following the woman toward the till.

Another assistant stood nearby, her attention focused on a distressed woman.

"I was waiting at the till," said the woman. "You know, while you were answering all those questions from that young lady who wanted to know where the train sets were made because she didn't want any of those German trains for her little boy, and—"

"Yes, I remember, madam. I don't think she believed me, even after I told her the train was made by *Hornby*. I assured her the company is British and the train sets are all manufactured here in England, but she still wasn't sure. I'm so sorry it took such a long time to help her."

The woman shook her head, tears rolling down her cheeks. "I wouldn't have minded that, but when I came to the till I know I had my purse in my handbag, and then by the time that woman left, my handbag was open and my purse was gone. I had three pounds with me today, and now I have nothing. I can't even get home."

"Are you sure you had the purse with you, madam? You could have come out without it. I know I've done the same thing."

Elinor watched the woman become even more flushed. "Are you suggesting—" She took a deep breath as if to quell her frustration. "Look, I had my purse with me when I paid the bus conductor. It was in my handbag when I came into the shop, because I checked. And I could still feel the weight of it just before I reached the till. What with all the people pushing and shoving past . . . anyway, someone stole my purse in this shop." She began to weep. "And now I . . . I don't know what to do."

"Madam," said Elinor. "Forgive me for interrupting, but I could not help overhearing this dreadful story. Would you be able to describe the woman to a policeman? If so—" She looked at the shop assistant and smiled. "If so, perhaps you could ask the manager to summon the police so the lady can make a statement."

The assistant nodded. "I'll get the manager."

"That's a start," said Elinor, as the assistant walked away at a brisk clip. "Now then—" She lifted the flap of her shoulder bag and took out her purse, which she opened to remove three half-crowns. "I think this should help out, madam."

"That's very kind, but—"

Elinor smiled, shaking her head when the woman tried to return the money.

"Just do the same for another person if you ever see the opportunity. I am sure the manager and the police will listen with all seriousness, though I doubt they will find the thief. Can you remember what she looked like?"

The woman nodded. "If it was the woman behind me, well, she was very nicely turned out in a pale-pink costume, you know, that sort of coral shade—yes, coral, I think that's what they call it. She had blondish-reddish hair. Black shoes, black handbag. She seemed very well-to-do, and as I said, she was behind me in the queue and then she was gone." She pulled a handkerchief from her pocket and wiped each eye in turn. "And I didn't feel a thing, nothing to make me turn around and look while she was lifting my purse—that's if it was her, and I'm sure it was."

"If she was a professional shoplifter, you wouldn't have noticed her move, so don't blame yourself. Indeed, she might well have been working in concert with the woman in front of you, the one who was so distracting with her questions about the origin of toy trains." *Just as she deflected attention at the Fenwick perfume counter,* Elinor wanted to add.

"Your Rosebud doll, madam." The assistant helping Elinor handed her a wrapped parcel. "The little girl will absolutely love her—there are even sweet curls molded at the back of her head. A doll made like this will last a lot longer than the old china dolls."

Elinor opened the purse she was holding and took out the requisite amount to pay for the doll, then placed the purse in her shoulder bag and secured the clasp. With the parcel under her arm, she bid farewell to the woman who had been robbed of her money, and thanked the assistant for her help in purchasing the doll. Leaving the shop, she knew that Elsie Finch was dealing in more than stolen clothing and perfume. She was a latter-day female Fagin, running her band of pickpockets. And they were attractive, "well turned out" thieves, the sort of women a good housewife would not try to avoid if she were standing close in the same queue waiting to be served while shopping in one of the most well-known stores in London.

CHAPTER 7

1917

War News Latest!
Passchendaele—Allies Capture All First Objectives
Haig's Great Blow on Wide Front in Flanders

You've done well, both of you," said Isabelle.

Elinor, now thirteen years of age, watched the woman whom they now welcomed to the house as if she were a family member. During the months since they had aided in the derailing of a German train, the De Witt sisters and their mother continued to observe trains when asked to do so, and reported to Isabelle on anything of note regarding the actions of their country's occupiers.

Cecily was almost sixteen and Charlotte seemed to be regaining the bearing and energy of a much younger woman, though she had passed her fortieth birthday that year. Elinor saw for the first time that, had it not been for the fatigue, worry and grief for the loss of her husband etched across her forehead and in the lines around her eyes and lips, Charlotte might have been taken for their older sister. She had heard it commented upon by neighbors before the war, but had never taken account of her mother as a beauty, nor her sister for that matter. Yet Cecily was indeed like Charlotte, with a more petite frame than Elinor, who still felt like her father's younger tomboy child. Cecily's rich chestnut tresses had been drawn back and braided, revealing heavy-lidded, nut-brown almond eyes. Elinor knew she had those same eyes, but her hair was lighter, with strands that became bleached in the summer sun, inspiring her sister to say she had a coat like a brindled dog.

Elinor and Cecily nodded by way of acknowledging Isabelle's praise, though when Elinor turned to her sister to exchange a brief smile—brief because laurels should never be rested upon—she noticed that her sister seemed to be paying more attention to a hangnail than it deserved, and she could also see that Isabelle too had taken account of Cecily's indifference.

Charlotte raised an eyebrow as she reached across and pulled her elder daughter's hands apart. "Cecily, it will get infected if you pick at it, and it will kill you. Plus it looks dreadful. Now pay attention."

"I am paying attention," said Cecily.

Elinor half expected her sister to flounce out of the kitchen. She had become very good at flouncing, according to Charlotte, who commented on the fact to Elinor only the day before. Cecily had rolled her eyes and left the house with a deliberate heavy footfall after her mother asked her daughters to run an errand.

"I wish your father were here," said Charlotte. "She could do with a strong telling-off from the head of the house. She doesn't listen to me anymore."

"But Mama, you are the head of the house," said Elinor, pushing back her chair ready to catch up with her sister. "Cecily is just going through that phase. I heard you talking to Papa about it, before he left."

Charlotte had reached for Elinor and wrapped her arms around her. "Thank goodness you're my same, stalwart Linni. Do try not to go through all this tantrum nonsense."

Elinor had no idea what the tantrum nonsense might feel like, but whatever it was, she was quite determined to avoid it. She brought her attention back to Isabelle, and became worried, having noticed how much weight the visitor had lost and the extent to which she appeared grey and drawn. Food had become more scarce than ever, and they knew even the German occupiers were hungry. "It doesn't do to leave young men with empty stomachs," her mother had commented. "They get angry faster than women."

"Your reports have been first class, and you've been brave, all of you," continued Isabelle. "But with the Germans pushing hard, we have to up the ante."

"What?" said Cecily.

Elinor ignored her sister and leaned forward. "What more can we do, Isabelle? Since the nuns and the old man were . . . were murdered, it's all become more difficult."

When Isabelle nodded, Elinor could feel both her sister and mother staring at her, as if their eyes could emit beams that pricked her skin.

"Good question," said Cecily, who was now picking at another hangnail. "I was about to ask the very same thing myself."

"Isabelle, my girls and I are already taking chances. If we 'up the ante,' wouldn't we be increasing risk to life and limb? I don't want to see my daughters out in the square, tied and handcuffed, then shot through the head."

Isabelle nodded. "Of course. I understand." She stopped speaking and regarded both girls again. "We have information—intelligence—to indicate that in the near future a train will be using the local route to transport one of the largest and most important shipments of arms, heavy artillery, explosives and men. More significant than any that have passed before. The Germans are losing ground—they want the war to turn toward victory in their favor, and to them it's crucial the end comes soon, that it is sudden and decisive. It's gone on too long, so a momentous push is vital for their success before the Americans come over in greater numbers."

"Won't there be more German patrols, more . . ." Charlotte rubbed her forehead.

"Surveillance?" said Isabelle. "Yes, there will. Which is why I want Elinor and Cecily to have some additional training."

"What sort of training?" asked Elinor. "We're in school all day until four, and then we have our homework."

Elinor heard her mother's sigh of relief and knew she was encouraged to hear her daughter countering Isabelle's suggestion.

Isabelle smiled. "Saturday afternoon is the best time. Hunters who have retained their rifles will be out, though only for as long as it takes to bag their dinner because they want to be home before the Germans come after them. No one will pay attention if they hear us. And there will be sporadic gunfire from the enemy doing their own shooting practice, whether the target is a dog, a cat, a live human being or just a cross on a wall."

"So no one will hear what?" asked Elinor.

Isabelle paused. "Linni, they won't hear you when you have your first lesson in using a handgun."

"A gun?" said Elinor, her eyes wide.

"And a couple of other weapons. One you use every single day."

"And what might that be?" said Cecily. "Because you won't get me touching a gun."

Elinor glanced down at her lap, embarrassed by Cecily's snippy tone. She was beginning to wish she could just get on and do what Isabelle wanted without any interference from her sister. She sighed, and as she raised her head, it was clear that Isabelle was looking at Cecily as if she were thinking the very same thing.

"A pencil, Ceci," said Isabelle. "A simple pencil."

It was the latter part of the following Saturday afternoon; the sun was low in the sky and dusk not an hour away as they walked along a well-trodden path to an area of woodland known to both girls. Following a detailed introduction to the weapon they would be using, it was time to begin. Isabelle stood at Elinor's shoulder and pressed the Webley MK VI into her right hand, then lifted her left hand to meet it.

"No, don't touch the trigger yet, whatever you do. Just lay your right forefinger alongside the barrel, like so." She lifted Elinor's forefinger and positioned it to demonstrate her instruction. "How does it feel?"

"It's heavier than I thought it would be. I don't know if I can keep my arms up like this and hold the gun," said Elinor, looking sideways at her instructor.

Isabelle smiled. "You don't go around holding up your gun all the time—that's for little boys playing soldiers with toy guns in the street. I'm going to teach you how to take out the pistol at speed, how to focus and to use your weapon to your advantage. Now, look at the target."

Elinor stared at the first bottle resting on a tree stump some fifteen feet away.

"Bring down your right arm by your side and do not touch the trigger. When I touch your shoulder, raise it to the point I've shown you—but don't shoot."

"I hope you don't think I'm doing that," said Cecily, standing to one side.

"Quiet please, Ceci—I'm already aware of what you will and won't do, but for the moment your sister is concentrating."

Elinor tried to ignore Cecily as she followed the instruction. She felt Isabelle touch her right shoulder. She raised the pistol, her left hand steadying the weapon, the forefinger of her right hand alongside the barrel. *The barrel.* She would have to learn these new words for something she never in her wildest imagination thought she would ever use.

"Good, and again," said Isabelle.

Five times Elinor repeated the drill at the command of her teacher. Her shoulder ached and her knees had locked.

"Excellent," said Isabelle. "Rest your body." She reached for the gun and took it from Elinor.

"You have to remain strong in your legs, but try not to lock your knees—if you have to run and move through trees while keeping focused on a target, you can't afford to have pins and needles anywhere in your body."

Elinor nodded while pressing her fingertips into the muscles around her shoulder.

"Let's start again. This time you're going to do that again from a crouched position. Like so." She held the Webley revolver and demonstrated the movement.

Three more times Elinor lifted and lowered the weapon on Isabelle's command. She glanced sideways and saw Isabelle smiling, but tempered her excitement at the woman's approval and waited for the next tap. Seconds later she felt the lightest touch on her left shoulder, lifted the revolver and eyed her target.

"Now, move your forefinger to the trigger, aim and fire." Her teacher did not shout, instead she uttered the command in a soft yet strong tone, as if she were one of the nuns instructing the girls to sit down in church.

Without pause, Elinor brought back her forefinger, rested it on the trigger and pulled.

Flat on her back on the ground, Elinor could hear her sister laughing.

"I'm sorry, Linni. I had to do that," said Isabelle, helping Elinor to her feet. "It's called a recoil, and I have found that I can tell people to prepare for it, but they never listen or they brace so much that they miss the target, so I just save my breath and let them learn the hard way." She brushed leaves away from the back of Elinor's jacket. "Everything in one piece? Arms still in their sockets?"

Elinor nodded.

"Then let's go again."

Five times Elinor felt the tap on her shoulder. Five times she lifted the revolver and drew back her forefinger while simultaneously imagining more strength in her shoulders to absorb the shot's upward kick. She held a vision of roots pulling her feet to the ground because she didn't want to set her knees and end up with pins and needles. She wanted to be ready to run. Five times she hit one target after the next.

"Excellent," said Isabelle. "We shall come again and practice, though I am very pleased with your progress, Linni." Elinor watched as she turned to Cecily, who was frowning. "Now, Ceci—are you ready?" Even before Isabelle had finished her question, Cecily was shaking her head. Isabelle nodded. "It's best not to do something if you don't want to do it, but I think you will both be very good at the next tasks."

"What next tasks?" said Cecily.

"The blade and the pencil."

Cecily giggled. "Sounds like something out of the handbook for nuns."

Elinor thought that was a pretty good joke, though most of their nuns were kind, despite the fact that since the executions in the square they had been solemn, and prayers had become more and more intense. Prayers that the war might end and life could go back to being normal before everyone forgot what normal felt like.

"That's a funny one, Ceci," said Isabelle. "Want to know how to use them to protect yourself?"

Elinor thought the pistol was a much easier weapon, as she didn't really think she could push a pencil straight into the eye of her attacker, or his ear, though with a fast move it could expedite a quick death. The knife was hard too. She learned that it took a great deal of effort to slide a knife into a man's heart, or into his side, and she didn't like the idea of being sprayed with blood as it pumped out of a jugular vein or an artery. But she knew one thing—if their lives were at stake, she would do all of these things to protect her family. There were only the three of them now, and though Cecily was a real pain in the neck at times, Elinor loved her. It was a fleeting thought that came to her as she lay in bed one night, but she suspected her father, mother and sister would remain the great loves of her life until the day she died.

"Elinor, any questions?" asked Isabelle.

"I hope not—I want to go home," said Cecily.

Elinor nodded. "Why are we doing all this? I mean, I know there's more risk—but why teach us this now and not before?"

"It's simple—because you weren't ready before. You had to learn the fear inherent in being prey—the fear that would keep you observant, careful and safe. That had to be ingrained before we turned the tables."

"What do you mean?"

Isabelle held the revolver and aimed it at Elinor, her finger alongside the barrel. "This clever piece of equipment transforms you from prey to predator, though the very best predators are those who understand how the hunted are likely to act. Predators who have felt the fear of prey are those with the best chance of survival."

Later, after they had returned home and after Charlotte had made tea for Isabelle and her daughters as if they had come from the market and not a lesson in killing, Elinor could not stop thinking about holding the revolver, feeling the tap on her shoulder, raising the gun, and moving her forefinger to the trigger. Aim and fire. Aim and fire again. And again. She fell asleep that night with a smile on her face. She liked the thought of being a predator. She liked it very much indeed, because it made her feel strong, and strength made her feel formidable. Elinor De Witt was a predator who understood what it was to be prey. With that knowledge, she knew she would survive—even if her shoulders hurt.

I wish you wouldn't do that," said Elinor as they made their way from the convent to their home.

"Do what?" said Cecily.

"Ceci, you must think I'm blind! I saw that German soldier just wink at you, and you smiled back. Mama says we must look away. Don't meet their eyes, and certainly don't encourage them. It's not safe."

"Oh, you're just imagining things," said Cecily. "I looked down."

Elinor stopped and pulled on her sister's arm. "Next time you do that, just remember what we saw in the square. He might look like a nice blond boy, but it could just as easily be him tying you up, ready for a gun to be put to your head."

"Linni, I didn't do it. I didn't smile at him. But even if I accidentally met his eyes, I'll be careful in future. I promise?" Cecily stared at Elinor. "Don't tell Mama. She will only fret about it."

Elinor nodded. "Come on. Let's get home. Mama worries if we're five minutes late."

When the sisters entered the house by the kitchen door, their mother was sitting at the table, pouring tea for Isabelle. Both girls stopped. Though they had been to the woods with Isabelle time and again, there had been nothing planned for today. During those lessons, Elinor learned how to fire the revolver while moving through trees. She learned how to hide, how to camouflage herself, and how to fight. Isabelle would become both predator and prey, testing Elinor time and again. For her part, Cecily still refused to touch the gun, though Isabelle reviewed her technique with the pencil and knife and considered her dexterity with both more than sufficient for the task of ending the threat of an opponent, should it be necessary. Elinor had been treated to one of Isabelle's rare smiles for her proficiency with all three weapons.

Now something more was to be asked of the De Witt sisters.

"I'll get to the point. It's time for you to go out into the field again," said Isabelle.

Elinor found it almost amusing, how Isabelle would refer to "the field," as if they were to take an afternoon amble through a meadow filled with buttercups and daisies. But there was nothing amusing about this field at all.

"Why the girls?" asked Charlotte.

Elinor noticed her mother's countenance was greyer than usual, and that Isabelle seemed even more weary, perhaps tired of all she was required to accomplish. They weren't the only women working on behalf of La Dame Blanche, so Isabelle must go from house to house training women young and old in the art of battle, the tasks they must complete if the Allies were to win the war.

"In the early hours of tomorrow morning, the train we have been anticipating will be passing along the railway line close to town. It's the same as your first assignment—but now the patrols have increased. It's crucial that this . . . this enormous shipment is delayed. Stopping it entirely would be best, but I would settle for simply setting the enemy back by the few days it would take to get the railway track cleared and another train through. The Germans have been moving materiel via different routes to avoid sabotage and to fool the Allies, but our intelligence suggests that this is the line they have chosen for such an important train." She paused. "You see, they can feel victory slipping through their fingers, but be aware—there is nothing more dangerous than a cornered bully."

Elinor stepped forward. "Tell us what you want us to do."

Isabelle explained that the plan was almost the same as their first assignment, with a vital difference.

"The train will go through at four o'clock in the morning. We must expect the time to be exact, because the Germans are always exact. The line will be checked approximately twenty minutes before the train arrives at the crucial point. You have only a very short time after the patrol passes to move the metal slabs. Then you must leave, but beware of other patrols in the area."

"Oh God, help me," said Charlotte, her head in her hands.

Elinor went to her mother's side and knelt at her feet. "It will be alright, Mama. Ceci and I know what to do. We're well practiced, well trained, and we will be home by sunrise. I promise all will be well."

"Ceci?" said Isabelle.

Cecily nodded. "I'm not letting my little sister go without me. And she's right—we know what to do."

"Sharpen your pencils then, ladies. Now, let's go over the plan. I won't leave here until you can both recite your every move. Is that clear?"

The sisters nodded.

"I said is that clear?"

"Yes," said Elinor, hearing her sister's voice echo at her side. She realized later that Ceci had spoken only after she had voiced her own positive response to the question.

At three o'clock in the morning, Elinor and Cecily left the house. Charlotte had wrapped her arms around each daughter, while Isabelle stood to one side. She had arrived half an hour before the stated departure time to listen to their recitation of the plan once more. Cecily had written the note to her fictional beau, ready to throw into the river and claim his love forever, should it be necessary. Both girls had string to hitch their skirts as soon as they were on the path, and they had kept underskirts to a minimum so that, if necessary, they could run with greater ease.

"Now you must go," said Isabelle, standing by the kitchen door. "Ceci, you're the eldest, lead the way."

Elinor stepped forward to follow her sister, but as she moved, she felt Isabelle push something into her pocket. She knew what it was.

"It's loaded," whispered Isabelle, as she reached toward Elinor's other pocket and slipped in more ammunition.

Elinor said nothing, but gave a brief nod. She pushed down the wave of nausea that seemed to rise from her core, and followed her sister.

The girls did not speak as they made their way along the path, though they reached out to one another and held hands as they walked. The river was to their left, with the railway line beyond the woods to their right. With her free hand, Elinor began to finger the tip of the sharpened pencil, but stopped, realizing that if it were indeed a weapon, she would need to keep the point as fierce as possible. She had tucked a sheathed knife into her belt, and as they set a determined yet almost silent pace, she was glad to feel the prickly sensation against her hip with every step.

With night vision established, they entered the wood on a route toward the tree with exposed roots. Earlier, in the strange comfort of the kitchen—which she now thought of as a kind of womb to which she wanted to return—she had asked Isabelle why they would choose the same place to hide the metal plates, because surely the Germans would search the area, given what had happened before. Isabelle explained that the invading army now expected an attack on a different section of railway line—this area had been dismissed as too dangerous for repeat resistance activity. They would still patrol it, though.

Having reached the tree, the girls rested. Cecily took out a packet of matches and touched Elinor on the arm. Elinor pulled up her sleeve. Together they sheltered the flame while they checked the time on the wristwatch Isabelle had provided, having synchronized the hour with her own timepiece. Elinor pulled down her sleeve, making sure the watch was secure. They sat for ten minutes more before Elinor cupped a hand around her sister's ear.

"Ceci, I can hear the patrol."

She felt Cecily nod. Elinor knew she was hardly taking a breath as they watched two German soldiers walk along the railway line, their torches flashing from side to side. Elinor tapped Ceci's shoulder again. The hour and minute were checked. It was time.

While practice had not made perfect since their first assignment, it had rendered them faster and more dexterous in their movements. They were quieter, knew how to move their bodies, how to bear weight and how to position a metal plate so that it was difficult to see, even with a torch. Ten heavy metal plates were placed along the track. Five times they went back and forth to the tree. Time and again they stopped to listen, hoping their luck would hold. Then it was done.

Without conferring, Elinor and Cecily entered the forest again, their footfall as light as fawns as they stepped out onto the path alongside the river. Elinor wanted only to get home, anxious to be cocooned in the kitchen watching Charlotte while she made breakfast. Would there be a special treat—an egg, perhaps, or a special pancake with fruit from the garden? Then she stopped, pulling Cecily to one side, into the lee of an ancient beech, a grandmother tree with a broad trunk and heavy branches sweeping close to the ground.

"What?" Cecily whispered.

Elinor touched her sister's ear, signifying that she had heard something.

"Halt! Who goes there?"

Elinor now knew what it meant when people said their knees had turned to jelly. She wanted to just fall down, but she couldn't. She wanted to run, but she couldn't. She wanted to be home, in the kitchen sipping weak tea. But she wasn't.

"Step out onto the path." The order was firm, aggressive.

Elinor wondered if the soldier was afraid, and then came another voice.

"Do as we say, or we shall shoot you dead."

Cecily began to move, but Elinor grabbed her arm.

"Linni, I'm not going to die," said Cecily. "I can talk us out of this—I have my letter, remember?" Elinor marveled at her sister's aplomb as she stepped out onto the path and called out. "It's only us—two girls from the town."

Now she wished Cecily hadn't said that—"two girls from the town" could be an invitation for bigger trouble. Was Ceci so stupid? In the distance Elinor could hear the muffled clickety-clack of the train approaching. They were as good as dead.

"Girls from the town, eh? Show yourselves now!"

Elinor followed her sister. Two German soldiers approached, their rifles held pointed downward. "What are you doing here? It's not the hour to be out walking—explain yourselves."

Elinor gave silent thanks that they had not yet asked for papers. Perhaps they wouldn't—after all, it was hard to read in the grainy light.

"It's an old tradition," said Elinor. "When a young woman is apart from her . . . her intended and is missing him, she writes a letter to him and floats it down the river under a darkened sky filled with stars. Of course she also posts a copy of the letter, but she's telling the river gods to take her love to him and bring him home."

The two soldiers began to laugh. "Well, if your intended is in the army, you can be sure he won't be coming home." There was more sniggering laughter, then the soldier who had spoken first held out his hand. "Come on, show us this letter. It'll be good for a laugh."

Elinor thought it strange that neither soldier had commented on the fact that both she and her sister were answering them in German.

"You can translate—read it for us."

"I can't see in the dark," said Cecily.

Elinor watched as the soldier holding the torch came alongside Cecily and directed the beam to the envelope she held in her hands.

"Come on, read it to us, sweet little lady who misses her boy." The soldier put his arm around Cecily's shoulder. "Hah! I recognize you—you're the pretty girl who smiled at me."

Elinor watched as her sister flinched away, but the soldier held her firm.

"I said read!"

"Please," said Elinor. "You're scaring my sister. Please don't."

The second soldier grabbed Elinor's arm. "Shut up, little girl!"

Cecily's voice quavered as she began to read her letter aloud.

"How I long to hold you in my arms again. How I long to run in the long grass with you, to go on picnics and to be your wife."

To go on picnics and to be your wife? Elinor could not believe what she was hearing. She was three years younger, but she could have done a better job of writing a love letter to float along the river toward river gods who didn't exist.

"You want to run in the long grass, eh?" The soldier looked toward his friend.

Elinor could hear the train coming closer. How far away was it? Sound was distorted through woodland. German trains heavily laden with arms moved at a slow chug toward the bridge, so perhaps . . . perhaps they had about ten minutes to get away. Fifteen at the outside.

"We shouldn't disappoint this young lady, should we?" said the second soldier.

"No, Hans, we shouldn't."

"But—"

Elinor felt the soldier's grasp tighten as she moved toward Cecily, who was now being dragged across the path by the soldier who had winked at her in town.

"No—leave her! Leave my sister—"

Elinor felt a sharp pain at the back of her head and fell to the ground.

"She won't get up in a hurry. Come on, Hans—be quick. We haven't got all night."

Elinor came to her knees, squinting to see the soldier who had hit her with his rifle shining a beam of light upon the other soldier—who was bracing Cecily so her face was buried against the tree trunk. He lifted her skirts and began to pull her underwear down.

"Come on—get on with it," yelled the second soldier, already un-buttoning his trousers. "I don't want to make do with this one."

Elinor stood up, pulling the pistol from her pocket. *Move your fore-finger to the trigger, both hands . . . both hands, Linni. Tighten your core, Linni . . . you are a predator, and there is your prey. Shoot. Shoot, Linni.*

In the beam of light, Elinor focused on the soldier who was pinning Cecily to the tree, and hit her target in the neck and back. And as the second soldier began to turn, still illuminated by his own torch, she aimed and fired, her eyes wide as blood erupted from his skull.

"Elinor . . ."

"Ceci, we must be quick. Help me drag these two into the woods. We don't have much time. I can hear the train. And please, please try to stop crying. We can do that later." Elinor felt herself becoming colder, a chill that seeped into her body, freezing limb, muscle and bone as her strength ebbed. "Come on, Ceci—pull yourself together. I need your help right now—he's heavy."

Cecily followed instructions, emitting a moaning as if her soul had been torn in two. And perhaps it had.

CHAPTER 8

1947

D riving from London to Shacklehurst proved to be soothing. Though the undulating countryside of Kent's High Weald was so different from the flat lands of her Belgian girlhood, just being close to farms and fields always brought calm to her thoughts. She wondered if it was because she associated fields with escape, and escape meant freedom—freedom from the past. There was also the ancient nature of a place, how it connected people and events, and how time moved on to heal wounds, for she knew that places bore scars as deep as those inflicted upon people who had suffered. Years after the first war, the one they said would end all wars, she had returned to Belgium and walked across land restored to the growing of crops, not the slaughter of human beings. Though many of the trenches had been filled or fallen in, white scars across the chalk soil exposed their former location, revealing what had once been no-man's-land threaded across fields of sugar beet, barley and maize. It made her ache, as if she were in the company of ghosts, and it crossed her mind that perhaps she was.

Elinor loved the names of places, curious about their origin and how they could change over the years. *Weeld. Wald. Weald.* Then there was Shacklehurst. *Shackle*. To impede progress. To bind. She wondered how the name came about and suspected it was something to do with prisoners—possibly French prisoners from the Napoleonic Wars. Could she never escape one war or another? Despite the limitations of village life, Elinor looked forward to being at home in her lair, the house at the edge of Denbury Forest. Yet there were times she felt both safe and vulnerable in her haven, dueling emotions that kept her on her guard. The surrounding trees offered shelter and seclusion, but the dense foliage could also hide an interloper, perhaps camouflage someone from the past who would take her quiet life and offer only a silent death in exchange.

Had she tried hard enough to keep hold of the settled existence her family had forged since they arrived in London, in late 1917? And as wartime descended again and victory seemed so far distant, did she wallow in indecision for too long when asked to take up arms once more? Yet within a few months, what began as a request had developed into an order, though the transition from respectful petition to command came at a point when she was angry, her mind and heart desperate enough to kill the enemy with her bare hands. Elinor knew she had little choice but to obey those orders, not least because there was an open account with her name on it, and it listed the deaths of those she loved most in the world—deaths that were hers to avenge. Had her enlistment been delivered with an element of emotional blackmail? Yes, of that there was no question.

It was time to talk to Jim and Rose. She realized that her immediate response to their plight was out of place, an emotional encounter akin to breaking an egg with a mallet. Yet she had been so incensed by Jim Mackie's rough treatment at the hands of his family that she had followed the men to London without applying much thought to the possible outcome. Though it was the least of her worries, in allowing her own instant reaction to get the better of her, she had broken the law when she exceeded the petrol allowance by some seventy miles over just a few days. It might have appeared to be a lesser infraction against the many other felonies committed and laws broken in Britain's dark, rationed postwar world, but it was still a crime. The Home Office permission note Steve had furnished her with would help if she were queried by the local constabulary—it attested to her use of a vehicle while on government business. It wasn't a Scotland Yard document, so not for the first time Elinor wondered about Steve Warren's field of influence.

As she drove through Sevenoaks, her concerns converged with memories and she smiled, recalling a linguistic error she made during a lesson at her new English school in west London. She had confused *influence* with *effluence,* and because the latter was often employed to describe the flow of sewage, the whole class had dissolved into giggles. Now she wondered whether her musings had returned her to the mistake for a reason, given that she was thinking of influence in connection with Steve Warren.

Though her attention had lingered on the countryside as she negotiated bends in the road, changed gear to slow on a hill, or tempered her desire to be home and therefore her speed, she was also aware of the black motor car now visible in her rearview mirror. She adjusted the mirror and slowed down. The motor car reduced speed—there was no other choice, but the driver had been quick with his reflexes, more so than a recreational motorist might have been. She could see there were two men in the motor car, a passenger silhouetted alongside the driver.

"I think it's time for me to stop," said Elinor aloud. She slowed again as she approached Goudhurst, then pulled across the road to park alongside the village pond. She cast her gaze to her left as the motor car passed, with both driver and passenger staring straight ahead. She waited, wondering if the driver knew there was another circular route from her stopping point to Shacklehurst. Slipping the motor car into gear, she eased onto the road and turned right, then left onto a back street that was used only for deliveries to the corner shop, the butcher and the pub at the top of the hill. She found a place to park, then locked and left the motor car while she continued on foot, looping around the back of the church to join the main road again. She carried a shopping basket, and as she approached the church she pulled a headscarf from her shoulder bag, which she put on and tied under her chin. Affecting the gait of an elderly woman, she emerged onto the pavement, and there it was to her right—the black motor car, parked under a tree. Walking any closer to the vehicle would have entailed an element of risk, so like an old lady deciding whether to step out onto the road, she glanced both ways and in those few seconds garnered more information. The driver was standing alongside the motor car, looking back. He shook his head, leaned into the vehicle and then took his seat once again. Elinor continued on, a woman of a certain age rendered invisible by her vintage, on her way to the corner shop. She appeared of no account, a grandmother of the village who had never left the house where she was born, except perhaps for a day by the sea.

Arriving back at her motor car, Elinor removed the headscarf, threw the shopping basket into the boot and her shoulder bag onto the seat next to her. She opened the flap and fingered the gun. Sighing, she shook her head, started the engine and reversed out of the narrow street and back onto the road, though this time, instead of joining the main thoroughfare to the right, she swung around to take the route to the left, a narrow lane that would lead to the little-known southern entrance to Denbury Forest. From there she would bump her way along an old drovers' road that terminated in Shacklehurst, close to home.

Elinor parked the motor car in the garage next to the house. The tape was still in place over the front door, but she left it where it was, and instead chose to enter via the kitchen door. Once inside, she used her binoculars to scan the woods and farmland to the rear of her house. There was nothing to cause alarm, though she could feel the muscles in her stomach clenching, a sign that her senses were alert, whether she chose such vigilance or not. She would sit and think before going to visit Jim and Rose, and when she left the house she would not walk along the road but would use the path just beyond the back garden, the one to the right that followed the perimeter of the field. She would check to make sure there were no idling motor cars, and only if the coast were clear would she clamber over the five-bar gate and approach the Mackies' cottage. No one would see her enter their home. In the meantime, there was much to consider, not least the identity of the men who had been following her—men, she thought, who might not have been at all happy with their task, and who—it appeared thus far—had given up the pursuit with rather more ease than she would have expected. Unless they hadn't, which meant she had to prepare for them to be very good at their job, whatever it was. She would be foolish to expect never to see them again.

At first Elinor had thought the driver and passenger were men from the Mackie family, yet when she studied the vehicle in the village, she realized the motor car following her was the same marque as the one she had seen waiting for Steve Warren in Whitehall Place. If she were not mistaken, it was indeed a motor car in use by the government, which in turn begged more questions. Why would someone in a senior government position want to know where she was going? She assumed "senior" because only a more powerful man would have access to such a motor car and the petrol ration required to send his associates on a mission to keep an eye on her during the long drive down to Kent. Was there a connection to the Mackie family? More than anything, though, what was Steve Warren up to?

R ose—Mrs. Mackie—is your husband home?"

Rose Mackie stood at the door to her cottage with Susie on her hip. The young mother looked as if she had been cleaning; her hair was tied back in a scarf and she wore a pinafore with the ties drawn around her back and secured at the front. On her feet she wore a pair of slippers that had seen a good few years of service.

"He should be back any minute," said Rose. "Is everything alright?"

Elinor smiled and nodded. She had no desire to concern Rose Mackie by adding more weight to that already upon her shoulders— though the conversation she had planned with the couple would in all likelihood escalate worries Rose harbored about her husband's family.

"I would just like to speak to you both. It's about . . . it's about the incident on Sunday. I have some . . ." Elinor knew she had to couch her words with care. "Let's just say that due to contacts I have in London, I think I might be able to help you."

"Jim's funny about strangers." Rose bounced her daughter on her hip. "But it can't do any harm, can it? Come in, Miss White—or is it Mrs.? Sorry if I've put my foot in it."

"It's Miss White, and even if I were a married woman, I would not take umbrage on account of such a minor slip." Elinor held out the package she had carried to the house. "I happened to be in London for a few days, and had to pop into Hamleys to get something for a friend. I saw this doll—she was so pretty, I wondered who might love her, and as Susie is the only little girl I know, I couldn't resist bringing it home for her. Apparently this is the most popular doll in the shop."

"That's so thoughtful of you, Miss White." Rose stood aside for Elinor to enter the beamed cottage. "Come on, Susie, let's open this, and then Mummy will make a cup of tea for the nice lady."

Much was made of opening the parcel, lifting the lid from the box and pulling away the tissue paper. Susie clapped her hands and grabbed the doll.

"What shall we call her?" Rose looked at her daughter, then to Elinor. "What do you think, Miss White?"

"Oh, that's up to you and Susie."

"Do you have a favorite name," asked Rose.

"Um, well, I suppose I do. Two, actually. My father always called my mother 'Lottie' because he said Charlotte was too much like a queen, and my sister's name was Ceci—short for Cecily."

Rose looked at Elinor and nodded. "Lottie or Ceci? What do you think?"

"Seh-si," said the child, clutching the doll to her. "Seh-si."

The back door opened and slammed, signaling that Jim Mackie was home.

"Love? You there? I've had to leave the dog out the back—she's got into that muck again. I tell you, they said she was a farm dog, but I don't know."

"We've got a visitor, love. Miss White from along the road."

"Just a minute."

Elinor heard Jim Mackie washing his hands at the kitchen sink. There would be no bathroom in the house. The kitchen sink was where everything from crockery to cutlery were washed, and where the child was bathed. Jim Mackie could be heard scrubbing away a day's work.

"Right then." He came into the sitting room, wiping his hands on a small towel. "Nice of you to drop in, Miss White." He bent over, kissed his wife and child. There was an hiatus while he made much of the doll, his daughter impressing upon him the name chosen.

"Seh-si? Sounds a bit Italian to me—you know, 'Yes, yes!' " Jim

Mackie laughed, laid the damp towel over the fire guard, and sat down in one of the threadbare armchairs. "I don't think you've come here to have a jaw about the late harvest this year."

Elinor appreciated the man's candor. "No, I haven't. I've come because I think I might be able to help you—or at least, I can try."

Jim Mackie frowned. Then, as if correcting himself, he smiled. "Oh, we're alright, Miss White." He turned to Rose. "We've got our heads above water now, haven't we, love?"

"I don't think Miss White is talking about money, Jim," said Rose.

Jim turned to Elinor, who did not wait for him to ask.

"Mr. Mackie—Jim. I am quite aware of what happened here last Sunday. I believe you are being pressed—bullied—into doing something you do not want to do. And I don't blame you."

"Thank you for your interest, Miss White. But this is my business, and I can look after it very well, if it's all the same to you." His demeanor had changed; his back was ramrod straight, his brow furrowed. "And I can definitely take care of my wife and child. All I want is to live a quiet life here in the country, away from all that."

"Jim, I don't want to offend you with this visit, but it was clear to me that they aren't going to let you stay away from all that." Elinor could feel Jim's annoyance rising, yet she held up her hand when she saw him about to speak. "Look, there is much I cannot tell you about my past and how I know things I know, but let's just say I have some important contacts where contacts count. I believe there is a very big . . . I suppose you would call it a 'job' . . . being planned, and that's why they want you back."

Elinor almost looked away as Jim and Rose Mackie stared at her. Susie saw her parents studying the visitor, and peered at Elinor, two fingers in her mouth, while she clutched the doll with the other hand.

Rose turned to her husband. "I was grateful when Miss White came along and helped me the other day, Jim. You know, when the boys came down." She fingered the place on the cheek where a liberal dusting of powder had been applied.

Jim nodded, though his frown remained as he stared at Elinor. "Are you with the police?"

"I know people in the police."

"Higher-ups?"

Elinor nodded. "High enough."

"Then you know there's rot everywhere, Miss White." He leaned forward, his pale-blue eyes cold. "There's something I'm going to tell you about my grandfather, and it's how our family goes about its trade."

Elinor watched as Jim Mackie looked over toward Rose and reached for Susie, as if cradling his child would provide the fortitude he needed to go on; as if she could gentle him. She could see that despite the strength he would show before his wife and daughter, Jim was a fearful and troubled man.

"My grandfather built the family business—that's what they call it, 'the family business'—through what he knows about the people he knows and the people he wants to know. That's the—what would you call it?" Mackie scratched his head as if searching for a word. "That's the foundation of his . . . his bloody empire."

"Jim—"

"Sorry, Rose. Language, I know. Beg your pardon, Miss White."

Mackie held his daughter tighter. Susie continued to stare at Elinor.

"Go on, Jim," said Elinor

"My father, his brothers and my grandfather have something on everyone who's anyone, whether they're in the police, the government, the House of blimmin' Lords, or members of your aristocracy," said Jim. "He has enough to make people go blind and not see or do anything about what's in front of their noses—if you catch my drift."

Elinor nodded. "Are you saying that any detective with the Flying Squad, or even a government minister, may have been compromised by your family?"

"Depends what their game is, what they're up to." He paused and handed Susie to her mother before drawing his attention back to Elinor. "You see, whatever they plan, whatever they want to take, they don't have to try that hard." He turned to Rose. His wife nodded for him to continue. "And it's always about taking, Miss White. They're not Robin Hoods, even though the people on the streets think they are. They only give if they want to receive, and they never want anything small." He looked at his wife again. "Rose, I like it here, and we've done well, haven't we?"

"You're a hard worker, Jim," said Rose. "You've put your back into making a go of it on the farm, and we have our lovely cottage. We just have to stand up to them. That's all."

Elinor cleared her throat. "I understand all this." She paused. "Jim, is there anything you can tell me about your aunt?"

"Elsie?"

"You seem surprised I asked."

Jim nodded. "I am. You know a lot about my relatives, don't you?" He sighed, as if resigned to Elinor's understanding of his family. "Sorry, Miss White, I can see you just want to give us a hand. I'm not taking offense—well, I am, sort of, but . . . anyway, yeah, Aunt Elsie's alright. She's got her little rackets going." He rubbed his forehead again and was thoughtful. "But it's funny you should mention her, because when I was a nipper, I always reckoned she was a bit of a dark horse, you know, among all them men. My dad and my uncles are protective of her, but on the other hand, they like to control everyone in the family." He held out a hand to Rose, who took it in both of hers. "We thought we were shot of them until my brothers came down here."

"Is there anything you can tell me—anything you know about what your family plans to do next that might help me to help you?"

"Well, there's definitely something on the cards. They wouldn't tell me what it was unless I agreed to go back and work for them. I said no and got a beating for my trouble—and they couldn't keep their hands off my Rose here either. I should have been able to protect her, but . . ." He looked away for a moment as if to compose himself before turning back to face Elinor. "You know, the only ambition I have now is to get behind the wheel of the new Massey-Ferguson tractor old Wicks said he was going to buy for the farm." He laughed, though Elinor could see it was false, an attempt at lightness.

Elinor came to her feet, ready to leave. "Thank you, Jim. If you're agreeable, I'll continue to do what I can to protect your life here."

Jim Mackie glanced at his wife, who gave a brief encouraging smile as he squeezed her hand. He nodded toward Elinor, stood up and walked with her toward the door.

"What I want to know," said Jim, opening the door, "is what you think you can do. To be honest, Miss White, I still can't get over how you know so much about my family. I'm flummoxed, to tell you the truth. I don't know how to take it, whether to be angry or thankful for you coming here, though I'm much obliged to you for thinking of us. But . . . but I wonder if you know what you're taking on—because, believe me, if you get involved, you'll see some terrible things. I mean, Rose and me, we're grateful you think you can help us out and all that, but why would you want to go up against my family? They're too powerful—and the more time I've spent away from them, the more I can see how blimmin' dangerous they are. I was brought up with it and thought it was the way everyone was, until I went into the army and met all sorts of other blokes who came from ordinary families. It's not normal that my dad has had people topped to protect the family's business. Even them as works for him have lost their fingers for getting something wrong on a job."

Elinor reached out and placed a hand on the young man's arm. "I know exactly what I'm taking on, Jim, and I suppose what I want to do is stop whatever is in the offing. I want to stop anyone who would try to intimidate a young family, a family with a lovely little girl like Susie."

Jim turned away, his back to Rose and Susie, as he lowered his voice to a whisper. "They don't care about Susie. And that's why I'm torn—if I do what they say, my family is at as much risk as if I don't." His eyes filled with tears. "They don't even care about me, just always what they want from me."

"Jim, perhaps they don't care, but I do," said Elinor. She reached for the door handle, and turned to Jim and Rose Mackie. "They are predators, and on my watch you will not be prey."

Elinor could not settle, which was why she was soon on her way back to London, this time on the train. She would not be venturing much beyond the West End, so train, Tube and bus would serve her well, along with the fact that she would not be breaking the law by using precious petrol, and her neighbors in the mews would not be disturbed—or intrigued—if they heard her motor car rolling into the garage below the flat.

Before taking the bus from Shacklehurst to Paddock Wood to catch the London train, Elinor stopped at the telephone kiosk, placed a call to the famed hairdressing salon, and asked if she could book a haircut.

"Shampoo and set?" asked the receptionist.

"Um, yes. Yes—a shampoo and set."

"I'm afraid Mr. Raymond's diary is full, but one of the assistants can do your hair—they're all trained by Mr. Raymond himself."

Elinor hoped she was correct in suspecting Elsie had a standing weekly appointment, and they would therefore cross paths in the salon.

"I don't mind. My hair is very easy to cut, and I don't require too much in the way of, you know, rollers."

"Don't worry, madam—we'll have you looking like a Paris mannequin by the time you leave."

Elinor thought about Elsie Finch. She had never seen anything less like a Paris mannequin, and wondered how easy it would be to wash out whatever the well-trained assistant put onto her hair.

From Charing Cross, Elinor proceeded straight to the salon. If she had not lingered when she saw the motor car draw up outside and Elsie alight and then enter, they might have bumped into one another at the door.

"Now then," said the young woman standing behind Elinor. "Madam has let her hair grow rather long, hasn't she?"

"She has? I mean . . . I have?"

"Not flattering, madam. Let's snip it a bit here and add some layers. 'Lift the hair and you lift the face,' I always say. Then we'll pop in some of the larger rollers to add some . . . some buoyance. You won't be under the dryer for long. There's a *Vogue* on the table, so plenty to read."

Elinor kept her eyes closed long after the shampoo was lathered and rinsed, and at one point the hairdresser asked if madam would please open her eyes so she could ensure the cut was correct and flattering for madam. Elinor's usual mode of keeping her hair under some control was to go to a barber in Tunbridge Wells who could be trusted to take off no more than an inch of hair and who would watch while she pinned it up in a French twist again and put on her hat before leaving. However, soon she was sitting under a hairdryer next to Jim Mackie's aunt. It did not take long to engage her in conversation, when they both reached for the latest copy of *Vogue* at the same time.

"Oh, please, you take it. Last month's copy is still here—I'll read that one," said Elinor.

Elsie nodded, smiled and expressed her thanks.

"Mind you," said Elinor, "I rather like the costume that model is wearing on the front cover of the new edition."

Elsie took up the bait. "It's very nice, isn't it? I've seen that one in Fenwicks. They've just got it in."

"Fenwick of Bond Street? Oh dear, I haven't crossed the threshold there since before the war. Is that where you shop?"

The woman nodded, and looked sideways at Elinor to the extent that she could, given the restriction placed on movement by the dome-shaped hair dryer.

"The war's over now," said Elsie Finch. "And as my late husband always said, 'Life is for the living to go on living,' so I make it my business to enjoy my days out across the water."

"I know what you mean. I try to come up to London regularly if I can. I live near Tunbridge Wells now—lovely town, but it's not London. Even with the bomb sites, our town has still got life in it, hasn't it?"

"That's what I always say," said Elsie, closing the magazine. "There's life in the old girl yet!"

Elinor laughed. "A woman after my own heart. I treat myself to lunch or tea somewhere nice, and then when I've walked along by the Serpentine or somewhere like that, I go to the station a new woman."

Elsie studied her watch. "Pity I have an engagement after this, or I would suggest we go to Fortnum and Mason for a cup of tea and a slice of something nice." She lowered her voice. "But I will say this, let me know if you'd like that costume on the front of *Vogue*. I have a special account there and can get something knocked off the price."

Elinor put her hand on her chest. "Oh, I doubt I could afford it even with a customer discount."

"Yes, you could. I'm good at knowing what suits people and the best size for them. When will you be here at the salon again?"

"You know, I don't think I'll wait too long. I'm having so much fun now I've added this salon to my day, I think I'll come again in a week."

"This is my day with Raymond, so tea next time it is!"

An assistant approached to turn off the hair dryer above Elsie's head, which allowed her to face Elinor.

"I beg your pardon—my name is Mrs. Elsie Finch. And yours?"

Elinor held out her hand. "Miss Elinor De Witt."

"French?"

"My father was Belgian."

"I hope you weren't there during the war."

"Oh no," said Elinor. "I was safely over here, thank goodness."

"Madam—" The apprentice indicated it was time for Elsie to move to the next stage of her coiffure.

"Better get on," said Elsie.

Elinor nodded as another assistant arrived to switch off her dryer and lead her to the chair where Belinda would lift her hair—and as a result, her face. Her hair was still being teased into the style imagined by Belinda when Elsie Finch approached and leaned toward Elinor.

"Lovely to meet you, Miss De Witt. I'm looking forward to tea next week. Oh, and I'm off to Fenwicks now—bit of window shopping. You never know what I might find there." She smiled, waved to her hairdresser and left the salon.

Belinda commenced styling Elinor's hair, then caught her attention in the mirror. "Looks like you've made a friend there, madam."

"She seems very nice."

Belinda leaned forward, lowering her voice. "Between you and me—she is when she wants to be. She's a good customer here, leaves a nice tip, but I would never want to be on her bad side."

"Oh dear, now you've worried me."

"No, she would be alright with you. It's the young girls she can be a bit off with. Had me in tears when I was an apprentice. No, I would never underestimate that woman, ever."

Elinor nodded, surprised the hairdresser would express her opinion in such a way.

"I wouldn't normally speak out of turn, madam. But you're a nice lady, so I thought it only fair to tell you. I am sure she wouldn't be a bit off with you—but I'm a believer in being forewarned is forearmed."

"Thank you, Belinda. I appreciate your candor."

Elinor departed the salon having left Belinda a generous tip, mostly due to the relief she felt when the new haircut was brushed and styled and appeared to be not too difficult to maintain. If all else failed, she could still sweep it up in a twist, which she was likely to do anyway.

Tea with Elsie would come much later than she would have liked, but it was Belinda's comment that remained with her, and something else she overheard as she was settling her account. The hairdresser had extended her warning to an apprentice—it might have been her first week, thought Elinor. Belinda had lowered her voice, though not enough to prevent Elinor from hearing. "Be careful of that Mrs. Finch. If she were a man they would call her a wolf in sheep's clothing. Don't put a foot wrong, or she will have you sacked. But if she likes you, you'll get a nice tip."

It occurred to Elinor that it was the sort of indiscretion that would one day result in Belinda being sacked from the posh salon. In the meantime it was a detail she could tuck away with all the other slivers of information she was gathering.

———

Elinor's next stop was Scotland Yard. The desk sergeant gave her leave to proceed straight to the office of Detective Chief Inspector Stephen Warren, where she noticed that the new blackboard had been set up in the corner, the white and colored chalks still in their respective boxes.

"Linni, I wasn't expecting you back so soon," said Warren. He gave a broad smile, came to his feet and pulled out a chair opposite his desk. With Elinor settled, he took his seat again.

"There was someone I wanted to see up here in town, and I thought I'd pop in. Do you have any news? I noticed Bob and Charlie are out today."

"They're always out, Linni—we've got more irons in the fire than just your suspicions about the Mackie family."

"Steve, I just want to do anything I can to protect Jim and Rose Mackie, and in the process—as I mentioned before—I think it would behoove you to investigate whatever is in the offing. It could be a feather in your cap—pulling out a thorn that's been in your side for some time."

"You have no idea how many thorns I have in my side, Linni." He sighed while pushing around papers on his desk. Elinor noticed that it was movement for the sake of moving, as the papers didn't seem to be in any particular order. "Let me give you another idea of what we're up against. Last year we had a gun amnesty, and can you guess how many were handed in?" He pushed back his chair and stepped across to the blackboard, where he ripped the top from the packet of white chalks. "No time like the present to use this thing."

"I would imagine—"

"Don't even try. I'll make it easy on you." He began to write numbers on the board. "There, it's just like school—the facts sink in a bit better if you can see them." He opened the colored chalks and underlined the numbers in red. "Seventy-six thousand guns were relinquished, along with over two million rounds of ammunition." He placed the chalks on the ledge at the foot of the blackboard, took a handkerchief from his pocket and wiped his fingers. "Now, you know what that means, don't you?"

She nodded. "There's still plenty out there."

"Bingo. And would you like to make some sort of stab as to one of the underlying problems we're having to deal with?" He pulled back his chair and slumped onto the seat again.

"Underlying problems?"

"I know, Linni—I sound like one of those psychiatrist types you'll find over in Harley Street." He shrugged. "Actually, to be honest, it was one of those psychiatrist types who told me what he thought was caus-ing our biggest battles with crime now the war's over. Met him at a do I didn't want to go to, but the fellow made sense."

"What did he say?"

"He said that the villains were suffering from an addiction to the adrenaline of battle—that these types who were dodgy even before the war did their bit when they were called up and that the blood running to their heads when it came to fighting, firing off their guns, was the same as what happened to them when they were pulling off an armed robbery. Only it was worse, because when they came back, they wanted even more of that adrenaline flooding their bodies."

Elinor met Warren's stare. She nodded. "I can understand that."

"I know you can, Linni. So can I. We both know it's why I do my job and why Bob and Charlie are good at what they do. But here's the problem—everyone else is suffering from war fatigue."

"Did the psychiatrist tell you that?"

"Didn't have to. But it's why the people just let them get on with it—and of course as we know, the villains look after their own streets. After all, a dog doesn't mess in its own kennel." Warren pushed back his chair and stood up. "So, Linni, when I see you come in here having rushed to the aid of the young couple down the street who just happen to have a little girl, I didn't even have to ask myself why. People like us can only live a quiet life for so long. We were trained for something different, and sometimes the something different doesn't quite go as planned. But we were trained for that too. And then we came home, and here we are." He shrugged. "Fiddling around with bloody blackboards and chalk as if we're kids playing schools."

"I don't think I need any adrenaline, Steve. I like my life in the country."

"I'm sure you do," said Warren. "But if the country is so damn quiet and comfy, why are you carrying a pistol in that bag you have over your shoulder?" He stared at Elinor. "Please, Linni, don't risk your life. You've gone through—"

"I'm right about the Mackies, Steve." Elinor stood up. "I'm your canary in the coal mine. But the difference is, I'm going to make sure the explosion doesn't take Jim, Rose and Susie with it."

"Then come back here when you've more for us to go on. Bob and Charlie are working on a bank job we've got wind of, but I've told them to keep sniffing around the Mackies, just in case." He paused, moving the pieces of paper on his desk again. He opened his mouth as if to say something more, but was interrupted by a knock on the door.

"Yes!"

Elinor looked around to see who had entered the office.

"Sir," said Val. "I've a message for you—the call you were waiting for just came in." She handed a piece of paper to Warren, who read the note, then crumpled the paper and pushed it into his pocket.

"Thanks, Val. Miss White is just leaving—and I want to go through these letters before you type them up for me." He lifted a folder and looked at Elinor.

"Yes, I must be on my way," said Elinor. "Off to run a few errands. I'll see myself out."

Elinor departed the office, closing the door behind her. She thought Warren's manner when the message was handed to him had been odd. She knew Steve Warren, knew he was master of the quick quip and capable of bluster—it was part of his charisma, what drew people to him, and she had been one of them, once. But the note had silenced what felt like a lecture in full flow. As she passed Val's desk, she noticed the white notepad from which the leaf of paper had been torn. There was no one nearby to bear witness as she tore the top sheet from the pad.

When she reached the ladies' lavatory, she rested the sheet of paper against the back of the door, took a pencil from her bag and, using the softest pressure, ran the pencil back and forth across the indentation left by Val's heavy hand until the words were revealed.

Sir Perry G-W. Six. The usual place. He said not to be late.

Elinor tore the note into small pieces and flushed them away into the toilet, where they would soon rot into nothing, swept away in the effluence of London's Victorian sewers.

Perry G-W.

A "sir," no less. A *member of your aristocracy*, as Jim Mackie might have observed. She would have to watch her back.

CHAPTER 9

1917

British Forces in Continued Drive
Bombardment on the Flanders Front Intensive

—*Daily Sketch*

Elinor could never quite recall every detail of the ensuing chain of events. When she tried to put together each lingering scene in her mind's eye, she felt as if she were struggling with a jigsaw puzzle. She could not identify the edge pieces that, once slotted into place, would create an outer frame to help her construct the complete picture. And there was not just one element but many, reminding her of the stereo-optic machines she had played with at the fair, a clutch of cards beside her on the table ready to slip into the viewer. Each card had two photographs that appeared to be identical, yet when she looked through the viewer, the images came together so she could see perspective through the lens, as if at any moment the people who had been photographed would begin to move. In the days to come a memory would sometimes make an abrupt entry into her consciousness without warning and, like lightning, interrupt whatever else she was thinking about.

In time she was able to recollect reaching the house after killing the German soldiers. Recollection brought with it the lightness of relief, a reminder that they were lucky—so very fortunate—not to see another soul as they returned to their home. *Home.* What a soothing word it was, wrapping itself around her, keeping her safe. They came home, though the comfort would not last. They entered the kitchen. Cecily was still moaning, louder now when she saw her mother. Isabelle and Charlotte took only a second to look them up and down before they began to move with speed. It was then that Elinor realized their clothes were smeared with blood and mud.

"Elinor, Cecily, remove your clothes. Now. Hurry. Charlotte, burn anything with even a speck of blood—use the stove, not a bonfire in the garden. Be quick. Girls, go and wash yourselves from head to toe." She looked at Charlotte again. "The boots don't have blood on them— but brush them clean and leave them by the stove. I want them as dry as bone."

"They . . . they tried to interfere with Cecily," said Elinor.

"Interfere?" said Isabelle.

"Oh no—no, my darling girl." Charlotte took Cecily in her arms.

Elinor watched as Isabelle touched Charlotte on the shoulder, and for a second wondered if she would begin to tell her mother how to use a pistol.

"Charlotte, there will be time for your tears later," said Isabelle. "You must do as I say with all haste, or your daughters will be paraded in the square and shot." She turned to Elinor. "The gun?"

Elinor handed over the weapon and ammunition. She had just killed two men in cold blood—and she knew even more German soldiers had lost their lives when the train derailed. Hungry young German soldiers, perhaps no more than boys who had no fight in them, had been crushed to death. But she had saved her sister from injury. To her body, at least.

Within twenty minutes, Elinor and Cecily were standing in the kitchen wearing fresh nightgowns. The floor had been scrubbed of any mud they had brought in. Forty minutes later the clothing they had worn on their mission to derail the train had burned through. Charlotte added wood to the fire so not even a scorched scrap of cloth would be discovered. Their boots were brushed clean and polished, then lined up with other footwear by the back door. Isabelle checked the garden and the house for any telltale signs that the De Witt women were saboteurs and murderers of German soldiers.

"I must leave now," said Isabelle, as the golden sunshine of early morning shone through the kitchen window. "Here's what you must do next."

Isabelle explained that Cecily must take to her bed. All the keening had given her the look of a girl with a very bad cold, so that was her alibi. Elinor must rest for an hour or two, then make ready for school and attend classes as usual.

"When they find the two soldiers, they will know they are looking for a woman. The state of one of the soldiers at least will indicate what he was about, and that means they will in all likelihood be searching the houses where there are women of an age to tempt young men who are far from home. Be careful. Say as little as possible. You all went to bed last night at the usual time, though Charlotte has been up ministering to Cecily, bringing her a hot water bottle and tea to ease the effects of her cold. And as Elinor and Cecily share a room, she didn't sleep well either. You're all tired—that is how you appear, and that is your story. Then we must get Elinor out of Belgium." Isabelle looked at Charlotte. "The Germans are ruthless. You've seen what they can and will do. I can't arrange for you all to leave at the same time. In fact, I think it would behoove Cecily to apply to become a novice at the convent." She looked at Cecily. Elinor followed her gaze and took account of her sister's countenance as the word "novice" was uttered. Cecily could never play the part of a nun. "And don't worry, Cecily, it won't be forever. I can make the arrangements. Now, the three of you— attempt nothing except the ordinary things you would do in your day until you hear from me." She looked at Elinor, Cecily and Charlotte in turn. "Understood?"

"Yes," they said in unison.

Isabelle stood up, opened the kitchen door and was gone.

Cecily leaned into her mother's arms. "Mama, no one will ever want me. No boy will marry me."

"Oh, of course they will, my poor darling. Don't fret. Now then, let's get you up to bed."

"Ceci, I stopped him before he . . ."

Elinor watched as Cecily began weeping again while Charlotte guided her upstairs. She stared at the cup of pale-grey watered-down tea set before her on the kitchen table, then stood up to gather her English leather satchel from the back of the chair. She checked her books and made sure her pencils were sharpened. Touching the tip of one pencil, she felt her nose prickle as tears begin to roll down her cheeks. She had killed two men. She had lifted a weapon and done what she had been trained to do. Yet as the days went on, she would come to realize that being a predator filled her with as much fear as being prey. She hoped Isabelle was right when she said fear could keep you safe.

Charlotte was adamant. "I've been thinking about it all day, Isabelle, and I can tell you now that I will not be separated from my girls. I am proud of what they have accomplished, though never in my most dreadful nightmares would I have seen this war, and I would not have imagined my daughter with a gun in her hand—and killing with it. I allowed this . . . this work to continue because the Germans have taken their father's life, of that I have no doubt. My husband would be proud of them both for avenging his death and the terror inflicted upon his country."

Elinor had never heard her mother speak in such a tone, and she wondered if it was the first time Charlotte had acknowledged that Thomas was dead. Yes, she had always been a woman who was strong of spirit, but as a rule Charlotte would wind her way around a problem, drawing people into her circle of influence rather than facing trouble head on, as if armed with a mallet. On the other hand, she knew Charlotte could be stubborn—a trait Cecily had inherited. Perhaps she too could be stubborn. She would have to think about it, one day, when there was time for thinking about oneself.

"You can't—" began Isabelle, who had arrived at the house just after dusk.

Elinor continued to watch her mother and Isabelle, though she knew in this instance who would win the argument. She sighed. Could so much have happened to them within hours? It seemed as if it were weeks ago that she and Cecily had lifted metal plates onto a railway line, had encountered two German soldiers. The train had indeed derailed, so at least they had accomplished their objective. They had carried out a successful mission—successful, that is, until they had been discovered by the soldiers. Isabelle had assured them their work had not been in vain, that whatever happened, they were heroines of Belgium. She let them know that she had already sent her report "along the line" to the British, so they knew a vital German transportation link had been all but destroyed by two girls—sisters. The Allies knew they were in the debt of two young women who were once again wearing their school uniforms.

Listening to Isabelle, Elinor realized she had come to think of the woman as something of an otherworldly figure, a Valkyrie from the realm of myths, or a sorceress who moved in the shadows; an operator in the half-light, half-dark grey and grainy tones of dusk or dawn. Now she was here with the plan, yet the conversation with Charlotte was clearly not going quite as she intended.

"Then we stay." Charlotte folded her arms.

Isabelle sighed and shook her head. "Charlotte, you know you cannot stay." Another deep sigh. "In that case I will make the necessary arrangements for all three of you to leave at the same time. Be ready to depart by nightfall." She came to her feet and, as was her habit, looked with intent at each of the De Witts in turn. "Do you girls have knapsacks, something of that order? I don't want you carrying cases or bags."

They nodded. Elinor heard her sister sniff and hoped she wasn't crying again. German soldiers had come to the house just as Elinor was leaving for school. They had pushed her inside, told her to summon her mother and sister and searched the house. Cecily looked awful, with a runny nose and bronchial cough that Elinor knew was not due to any skill in the art of acting on her sister's part, though it served a purpose and the trio were given leave to continue with their everyday ordinary lives in a small town in occupied Belgium.

Charlotte hesitated, then nodded. "We will be ready, Isabelle. We tried to flee once before, so we know we must leave almost everything that ties us to our life here."

"Good. Because in moving all three of you, others will be put in grave danger. They will be risking everything to give you a chance of escape, so don't take anything more than necessary. We will leave before dawn. The Germans might have left you alone for now, but I believe they will be back."

Remember what happened to Nurse Cavell," said Cecily, packing underwear, a fresh blouse and her hairbrush into the knapsack she usually employed to carry her sketchbook, paints and pencils.

"I know very well what happened to Nurse Cavell, Ceci, but this isn't the time to dwell on it," said Elinor. "Remember, you can always go along to the convent and become a novice."

Ceci blew her nose, which was red and sore. "I'm scared."

"Ceci!" Elinor threw down her knapsack. "And I'm terrified! But I am also fed up with listening to you and feeling as if I have a sister in kindergarten and not one who is older than me. Please, help us both and stop whining!"

"That's enough, Elinor." Charlotte came into the bedroom shared by the sisters. "But your sister is right, you should stop whimpering, Ceci. We don't have time for it. Find some of the bravery you had at your fingertips while moving those metal plates."

Cecily nodded. "Yes, Mama. I'm sorry. It's just—"

"Just nothing. Do you have your petticoats with you—the special ones?"

Both girls nodded.

"Good. Don't take them off at all until we get to wherever we're going—until we know we're safe. And remember you're to put on your boots again. Thank heavens Isabelle didn't make us burn them. We'll be traveling some distance on foot."

sabelle came to the house at the appointed hour, and within minutes the women were walking at a determined pace through the town, using doorways to linger for a few moments if a patrol were spotted. Then they continued on. They walked for miles with not a word uttered, following Isabelle in silence. Not for the first time, Elinor wondered how old Isabelle was. She'd settled on twenty-five. An old twenty-five. And not only that, but she had come to realize that there was an occasional inflection in her pronunciation, and she sounded a little like Charlotte.

In time Isabelle held up her hand. They were in farmland now, making their way around the edge of a field close to dense woods.

"Wait here, behind that hedge," said Isabelle. "Do not make a sound. Is that clear?"

"I need to—"

"Then relieve yourself behind a tree, Ceci. Elinor, keep watch. I will return in twenty minutes."

As the sun rose, they watched Isabelle make her way around the field, maintaining her usual marching momentum. She never seemed to run, but could move at a speedy walk. Elinor wondered whether she had perfected the gait to avoid the risk of falling, or being seen. Was it harder to spot someone striding out than someone running? She thought it might be. Speed can lead to errors, and errors can lead to death. Prey run while predators stalk them.

Focusing on the route Isabelle had taken, Elinor soon identified a speck in the distance and knew the woman in whom they had placed so much trust was returning. Isabelle reached the hedge ten minutes later and climbed through.

"Now, we have to be very, very careful. I am going to lead you to a farmhouse where we will meet the couple who will be taking you across the border."

"You're not coming with us?" asked Cecily.

Isabelle shook her head. "Not to the border, though I am sure I will see you all again soon. Come along, we don't have much time—and keep up with me."

At the corner of each field Isabelle stopped, lifted her binoculars and scrutinized the land around her. Only when she deemed it safe and clear did they move again. Soon they approached a farm at the corner of another field. Once again Isabelle indicated they should remain in place as she went ahead. Elinor watched as she knocked on the farmhouse window and stood back. The door opened to reveal an older man, tall with grey hair. Even from a distance she could see that his clothing had known better times, with trousers baggy and worn, a jacket over his collarless shirt and a scarf tied at his throat. His neck was folded forward, as if he had sustained an injury or fallen from a height, and when he turned around to step back inside the house, Elinor thought it seemed as if he had no head, that she was looking at a man walking into the house with nothing above the shoulders. The headless horseman in his home. Isabelle beckoned to the women and chivvied them into the farmhouse. Inside the man and his wife stood side by side to greet them.

Isabelle pointed to each of the De Witts in turn. "Charlotte, Cecily and Elinor—I would like you to meet Uta and Tim. Uta and Tim are my heroes."

The couple smiled, looked at one another and laughed. Elinor wondered when she had last laughed. When had she even heard someone happy, or seen something comical? When was there anything to be lighthearted about?

Uta, with grey hair pulled back into a tight bun and wearing clothing that could have belonged to her husband, nodded and greeted the women, first in perfect English and then in French.

"I am from Amsterdam, so I learned English and French because . . . well, who learns Dutch, apart from the Dutch?"

Tim smiled at his wife again. "I learned it, dear Uta."

Isabelle cleared her throat. "Uta and Tim are known at the border because they visit their children and Uta's family when they can. The farm keeps them busy here, though, and the border guards know they will return." She reached into her jacket and handed an envelope each to Charlotte, Cecily and Elinor.

"You are now Uta and Tim's family. Everything there is in order. Charlotte is the wife of Uta and Tim's son, Piet, who lives not far from the border, and Elinor and Cecily are Uta and Tim's granddaughters."

"Won't they know these are forged?"

"They are not forgeries, Charlotte. We just had to get your names on the correct documents. Now then, may I have your existing papers?"

For a moment Charlotte wavered and clutched her knapsack to her chest. Then she nodded, unbuttoned the clasp and took out the three sets of documents attesting to the identity of each of the De Witts. She gave the papers to Isabelle, who handed them to Uta. Elinor craned her neck to watch as Uta turned around and lifted a cast iron fork to open the door of a blackened stove, then pushed their identity documents into the flames.

"When will we leave?" asked Charlotte.

"There's often a fair amount of movement across the border in the morning and evening," said Tim. "And as we want to get you home for supper, we will leave in an hour. It's a bit of a walk to the crossing, but many will be on their way at the same time. And your papers will attest to the fact that you have gone back and forth several times."

Uta looked at Charlotte. "Charlotte, dear, to make you feel better, we know of one twelve-year-old girl who accompanies disguised British soldiers across the border with some regularity. The guards do no more than glance at her papers and those of her 'old uncle' and she's through. Then she comes back again to join her parents."

"Do we have to see Germans?" asked Cecily.

"I'm afraid you do," said Tim. "But for the most part they are boys doing a job they really don't want to do. They are hungry too, so we try to take them a small gift of bread. All the Germans are wanting for food now—even in Germany. Perhaps you've not heard about the food riots there. If there's hardly enough for the people, you can be sure sustenance isn't getting through to the army here. We're known to be friendly, sympathetic and our good reputation means we cross the border without incident, no matter who is with us and in what guise." He paused. "And there really is no longer any other way. The fences are all electrified, and I have had enough shocks in my life, so we won't risk that route anymore."

Isabelle nodded toward Tim and Uta then turned toward the door. Elinor looked at her mother and Cecily, who didn't seem to be paying attention—they were instead studying their papers, while Uta set about making tea and Tim pulled out chairs. Elinor ran out of the farmhouse and caught up with Isabelle.

"Isabelle!"

"Elinor—for heaven's sake, go back inside!"

"But I wanted to say goodbye. I wanted to thank you—thank you for everything you taught me."

Isabelle stared at Elinor. "Linni, I taught you to use a weapon and put you in a position where you had to kill two men. That is not something to be lauded."

"You taught me how to be brave, Isabelle."

Isabelle shook her head. "No, Linni. My job is to see bravery in people and then give them a good reason to use it. You are a very brave young girl."

"Will we ever see you again?"

Isabelle smiled. "Oh, I think you might." She stared across the fields. Both could hear the echo of cannonade in the far distance, the unrelenting thunder of war ricocheting for miles and miles across the flat lands of Belgium; an almost constant rumbling that could even be heard on the other side of the English Channel. "Who knows what might happen before this war is over."

Uta and Tim's lightness of spirit was almost worrisome to Elinor as they led the way across even more fields—fields now bereft of whatever crop might have grown there.

"When the harvest comes in, we make sure we keep enough for us and any visitors," said Tim. "We knew the Germans would take everything they could for the soldiers, so we have to be quick. Our food for the winter is down in the cellar, through a door that only we know." He smiled at his wife as they joined the road—a road where a few other travelers were ambling along toward the border. "Though I think we might be rather tired of vegetable root soup by the new year. But people are always hungry when their country is at war, so we think ourselves fortunate that we at least have something to warm the belly."

Charlotte nodded, while Cecily looked down as she walked. Elinor could not stop thinking about Edith Cavell—now they were on their way, the English nurse came to mind time and again. The Germans had dealt with the woman in a brutal fashion. Is that what would happen to them? Was she now listening to Tim and Uta tell stories as they walked toward the border, only to be shot for trying to escape? What would happen to them all? Would her life end within the next hour?

Some sixty-five minutes later, Elinor was not only still alive, but on the other side of the border. They had reached the Netherlands, and now she was standing in a queue with Tim, Uta, her mother and Cecily, and they were waiting for an omnibus as if it were the most normal thing in the world. Elinor tensed. No, she would not become complacent. She would not settle her nerves. Surely the soldiers could still catch them all; it had been too easy. Well, perhaps not easy, but then, easy was anything that wasn't a trial and didn't compel her to tell lies. Though of course she was telling lies—but it was a truthful lie, because in her heart she now felt so close to Tim and Uta that she wanted to call them Nana and Grandpa. She wanted to sit in front of a fire with them listening to stories, and here she was seated between them on the bus, their old shoulders next to hers, as if she were tightly held by two ancient oaks. Her mother had taken the seat in front of them with Cecily. Ah, Cecily, who had looked down when a German guard at the border—who could have only been a year or two older—smiled at her and flirted. Her blushes were so pink, the German apologized for upsetting her, at which point Ceci began to weep.

"She misses her father," said Charlotte, putting her arm around Ceci and leading her away.

As they passed the border crossing and began to walk on, Elinor thought they were bound to be called back, sure to be challenged, and became afraid that her surprise might give them all away. Then Tim put his hand on her shoulder. "Come on, child. Hurry up—there are other people trying to get through." He lifted his hat to the soldier as

Uta handed the boy fresh bread and a pot of honey, and they moved off, shuffling away from their occupied country.

After an hour on the bus, Elinor woke up from a short but deep sleep when Tim moved to tap Charlotte on the shoulder.

"Your stop is coming up next."

Charlotte turned around. "Our stop? I thought—we thought we would remain with you until we settled ourselves."

Tim shook his head. "Someone will be meeting you. Do not fear, you will be home soon."

"Home, but—"

"You're from England, Mrs. De Witt—London?"

Charlotte nodded.

"Yes, you will be home soon."

"What will we do—who will meet us?"

"You are safe now. Miss Isabelle has arranged everything. You must have done your country a great favor."

"My girls—" Charlotte began, then reached forward, lifted her sturdy walking skirt enough to reveal a mud-splattered white petticoat. With nimble fingers she prised out a small, clear stone, then reached for Tim's hand. She pressed the diamond into his palm. "Thank you— from we three De Witts."

Uta leaned past Elinor and took her husband's hand in hers, where-upon he opened his palm so she could see what Charlotte had given him. She closed the palm and nodded her thanks.

"We will take very good care with this, perhaps not use it until after the war. We're simple people—we don't know quite what to do with your gift."

Through sleepy eyes, Elinor watched as her mother passed a small folded note to Uta.

"I know—but here's the name of a man who will help you. Put the stone and the note away in a safe place and use it when you need to," whispered Charlotte.

The bus came to a slow halt. Farewells were expressed, and when Elinor, Ceci and Charlotte alighted the omnibus, they waved to Tim and Uta. Then their protectors were gone. Elinor watched for a while, committing the two faces to memory, hoping she would see them again.

"Mrs. De Witt?"

The De Witt women turned at the same time to see a man of about forty standing before them. He lifted his hat and smiled, leaning forward as if he might bow.

"Good, I've found you. Now come with me. I'll get you settled; however, I'm afraid there will be a debriefing, after which we'll go over the plan for your repatriation." He looked at Cecily and Elinor. "Very clever of you to register your daughters as British subjects when they were babies, Mrs. De Witt. Made things rather easier for us."

Elinor could see fatigue claiming her mother. Charlotte said nothing by way of reply, but simply nodded. The man had noticed.

"Might be a bit of a stretch, you know, the debriefing and all that. We've rooms for you, so I'll take you over to the house now. Give you a chance to put your feet up before we begin."

"What's your name?" asked Elinor.

"Mr. Strong."

It was clear Mr. Strong would say no more as he turned, indicating with his hand for them to follow. Elinor doubted his name was Strong. She thought they must seem like a trio of ducklings following in his wake as he led the way across a street. It occurred to her, then, that she had no idea where she was. Yes, she was in the Netherlands, but was she in Amsterdam? Rotterdam? Perhaps another town altogether. Had she seen a sign for Breda when she looked out the bus window? Or had she imagined it? She knew only that she had walked miles across fields and along roads. Miles from there to here. Many hours trudging on foot to escape something that might have happened years ago, so distant was it in her mind. Except the killing wasn't far away—it was there, staring her down every time she closed her eyes.

W hy do they call it a debriefing?" asked Cecily of her mother, as Charlotte came from the room where Strong and another man— Hitchen—had asked questions of her.

Elinor looked at her sister, who had already been into the room for her debriefing. It was clear that Ceci was more like her old self. Her old contrary self.

"Miss Elinor De Witt?" Strong stood at the door and curled his finger toward Elinor, an instruction to join him.

"Well, you're a very brave young lady," said Mr. Hitchen, who stood up when she entered the room and extended his hand.

Elinor nodded and shook the man's hand, which he then held out toward the chair on the other side of the table.

"Just want to go through a few things—mainly regarding the train incident." He looked at her as if expecting a response. Receiving none, he cleared his throat and began again. "Right then, I take it you did not see the train."

"We had left by the time it came along the railway line close to town."

"Yes, of course. Did you hear anything to indicate the operation's success?"

Elinor looked out of the window, then back at Hitchen.

"Yes." She took a deep breath; she had no intention of repeating herself. "We executed the task, but on our return journey, my sister and I were seen by German soldiers. One of them began to attack my sister, and I was thrown to the ground by the other. As I regained my senses, I could see they were about to . . . about to take her honor, so I stopped them. I used the weapon given to me by Miss Isabelle. I had no other choice." She cleared her throat, but continued because she did not want to be cross-examined. "We began to run back to our house, which was when I heard the train derail. We were less than a mile away, but I could hear the sound of every carriage and wagon on the train crashing. It was very loud."

Hitchen and Strong looked at one another, then drew their attention back to Elinor.

"You carried out your task to the letter," said Hitchen. "We will miss you in the field."

"I won't miss the . . . the field, though. Can we go now? Please."

And with that, the ordeal was over. Elinor, her sister and mother boarded a freighter bound for Harwich the following morning. They had been given fresh clothing and enjoyed hot baths and a good meal. Then it seemed that all too soon they were on a train from the port of Harwich to London, and once in London they were at the home Charlotte had grown up in, a Georgian terrace house close to Brunswick Square. There was a cook and a daily who came in to clean. Elinor wondered why her mother had ever left London.

"If there weren't so many people wearing their mourning black, Britain wouldn't be far off normal," said the now-widowed Lillian White. "But at last you're here, and I'm so glad those men from the government arranged for you to come home, Charlotte, dear."

Elinor was shown to a bedroom she would share with her sister, while her mother moved into her girlhood room. She fell asleep that night with her grandmother's words echoing through the memory that now would not be banished, of lifting the pistol and firing toward one soldier and then the next, blood blooming across the back of the first and then exploding from the shattered skull of the second. Perhaps they weren't far off normal, though she could not remember what normal felt like. Normal was running through the woods with Polo, before the war. She wondered if people talked about normal because it felt safe. But Elinor didn't know if her life would ever feel secure again, or if she could trust normal, if it came.

CHAPTER 10

London
September 1918

Elinor sat at the back of the classroom and stared out of the window to a point beyond the quadrangle, past the netball courts and the hockey pitch to a place under the trees where she imagined herself lingering with a book. Or perhaps just resting, her mind empty, vacant, without a single thought to bother her.

"Elinor White, you've been in the midst of yet another dream since you walked into my classroom," said Miss Doncaster, the mathematics teacher. "Apply yourself, my girl. Apply yourself, or you will never complete the test."

Elinor turned to face Miss Doncaster. She did not roll her eyes, but both she and the teacher knew she might as well have.

"What do you have to say for yourself, White?"

Elinor pushed back her chair with an audible scrape and lifted the six sheets of paper handed out forty-five minutes earlier to each of the twenty girls in the class. She stood up, proceeded to the front of the classroom and handed the papers to the teacher.

"I've finished."

"Finished? Finished? Mark my words, I do not appreciate sloppy work from any girl in my class." Doncaster pronounced the word "gel." "I will hold you to the highest standards of academic accomplishment."

"I did not find the test particularly difficult, Miss Doncaster," said Elinor.

"Well, everyone else in this class admits to at least some difficulty with mathematics, so why you are any different is quite beyond me."

Elinor offered no immediate response, instead waiting a second or two before voicing her request. "Miss Doncaster, may I go to the library to read? I believe it will be a far better use of my time."

"That's it!" Doncaster stood up and leaned forward, resting her knuckles on the desk before her. "Class! Put your pencils down and pay attention. White, return to your desk."

Elinor did as she was told, feeling all eyes upon her as she took her seat once again. Tempted as she was to fold her arms, she knew Miss Doncaster would interpret the gesture as an inflammatory action. Instead she clasped her hands on her lap.

Doncaster stepped out from behind her desk and looked from right to left, eyeing each of the twenty girls in the classroom.

"Ladies, our country has endured four years of war. Though we hope there will be an end soon, it has not yet come. How many of you have lost your fathers to this war?"

Seven girls, including Elinor, raised their hands.

"And how many of you will never see your brothers again?"

Twelve girls raised their hands.

"How many of you have received news that a male relative has perished?"

Fifteen girls raised their hands; twelve of those raised both hands.

"And finally, how many of you know of young men who have given their lives for our country—perhaps neighbors, or friends of your brothers and cousins?"

Every hand in the room was raised.

"Ladies, look around this room at the show of hands. You may not realize it at this particular juncture, but you have before you a mathematical truth that only the most foolish will ignore." Doncaster focused on Elinor, who stared back. "Given what we know—and what is evident in your responses to every question I have put to you—the loss of life our country has sustained, notably the passing of young men in their prime, it would be fair to say that girls of your age who are on the cusp of womanhood will have only a one-in-ten chance of marriage as time goes on. One. In. Ten." She paused, again looking from one girl to the next. "So, where does that leave you?" Doncaster did not wait for answers, nor did she show any indication of a willingness to listen. "That leaves you to prepare as best you can to make your way forward alone, which in turn means you will have to become responsible for your own financial security. Your future prospects are in your hands, and you must build a sturdy academic foundation for the years ahead, so you may forge connections, friendships and the valuable associations that will carry you through your lifetime." She glared at Elinor again. "Miss White, are my calculations right? Given your mathematical prowess, I believe you should know."

Elinor nodded. "Yes, Miss Doncaster. Your reckoning is correct." She did not blink as she answered the teacher. "And to support your hypothesis," continued Elinor, "I believe women bereaved during the

Boer War found themselves in similar circumstances, so their progress should be an example to us all."

Doncaster reddened, and was about to say more when she was interrupted by another girl in the class.

"Miss Doncaster," said the girl, raising her hand.

"Yes, Sophia Wallace, what is it?"

"Miss Doncaster, it's not only our brothers, cousins and their friends who are dead. My sister, Delia—she was one of your pupils a few years ago—well, she was killed while driving an ambulance in France." The girl pulled a handkerchief from her sleeve. "So it's not only the boys we know who are gone."

Doncaster glanced at the ground. "Yes, of course. Delia Wallace. Excelled at physics and chemistry. First class, absolutely brilliant academics—Delia should have gone to Cambridge. I expect you to attain a place in her stead, Sophia." She cleared her throat and began again. "However, I was simply making a point for the benefit of anyone who thinks they can swan through a vital test of accomplishment and ability. None of you can afford to be so cavalier." She walked to the other side of her desk and checked the clock. "Continue with your test—in silence! And Miss White, given your swift progress, you may be excused to go to the library." She sighed. "As may anyone else who has completed the test. Every. Single. Question."

"Thank you, Miss Doncaster," said Elinor, gathering her books and pencil case and placing them in a brown leather satchel.

As Elinor reached the door, she heard another chair being pushed aside and footsteps moving toward Miss Doncaster's desk, but she did not look back. And she did not proceed to the library. Instead she walked along the corridor, with its oak-paneled walls and polished parquet floors that smelled of lavender and beeswax, and upon reaching the main entrance, she left the building. She took neither bus nor tram, but continued taking one step after the other until she felt pain from the effort, from her feet to her head. She did not want to stop and she did not want to talk to anyone as she made her way some two miles along the London streets to Kensington Gardens. Once there, she would find a quiet corner to be alone, avoiding the area that had been given over to the army, who had built trenches and dugouts, and brought in sandbagging for the training of soldiers bound for the front.

Alone had become Elinor's preferred place. Alone and away from her grandmother, with her suggestions and opinions that could only come from one who has been at home and safe while others were at war. She wanted a rest from her mother, who had become a daughter again since returning to live under her own mother's roof. Charlotte was often fussy, wondering aloud what might become of them all. Cecily had been persuaded to undertake a clerical course, but had left the Secretarial School for Young Ladies in favor of teaching and perhaps employment as a governess. Who knew how long that would last? Elinor thought it obvious that Cecily did not care for work at all and would rather languish in their shared room all day, worrying about herself, which caused more fussing from Charlotte, more arguments and more apologies. Oh, how Elinor wished her father were there. He would temper her mother's moods and give Cecily the gentle push that in his clever way always worked with her sister. She wanted her beloved father home again.

In truth, Elinor was torn; she loved her family with a fierce protectiveness, but it left her weighed down by guilt that wrapped itself around her whenever she dreamed of being far away from this coterie of women among whom she just didn't seem to fit. Would it be too much for her mother and Ceci to grasp that no one can ever be ordinary ever again after they have killed a person? And she had killed two men.

Elinor dropped her satchel on the grass and lay on her back, eyes closed against the low autumn sun. It was predicted the war would be over soon, though she doubted that the moving pictures in her mind would vanish forever when peace was declared. And what about this restlessness she had felt since they arrived in London? It was a feeling inside her very spirit that nothing mattered yet everything mattered, that she had to be on the move and could not tarry. If she stopped, what then? The more settled their situation, the more unsettled Elinor became. And why were mathematics, geography, history, chemistry, English literature and the study of everything else so important when she had derailed two locomotives, when she had crept out of her house in the blackness of night to count the carriages on a passing train, estimating the number of tanks, of cannons, of guns that might be on their way to the German army at the front? People had been slaughtered as a result of her actions. What might it take to calm her from the inside so she could be normal on the outside? And would anything ever be plain ordinary anymore? She pressed her fingers against her eyes as if to push away the torment.

"There you are. I thought that was you."

Elinor sat up, now a little dizzy, shielding her eyes with her hand and squinting to see who had spoken to her.

"Sophie Wallace, what are you doing here?"

The girl, wearing the same long navy-blue tailored jacket, the same mid-calf-length skirt and white blouse with a navy-blue tie, sat down beside Elinor. She removed her brimmed turquoise-blue hat with the darker grosgrain band bearing the school insignia and pulled pins from her red hair. "Same as you. Had to escape St. Joseph's Academy for Young Ladies—and bored mathematicians."

"How did you know where to find me?"

Sophie shook her head and ran her fingers through a cascade of sun-burnished chestnut curls. "I didn't. I just happened to see you." She pointed to a place in the distance. "My brother was stationed here for a while, training over there before they sent him off to fight. I used to sneak out of school to meet him. I did it almost every day because I was scared I'd never see him again after he sailed for France."

Elinor waited. The other girl shrugged.

"And I was right. He was killed about a week after he landed," said Sophie, who seemed to be sprouting more freckles in the sunshine. "Just one week."

"You said you'd lost your sister too."

"That's right." She smiled. "There was a bit of a gap between Robin Delia and me—I was the afterthought child, or a mistake, depending on how you look at it. Now I'm the only one left."

"That's terrible." Elinor paused. "My father was killed in Belgium."

"You're originally from Belgium, aren't you? Your English is really good—you'd never know you're from over there."

"My mother is English."

"And I know you speak French and German—I've heard you rattling it off in class. Do you speak that funny Flemish language too?"

Elinor nodded. "And a fair bit of Italian. We had a lot of language lessons where I went to school."

"That'll be useful, won't it—if Dopey Doncaster is right, you can get a position as a teacher."

"Sophie, she's not so dopey—Miss Doncaster hit the nail on the head."

"I suppose I should do some of that galvanizing and think of something to do so I don't languish in a dark, dismal chasm of bored and bereft spinsterhood. Perhaps I could become a nurse, though my father will have a fit. I can see him now going on and on about how only poor girls go into nursing, that it's for young washerwomen. My mother would complain about what people might think. You should

have heard them when Delia joined the First Aid Nursing Yeomanry."
She shrugged. "Father just cannot grasp the fact that everything has
changed. We shall never be the same, and I'm not going to languish
at home waiting for a husband who will probably never come along.
You're right—you can't argue with Doncaster's calculations on that
one."

Elinor nodded and they sat in silence for a while, both girls replac-
ing their hats to protect pale skin from the warming sunshine.

"What was it like in Belgium, Elinor?"

"You'd never believe me if I told you."

"Why not? I think I'd believe anything about this war now. Most of
the women you see on the street are clad in black, or they're in some
uniform or another and wearing a black armband so you know they've
lost someone. We're a land in mourning, women wrapped in widow's
weeds." Sophie sighed. "It's like that poem by Walter de la Mare—you
know, we read it in English last week. 'Weeps she never, but sometimes
sighs, And peeps at her garden with bright brown eyes, And all she has
is all she needs — A poor Old Widow in her weeds.' " She pointed into
the distance. "Do you know that every single one of the boys who was
over there training with Robin was killed? Every. Single. One—as Miss
Doncaster would say. So, yes, Elinor, I would believe whatever you told
me about Belgium."

"Another time, perhaps," said Elinor, coming to her feet.

"Are you going back to school now?" Sophie held out her hand toward Elinor, who grasped it and helped her up from the damp ground.

"No."

"Home?"

"No."

"What will you do?"

"I think I'll just wander."

Sophie regarded Elinor and without warning, opened her arms and embraced her. "That's for being honest and for being brave."

Elinor shook her head. "I'm not brave, Sophie. If I were truly brave, I would go back to St. Joseph's. I feel . . . I think being a schoolgirl was in the past even before I left Belgium."

Walking away, Elinor could feel Sophie's bright brown eyes upon her, but when she turned around, her classmate was making her way across the park in the direction of the training trenches, as if she might encounter the returning soul of her lost brother.

WORLD WAR ENDS

ARMISTICE IN FORCE

HOHENZOLLERNS TAKE TO HEELS, KAISER RUNS TO HOLLAND

—*The Daily News*, November 11, 1918

"Just hold my hand so we don't get separated, Ceci," said Elinor. "Oh, look over there—the soldiers are jumping in and out of the water! Oh my goodness, look at them!"

Elinor felt Cecily clutch her hand as the crowd gathering at Trafalgar Square pressed in, laughing, drinking, happy beyond any measure since eleven that morning, when bells began ringing across the land to let everyone know that at last, after four long years, the Armistice had come. Peace was declared.

Soldiers from Australia and New Zealand were whisking up girls to dance around the fountain, and then the Canadians joined in, with more soldiers from across the British Empire taking the hands of anyone who was game to be part of a conga line. Elinor looked at the men, women, soldiers, children; at the masses converging in jubilant accord. Yes, she was relieved, happy. She was now fourteen years of age, and though she was joyous at the news, there was another feeling she could not pinpoint. She had so much to be thankful for. They had escaped Belgium with their lives, given help along the way by strangers who risked so much to assist them. They were not poor in London, thanks to a number of diamonds taken one by one from their petticoats and a grandfather who was clever with his money. Despite the near-constant ache of grief and loss, Elinor had done well at school since coming to England; it seemed the nuns in Belgium had given her a first-class foundation, so she was ahead in her studies. In time, if the gods remained with her, she would be bound for university with Sophie.

It was later, as she walked with Ceci back to their home, joining in street parties along the way, that it came to her in an instant why she felt as if she were on the edge of a precipice. She still could not escape the truth that she had killed two men to protect her sister's honor. The act had saved both their lives, but didn't taking a life require atonement? If that were so, when would Fate come for her? Where was her personal armistice? What might it feel like, and how would she know when she was free? Because that was her fear, that the piper must be paid, and war or no war, necessity or not, Fate was coming to settle the account.

Elinor White returned to St. Joseph's for her final years at the school, and having made a friend—her first ever best friend, someone who was not her sister or mother—she felt as if she were following in Sophie's wake, learning from her, adjusting her ambitions as she became more familiar with academic life in England. Every day she seemed to become a little more English, with a greater understanding of what might be possible if you could negotiate society's structures, its opportunities and dead ends.

It came as no surprise when Sophie announced she was bound

for Newnham College, Cambridge. Elinor had applied to Cambridge and was deemed the perfect candidate by no less than Miss Doncaster. She was therefore crestfallen when Charlotte objected and her grandmother complained, both suggesting that Elinor should remain in London. Cecily said little, though Elinor thought she didn't need to—her pout was enough. Yes, she could see that Ceci had been caught betwixt and between, as the saying went, and might feel as if opportunity had passed her by. There had been many new sayings to be learned since coming to London, aphorisms to describe this or that feeling or situation, or someone's character. Ceci had indeed been "betwixt and between"—she was too old for St. Joseph's and at first a little too young for the secretarial college, though even her grandmother suggested the night schools established decades earlier, when rural workers had flooded into London seeking employment in new factories being built alongside the river. The night schools offered opportunity to those who had been left behind by the circumstance of age, available funds or their station in life. Ceci was slow to apply, and Elinor knew why—she saw it on Armistice Day, when an Australian soldier grabbed her sister's hand to whisk her into a dance. There was a flash of panic writ large across Ceci's face, and in that moment Elinor too was transported back to the path by the river, in the dark. Though she carried only her jacket on that glorious Armistice day, she could feel the pistol's weight in her hand.

Elinor and Sophie kept in touch, visiting one another throughout the years of their tertiary education—Elinor's at the University of London—though those meetings became fewer when Elinor won the opportunity for further study in Paris, at the Sorbonne. Of course, there was no such offer without making an application, so this time Elinor said nothing until her plans were set. Life beckoned. The future teased her with possibility, and she had an objective. She would make a life in Paris. The past was gone, and she had endured enough of the depression that had wrapped Britain in a cloud within days of the Armistice, as if the people had overnight realized the dead weren't coming back. They were gone, never to return.

As soon as she arrived in Paris at the age of twenty-two, Elinor determined one thing—she would never, ever look back. She would remain in Paris and make a life for herself. Visits to see her family in London would be kept to a minimum. If she turned her head toward the past, she might see Fate coming for her.

CHAPTER 11

Paris
January 1940

Germans Invade and Bomb Poland
Britain Mobilizes

—*Daily Mirror*, September 1, 1939

Elinor De Witt—she had resumed using her former surname—entered the tall building, stopping in the entrance hall to collect her mail from a heavy carved oak table before making her way up a curved staircase to her rooms on the second floor. Throwing her leather document case and an armful of books onto a chaise, she looked at the letter—the latest missive from her mother in London. Without taking off her coat, she leaned against the window frame and stared down onto the courtyard at the rear of the building. Bracing herself for what she knew would be another plea from her mother, she slipped her finger underneath the flap and tore open the envelope.

Dearest Linni,

I won't beat about the bush, but I think it's time for you to come home to London. The newspapers are saying that Herr Hitler has his eye on France, and Paris will be occupied before the end of summer. We know you've done so very well since university (not many women can boast two degrees from two countries) and we understand that you love your work there, but your grandmother and I think it's time. She's becoming quite infirm and I fear you might not see her before she goes—I don't need to tell you she's getting on. Both Ceci and I miss you and worry about you.

They're calling it the "Bore" war over here because it's quite boring and nothing much has happened since last September. The sirens go off but mostly they're just for practice, so we will know what to do when London is under attack. Sometimes people just ignore them. Mind you, there have been a number of bombs dropped by the Germans, so we three have made the cellar comfortable enough, just in case we must descend the stairs for safety. Nana finds going down that rickety staircase very hard. I can imagine us just getting her settled when the "all clear" is sounded and we then have to get her back up the stairs again. To be honest, dear Linni, I'm not so young myself now, and could do with you at home to help out.

Ceci is still working at the library, for which I am filled with gratitude. I don't know if I ever thanked you for suggesting librarianship during your last visit home. Poor Ceci does not have any friends to speak of who might have made the necessary introductions to a nice young man. I confess, I sometimes think it would be awfully fortuitous if she met a widower, though she isn't the best with children. Nana keeps asking if she'll ever have great-grandchildren (she forgets she asked the same question the day before). Her mind is wandering, and not only do I have to remind her that Grandpa has passed on now, but that neither of you are in the first flush of youth anymore, so we're not likely to see babies in this house.

Elinor closed her eyes, rubbed her forehead and sighed. "Poor Ceci? Poor Ceci? Ceci's in sweet clover, if you ask me, with Nana and Mama at her beck and call as soon as she walks into the house." She opened her eyes and went on reading the letter, which continued to press the issue of her possible return.

Linni, we both know only too well how war goes and we know the depth of solace to be found when family are together. We are worried about you, and we three feel quite at sea without our fourth White lady in the house. Please come home. I am sure you could secure a teaching position or perhaps even something with the government. I've heard they need translators due to the war, and there's no doubt your references are most excellent.

Elinor put the letter to one side and leaned back in her chair. She was now almost thirty-six years of age. As Miss Doncaster predicted, she was indeed a spinster, yet unlike her sister, she had made that choice—though she suspected Ceci liked the idea of marriage more than the reality of a union and what might be demanded of her. As far as Elinor was concerned, a lover was a far less troublesome prospect than a husband, though Alex Blake had become something of a problem. He wanted more than Elinor was prepared to offer, which amounted to her freedom to do what she wanted, when she wanted. Alex was honest about his desire for marriage, for her to return to New York with him as the wife of an international man of commerce with political aspirations. But a diamond ring held no fascination for Elinor. In her world diamonds had been a necessary currency of survival in wartime. Alex wanted a hostess of note who could converse with ease when they were entertaining ambassadors or important men from overseas and their wives. In return she would have servants to attend to her every need or desire and money to spend on whatever she wanted, when she wanted. She would be a woman of substance, a feature of the society pages. The thought of it all exhausted Elinor, yet the more she refused, the more Alex pressed her. He was a man used to winning, after all.

Alex had been fun at first, another expat in Paris. He was handsome, well dressed, athletic in the way that Americans seemed fitter than anyone else. He had been light of character, with no questions asked so no answers given. He had spoiled her, but she had been able to keep her work and private life separate; one had nothing to do with the other. Now she had tired of Alex. She had even tired of flowers delivered every Friday. She lifted Charlotte's letter again.

Please come home.

Perhaps her mother was right. Yes, perhaps it was time. She looked around the modest but comfortable apartment, her home for some five years now. It had been a little beyond her budget, yet in a good area, when she had first viewed it following receipt of notice to leave her previous rooms because the owner was selling the property. But she had been careful with her money, never profligate, and having a pleasing place to live had become more important to her than a visit to a seamstress—and to help her out, there was the money from her grandfather that had been held in trust until she was twenty-one. That had been a surprise—the gift of a bank account with a tidy sum to see her on her way. Even after paying for her education, the lion's share was still in that account, squirreled away and building interest.

Elinor finished marking assignment papers in preparation for the following morning's classes. Taking a deep breath, she lifted a sheet of good stationery from her desk drawer, took up her fountain pen and began to write to her mother. Yes, she would indeed return to England, though it would take some two months; she was required to provide sufficient notice to the school and would therefore be expected to remain in her post until the Easter holiday. She would try to arrive in London by Good Friday.

Elinor knew Alex would be shocked when he heard her news, but it could not be helped, though his ego would be bruised because he had not ended the courtship first. Alex liked to be first, though she doubted he would pursue her to London in a bid to press her to continue seeing him. And perhaps her mother was right; she could get a good job in London. Sophie Wallace might know of something. Sophie—now Sophie Hunt; she had married after all—was a lecturer in mathematics at Bedford College, a women's seat of learning that was part of the University of London, so she could alert Elinor to any academic positions open, especially given the number of men going off to war. That was always when women were needed most; when men went to war. Thank goodness her old friend had decided not to pursue the nursing profession after all, though in her last letter she had said something about doing special war work. Elinor couldn't imagine Sophie engaged in war work. In her experience, war work was an exercise in brutality, and Sophie had too soft a heart.

As Elinor slipped the letter into an envelope, addressing it to her mother, she could not help wondering how it would be to live in London once more. Thoughts of Sophie and her work—whatever it was—inspired another memory to come to mind, one she had pondered at the time of the event, but was diminished by her mother's insistence that she had been quite mistaken.

In a ceremony at Buckingham Palace, held in secret after the 1918 Armistice, Charlotte, Cecily and Elinor, along with other members of La Dame Blanche network, had been summoned to an audience with the king where they would be awarded a medal in recognition of their service. The resistance work of La Dame Blanche had been financed by Britain, and Britain was indeed grateful.

The day passed in a blur, and at the time the medal had not meant very much to Elinor, given what she had done to earn the thing. However, she was taken aback when a woman who looked very much like Isabelle, accompanied by a man in uniform, entered via another door on the opposite side of the ballroom—which was the largest room Elinor had ever imagined. The Whites—the name De Witt had been jettisoned into the past so they would not be not mistaken for alien spies in London when they arrived in 1917—were clustered together and had not seen other medal recipients enter or depart, a move they assumed was to protect identities. Charlotte and Cecily whispered together as Elinor kept her eyes on the king, the man in uniform and the woman. Did Elinor imagine the woman's smile, the nod of acknowledgement? She nudged her mother and sister, who both admonished her with sharp looks as if she were a young child misbehaving in church. Elinor crept forward a few steps, so she might hear when the woman she thought resembled Isabelle spoke to the king. She watched another man in uniform beckon the woman to approach the monarch.

The uniformed man announced her name, which seemed to echo in Elinor's direction. *Clare Fields*. And when the woman curtsied and replied to the king's greeting, it was clear she was British.

"Linni, come back here," said Charlotte, sotto voce through

clenched teeth as she grabbed the top of Elinor's arm and pulled her into line. "You know better!"

"I think that's Isabelle," said Elinor.

"Don't be ridiculous," snapped Cecily, her voice low.

Then the woman was no longer there. Now, in Paris, decades later, Elinor could see everything about that day in her mind's eye. It might have been yesterday. There was the uniformed man who beckoned them to approach the king, who expressed gratitude for their service before the pinning on of medals. Charlotte and Cecily curtsied to the king, and she forgot to do the same because she had turned her head in case Clare Fields stepped back into the room. Her mother had grabbed her arm once more and almost pulled her to her knees in deference to the monarch.

She wondered about Clare Fields, and if indeed she had made an error due to nervousness about the occasion. But was she at all anxious on the day? She remembered being a bit bored by it all, and there was of course the argument with her mother when they left the palace.

"I cannot believe I was so humiliated by a daughter of mine in front of the king himself." Charlotte pressed a handkerchief to her brow.

"Why?"

"Because, idiot," said Cecily, "we practiced the curtsy a million times so we all did it together, and then you forgot because you were gawping around looking at other people instead of concentrating on what you were supposed to be doing."

"But I did curtsy!" protested Elinor. "I was only a little bit late, not even a second. I was looking for that lady—I'm sure it was Isabelle."

"I saw her—she had short black hair, so I know it wasn't Isabelle," said Cecily. "Anyway, Isabelle was Belgian."

"We don't know that, do we? She always spoke in French."

"Girls! Our work was recognized by no less than the king! Now, let us forget Linni's faux pas and go for a nice tea. It's a lovely afternoon, the war is over. We never expected to see this day, yet here we are safe and well here in London, and your father would be so proud of us because we served two countries. Now it's time to celebrate and forget. Is that understood?"

"Yes, Mama," the sisters replied in unison.

As she made tea in her Paris apartment, Elinor De Witt, a woman who spoke five languages, who had earned two degrees, landed a good job and attracted a lover who bored her, wondered if her adolescent self was indeed wrong about Clare Fields. It had been a heady day, a strange event, and perhaps there were a few butterflies in her stomach after all, so it was possible she had been mistaken. She cut a slice of lemon into the tea and stirred it together with half a teaspoon of honey. Elinor had done her best not to think of Isabelle over the years, and now she wondered if she had survived the war. And if so, and by whatever name, had she suffered nightmares about what happened in Belgium during that terrible time of want and death? If still alive, she would be in her mid- to late forties.

Elinor wondered if Isabelle had ever struggled to balance herself when the war was over. Would she have been happy if consigned to live an ordinary life? Elinor remembered a feeling she had experienced the previous summer, when she joined Alex on his yacht in Cannes. Though the sojourn started well in calm seas, inclement weather soon closed in, and they had sailed through a storm for what seemed like hours before emerging into steady waters once again. When they came ashore, she struggled to find purchase on land, as if any equilibrium had deserted her and she had lost the sense of where to put her feet. It was a strange feeling, and she thought, then, as she reached for a guardrail to steady herself, that it was how she had felt after they escaped Belgium in fear for their lives, yet just days later were living a quiet life in London. The setting of her feet on solid ground was almost harder to bear than the storm.

CHAPTER 12

London
April 1940

FIFTH COLUMN WAR OPENS HERE
TOWN BOMBING HINT BY NAZIS

—*Daily Mirror*

Miss White, I must say, when I placed an advertisement for a teacher of French and German, I did not expect to receive an application from you."

After Miss Doncaster held out her hand and invited Elinor to be seated, she wondered if her old teacher would add, "of all people" to the stilted welcome.

"Sophia Wallace—now Hunt—sent me the details, Miss Doncaster," she said. "We're still in touch. She'd seen the advertisement in *The Lady* and thought it might suit me, given my planned return to England." Elinor rubbed the palm of her right hand across the top of her left hand. "I know I was probably not the easiest pupil in your charge, but . . . but coming here from Belgium in the midst of war was difficult, a troubling transition for a young girl. I'm afraid I didn't rise to the occasion terribly well while in class."

Elinor still felt a certain awkwardness when using English locutions, a manner of speaking designed, she thought, to give an impression of respect that she didn't always feel. There were words that seemed to be used to emphasize an emotion, and thus to bolster the speaker's case—or their contrition. *Terribly. Awfully.* I'm *terribly* sorry. I'm *awfully* pleased to see you.

In Elinor's estimation, awful was awful, as in terrible. And then there was *dreadful.* After a few months in London, she decided such words rendered the speaker nothing less than obsequious, and should therefore be avoided. "I'm *dreadfully* proud of my daughter," Charlotte had exclaimed during Elinor's entrance interview for St. Joseph's. Elinor thought her mother might as well have declared that she found her daughter dreadful, and wondered if she would ever be awarded a place based upon her mother's entreaty. It would not have surprised her had Charlotte said something about being *absolutely* dreadfully proud— after all, since the return to England, Elinor sometimes thought her mother had become another person, at times almost a stranger.

"She's devolved into being English again," Cecily had observed.

When she was seventeen and preparing to leave St. Joseph's, Elinor had wondered if this way with language helped gird Charlotte to put her foot down, countering her younger daughter's future plans. "I'm *dreadfully* sorry, I *simply* cannot countenance my daughter going off to Cambridge when we *absolutely* need her at home."

Elinor was sure Charlotte was not as dreadfully or simply anything as much as she herself felt *absolutely awful, terrible, dreadful* when it was clear she could not take up the offers from the universities of Oxford and Cambridge, and would instead be stuck in London when she wanted so much to be on the move, to run in case Fate found her. She wanted to be among people who would never know her past. In London she had felt like prey, without a safe lair in sight.

Miss Doncaster, now headmistress of St. Joseph's, clasped her hands on the leather-topped desk. Although the woman had aged, it was clear to Elinor that she had retained her bearing, as if early lessons in deportment had remained with her, so neither grief, loss nor fear had the strength to cower her, to round her shoulders or diminish her step.

"Miss White—Elinor." She smiled. "You were an excellent student, and you have made a very good account of yourself. I am proud of all of my girls—Sophia has done incredibly well, and you are her equal, though in a different sphere of endeavor."

Doncaster paused, sighed and leaned back in her chair to stare out of the window, as if deciding how to voice thoughts that had come to mind as she prepared for the interview. She turned to Elinor again.

"Our girls are quite a different breed now, you know. The years since you graduated university and went on to further study in Paris have been somewhat tumultuous for the young—admittedly no more than it was for you, or even in my day, but all the same giving rise to an element of doubt, of unknowing that can in turn lead to undesirable words, thoughts and actions. There have been good times and bad. Some of our pupils are the daughters of bankrupt men—and women—and I don't mean bankrupt only in a financial sense, I'm sorry to say. The years after the war changed our society, and that is reflected in the attitudes and behaviors of our young women. As their teacher, you are here not only to ensure that they are proficient in two languages—and by the way, I'd like to see another Romance language added to the curriculum; Italian comes to mind. As I said, you are here to do more than teach languages—you are to uphold a strong moral code and to support the standards impressed upon your pupils by the school; principles that will become the backbone of everything they do in life. Every. Single. Decision. I have found that when one remains true to one's established values, life's squalls, storms and doldrums become easier to navigate."

"Does this mean—"

"Miss White, I really do not need to extend this interview into the afternoon. I am a woman of resolute decision, and I am delighted to offer you the position. You will begin your tenure at St. Joseph's when the girls return to school for the beginning of the summer term. You will teach French and German language and literature to the girls in both the lower and upper schools. As I said, I'd also like to see Italian added to the curriculum." Miss Doncaster placed a pair of spectacles on her nose and studied the notes in front of her. "Ah good, you have also taught Latin in a previous position." She regarded Elinor again. "Such a fundamental lesson for our girls. They think Latin is ancient history, but as time marches on they will understand the value of at least one year of that remarkable language. We begin instruction in the second year, which we have found is a perfect time for such immersion."

"Yes, of course. Regarding the timetable, Miss Doncaster, I—"

"My secretary will give it to you on the way out, along with your contract and other documents requiring your signature."

"Of course." Elinor came to her feet and held out her hand.

Miss Doncaster smiled as she returned the grasp. "You know, Miss White, I rather admired your pluck when you were in my class. *Pluck.* People don't use that word much anymore, but I like to see it in a young woman. I don't care for disrespect, and I will use my cane across any girl's palms for a display of outright insolence, but pluck is something quite different. It shows resolve and is a hallmark of resilience. We are at war again, Miss White, and our women in the making will need such qualities to see them through."

Elinor smiled, ready to leave the interview.

"Oh, by the way—I really should have queried this earlier because it's such a crucial point, but even though your interview has taken place here in London, I hope you understand that now the school has moved, we are situated in Surrey, just outside Reigate. All the pupils are required to be boarders and will be so until it is safe for the school to return to our London premises, when I expect some to revert to being day pupils. Reigate is not terribly far on the train, and if you do not wish to commute, then rooms will be provided for you—in fact, we need a housemistress for the Jane Eyres. I think you were with the Lorna Doones, weren't you?" Doncaster rubbed her forehead. "I really should have said something at the outset to ensure you are able to leave London—I'm dreadfully sorry."

Elinor stifled a laugh upon seeing Doncaster so contrite. "That's perfectly alright, Miss Doncaster—I was aware of the school's move. And yes, I would be delighted to take you up on the offer of rooms, though I would appreciate permission to return to visit my family from Saturday afternoon until Sunday evening."

"Excellent! Then everything is settled. Welcome back to St. Joseph's, Miss White." Doncaster gave Elinor the broadest smile she had ever seen expressed by her former teacher. "Now then, Miss Harding, my secretary, is waiting in the office with your employment contract and timetable, plus the languages curriculum adhered to thus far. Please inform me of any suggested alterations within the week, along with your reasons for making those changes. In addition, I would suggest you visit the temporary school before term begins—it's a rather lovely and very grand estate close to Reigate Hill. There's a stables too, which some of our more accomplished horsewomen have very much enjoyed. The whole estate was mothballed when war was declared and the family departed for their equally large estate in Scotland—but as luck would have it, the lady of the house is a St. Joseph's old girl, so the entire property was offered to us free of charge. I would add that we're asking the girls to be as careful as possible, as the school will be responsible for any necessary restorative work when we return to London. I dread the thought of holes in walls or broken chandeliers."

"I'm just thrilled to be joining your staff—thank you, Miss Doncaster. I'll journey down to Reigate tomorrow to view the school."

"Good—I'll see you there. I'll be in situ when you arrive. Miss Harding will provide you with the address and everything you need to know. You should find out which train she's catching—you can travel down together."

Elinor smiled again, but as she was about to turn and depart the office, she stopped and turned to her former teacher. "Oh, Miss Doncaster—by the way, I was with the Catherine Earnshaws, not a member of Lorna Doone House. So was Sophia."

Doncaster nodded. "She's a good friend to have, and I believe the connection was beneficial for the two of you, given all that had come to pass for you and Sophia during the last war. And you were both very good at mathematics, though I will say, Sophia excelled at her number work in the way you eclipsed everyone when it came to your innate ability with languages." There was a pause while Doncaster regarded Elinor, as if to gauge her integrity. "Miss White—Elinor—a word of advice for you. I know you were close, but don't ask Sophia about her work, will you? She can't tell you, and it would put her in a compromised position to be questioned about it."

Elinor was surprised at the warning. "Do you know—"

"Remember, I am a mathematician too. During a time of war the government cannot afford to let talent remain unused, whether the gifted are women or men, or indeed whatever their station in life might be." Another pause. "And I like to think all my girls leave St. Joseph's accomplished in at least one useful skill. Yours is languages." She tapped a buff-colored folder on the desk. "Which is why I will be retaining all other applications for the post I have just offered you. I fear I may be required to study them again sooner rather than later."

The first month at St. Joseph's in Reigate allowed Elinor little time for reflection on her decision to return to England, though to her surprise she found she did not miss Paris. As April canted into May, the threat of Hitler's army reaching the French capital loomed, and Charlotte's demand that she return home to London had seemed more prescient. Elinor was glad she had acquiesced.

The Surrey hills provided solace for Elinor, who had taken to riding out across the North Downs on a Saturday following her final class of the week, which was to introduce a class of twelve-year-old girls to the study of Latin. It was their last lesson of the academic week, so Elinor's classes were lighthearted in nature, and usually began with a humorous poem she had translated into Latin and required the class to translate back into English. Once she had their attention, learning could ensue, though the speed with which the girls departed the classroom indicated that Latin might well be deemed useful by Miss Doncaster, but not by the second-year pupils.

A groom who had remained at the estate to care for the owner's horses had Jasper tacked up and ready for Elinor when she arrived at the stables.

"There you are, Miss White. I'd say he's raring to go today, but watch the footing on account of that rain we had last night."

"I'll look after him, Dave, don't you worry," said Elinor, stepping up onto the mounting block.

Dave held on to the reins until Elinor was seated. "Off you go then, Miss White—see you in a couple of hours."

Elinor had set off at a walk toward the archway leading away from the stable block, in the direction of a bridle path that she planned to follow up a hill then onto the North Downs, when she was stopped by Miss Doncaster, who called out and waved to her as her pace became a determined trot from the main house.

"Miss White! Miss White! A moment, if you please."

Elinor turned Jasper in the direction of the headmistress and was about to dismount in order to conduct a respectful conversation when Doncaster shook her head.

"No, stay where you are. You deserve your ride across the Downs. I just wanted to let you know of an adjustment to your Monday-pm time-table for the next three weeks."

"An adjustment?"

Doncaster looked up at Elinor, then around her. "Perhaps you'd better get off that horse. Young girls love to eavesdrop, and I can never be sure where one or two of them might be hiding on a Saturday after-noon."

Elinor dismounted as Miss Doncaster came closer.

"Miss White, given the increased preparations for an invasion by the Germans, it appears we must consider how we might best protect our charges in the event of an incursion into the grounds by the Nazis."

Elinor nodded. "I see—yes, indeed, there should be a plan in place. The girls already demonstrate a remarkable sense of calm when we have to go down to the cellars at the sound of the air raid warnings, so I am sure they will take well to drills in case of invasion."

"Indeed, yes, but this is something else." Doncaster looked around her once again. "Truly, Miss White, I will be honest, I cannot believe I am going to ask this of you."

"Please go on, headmistress."

"I have selected four members of staff to learn how to use a gun."

Doncaster cleared her throat as if the word *gun* were so distasteful to her that she could not digest what she had said and might choke at any moment. "The owner of the house has a gun room—as soon as the school moved in, I had the sign removed and ensured that the door was always locked. However, upon advice from the local constabulary and Home Guard, we will be making the weapons inside"—she coughed again— "we will be making the weapons inside available to the four teachers I've selected to practice marksmanship. The gamekeeper, Mr. Jessup, has offered to teach you. He's also a member of our Home Guard— and I should let you know he's a crack shot. He was what they called a 'sniper' in the last war and was also decorated for valor." Doncaster gave Elinor a broad though forced smile. "So, Monday it is. Meet him by the kitchen doors after lunch. To be perfectly honest, you will need a meal in you to have to do this. Most unladylike." There was a pause. "Now then, let me hold on to the opposite stirrup so you can mount up again."

Elinor trotted out of the gate and onto the bridle path. Jasper was hot to go, so as soon as they reached the wider path, Elinor let him have his head, galloping across the Downs until they reached woodland, where she brought him to a trot, stopping at the place where a marker signaled the very spot where a hunter had fallen from his horse decades ago, and—as Dave had informed her—"They planted him headfirst where he landed."

"They should have planted me when I landed," said Elinor aloud. She dismounted, leaned into Jasper's neck and shed tears of frustration. She did not want to take up arms. She did not want to go on a target-practice jamboree with three other teachers, and she knew only too well that if there was a Nazi invasion, four teachers among a school of girls had better have more creative ideas up their sleeves to protect them all.

As Elinor became calmer and wiped her cheeks, she realized she had not wept since Belgium, not since the day she accepted the truth that her father had died. She had never once broken down—unlike Cecily, who had snuffled into her pillow every night for weeks after their arrival in London. She dried her tears, took a deep breath and, stepping up onto the trunk of a fallen tree to give herself a few more inches of purchase, slipped her foot into the stirrup to take her place in the saddle again. She continued on at a walk. The horse seemed just as happy to amble after the long gallop, though she would give him one more canter before easing into a trot and another walk to cool down before she handed him over to Dave. Then she would look for Mr. Jessup.

The gamekeeper's beamed sixteenth-century cottage was set among trees at the far end of the estate. A wisp of smoke rose from the chimney, and even from some yards away, Elinor could smell the aroma of baking. Had Mrs. Jessup managed to obtain the ingredients to make her own bread? On the other hand, if anyone could use the black market to his advantage, it would be a gamekeeper.

"Hello, Mr. Jessup," said Elinor when the gamekeeper answered her knock. "I wonder if I could have a word with you. A private word."

"Let me just get my cap," said the man, who looked to be in his fifties, though Elinor thought he might have been younger. A life spent outdoors with his face exposed to the elements had left Jessup with skin that mapped the trials and tribulations of a life that was far from easy.

Jessup walked with Elinor, listening to her with a hand cupped around his ear, testament to hearing compromised by years of proximity to guns—especially heavy artillery during the last war.

"So if you don't mind, I'd rather not attend the lesson; however, if you allow me to do so, I will demonstrate that I can use a gun, and then you can let the headmistress know, so that will be the end of it."

Jessup nodded. "Where did you learn?"

"You know what they say, Mr. Jessup." Elinor smiled at the man beside her. "Ask no questions, hear no lies."

"Right you are." He touched his cap with two forefingers in an informal salute of understanding. "You wait there a minute."

Elinor leaned against a tree, the late-spring sunlight filtering through the canopy of branches above with a welcome warmth; until that point, she had been freezing cold. Jessup approached again, a sack slung over his shoulder. He pointed to a path leading into woodland and instructed her to follow him, stopping in a clearing where a make-shift target practice had been set up using fencing and bottles.

"Let's try you with the Webley first," he said.

Elinor had not handled a weapon since Belgium. She fought to keep the image of lifting her gun toward two German soldiers, seeing them fall, running with Cecily, dragging her by the scruff of the neck because at first her legs would not move. Instead she envisioned Isabelle at her side, felt her position her hands around the gun, heard her voice, the instruction to brace, to use her core. *I will not be prey. I will not be prey. I will not be prey. I am the predator.*

"Where did you learn to shoot like that, Miss White?"

"What?" said Elinor.

"You just emptied the Webley, and you got every single bottle—and I deliberately stood you back here, not close."

Elinor nodded and handed back the Webley.

"Can you do this with a rifle?"

"Yes."

Jessup rubbed his chin as he dropped the gun into the sack.

"How old were you in the last war, Miss White?"

Elinor stared at him, then looked away.

"I thought so," he added. "Too bloody young. Come on. The missus has just done a bit of baking. You'll come in for a nice cup of tea?"

"I must be on my way, Mr. Jessup. I return to London on Saturday afternoons—you know, to see my family."

"Mother and father still alive?"

"Just my mother, and there's only the four of us. My gran, my mother and my older sister, Cecily."

"Right, well, I'll let Miss Doncaster know you passed the test with flying colors." He paused, his grey-blue eyes staring at Elinor. "You're a blimmin' good shot, Miss White, no doubt about it."

Despite the fact that war was ever present, that air raids and drills were part of life at the school, Elinor valued the daily rhythm her position provided. She had been drawn to teaching because it was a profession with an anchor. Timetables, curricula, terms, examinations, rosters and rotas. Christmas, Easter, summer. Every hour mapped out for every single day of every single week. Homework, bedtime, breakfast, lunch, dinner. Then Saturday Latin followed by a ride into the hills on Jasper and back again before running for the five o'clock train into Victoria. Grandma sleeping away her days, Charlotte cooking, complaining, chivvying her along, and Cecily resigned, but now at least conversing about books, about her work at the library, about the light romances, so-called literature flooding the market, cheap escape in a paperback book to take to the shelter.

Elinor did not argue. She drew back and never crossed her sister to press the point that perhaps people needed "light" at a time when death was raining down from above. Perhaps there was something to be said for stories of sheiks running away with princesses or doctors falling in love with nurses and vice versa. She tried not to rise to a row with

Cecily; there was enough war everywhere without a battle across the no-man's-land of the family dinner table.

A term passed, then another. Home for Christmas, down to the shelter, up from the shelter. London was a life spent waiting for the all clear, the second siren letting people know the bombers had gone, so they could emerge from their underground lairs like rabbits seeking sunshine. Soon January 1941 hove into view, then February, March, and before long it was Elinor's one-year anniversary at the school, though she elected to remain at the estate, with only a short visit to see Grandma, Charlotte and Cecily for Easter. Yes, that would be best— she would go up to London on Thursday, April 10th, and return to Reigate on Tuesday, April 15th.

LONDON BOMBED FOR SIX HOURS
CASUALTIES NOT COUNTED—IN THE HUNDREDS

City Gazette

In years to come, Elinor would never quite find words to describe how she felt that day, the day before Good Friday, when she boarded the train bound for Victoria to spend the holiday in London with her family. There came a point during the journey when she knew she had to make her peace. It had seemed the best time to start pulling the White ladies together again, and after all, wasn't Easter the celebrated anniversary of new beginnings? Of resurrection? Yes, she would take the lead. She would not allow Cecily to bother her, even if her sister was spoiling to create discord. She would put her arms around her beloved family, bringing them close together once more, because even though in 1917 they had arrived in London to the cocooned comfort and safety of a welcoming house, in truth the chaos of war had splayed them apart, had removed the glue of familial connection. Sometimes they could not even hold a conversation over dinner without an argument. How many times had her grandmother walked out of the room saying, "I'll leave you three to it!" It would not happen again. The love between them had not been enough, but Elinor knew it was well past time for her to gather her family in her heart with compassion, for her to be steadfast in her care for those who shared her blood.

Charlotte's anxiety, having escalated during their escape from Belgium, had never quite abated. She coddled Cecily, indulged her nerves when in male company—which was rare anyway. Elinor knew that Cecily was caught in a vicious circle of behavior, but over the years she could only manage her own survival. Now, filled with empathy, she acknowledged that perhaps she might have invited Cecily to Paris, offering encouragement and opportunity as she eased her sister into a life independent of Charlotte's apron strings. She could have aided her as she slaughtered her demons and banished her fears, because Cecily surely continued to feel the terror of attack in the same way Elinor saw a shattered, bloody skull lit up by a torch every single day. Yes, she would make amends. She would help dear Ceci cross the bridge into a better future—they might be older, but it wasn't too late.

At first the journey to London was uneventful, but somewhere in the region of Croydon, the train halted. A guard came through the carriages, informing passengers that they were being held up as a precaution due to a daylight raid by German bombers. The heavy, lumbering angels of death had approached the capital from the east, the Thames once again pointing the way to the docks and the City, then onward to the West End. The train would commence the journey as soon as they received the all clear.

Elinor was used to interrupted journeys, so she took out a book she was considering for her third-year Italian class. In time the train moved on, and at Victoria all seemed calm. From there she ran to the Tube—she had promised to be home for tea—but began to worry when there was a delay at Tottenham Court Road station. She decided to walk the rest of the way. The house was not too far from Brunswick Square, so it was easy enough, fifteen minutes at her usual clip. Her grandparents had moved into the house soon after their marriage, helped by family money. Charlotte had been born in the first-floor bedroom, and it was where she had brought her own daughters home to safety from Belgium. Yet as Elinor came closer to the family home, she began to slow her pace. A feeling of dread seemed to envelop her. Approaching the street, she was aware of an escalation in activity, of people rushing to and fro. There were sirens, fire tenders, police vehicles, bells ringing. Air Raid Precautions men pointed here and there while firemen directed hoses at burning buildings.

Stepping over fallen masonry, she saw the Women's Voluntary Service van opening up, ready to provide tea, cakes and sympathy. She stopped walking, not knowing quite what to do; she knew, then, even before turning into the street where her family lived—before dropping the bag holding fresh hot cross buns from Mrs. Jessup, unmarked papers from the Latin class, a book for Cecily and new embroidery silks for Charlotte—she knew they were gone.

Are you sure you don't need a little more time, Miss White? You've endured a terrible shock." Miss Doncaster regarded Elinor as she poured more tea. They were in Doncaster's private rooms.

Elinor shook her head. "No, work is really the best medicine, Miss Doncaster, though I appreciate the offer." She lifted her cup from the saucer. "Teaching gives me a . . . a framework. A daily round. It's my mainstay, and I don't know what I would do otherwise, to be perfectly honest with you." Perhaps she should have said *awfully* honest. *Dreadfully* honest. Or *crushingly* honest. She wanted to use the most mournful adverbs, even if she had to invent them. *Deathly honest.*

"Right you are. But do let me know if you change your mind. Arrangements can be made." The headmistress paused. "You know, I have a sister in Cornwall, if you wanted—"

"That's very kind of you, Miss Doncaster, but I promise, I will be alright."

"Of course. Now then, in the vein of carrying on, do tell me about your new ideas for the sixth-form French conversation classes."

Hacking out on Jasper had become balm for Elinor's soul. The lighter evenings gave her an opportunity to ride after classes ended for the day, and now she had nowhere to go in her free time, so on Saturday and Sunday afternoons she discovered new bridle paths, fresh places to explore from the estate. She was often away for hours, losing all sense of time. Jessup had come to her aid too. He hailed her from his cottage as she was trotting toward the path one Saturday afternoon, removing his cap when she approached.

"Good afternoon, Mr. Jessup."

The man nodded. "Head above water, Miss White?"

Elinor looked down at the man and saw pity in his eyes. "Yes, I think so, Mr. Jessup."

There was a pause, and Elinor wondered if he was going to say more, and whether she should thank him for asking, wish him a good day and ride on.

"You know, Miss White, I reckon sometimes we have to get rid of the big black hole right in here." He put his hand against his middle. "You can't have that filling up space in there, because if it doesn't get out, it can take you down. Grows like a cancer, that's what anger does."

She stared at him.

"So, what I do," continued Jessup. "I take my gun and I go into them woods, and I shoot them bottles time and time again until there's nothing left of them." He sighed and kicked against a stone. "You can come and take one of them guns any time you want. You put as many bullets as you like into those bottles, and you kill the demons one by one. If you let them take you down, they swoop in again and they won't let up—I know that because of how I came home from Flanders, after the last war. Don't let them Nazis beat down your heart. Never let them win." He lifted his cap and put it back on his head. "And anyway, you never know when you might be grateful you kept your hand in. I'll bid you good day, Miss White."

"Good day, Mr. Jessup." She turned Jasper away from the cottage, but looked over her shoulder and called out, "And thank you, Mr. Jessup. Very much."

Cantering up Colley Hill, Elinor brought Jasper to a halt at the Inglis Memorial, a folly affording views across the land. People said there were military "goings on" in the area, though Elinor did not care to look for anything untoward. She had never seen activity that might concern her, so she remained in place for a while, pulling up Jasper so he didn't eat the grass.

"If your bit is mucky with green slime when we get back, Dave will never let us out together again!" She leaned into the horse, who of late seemed to know her despair and tolerated the weight of her against his neck. She hoped he didn't sense her anger, because Jessup was right—

there was a fury inside she could feel as if it were a ball of hot coals. At times she could even rest a hand on her ribs and feel the heat pressing back against her fingers.

With one final look across the Downs, she picked up the reins and trotted back to the stables.

"I was about to send out the cavalry for you, Miss White," said Dave, holding on to Jasper's reins as Elinor dismounted.

"You know I'll be alright, Dave—unless Jazzie gallops home alone, then you can come out to find me. Sure I can't rub him down and put him away?"

"I like to do it myself, Miss White, though I'm not disputing your ability."

Elinor pulled two sugar cubes from her pocket.

"Wasting good sugar on a horse?" said Dave.

"I don't take sugar in my tea, so I sneak some out for this boy—he deserves it."

"Won't argue with you there. Oh, I should have mentioned it first, but a lady came along a little while ago, looking for you."

"Me? Was it one of the parents?"

He shook his head. "I don't think so. And I don't think she went to the office first, either. I reckon she came here directly—so she must know you ride on a Saturday afternoon."

"Hmmm, perhaps it's my friend Sophie. Any idea where she went?"

The groom turned and pointed toward the wood. "You know that bench just inside the wood, near the pond, the one with the brass plaque with a name on it? Mr. Waters, the owner of the estate, had it put there in memory of his sister who died young. Well, when the lady told me she didn't want to wait over at the manor house, I told her that if she had time to hang on for a bit until you came back from your ride, that bench was as good a place to sit as any on a lovely day like today."

"I'll go over there now, thank you, Dave."

Elinor turned and walked along a path that led to the bench where a woman she knew very well would not be Sophie waited for her. Sophie would have paid a visit to Miss Doncaster if she had to linger for a while.

As she came closer, she could see a woman with short dark hair, wearing a tweed jacket and brown trousers. She had no doubt the woman's footwear was suited to walking across a field, and even from a distance she noted the fine ribbon of smoke from her cigarette. The woman did not wave when Elinor approached, nor did she come to her feet. Instead she tapped the place alongside her on the bench.

"Hello, Elinor. It's been a long time, hasn't it? You've grown into quite an accomplished woman."

Elinor nodded. "What are you doing here, Isabelle?"

"Clare Fields—actually, it's Commander Clare Fields. And I think you already know that name, don't you? I hope recognizing me at the palace hasn't bothered you too much over the years." She sighed, shrugged and gave a wry smile. "Sadly, Isabelle had to die in 1918. Poor woman." She flicked her cigarette down at her feet and ground it into the earth with the heel of her stout brown walking shoe.

"Well, *Clare Fields*—sorry, Commander Clare Fields," said Elinor, feeling the knot in her stomach become tighter. "Let me ask again— why are you here?"

"I'm here to give you the opportunity for revenge, Elinor, because—as good old Lord Kitchener said in his finger-pointing way last time we were in this sort of pickle—'Your country needs you.'"

Elinor shook her head and stood up. "No. With respect, Commander Fields. No."

Fields came to her feet and held out a hand to Elinor. "You don't mind if I try again, do you, Linni? It's not often someone with much-needed skills turns down an opportunity to serve their country when the chips are down." She smiled. "I know you. You'll do the right thing eventually. Until the next time, Miss White."

CHAPTER 13

London
1947

would like to have had a sister, instead of all those brothers." Elsie
Finch buttered another scone and lifted it to her lips, followed by her
table napkin, with which she appeared to be hiding the fact that she
was chewing.

"Oh, I don't know about that," said Elinor. "As girls Cecily and I
didn't always get on, and our arguments upset my mother terribly, especially after we came to England." She set down her cup in the saucer
and looked around at other ladies taking tea at Fortnum & Mason, then
back to the woman before her. "Though I have missed her since . . .
well, since she died."

"Horrible, losing your mother and sister on the same day."

"And my grandmother. I was at work when it happened, and it was
only when I walked down the street toward the house that I realized it
was gone. The whole street had been destroyed."

"They dropped those heavy bombs like they were eggs, didn't they?
Mind you, I think the doodlebugs were the worst—you'd hear that buzz-
ing, and when it stopped you knew it was coming down and you didn't

know which way to run. That's what took my Abe. He was a good man, my late husband." Elsie fluttered her ring-laden fingers over a plate of petits fours before lifting one topped with pink icing. "You'd never know there was still rationing going on when you come in here—that's why I always treat myself, you know, after Raymond has given me a new hairdo."

Elinor thought the "hairdo" was the same as last week's version. "He does a lovely job, doesn't he? Mind you, the girl who set my hair has a good eye, though she was rather insistent about what she thought would suit me."

"Raymond trains them all, you know." Elsie sipped her tea and stared at Elinor. "So, what did you do in the war? You said you were coming home from work."

"Teaching," said Elinor.

"I thought most of the London schools were closed," said Elsie.

"It was a small private girls' school in Kensington."

"What did you teach?"

"Languages. French, Italian, German, and some Latin, which the girls didn't care for at all. The school moved out of London when war was declared, then we brought the senior pupils back into the old school in 1944. Not the best decision on the part of the headmistress, but fortunately we weren't bombed."

"I would have liked a profession, but my father was old-fashioned, you know—the only work women were supposed to be good for was in the kitchen."

"The war changed life for many women, Elsie."

"Well, the old boy is Italian—and still alive, I might add. He rules the whole family." She grinned. "But I'll have the last laugh on him, and those brothers of mine."

"The last laugh?" Elinor lifted a hand to brush back her hair. Though she had complimented the hairdresser, she wasn't sure about the Veronica Lake look styled by Pauline, who was assigned to her that day.

"Dad is losing his marbles," said Elsie. "Mind you, he can still give orders." She leaned back and grinned. "Though my brothers don't know who's giving Dad the orders he gives out—more fool them, for assuming the only thing I'm good for is keeping an eye on the old boy and making sure the nurse changes his dirty knickers." She paused, nodding toward Elinor. "I'd pin that back, if I were you—I can see you don't like that bit of hair flopping everywhere."

"You're right," said Elinor. She reached into her pocket, found a hair grip, and clipped back the long curl styled down one side of her face. "That's better." She smiled and poured more tea into both cups. "Do your brothers listen to your father? I mean, they're grown men, aren't they, with children of their own."

"You don't know what Italians are like, Elinor. There's the boys—my brothers—and then there's *their* boys, and all of them are in the family business."

"Any girls?"

"I've four nieces. I'm taking them under my wing, though, so they don't end up idle and brainless." She chuckled. "That's five of us girls, and five is my lucky number."

"What's the family business?"

Elsie Finch shrugged. "Warehousing, storage, removals, that sort of thing."

Elinor nodded. "I suppose there's quite a call for it, people having been bombed out and needing a place to put their things, furniture and whatever they could salvage, and then moving into a new house or flat when they've found one—if they're lucky enough to find one."

"Yes, as I said, that sort of thing." Elsie glanced at her gold watch, which Elinor noticed was studded with diamonds around the dial.

"Goodness, you're right to look at the time," said Elinor, checking her own plain watch. "I've a few errands to run, and I mustn't be late to catch my train."

"Where is it you live, my dear?" asked Elsie, pushing back her chair. She came to her feet on unsteady legs.

"Tunbridge Wells," said Elinor. "I thought I told you."

Elsie nodded. "Oh yes, I remember now. My nephew, Jimmy, John's youngest, he lives down in Kent—much farther down into the country though. Place called . . . oh, what's it called? Something-hurst."

"There are a lot of something-hursts in Kent," said Elinor, smiling. She had already settled the bill.

"I know. His father didn't like it at all—my brother is too much like Francisco."

"Francisco?"

"The old boy—that's his name. Our father who art in his wheel-chair. The patriarch. Jimmy's dad is too much like him, if you ask me—in fact, my brothers are all the same. As I said, they think women should be in the kitchen, but I'll have the last laugh on those boys—you mark my words."

"I won't ask how you intend to do that, Elsie," said Elinor, smiling, as the women began to walk toward the exit. "When I planned to have the last laugh on my sister, it usually meant putting spiders in her bed."

"I wish I'd've thought of that," said Elsie. She turned to Elinor. "Lovely of you to treat me to tea—I didn't expect you to pay when I invited you to join me here. Very kind of you. I don't get out as much, not since my husband died, so it's lovely to have a chat with another woman."

"For me too, Elsie."

"Are you sure I can't drop you anywhere? My driver is waiting just outside."

"I've a spot of shopping to do, and I fancy a walk after that tea," said Elinor. "But thank you. I hope we can do this again."

"Next week?" asked Elsie.

Elinor pointed to the forelock of hair now pinned back. "As long as I don't get the Veronica Lake. I was hoping for more of a Rita Hayworth."

Elsie Finch laughed, gave a short wave and turned to walk toward the motor car double-parked outside, the driver ready and waiting with the rear passenger door open. Elinor felt a wave of sympathy for Elsie, a short, round woman who, she thought, ached for the elegance of those mannequins who could carry off Christian Dior's New Look. It had been launched in an edition of *Harper's Bazaar* earlier in the year, with photos of a whippet-thin young woman wearing a black skirt with a lower-calf-length hem complemented by a cream jacket, its nipped-in waist and soft rounded shoulders in direct contrast to the masculine look of wartime. Elsie must have been one of the first women to wear the sought-after costume, yet instead of stunning onlookers with her fashionable attire, she appeared more reminiscent of Queen Victoria in her later years.

"No wonder she has a chip on her shoulder," Elinor whispered to herself as she stepped away from Fortnum & Mason and set off in the direction of Piccadilly Circus and the Tube station.

Elinor caught a Bakerloo line train to Charing Cross, which put her in the right place for an easy walk along to Scotland Yard. Once again, Steve Warren was not at the Yard, though she bumped into Detective Sergeants Bob Mills and Charlie Kettle as they were leaving.

"We're off to Catford dogs, Miss White." Charlie Kettle grinned, then glanced at Bob Mills with an almost imperceptible wink before turning back to Elinor. "Want to come with us, observe what it's all about at the sharp end of our sort of police work?"

Elinor had taken note of the exchange, and suspected there would be a benign attempt to shock her, what the detectives might consider a bit of fun.

"There's an offer I can't refuse, Charlie," said Elinor. "Count me in."

She had never been to a dog racing stadium and wasn't sure she really wanted to see greyhounds running at speed around a circuit chasing a hare, even though it was fake. Or was it? The question disturbed her.

"The hare isn't real, you know—it's driven by electricity," said Bob, as if reading her mind.

"Bob, I know that!" said Elinor. "Let's get on our way then, shall we?"

The drive to Catford in southeast London took longer than it might have, given the city traffic and the time of day. As soon as they were south of the river, horses and carts vied for a place on the road, along with trams, lorries and buses, and because flesh-and-blood horsepower still had right-of-way over other vehicular traffic, it was slow going. The journey gave Elinor a chance to ask a few more questions and to get to know Warren's detective sergeants a little better—and she was aware they intended to use the time spent in the motor car to find out more about her.

"So, you knew DCI Warren in the war, did you?" asked Charlie Kettle. "Weren't you in the same department, something like that?"

"I'd better be careful," said Elinor, as if she were teasing the men. "What did he say?"

"Not a lot. We reckon it was all a bit hush-hush."

Elinor shrugged. "It probably was—I can't say I know. Everyone had different jobs."

"Oh?" said Bob.

"But before the war I was a teacher of French, German and Italian, then when the evacuations began, the school moved out of London. I met Detective Chief Inspector Warren when I was called up—and, well, you know what it's like in the services. You meet all sorts, don't you?" Giving the impression that they had crossed paths in the regular army without telling an outright lie was deliberate. She knew it was better for any cover story to run as close to the truth as possible, because the person asking questions might well be trained in the identification of lies. The phrase rolled around in her mind for a few seconds. *The identification of lies.*

"But didn't he say you could look after yourself? We assumed it was something do to with your job." Charlie turned around from the front passenger seat of the Humber motor car to query Elinor.

Elinor laughed. "All the women had special training, didn't they?" She left the thought hanging as if it were proven truth, then continued. "But I'd already taken it a step further, because being a teacher responsible for girls coming into womanhood during a time of war, well, you have to make sure they're the ones who can look after themselves. What with all those troops from overseas coming into the country, attacks on women escalated. It was hushed up, but we all knew it was happening, didn't we? And we know British soldiers weren't above suspicion in that regard either." Another pause as both men seemed to shift in their seats. "Anyway, the headmistress brought in a teacher of martial arts, and the girls learned a few things about self-defense, so I joined in with a couple of the other women teachers so we could practice with them after school. And I was glad I'd done it, because I worked late sometimes, and I hated walking along the street in the blackout. I was terrified a gang of drunk squaddies would come stumbling toward me thinking I was one of those Piccadilly Commandos. Not that I was in that particular area, but it's fair to say a woman alone wasn't safe."

Bob glanced in the rearview mirror and nodded. "There's a description that went around fast, eh? 'Piccadilly Commandos.' The Messinas were running those girls. The Americans, especially, would roll out of Rainbow Corner and the other pubs and clubs, and there were the Messinas' Piccadilly Commandos ready and waiting to do business; ladies of the night dolled up to the nines, raking in the money and having to give most of it to the Messina family." He shook his head. "You were right to be worried, Miss White, and good for you to be prepared to look after yourself, because no woman or girl was safe."

"Didn't DCI Warren say you could handle a gun? Where did you learn that?" asked Charlie.

Elinor laughed. "Steve Warren was having you on a bit there, Charlie. We had a chat one day and—gosh, I can't remember how we got onto the subject, but I told him my father had been an excellent shot. Dad was a hunter, so as soon as I was old enough I went along with him and he taught me how to shoot straight. Can't say I've as good an eye as my father—God rest his soul—but I had a go, and I know I wasn't half bad. You know what it's like when you're a youngster, you don't want to disappoint your father, and I looked up to him." She paused, her demeanor now more serious. "But I do know a bit about the Mackies and that they're up to something, if that's what you're worried about, which was why DCI Warren asked me to join you for a . . . for a parley. And because of where I live, I'm in a position to find out more for you to go on, though with due care; you're the experts, and I defer to your better knowledge. You're the men of the moment, so to speak."

The detectives both shrugged. "What the boss says goes. We trust him," said Charlie.

There was a lull in conversation before Charlie spoke again. "The first people to be liberated by the British during the war have been our biggest problem, plus the fact that they're now back among us since demob."

"I'm not sure I understand," said Elinor.

"It was the blimmin' criminals, the villains," said Charlie. "The government liberated even the worst of them, giving them the choice of forestry work, joining the army or having more time tacked onto their sentence if they refused those offers—and of course no one wants to stay inside at His Majesty's pleasure, do they? They get themselves out given half the chance, and if it's the government doing it, well, there you go. Anyway, if the con agreed to do their national service, more than likely the sentence was repealed or they only had to do a few weeks or months back inside when they were demobilized after the war, especially if they went into the forces and fought on behalf of king and country. So, like I told you before, off they went into the army or the marines—and what did they do there? Let me tell you what they did— they learned more killing skills to add to the ones they already knew, then they came out ready to do business, and more often than not with a stash of Lugers and what have you left behind by the Germans and Italians when they ran off—and not only that, after the war the Yanks went home, leaving half their weaponry behind, and a lot of it fell into the wrong hands. I bet the boss already told you about that."

"But the real trouble—" Bob glanced again at the mirror to make eye contact with Elinor. "The real trouble is in their minds." He took one hand off the steering wheel to tap the side of his head. "All that business of killing—they miss it. It's the adrenaline, isn't it? It's sort of—what do they call it? Addictive? Yes, addictive it was. They couldn't settle in to becoming reformed men, going out to a proper job every day, not when being on the wrong side of the law gives them the promise of easy money, and that rush-headed feeling all over again."

Elinor nodded as she took the pin from her hair and repositioned it again. "Yes, I understand. DCI Warren has mentioned the same thing."

"Yeah," said Bob. "He had a chat with some sort of 'ologist' bloke, told us all about it." He laughed, "Trouble is, he's a bit like that himself—rush-headed, running off and sorting out—"

"Reckon knowing how to protect yourself, how to go on the attack with all that Chinese whacking around, does the same sort of thing." Charlie's interjection came with a swift glance sideways at his partner, before he turned to Elinor. "Feels pretty nice, knowing you can take care of yourself. Gives you confidence."

Elinor smiled, though she was curious about what Bob might have divulged had he continued. "I'm not so sure I could have done much to help myself if I came across a gang, Charlie." She half frowned as she faced Charlie Kettle. "But I would imagine it's not just the boss, but you experience that sort of feeling too, because you were both in the army—and at least if you get 'rush-headed' now, you're on the right side of the law." She looked out of the window. "Are we nearly there yet?"

Detective Sergeant Bob Mills parked the Humber on Adenmore Road, a short distance from a row of idling buses. Hopeful punters were alighting and either running or walking at speed toward the entrance to the stadium.

"See that?" Charlie pointed to the buses and the people lining up to enter. "That there is money made from people doing their best to spend whatever they've got handy because they think they're onto a winner—or two or three. They go in there planning all the wonderful things they're going to do when they come out clutching a few more guineas than they went in with."

"Here, Miss White," said Bob Mills. "Would you mind putting your arm through mine when we get out of the motor and walk down the street? There are times we might as well have signs above our heads letting everyone know who we are and why we're here."

"Not at all—I'm happy to be part of your disguise." Elinor looked around at her surroundings. "Bit dismal here, isn't it?"

"See right over there?" said Charlie. "Last year the express train from London to Ramsgate came off the rails, and five carriages tumbled right down onto where all them motors are parked. Only one person died—a miracle was that, only one person killed."

Elinor looked back at the railway—the stadium had been built on Southern Railway land, so it was between two railway bridges. It seemed a dark, miserable place.

"Come on, we'd better get a move on." Bob held out his elbow toward Elinor as they stepped out of the Humber, and she slipped her arm through his.

As they walked, Elinor noticed a few uniformed policemen along the way, and that Charlie nodded to each one. It was not an obvious movement of the head, but she was aware of it all the same. Other men lingered near the entrance, either alone or with a companion, while another was pointing out something on a folded newspaper, or laughing and sharing a joke. The almost imperceptible acknowledgements as they passed might have been invisible to most, but Elinor knew these were plainclothes policemen, already in position.

With tickets purchased, the trio took their seats, well chosen, close to both an aisle and exits, with views across the stadium. Elinor waited until a few minutes after they were seated before speaking.

"So, gentlemen, you have both uniformed and plainclothes policemen outside, and I can see them inside the stadium too. I imagine people are used to seeing a few uniforms present, so nothing amiss there. But the plainclothes men? What's going on?"

Charlie and Bob exchanged glances.

"Doping, for a start, Miss White," whispered Charlie. "Or deliberate overfeeding so the dog can't run—with the risk of a ruptured stomach into the bargain. And one of our ways of catching the men in the act is to catch the dog in the act, so to speak—the four-legged innocent bystander, who isn't actually standing anywhere."

"Is there that much money in it?" asked Elinor.

"Is the pope Catholic?" said Bob, running an arm along the back of the seat, still playing the part of affectionate husband or lover.

Charlie kept his voice low. "Here's how it goes. You've got your favorite to win or a dog with promise and good odds, and those dogs attract the bets. Everyone loves the top dogs, and only a few punters ever pick the right outsider. Every year hundreds of thousands of pounds—and I mean hundreds of thousands—are placed in bets at the dogs, and most of that stays in the coffers of whoever's pulling the strings."

"It's a cruel sport, isn't it?"

"You think this is cruel, you wait until you get to the horses," said Bob.

"But you're right, Miss White," said Charlie. "A racing greyhound isn't good for much afterward—don't get me wrong, they're lovely animals, but once they're taught to chase, it's not as if they can suddenly become the dog that little Timmy can run about with in the park. They always have to be kept on the leash, and a lot of people can't be bothered with all that—if they've got a dog, they like to see it run. Most of these racers are put down when they stop making money, and the putting down is not done in a nice way."

"Then there's the injuries, some of them terrible," said Bob. "Couple of months ago there was this lovely dog—Cloudbreak, she was called. Sweet girl by all accounts, but what a racer! She was doped and went down in the second lap—but as she fell, her front claws went up under her, pierced her stomach and ripped it open. That dog died a terrible death before the vet got to her. Terrible."

Elinor put her hand to her mouth, at once remembering the ache she felt as a girl when told that Polo had been taken away to a man named Arthur.

"Sorry, Miss White—that was a bit graphic, wasn't it?"

"That's alright, Bob. I was just thinking of a lovely dog I had when I was a child. He had to be put down too."

"Here we go," said Charlie, pointing to the track. He took a pair of binoculars from his pocket. "Keep an eye on a black dog that'll be moving up on the inside to the front really fast."

After three races focusing on a black dog, then a brown dog and a grey-and-white dog, Elinor thought she would see running dogs even if she closed her eyes, and wondered what she had let herself in for when she agreed to accompany the men.

"Right, this is one to watch. Sunshine Baby is her name—the brindle with a white chest and four white paws. Smashing little runner, she is—good odds and a favorite for the first time. Lots of money on this one."

Elinor squinted and leaned forward. In an instant the hare passed, the gates opened and a row of dogs began the chase. Sunshine Baby took the lead within a second. Shouting and screams from the crowd escalated, people stood up, and some ripe language accompanied the cacophony. Then the tone changed. Anger, disappointment came with a sudden burst as Sunshine Baby lost the lead, then relinquished second place.

"Bob—"

"Yep, I've seen it, Charlie—she's down."

The men stood up and moved into the aisle.

"Best you stay here, Miss White," said Bob.

"Don't worry, we'll find you later," added Charlie.

Elinor waited two seconds, but before she lost sight of the detectives in a sea of waving arms and bad lighting, she stepped into the aisle and began to follow the men. Ahead she could see them joined by two uniformed and two plainclothes policemen, and as she looked to the right and left, others were moving. She walked in the same direction.

The race ended, and two stewards went to the aid of the fallen Sunshine Baby. Elinor was close enough to see the dog, limp with her mouth open, tongue lolling as white, blood-spotted saliva coated her lips.

"It was too much for her," said a trainer to those gathered. "One of those who burns out too young—she's done her bit, better let her go."

She watched as Charlie Kettle stepped forward, his identification badge held high.

"Police! Not so fast—and no one move, or there will be a lot of trouble."

"Routine testing by a police vet," added Bob, holding up his own identification.

"Bent police vet, and probably bent police as well." A man spoke out from beyond those clustered around the dog.

"Your mouth has just got you into a bit of trouble, sir—though I would imagine you're in it anyway." Charlie nodded to a uniformed constable, who moved toward the man.

"Alright, alright, I'm sorry. Didn't mean it." The man held up his hands. "I'm just upset, stricken, that's all."

"This your dog?" asked Charlie.

The man nodded.

"Well, let's all get out of the way so the vet can help her out—see if he can't save her for you," said Charlie. "She might even make a good lap dog now—if you'll forgive the pun." He waved to another man, who might have been taken for a teacher, with his tweed jacket, Viyella shirt, brown corduroy trousers, and his hat askew.

Elinor watched as the man knelt alongside the dog. He lifted her head and flashed a penlight into her wide eyes. With speed he opened his leather bag, took out a syringe and passed a test tube to Bob Mills, who held it for him as he inserted the needle into the dog's vein to draw blood. He flushed the blood into the test tube, and Bob pressed home the stopper, placing it back in the veterinarian's bag. With another syringe, the vet drained a clear liquid from a small bottle and injected it into the dog's thigh muscle while looking up at the owner.

"A little adrenaline—just enough to help her out. She's been doped and overfed before the race. If you don't want to watch your dog's stomach pumped, you should look away."

"Why are you even bothering?" asked the steward who had been first to reach the dog. "Better to let her go. Kinder thing for a vet to do, I would have thought."

The vet, who was taking a long red rubber tube from his leather bag, stared up at the steward.

If looks could kill, thought Elinor.

"I'm trying to save this creature because people like you"—he looked around, focusing first on the steward before directing his gaze toward the owner and a man standing alongside him—"and you, and you, you make me sick." He continued working as he spoke, holding open the dog's mouth and extending her neck as he pushed the tube into her gullet. "You make me sick because you will kill an animal for the money."

"Dr. Adamson, we'll sort this lot out—you look after that poor dog." Charlie stepped forward and placed his hand on the veterinarian's shoulder. "I'll get the blood sample run over to the lab, but I want to confirm that you believe the dog has been doped."

"No doubt in my mind," said Adamson. "Not a bloody shred of it."

Elinor continued to watch the veterinarian as he pumped half-digested matter from the dog's stomach, taking samples as he worked. Around her men were led away, two in handcuffs. Another steward, younger than the first, remained.

"Son," said Adamson, looking up at the steward, "if you know of any other poor creature that might end up in this state tonight, you might as well tell me now so I can do something about it."

The steward reddened and shook his head. "I'm new."

The doctor sighed. "Then I'd advise you to get out of this job while you can. Find yourself something a bit less miserable. This is a bloody nasty business to get into."

Removing the tube from the dog's mouth, Adamson rested his hand on her sleek head and began stroking. The greyhound stared up at him with wide eyes and turned her nose to lick his gentle hand.

I had a feeling you wouldn't stay in your seat, Miss White." Once again Detective Sergeant Bob Mills looked at Elinor's reflection in the rear-view mirror as he spoke.

"I wasn't in the way. Anyway, you men invited me to come along and see what your work was like at the sharp end, so I thought I'd make sure I followed instructions to the letter. No good my being squeamish, is there?" Elinor stared back at Bob, who reached forward and started the engine. "What will happen to that dog?"

"Sunshine Baby?" Bob shook his head and pointed to a motor car parked some six yards ahead of them. "That's Dr. Adamson's motor car. Any minute now he'll come out, and you'll see exactly what will happen to Sunshine Baby."

"If I was going to put money on anything," said Charlie, "it's that our trusty vet would be doing exactly what he's doing now." He pointed toward the stadium exit.

Elinor watched as Adamson emerged, followed by the neophyte steward, who was carrying Sunshine Baby wrapped in a blanket. Adamson opened the back door of his motor car and nodded toward the steward, who placed the dog on the passenger seat. Adamson closed the door with care, not a slam, as he turned to the steward and spoke to him for a moment, lifting his hand to rest on the young man's shoulder. Then he turned, opened the driver's door, took his seat, and was soon maneuvering the vehicle onto the road.

"There you go. Another dog going home with Doc Adamson. When she's better she'll end up in clover, because he'll find a good home for her—probably a woman widowed in the war who needs a bit of company, or a soldier who came back from hell wounded and needs a good friend who won't leave his side. Adamson's got a way of putting injured souls together so they can help each other out. Pity he's moving away. Mind you, he's wanted to get out of London since he lost his wife."

Elinor nodded. She was looking ahead, still watching the veterinarian's vehicle.

"You're looking wistful, Miss White. Did you want the dog? We could put in a word with Doc Adamson for you."

"No, it's not that, Charlie. I think the motor car that pulled out behind Doctor Adamson's might have been the same one . . . Charlie, Bob, I think the Mackies might be following Dr. Adamson."

The speed with which the two men acted surprised Elinor. Bob swerved out into traffic, while Charlie began shouting orders via the police radio. *Calling all cars. Calling all cars.* She held on to the leather grab strap as Bob turned the steering wheel to make a sharp maneuver under the railway bridge in pursuit of the Mackies.

"Hold on, Miss White," said Bob. "We'll sort it out—we look after our own, and Adamson is a bloody good vet. He's not a bent vet ei-ther. People like the Mackies can buy a lot of people, but I can tell you right now, none of them have enough money to buy Dick Adamson. He doesn't give a flying you-know-what about money."

"That doesn't mean they won't try though, does it," said Charlie, taking up the handset again. "Calling all cars. Calling all cars . . ."

CHAPTER 14

Tatton Park, near Manchester, England
1942

WAR ON TWO FRONTS

NATIONAL SERVICE ACT PASSED

WOMEN CALLED FOR DUTY

—*Daily Pictorial*

W hen you land, I want to see you curl and roll to the side, and for bloody hell's sake, don't put your arms out as you hit the ground." The instructor stared at the three women in particular. "If you do, you'll end up working as a shorthand typist." He drew in his arms and wiggled his fingers as if he no longer had elbows, just hands attached to his shoulders. "Shorthand typist, get it?"

The four men in the group laughed, while the women exchanged glances and offered desultory smiles.

"Gaw blimey, have a sense of humor, ladies."

"Heard it all before," said Elinor—though she spoke in German.

"Right then, that's it—you won't mind being first up the tower, will you?"

"Not at all, sir," said Elinor, this time in English, while hoping no one would notice the tremor in her voice. "Ready to set an example, sir."

The seven prospective Special Operations Executive agents had arrived at Tatton Park—where RAF Ringway was based—a few days earlier to begin parachute training. Knowing what would be demanded of her, Elinor was now fitter than she had ever been in her life, though she was older than the other women training alongside her. One was twenty-two, the other twenty-five. Elinor was thirty-eight, but more than one instructor had observed that she could have been taken for a woman ten years her junior.

It was her second jump from the tower, a tall wooden structure set up in an aircraft hangar for the recruits to practice landing without injury. The first jump was without the weight of a parachute strapped to her back. For this one she wore a heavy pack on her back with a cord attached to practice releasing a parachute. Tomorrow would mark her first real exit from an aircraft, though the chute would open automatically. At least she hoped it would. Two more practice jumps would follow, but for those she would have to pull the cord releasing the chute. Now, as she climbed the ladder up to the top of the tower, ready to jump and land on the padded mattress below, she felt as if her life over the past year was rushing before her, with a fleeting return of the same weakness she had felt in her legs when she began running toward the bombed and broken house, the home where her mother, grandmother and sister lived.

———

Not a night passed without Elinor dreaming of the moment she stumbled, falling as she knelt down to pick up a scrap of thick scarlet fabric. It had come from her mother's favorite dress—her "holiday dress," the one she wore for special occasions and would have been wearing to welcome Elinor home for Easter. Charlotte loved every moment of the holiday, the precious days from Good Friday to Easter Sunday. Looking up, Elinor had seen the remains of painted eggs and Easter decorations strewn among the rubble, along with books, china, splintered furniture and all manner of broken and twisted household effects.

"What are you looking for, miss? Perhaps we can help. But you should leave now—it's too dangerous."

Elinor stared at the Air Raid Precautions man in his uniform, at his helmet with ARP in big letters across the top, and his smile. It was a pained and mournful smile, as if etched onto skin in an instant when he had to chivvy the brokenhearted and grieving on their way.

"My mother's jewelry box. It was beside her bed. It was very precious—it's where she kept letters from my late father." She wiped the back of her hand across her wet cheeks.

"Jewelry box? Nah, haven't seen anything like that, miss." He shook his head, as if for effect. "If we had, it would've been turned in, you know, for you to collect from the police station."

"Oh dear—I really hoped I could find it." Elinor stared at the ground and kicked at some fallen masonry. She knew she would never see the jewelry box again. It had gone. Most likely discovered and taken already. So it was true, about the looting.

"If you find my father's letters, would you—"

"Of course, miss. Now then, you go and get yourself a nice cup of tea. The WVS ladies will look after you."

The loss of diamonds had no meaning for Elinor, but she would have loved the letters.

And when you've all done this jump, you can go in and get yourself a nice cup of tea—and a clean pair of trousers. The laundry room is on standby." The instructor laughed at his own joke again. "Right then—up you go to the top of the tower, Snow White. Show this lot how it's done."

Elinor ensured her helmet was secure, positioned well down over her ears with the strap tight. She stepped toward the tower and began climbing up the ladder toward the platform at the top. Reaching the launching point, she braced her shoulders, looked down, gave a thumbs-up and imagined a bird on the wing. She opened her arms, jumped, pulled the cord, drew her elbows in again and a second later landed, curling to one side as her feet touched the ground, her arms now firm against her chest when the instructor reached out to pull her up and off the mat.

"Stellar display. Stellar. Now then, who's next? I see that brave man is already at the step on his way up to prove he can do it. Let's see if you can best the lady here—and you youngsters, keep an eye on these two oldies, because they're making you look like blimmin' trainee clowns."

Looks like we're the two mature clowns in this round. Buy you a drink, Snow White?" Stephen Warren leaned on the bar next to Elinor.

"We should be using our assigned operational names. You know, to get used to them," said Elinor. "And a joke is rarely funny second time around, especially if the joker isn't amusing."

"Sorry about that—and yes, you're right, we should be using operational names. Now, what's the heck is your name?" He had forgotten every time their paths crossed since preliminary training at Wanborough.

"Marianna. And our jolly instructor shouldn't have mentioned my real name today."

"Poor sod probably can't remember the new one."

"He's got a difficult job on his hands, so I wouldn't disparage him, eh, *Luc*?"

"I'm glad one of us has good recall. So, what's it to be, Marianna?" Warren winked.

Elinor laughed. "Gin and tonic, thank you, Luc—oh, and just to remind you, I've heard they try to get us drunk to find out if we tell secrets under the influence. Watch what the soldier barman puts in the glass."

"That's better—a smile from the serious one. A nice G&T coming up—and I'll make sure it's not spiked with anything." Warren caught the attention of the soldier tending the mess bar, ordered their drinks and watched as the man prepared two cocktails before turning to Elinor again. "So, what did you do before the war? Housewife? Lady of leisure?"

"Luc! You're not supposed to ask me questions about before the war. Suffice it to say I speak several languages and was recruited based upon those skills. Apparently the fact that I was a teacher helped."

"How on earth does that help?"

"Well, Luc, there's the ability to assess up to about thirty personalities in double-quick time, as well as being able to explain a tricky concept so that even the most troublesome perisher understands." She smiled. "The 'Lucs' of this world."

"Alright, alright, I get your point. But you're not too shabby with the firearms either. I was with the police, so take that as a compliment!"

"You can't stop yourself, can you? You've given me a hard job, Luc, because now that's something else I've got to forget, plus I've told you too much already. Let it be said it's best we keep quiet about our past lives."

"Bloody hell—I've done it again! It's like being at school. I was forever walking on tiptoes as a lad, wondering what I could say or not say without getting a clip around the ear."

Elinor sipped her drink. "It's called discipline, and it can save your life—and mine, if we're sent out together. Bad for me, as it looks like that's exactly what will happen."

"I'll ignore that one. But what do you think of the girl with the radio—you know, the blonde? I think she's supposed to be coming with us."

"As long as she can do her job and do it well—that's the most important thing."

They were silent for a moment or two.

"You want to ask me something, don't you?" said Warren.

Elinor smiled. "I suppose so, but it's an out-of-bounds question."

"Go on."

"Why are you being deployed to Belgium? Why not France?"

"It's my accent. I was a scholarship boy at a good school, and by some miracle became fluent in French, but because my mother was Dutch, when I natter in French I have this little touch to my locution that's a bit different, and the powers that be decided I would be better suited to Belgium. Apparently there's a number of recruits who happen to speak French or Belgian because their fathers brought home brides after the last war, so they learned another language. Now the Special Operations Executive has nabbed them. As for me, I don't actually speak Dutch— well, I managed to get by for the one afternoon spent with my gran in Rotterdam, but I'm not exactly fluent. You?"

"Born in Belgium. I was fourteen when I came to London."

"Oh, so you were there during the last war; the German occupation."

"We should stop before we say anything else about the past."

"You've got what we call 'previous' then."

"What?"

"Copper talk for a con with a conviction or two under his belt. You could say a prior experience of something. It's your second occupation go-round, so you've got previous."

"Oh."

"Another one?" He lifted his glass.

"I've barely touched this one yet."

"Drink up then, Lieutenant, don't let the First Aid Nursing Yeomanry down!"

"*Marianna*—I hope I don't have to keep reminding you."

"Sorry. And if you don't mind my saying so, I think a Wrens uniform would have been a better cover for you on home turf, not the FANY. Navy is more your color."

"Oh, give it a rest, Luc, or you'll be the first casualty next time we're on the firing range."

Following parachute training, Elinor and other members of the group were sent to Beaulieu in Hampshire, the country seat of Lord Montague, though it was now requisitioned by the government for what was described as the finishing school for SOE recruits. It would be their base while they endured an advanced skills course designed both to save their own lives and bring an enemy's time on earth to a swift end.

Having commenced her preliminary training at another grand estate—Wanborough, near Guildford—Elinor at last understood why recruits and instructors alike referred to the SOE as "Stately 'Omes and Estates" in jest. They were being trained for the ultimate in discomfort, the worst that might befall them as they worked to set Europe ablaze, yet while facing one test after another, they were domiciled in manor houses offering a level of splendor that had hitherto been reserved for the exclusive comfort of the aristocracy. Or discomfort, given that most of those manor houses were cold and drafty.

At the end of each day, Elinor felt as if her joints were being pulled apart; the intensive training taking recruits from shooting—where they were introduced to the Sten gun, the Liberator pistol and a plethora of other weapons—to the skills required to kill someone in silence, which for Elinor was not a new lesson, instead more of a refresher course. A key to their future, however long it might last, was preparedness for a clandestine life while having to appear ordinary every single day in a country occupied by the enemy.

Falling into bed one night, beyond tired and having only picked her way around a fish supper, Elinor listed into a deep sleep only to have her arm almost pulled from its socket, while a light so bright it all but pierced her brain was directed into her eyes. Hauled from the bed by the Gestapo, she was dragged down a staircase she never knew existed and thrown into a dark cellar, enveloped in blackness until another light illuminated the dank, fetid space around her and she was tied to a single chair, with a German guard at the door. So began her interrogation. Hours passed. Darkness. Light—sometimes too much light—at the whim of her captors. Her chair taken so she crumpled to the floor, with only thin pajamas between her and the frigid night. Or was it day? Time and again she was questioned. State your name. Your nationality. Where do you live? What do you do? Tell me your name. No, your real name. Then the tactic changed; a kindly Gestapo officer entered with a chair, helped her to take the seat and offered her a cigarette, shrugging when she shook her head. "Come on, my dear, do answer our questions—then you can go home." The officer left the room and another replaced him, walking to her, slapping her across the face and dragging the chair away again so she hit the ground hard. Names. Expletives. The officer speaking in German, French, English, and she only ever responding in Belgian French. He kicked her again, threw a lighted cigarette down so it hit her on the back, singeing the fabric of her pajamas, and left the cellar, turning out the light as he departed. She coughed, phlegm racked hard from her lungs, the bitter cold leaching from the floor into her skin. Was she in France? Was this a nightmare? She slept.

Sounds outside filtered into the cellar. Elinor braced, ready for more brutality, more blinding light, more questions. She sat up and pulled herself into the corner alongside the door. She massaged her legs, thumped her thighs, found her strength and came to her feet. She waited behind the door. The handle turned, the door opened. The single bright bulb flickered into life. The first Gestapo officer entered the room. Elinor summoned all her remaining strength to move fast, and in a split second his neck was held tight in the crook of her elbow. With another swift move, she slammed him into the wall and kneed him in the groin. The officer doubled over.

"I say, old girl, steady on." The "officer" coughed. "I was only coming in to free you up. You don't want to miss another supper." He came to his feet, clutching his crotch. "Good Lord—you almost took my manhood."

"Sorry, sir." She caught her breath, sweeping a lock of sweat-soaked hair from her face. "But you had it coming."

"Marianna, take this as a warning—yes, you've done well. Not every SOE recruit can endure some thirty hours of intense interrogation. But ordinary Belgian women going about their business don't usually know how to get one over on the Gestapo. And what would you do then, after you've crippled Gruppenführer Lostballs? Think you can knee your way through an army of guards? They'll know everything they need to know about you as soon as you wrap an arm around the guard's neck and whack him in the kidneys, so let's call that a lesson learned, eh? The last thing we want is you in front of a firing squad and an entire resistance line shredded." He blew out his cheeks and shook his head. "Mind you, that knee will come in handy if you're stopped by a lonely Nazi while you're riding your bike along a country road."

"Doesn't every father show his daughter how to use her knee?"

"Did yours?"

"No—but someone else taught me a couple of handy lessons."

Nathalie, the young woman Elinor thought might become the radio operator accompanying herself and Warren—Luc—to Belgium broke her right clavicle, scapula and ankle during her second parachute jump. She had been sent to another location to recover, and in all likelihood to end up in a desk job—though, Elinor hoped for the woman's sake, not in a clerical role; by now everyone knew the parachute instructor's joke. Another radio operator would be assigned in due course, but selecting an agent for Belgium was not as straightforward as it was for the French section. In the meantime, Elinor's role was clear. Her remit during deployment into occupied Belgium was to strengthen a resistance line that included establishing new escape routes for Allied airmen who had been shot down and survived. The resistance line would also carry out acts of sabotage and intelligence gathering, and in time would prepare for the Allied invasion of occupied territories—the end goal that everyone expected. And soon, they hoped.

Given childhood memories of her work with La Dame Blanche, Elinor was under no illusions regarding the difficulty involved in every single operation.

The training had been long, and arduous at times, and now she just wanted to get over to Belgium to "do her bit," as the British said. She considered it a strange phrase, not least because it leveled the risking of life on the battlefield, in the air or at sea into something quite small—a "bit." Not a lot, just a bit. It was the limited portion anyone could be expected to accomplish in a time of war—though it was a phrase used in peacetime too. "Go out and do your bit," Miss Doncaster had instructed the hockey team at St. Joseph's. On the other hand, perhaps the "bit" was typical British understatement. After all, every citizen was expected to serve, to do their bit and charge an invading enemy with whatever they had to hand—hockey sticks included. Even children were being trained in unarmed—and armed—combat, just in case. But this was far from a game.

There had been no beating about the bush during her training— the life expectancy of an agent in the field was about six weeks. Six weeks. Could she expect that in just six weeks she might be free of the stiletto of pain that had run through her heart and taken up residence when she stared at the remains of her grandmother's house while holding a shred of scarlet fabric in her hands? If so, she might greet death as a blessed release. In two wars she would have done more than her bit.

The newly minted Special Operations Executive agents were now situated at another manor house in Hampshire, where they waited to receive orders. Each morning they came down from their well-appointed quarters, and as they entered the dining room where breakfast was served, they would stop to look at the blackboard. If their name had been chalked on the board, they were now on the flight plan to depart for the field of operations that night under cover of darkness. It was their time, and from that moment the clock was ticking.

Elinor, Stephen Warren and two others had been at the house for some ten days. Ten days during which Elinor went for long runs every morning to maintain fitness for deployment. Ten days when she saw men and women, one by one or in pairs, stare at the board before break-fast, knowing it would be their last in England for some time—perhaps even the last of their lives. Lives that might only extend for another six weeks. Or six days. To kill time, Elinor engaged in more target practice, and with a willing partner she became even more skilled in unarmed combat; faster, more precise and effective with every move. And against her better judgment, she and Stephen Warren became lovers.

Returning from a ten-mile cross-country run one day, Elinor took the stairs two at a time and went directly to her room, unlocked the door and was only half surprised to see Clare Fields seated in an arm-chair alongside the window, now open wide to allow the escape of cig-arette smoke. Fields came to her feet, pinched the end of the cigarette and ran it under the cold tap at the sink in the corner of the room, then threw the remains into the wastebasket.

"I should check to make sure you haven't left any vital information scribbled on those discarded papers," said Fields.

"You know better than to suggest such a thing to me, Clare," said Elinor. "You know I wouldn't be that stupid. Why are you here?"

"I thought I should pay you a visit for old times' sake, Linni."

"My name is Marianna."

"Yes, of course, sorry about that. And you've forged a friendship with Luc—in fact, I believe you've become best mates."

Elinor looked away.

"If I didn't need you both in Belgium sooner rather than later, be-lieve me, one of you would be out doing some sort of boring menial fieldwork in deepest Wales, and at this very moment, I am sorry to say it would not be you." Fields, dressed in the uniform of the First Aid Nursing Yeomanry, approached Elinor and stood in front of her. "It took me a while to recruit you, but I persisted because I knew you would be one of the best—so how could you be so bloody stupid? You of all people, Linni. And I'm using your real name because never in my wildest dreams did I think you would make such an error. Elinor De Witt, you've shocked me. I would have trusted you above everyone else I've recruited for this work."

"I'm sorry, Clare, I—"

"Commander Fields."

"Yes, Commander Fields. I will disengage myself from any further involvement with Luc beyond our work in Belgium."

"Nicely said. Textbook apology. Now for bloody hell's sake keep your promise. I didn't bring you out of Belgium in the last war to make an idiot of yourself years later in the SOE. I've put my trust in you, Captain White." She turned away, shaking her head. "And yes, you've been promoted, though god knows I'd like to roll back my reference on that one."

Elinor said nothing. She knew there was more to come.

"There's something else," said Fields, now facing Elinor once again. "You must keep to your promise and end the liaison because I need— yes, *need*—oh dear, unfortunate word, that one. Anyway, I need you to be absolute in your independence of mind."

"I don't understand, Commander Fields."

"Of course you don't, which is why I'm going to explain myself." Fields folded her arms as if to form a shield. "Oh, for god's sake, sit down."

Elinor followed the instruction, taking a seat on the second armchair set underneath the window. Fields took the other chair once again, facing her.

"Here's a nagging problem we are dealing with at SOE HQ. As you know, the prime minister instructed us to 'set Europe ablaze' with our irregular methods of intelligence gathering, sabotage of the enemy, resistance to their occupations of Allied countries, and the protection of our airmen who find themselves on the ground, vulnerable and far from home. And as you also know, the PM believes women to be as good if not better than men when it comes to the execution of the Section's plans. We work well alone, and we know how to keep secrets."

"Yes."

"Right. Well, what you may not know is anything about the competition and often downright rancor with which we are viewed by other government departments." She shook her head. "The Secret Intelligence Service—SIS—has their knickers in a twist, claiming we're nothing but incompetents comprising felons, failures and—well, pick any disparaging word beginning with F, and you pretty much have it. Naval intelligence is on the warpath along with every known Allied intelligence department—half the time we don't know who's for us or against us. Intelligence has always been an old boys' network of disparate offices, so they don't take kindly to us recruiting from what they consider to be the lower classes—women fall into that category—and the fact that we've found a very motley assortment of first-class operatives who have linguistic and other skills has bent the old boys out of shape. Mind you, the Americans are interested and have taken to the idea of the SOE. For all their pomp and bluster, the Yanks like a maverick approach to war and are following suit."

"Commander Fields, what has this to do with me?"

Fields sighed and shook her head, her lips pressed together. Elinor thought the woman she had known for a long time was in a personal tussle to stop herself saying more. She knew her superior would fail in the attempt.

"White, I have known you from valiant young girl to courageous woman, and I believe there are even greater resources of spirit inside you to draw upon as you keep yourself and others in your circle safe and operational. But you must not reveal this conversation."

"It will remain between us." Even as she offered words of reassurance, she felt Commander Clare Fields staring at her, testing her with her eyes.

"I can't put my finger on it," said Fields. "But I don't trust your lover any farther than I could throw him."

Elinor stared at Fields and thought she might laugh. "Commander Fields, I've already thought working with Steve—I mean Luc—might occasionally be difficult because he sees things in such a lighthearted way. He's a bit too much of a jester at times, but throughout our training he's taken each task very seriously—he knows the gravity demanded of his job."

"It's the joker that worries me. I saw it when you were based in Beaulieu, and I saw it on every occasion when I was engaged in monitoring training—sorry, you didn't even know I was there. All part of *my* clandestine work. Yes, I'll concede he kept everyone's spirits up, and yes, every word out of his mouth was passable French in a serviceable locution for Belgium. However, he is very well connected, and it was a reference from another department that secured his entry to the SOE."

"Who recommended him?"

"You know I can't tell you that—suffice it to say it's the old school tie again—but his exemplary if somewhat nonconformist police work with Scotland Yard's Special Branch was also considered before we recruited him. He's just a little more 'irregular' than the rest of us." Fields stood up and glanced at her watch. "Be careful. Watch him. I hope I'm wrong, but there's something amiss. As I said, it's an element I cannot put my finger on, though I have my suspicions. There are secrets kept from me too, so I sometimes engage in rather wild thinking. It's surprising how often I'm right, though I'm always more than happy to be wrong."

Elinor came to her feet. "You can depend upon me to be vigilant, Commander Fields."

Fields nodded, placing a hand on Elinor's shoulder. "Yes, I know that, Linni—Captain White." She smiled. "You will do us proud, Marianna. I would trust you with my life."

"And I would trust you."

Clare Fields smiled again. "Thank you." She stepped toward the door and stopped as she reached for the handle. "Have a good supper and get a good night's sleep. You leave for Belgium tomorrow evening."

It was the shovel strapped to her leg that concerned Elinor most. The tool was one of several items of equipment she would have about her person as she jumped from the Westland Lysander aircraft. On her practice jumps she had worried that the shovel might be a liability as it pressed against her shin like a splint against bone. She wore day clothing underneath the overalls—every item of attire and her shoes had been checked and checked again for anything revealing her country of origin. She had heard about the recruit reprimanded when an officer went through his pockets before he boarded the aircraft, only to find a London bus ticket.

She felt the parachute bulky at her back and knew she would be lying if she said she had no fear. Taking another deep breath in an effort to settle her fast-beating heart, she felt for the semiautomatic pistol and knife issued in preparation for her departure. She could still hear the instructor's words. "Shove that dagger in hard, right between the enemy's ribs, and then bring it up fast with a strong thrust—it'll be harder than you imagine. Or just stab the bastard and keep on going at it once he's down. Save your bacon, because I want to take you to the pictures when the war's over." Another joke, another verbal sheet of festive paper wrapped around the gift of training designed to save her life.

"Time for the off," said Warren, leaning toward her. "See you down there, Marianna. Remember you were the best of the bunch in training for this falling-out-of-aeroplanes lark."

Elinor nodded and gave her fellow operative the thumbs-up. Since the unannounced visit from Clare Fields, she had felt herself gnawing away at the woman's warning as if she were a dog trying to suck marrow from a bone. Yet in that moment as Steve Warren leaned toward her, offering words of encouragement, she trusted him. *She's wrong this time,* thought Elinor as the aircraft door was drawn back and the sharp, cold wind hit her face. She took her position, gave the thumbs-up again and did not look down as she jumped, pulling the cord to release the parachute at the perfect moment when she was clear of the aircraft.

Seconds later she made a faultless landing. She was quick to free herself from the parachute, to catch and roll up the white billowing silk and to unstrap the shovel ready to go about the business of burying everything but the clothes she stood up in and the small suitcase brought down with her. It had taken only minutes for her to make herself presentable in attire and footwear more suited to a woman selling cosmetics door-to-door. As she waited for Luc to join her—he had landed some yards away—she exhaled. The first part was done. Yet as a reminder of what might come next, she touched the pocket close to her chest where she had slipped in the "L-pill" issued before departure. It was the lethal cyanide pill she would use to take her own life if any part of her remit failed and she was captured by the Gestapo. But now she was on firm ground, ready to get to work.

"Thank heavens that's over," whispered the newly christened Marianna. "I'd make a terrible shorthand typist."

CHAPTER 15

1947

Elsie had suggested a "little afternoon tipple" instead of tea at Fortnum & Mason. Now they were in a small pub tucked away along a street Elinor would never have known existed had she not met Elsie according to her instructions and at the appointed time. As before, Elsie's motor car waited outside.

"Meet me at the Queen's Head—the ladies' saloon." Elinor had been seated under the domed hairdryer when Elsie tapped her on the wrist and handed her a note, leaning over to be heard above the fan. "Any taxi driver will know where to go."

Elinor liked the idea of a pub with a "ladies' saloon," but was taken aback when Elsie Finch soon became tipsy. Elsie's swift loss of sobriety surprised Elinor; she assumed anyone from the Mackie clan would be better able to hold their alcohol. However, it had not taken long before the woman's hat was askew and she was slurring her words. Elinor wondered if Elsie suffered from a metabolic disorder of some sort. She remembered Charlotte admonishing her once for serving her grandmother a larger than usual glass of sherry for a toast before Christmas dinner. "She can't take her drink, Linni—you shouldn't have given it

230

to her." The image of her grandmother facedown on the table almost caused Elinor to laugh, but given that Elsie was on her way to a similar position, instead she rested her hand on her companion's shoulder. At once she felt sorry for the woman—perhaps Elsie had let down her guard because she thought she was with a friend.

"Elsie, are you alright?"

Elsie rubbed her forehead, knocking her hat even farther to one side. "You know what they call it? What they call gin? Mother's ruin. I'm not a mother, but I should've had a bite to eat before I had a drink. I could do with a packet of crisps."

"I'll get them, Elsie, and I'll see if they can rustle up something more filling for you to eat—you need something inside you."

Elsie came to her feet, swayed and grabbed the back of the chair. "I'll just nip to the khazi," she announced in a loud voice.

Elinor cringed as she watched Elsie stagger and then right herself while making her way to the ladies' lavatory, her crimson Robin Hood–style hat with bright blue feather slipping farther to one side as she half-stumbled into the door. The London slang for *lavatory* was a word that grated on Elinor, though she knew its Italian origin was probably more familiar to Elsie—*casa* was, after all, the house. In witnessing Elsie's meander across the beer-stained carpet, Elinor felt another surge of empathy for the woman. Elsie had been raised within a brutal family, an unforgiving territory where she watched her brothers trained to assume the family business as if they were raw recruits into an army. Elsie grew up in a man's world, and the only person who had ever set any account by her was Abe Finch, and he was dead.

As she considered Elsie's upbringing, Elinor realized why she had been so curious about the woman. They had something in common, after all. Circumstance had rendered them both outsiders from a young age, and with that understanding, she was filled with compassion for Elsie Finch.

Having purchased a packet of Smith's Crisps, Elinor took her seat again and looked toward the lavatory door, waiting for Elsie to emerge. Elsie's inebriation had put Elinor off taking even one more sip of the cream sherry, but as she pushed the glass aside, she glanced down at the floor and realized that Elsie had left her handbag. She looked toward the door leading to the lavatory again, and hoped that her companion might be a good few minutes before emerging. Making sure no one was watching—it was fortunate they were alone in the ladies' saloon—she picked up the bag and unsnapped the clasp. There were several items inside—a purse, a lipstick, a bottle of Chanel No. 5 perfume, a powder compact and a pressed handkerchief, together with a pen and a thick notebook. She opened the notebook.

The book had been separated into sections, each with a woman's name inscribed in small, exact handwriting. It seemed as if the writer was a girl unfledged, a young woman who had entered adulthood never having graduated to a mature script. Underneath each name was a list of clothing and other items—she suspected stolen goods—their value set alongside a figure indicating the price for which it was sold and the amount paid to the woman in the middle of the transaction; remuneration for both the shoplifter and the receiver who would take the stolen items and find willing buyers. Elsie Finch monitored the worth of each woman who worked for her. Hardly surprising, thought Elinor. A final section seemed to be more personal, though it reminded Elinor of the diary an adolescent girl might pull from under her pillow each night before going to sleep, to pen every secret thought and feeling. She had never kept such a journal, though she had once read Cecily's, having found it while making the beds. In Elsie's diary, the section entitled "Plans" and "Future" were penned as if written by someone who had not quite reached even the cusp of maturity, with all the hopes and dreams such a passage entailed—except, though written in the language of adolescence, the entries were dark.

My brothers have under-esteemated me. They're all the same. But they don't know I can get one over on them any day. Abe told me I was better than the lot of them and he was right. He told me the future was in my hands. Bless him, he made me realize I could do anything I wanted and I won't let him down when the time is right. I will show the snots who I am. I miss Abe. I'm not a Mackie anymore and I will have the last laugh on them—you see if I don't. I am Elsie Finch and five is my lucky number.

While "esteemated" left Elinor wondering if Elsie meant to make such a telling error or whether it was a laughable mistake, the list following her declaration of intent revealed something Elinor had considered from the time she observed Elsie's girls at work in Bond Street. Elsie Finch was not a woman to be underestimated—or under-esteemated—and as things stood, both DCI Steve Warren and the men of the Mackie family had viewed her as if she were no more than a related though less venomous spider crawling out from under a stone.

Hearing the door to the lavatories rattling, Elinor returned the notebook to Elsie's handbag and set it on the floor alongside her seat again. She stood up, walked over to the door and opened it.

"Thank god you heard!" said Elsie. "I thought I'd never get out of the bleedin' khazi."

"I think you were turning the handle the wrong way," said Elinor. "Do you feel better now, Elsie?"

Elsie nodded, and as she opened her mouth to speak again, Elinor could smell the sourness of vomit.

"Let's ask for a glass of water for you," said Elinor. "There's a packet of crisps on the table—the saltiness will make you feel better. It's so easy to get dehydrated under those hair dryers when you're having your hair done."

"De-hy-what?" said Elsie.

"Your body needs some water. Here, you sit down and I'll get it for you so you can have a bite or two of the crisps—then perhaps you should tell your driver to take you home." Elinor paused. "I don't think you had too much to drink, Elsie—you're probably about to go down with a cold or something, so you should rest. Hopefully it's no more than a twenty-four-hour summer sniffle, but best not to take chances." The lie almost stuck in her throat—Elsie Finch had knocked back several gin and tonics before Elinor had even lifted her own small glass of sherry for a second sip.

"Yes, you're right, my dear," said Elsie. "I'm not one to lose my insides over a drink or two."

After watching Elsie Finch's driver transport her away to her home south of the river, Elinor set off toward Scotland Yard, where she was soon ushered in to see Detective Chief Inspector Steve Warren.

"Linni, before you start, I've too much on the boil right now to give your . . . that lead about the Mackie family any more time than you've had from my men already. I mean—going off to Catford dogs, and then, what was it? Down to Goodwood the following day so you could see what a doped-up horse looks like when it falls and breaks its neck?"

Elinor felt her eyes grow wider and fought to compose herself. "Just so you know, Steve, Bob and Charlie asked me if I wanted to go to Goodwood, and I had no idea I would see a horse with a broken neck and the vet have to do the right thing with a bolt through its head."

Warren shuffled papers on his desk. "I know you too well, Linni—you probably hinted, and—"

"Yes, I hinted more than once about seeing a horse race, Steve, and they were bloody big hints too, but I didn't plead and I didn't get in the way."

"Unlike at the dog stadium."

"I wasn't in the way there either—in fact, I kept well out of the way. And had it not been for me, they wouldn't have seen the Mackies pull out in their flash new Ford after the vet had passed."

"The Mackies peeled off and away when they saw one of the police cars, as you know, and I'm sure you are aware that we can't nail them just for being at Catford Stadium."

"Of course they diverted when they knew there was more than one police vehicle after them, but they didn't get the dog doctor, did they?"

Warren threw down his pen and leaned back in his chair. "Linni, enough! I have had more than enough. You come in here with your big ideas about the family gang just because a couple of John Mackie's boys were roughing up their brother. I mean, for two pins I'd rough up my own brother, if I could."

"Says a lot about you, Steve, doesn't it?"

"You know what I mean, Linni." He shook his head, staring at her. "Look, Linni, more than any other person on earth, I understand how it is for you. If you're bored, get yourself a job. Find a nice little school down there in Wattlehurst—"

"Shacklehurst."

"Whatever hurst the bloody place is called. Go back to teaching posh girls how to speak another language and take that useless blackboard with you. Forget you were ever good at anything else. I should never have indulged you in the first place. I blame myself."

A curtain of silence lasting a minute seemed to envelop both Elinor and Warren, until she spoke again.

"What's really going on, Steve?" Elinor's voice was low. "You're pulling back, yet given the information I brought to you, it's evident that something is in the offing that should be of interest to the Flying Squad." She took a deep breath. "Elsie—"

"Please, Linni—not Elsie Finch again. Not that little fat thing with her merry gang of shoplifters. Didn't you hear me? I said I have enough on my plate."

Elinor nodded. "I know you do, Steve."

"So let it go—let it go because we both know why you're pushing."

Another silence.

"The thing that interests me most, Steve, is why you're now ignoring the evidence I've brought to you."

Warren pushed back his chair and stood up. "And that's where we stop this merry-go-round right now. I truly don't know how to explain this to you anymore, and I've tried a good few ways in this conversation alone. You do not know my world, Linni. 'Evidence' is more than a thought, a suspicion. *Evidence* is solid information, solid intelligence brought to us by people on the inside. Bob, Charlie and me, we all have our informants and they are gold dust to us. You could say it's a bit like running an escape line, choosing the right people to usher everyone along on the way, only in this department, we're trying to get in, not get people out."

Elinor looked behind her and then at Warren again. "Just as well the door is closed, Steve. You've just let fly about part of what you and I did, and it's still classified." She came to her feet. "So, would you like me to come to you when I've more information?"

"Oh yes, and where might you get this valuable intelligence of yours?"

"Don't your people keep their sources to themselves?"

Warren ran his fingers back through oiled hair. "Please, Linni, stop all this and go home before you give me a heart attack. All I want now is for you to be safe, so please leave well enough alone. You've got a cushy life, so enjoy it. Go and work in your garden. Teach girls to natter in French, or Italian—just not bloody German, for all our sakes. And stay away from the Mackies. You've a nice little grace-and-favor house down there in the sticks, so go and live a quiet life furnished by His Majesty's government."

Elinor was about to turn away and leave without responding when Warren spoke again.

"It was the war, Linni. It wasn't your fault—what happened over there. It was the war."

Elinor met the detective's gaze. "And this is now." She stared at the man before her and went on. "You know, a few years ago a very wise woman told me that everyone has special talents, and in a time of war, those with unique skills would be sought out. I soon realized that she had given me a warning of sorts, because I had a special talent that was indeed sought out—and we know it was my skill with languages. But I think she knew I had something else up my sleeve, something I was blessed with since I was a girl—because without it I would be dead." She took a deep breath. "So know this, Steve—I have just enough fear in me to keep me alive. I have enough fear not to do anything stupid, but I have absolutely no fear of those who would see fit to scare me— and that means you, the Mackies and anyone else who comes after me."

Warren was quick with his retort. " 'Enough fear not to do anything stupid,' eh, Linni?" He gave a half-laugh. "It seems you can put the past in its place after all—in fact you've made up a completely new story about the past." He shook his head. "Well, well, well, Elinor White doesn't do anything stupid. Funny, I remember something very stupid that came of you and your fear during the war. It was so bloody stupid that—"

Without lingering to hear DCI Stephen Warren finish his retort, Elinor turned and left the office, slamming the door behind her.

Elinor stood still, as if she were another statue positioned along the Embankment, overlooking the water. The sounds of traffic, of people and pigeons, were muffled behind her, echoing as if her ears were filled with cotton wadding. She watched a police vessel motor past toward Westminster Bridge, and in the opposite direction a Thames barge showing every one of its many years was taking advantage of an outgoing tide on its journey toward the docks. Was the barge a home now? She had heard some of the remaining barges had become dwellings, and thought it might be calming to live on the water, waking to the sound of small waves lapping against the sides of the vessel and waterfowl heralding morning. She took a deep breath and tried to render her mind empty.

There were landmarks in her past that could never be erased, though she had made a measure of peace with all but two: her first killing, and the last. The passage of her womanhood was bookended by death, and entry into maturity had come early. With those ghosts still haunting her, how might she live until her own passing? When would it come, and how? Would she be in her bed, alone except for a nurse? Or would she fall in her garden, to be found among the roses? Elinor suspected, though, that Fate might be holding a loaded gun when she found her, when she decided it was time to pay up. There were interludes when she wished Fate would just hurry up, get the job over and done with. She was tired of the torment.

Feeling the wind against her face, Elinor turned around. She was about to take her first step in the direction of Charing Cross when she saw a chauffeur-driven black motor car draw up outside Scotland Yard—the same black motor car she had seen in Whitehall Place and on the Goudhurst road. Only a second or two passed before Detective Chief Inspector Stephen Warren emerged from the building and stepped into the idling vehicle, the passenger door barely having closed before the driver pulled out into traffic.

"Afternoon, Miss White."

Elinor turned, startled by the greeting. "Val—you made me jump."

"People always say that. It's because I wear these flattie shoes. I know it's not exactly stylish, but I can't wear high heels at work, what with all the running about and up and down the stairs, so I wear these. They're very quiet on the pavement."

Elinor nodded, composing herself, ready to meet the secretary's jaunty demeanor. "I'm the same, Val. Cannot abide the things a heel does to my back."

Val nodded toward the motor car speeding off into the distance. "There he goes again, the boss on one of his afternoon bigwig chat sessions."

"Bigwig chat sessions?"

"I've got a minute before I go in." Val took a packet of cigarettes from her handbag and offered one to Elinor, who declined. "I shouldn't," said Val. "You know, I've read something about these things and cancer. To be honest, I can't see them doing that much harm. Anyway, I reckon having a few puffs helped all our nerves during the war, what with the bombs dropping—and smoking probably saved the looney bins being overrun with all us nutters scared out of our wits." She lit the cigarette, shook out the flame on the match and threw it over the wall.

"So what are bigwig chat sessions, Val?"

"Oh, it's DCI Warren and one of his old mates. They were at school together, apparently. Steve—sorry, DCI Warren—was a scholarship boy, and that bloke in the flash motor car was his best mate, the one who stopped him from getting his head knocked in by all them other posh boys."

"Really?"

"I think they worked together in the war, something like that."

"Oh. What's his name?"

Val cleared her throat, as if for dramatic effect when she mimicked a more upper-class accent. "Sah Pereh Gordon-Williams."

"Perry?"

"Short for something. Probably Percival. In fact, it might be Sir Percival Gordon-Williams, but it's the way he says it. 'Be a good gel and tell Stephen it's Sah Pereh on the line.'"

Elinor nodded. "A bit familiar of him."

"And then there's that double-barreled name a lot of them toffs have, like they have to drag their ancestors up from the grave so we all know who they're related to."

Elinor laughed. "You should write that in a column for the *Sunday Pictorial*, or the *Mirror*, one of those papers."

Val looked around as if to check no one else with soft heels might be approaching. "Actually, Miss White, I am applying for another job. At the BBC. Secretary. I reckon there's a chance I could work my way up—and I won't get that over the road there." She nodded toward Scotland Yard, drew on her cigarette, pinched the tip and pressed the unsmoked half back into the packet. "You see, I thought about what you said before, you know, about DCI Warren, and on the way home I said to myself, 'Val, love, it's time to get away from this lot and out into something with more opportunity. Away from all this crime and these miserable coppers.' Even if I don't get this job, there will be another one—perhaps at *Vogue*. I hear a secretary can work her way up there too."

"If I hear of anything, I'll let you know, Val. It's not quite as colorful, but I have a friend who works at the university, and there might be a secretarial position open."

"That's interesting. I wonder if I could get some lessons free too. You know—move up in the world, get more education to better myself."

Elinor nodded. "Always a good idea to better oneself—like DCI Warren at that school he attended. What did you say it was called?"

Val's smile developed into a knowing grin. "I didn't say, Miss White, but I think it was somewhere in Sussex. Down near Hove, that way. I remember DCI Warren telling me it was called something or other Abbey." She consulted her watch. "I'd better get going. I went on a late lunch break to meet my new bloke. Took your advice there as well— found myself someone my own age." She looked both ways, ready to cross the street. "And that's another reason for leaving that lot over there. Bye, Miss White."

"Bye, Val—and thank you."

"Miss White—I've just remembered. Standing Abbey. That was it—the school in Hove. Standing Abbey." Val gave a short laugh. "I've no idea if it's still standing, but you never know what you might find out if you hove down there." She laughed again. "Get it—*hove?*"

Elinor smiled as she waved to Val, and whispered as if to offer a blessing. "You're a very clever young woman, Val—don't throw it away, whatever you do."

When the war ended, Elinor had promised herself that her life would become monotonous, that she would find the same rhythm to her days that teaching had provided. Once settled in the countryside, she would welcome an existence of ease in her self-styled hermitage. She would make no instant decisions. She would not treat her life as if it were a target and she a sniper in pursuit of something more.

The altercation between Jim Mackie and his brothers had interrupted the tempo she had constructed with such care, and though she was intrigued by the hunt she had embarked upon, the way she had jumped in with two feet was nagging at her, leading her to a boundary between the present and a past she had hitherto only viewed through a lens seared with pain. Now another path had opened up, and she was curious enough to follow it, beating back undergrowth along the way if she had to. She had known Stephen Warren for five years. It was not a long time, not an expansive period that would suggest the loyalties wrought by a long-term friendship, but those years of their shared war had been hard enough to flay the outer skin from any pretense. The essence of character, the good and the bad, the strong and the weak, had been laid bare. They knew one another too well.

Elinor made an instant decision as she walked away from Scotland Yard. It was so swift that it surprised her as she hailed a taxicab to take her to Victoria Station, where she purchased a ticket for Hove railway station. She realized how far she would go to bring order to the nagging doubt and deep frustration she felt when the jigsaw pieces of gathered information refused to slip into place.

I t's so good of you to see me, Father Ignatius."

"Anything I can do to assist you, Miss White." The elderly priest, headmaster at Standing Abbey School for Boys, held out his hand toward a worn leather chair in front of the cold fireplace. He did not take his own seat until Elinor was settled.

"Father, I would very much appreciate this meeting being held in confidence."

Father Ignatius smiled, his grey eyes soft and clouded with age, his hair silver, though the skin on his hands and face remained youthful, with none of the liver marks, folds and lines Elinor expected to see on a man of his years.

"Miss White, every conversation in this room is conducted in confidence." He pointed toward the ceiling. "With one exception."

"Of course." She leaned forward. "A dear friend of mine was a pupil here some years ago—he's about forty-six now, so it would have been during the Great War. His name is Stephen Warren, and he was a scholarship boy."

Father Ignatius drew a hand across his eyes, as if the friction might stir his memory. "Warren . . . Warren. Stephen, you say?" He paused, then settled his hands together in his sleeves. "Yes, I remember now. I remember almost every boy here, you know, though sometimes it takes a little time, as if my brain were sifting through a series of folders in the filing cabinet. But I tend to recall the scholarship boys in particular, because the school's governors award only one scholarship every year." He looked up at Elinor. "Not an easy passage of entry for some." He rubbed his chin. "Hmmm, yes, Stephen came here at age twelve. Very bright boy—taller than most, but of course they tend to even out with the years. Young boys are like giraffes—ungainly for a long time, growing in spurts that beggar belief. But is he in trouble?"

"Mmmm, no, not really trouble. Stephen is an accomplished man, but . . . you know . . . the war."

"Yes, of course. The war. War inflicts such terrible wounds, most of which cannot be seen."

"Indeed." Elinor cleared her throat, wondering how to parse the lie. "I know Stephen—Mr. Warren—had a very good friend here, and I wondered if you could tell me about their early friendship. I'm curious about it, and I have a feeling—" She looked upward for effect, as if seeking divine counsel before bringing her attention back to Father Ignatius. "I have a feeling there was some element of the connection that might offer a clue to Mr. Warren's approach, his ability to . . . well, his ability to live a fulfilling life."

There was silence, as Father Ignatius stared at the fireplace as if he were a cat peering into flames, though there was no fire on a summer's day. Elinor wondered if she had gone too far, if she were chasing a rabbit down a never-ending hole and would fail to find her way out again. Steve was right—this wasn't her world. It was none of her business, an investigation was something she didn't understand. Nor did her own lies sit well with her.

"Yes, Miss White. I think I can help you there." Ignatius looked up at Elinor.

"You can?"

"I recall that Stephen Warren's best friend was a boy named Peregrine Williams, though I believe he has since used a middle name and honored it with a hyphen, so it's now Gordon-Williams. Sadly, he was the sort of boy one could never forget, and not because he was an outstanding scholar." He looked at Elinor, almost staring as he made his point. "While we imbue our pupils with strength of character, we also counsel against hubris—a lesson Mr. Gordon-Williams clearly missed." He smiled. "Oh dear, my error—I understand he received a knighthood after the war for service to his country, so is no longer a 'mister,' though he was in line to inherit a title when his older brother was killed at Passchendaele, in 1917."

"Oh dear—how sad."

"I don't think the younger Williams thought it sad at all." The priest looked up again, his gaze direct. "He rather crowed about the title—that's why I remember him. Hubris, you see. He was a boastful boy, and he was one of those I prayed for, hoping the Lord might look down and soothe a troubled mind."

"Troubled?"

"Miss White, people in pain can be terribly harmful, and he could be a bully, but not in the sense of using physical might. No, Peregrine was a manipulative boy. One of those who kept an account. If he helped another pupil, then he would call upon that boy when he needed his assistance."

"How would he do that?"

"Writing an essay for him when he couldn't be bothered to do the work. Completing homework, petty pilfering in the town, telling lies." Ignatius shook his head. "He had his own little fiefdom."

"How did that affect Stephen Warren?"

"Ah yes, of course—Stephen. Miss White, I don't know what you might know of this sort of school—"

"I was a teacher at a private girls' school."

"Well, there you are. I would hope young women aren't quite as questionable as boys of a certain type can be when it comes to their treatment of those less fortunate—those they do not consider their equal. Suffice it to say, Stephen's first year was not pleasant for him. When we encounter that sort of situation, we tend to wait to see if the boy will sink or swim. If we see fit to act too soon, it puts them at even more of a disadvantage, and of course there is the question of character. As it happened, Peregrine came to Stephen's rescue; his innate charisma and power over other boys became a protective shield around Stephen."

"And?"

"The piper must be paid, Miss White. An old aphorism from a

well-known story, but there is so much truth to be found in children's tales, though there is always a suitable passage from the Bible." Father Ignatius shook his head. "There was an occasion when young Mr. Williams had to be reminded of the First Commandment, because he appeared to think and act as if he were a god." The priest closed his eyes, fatigue writ large in a grey pallor without any blush to the cheeks. He sighed, opening his eyes to stare at Elinor. "I suspect your friend Stephen Warren might still be suffering the slings and arrows of his early years, and I can only surmise that the war has exacerbated those formative experiences of powerlessness. You see, even though his savior's interventions gave him a level of peace enabling him to excel at the school, it would not surprise me if he were still paying off the debt."

Elinor was thoughtful. "Yes, that might well be what ails him."

Father Ignatius came to his feet. "But the other side of the coin is that I do not have any instant solutions to help you in your quest to assist Stephen. I should add that Peregrine petitioned his father to give Stephen a reference so they could both study at Oxford at the same time, and he might well have provided financial assistance, as the Williams—or should I say, Gordon-Williams—family was very well-off. Stephen was of course the recipient of bursaries and so on, but still, tertiary education comes at a price."

"Thank you, Father Ignatius; you have been most generous with your time."

"Let me walk with you. Do you have a motor car here?"

Elinor shook her head. "I came down yesterday evening on the train and stayed overnight at a local guesthouse. I can walk back to the station."

"Right you are." Ignatius held out his hand to direct her. "Along the cloister here." As they walked, he continued the conversation. "I understand Stephen joined the police."

Elinor nodded. "Yes, and rejoined after his wartime service. He's in a very senior position."

"I see. Yes. Peregrine Williams entered the foreign service. I would imagine he was in a sensitive position during the war—he seemed as if he would grow into the sort of man who would be tagged for that level of assignment."

"Really?" said Elinor.

"It's just a thought, Miss White. Do not take my observations as truth, whatever you do, though by the same token, do not for a minute think being a teacher here in a boy's school is a recipe for ignorance. No, we're very much of the world at Standing Abbey. Our boys are tasked with going out into life to succeed, which means we must understand all prospective professional avenues to prepare them for what might come next. But Peregrine would have been suited to what I can only describe as sensitive work. You see, if anyone could pull one over on the Nazis, it would have been Peregrine Gordon-Williams. Clearly he did something of note to receive a knighthood."

"Yes, of course." Elinor stopped as they reached the main entrance. "I'm not sure how I can use everything you've told me, but at least I can be a better . . . a better, more informed friend to Stephen."

The priest nodded, drew open the door and folded his arms into his copious sleeves as he bid Elinor farewell. She had reached the bottom step and was about to walk toward the main road when Father Ignatius called out to her.

"Miss White. Be aware of one more element. Young Peregrine had the ability to achieve his aims and not look back at the detritus in his wake. He would win at all costs. I doubt it's a trait he would have grown out of. Hubris, you see."

———

Elinor caught the train at noon, her ticket to Shacklehurst requiring two changes. The side-to-side movement of the carriage soothed her as she considered conversations she'd had over the past two days and the things she had seen. She wondered what might still be binding DCI Stephen Warren to the boy—now a man—who had protected him at school, and what any overdue account might include. Was Warren indebted to Peregrine Gordon-Williams? Or did they just enjoy the longevity of a shared friendship? No, she thought, there was more to it. There was an air of urgency about the way Warren had rushed to join his friend; an atmosphere of risk. The circumstances of their meetings seemed clandestine.

Clandestine. There was a word she had hoped never to use again. *Covert. Secret. Furtive.* All words suggesting a wall, a division, a line between truth and lies, life and death, the world above ground and below. Clandestine was hell. The speed with which the chauffeured motor car had braked outside Scotland Yard suggested something to be hidden. And both those meetings she had witnessed—each requiring Warren to climb into the back of the vehicle, as if he were being granted an audience—had taken place soon after she had seen him in his office.

Sir Peregrine Gordon-Williams. She continued to stare out of the window, watching as a farmer ploughed a field, birds settling in his wake to find a tasty worm turned over with the soil. As she relaxed, studying the bucolic scene, a hawk swooped down, the sparrows and starlings scattering into the skies, flapping their wings in a fury to escape. And in that moment, as she watched a farmer continuing to plough, unaware of the melee behind him, a piece of the jigsaw slipped into place—and she wondered why she had not seen it hours ago.

Peregrine. Peregrine falcon. The falcon was a bird of prey. Peregrine Gordon-Williams was one who intimidated others. A predator.

She pressed her fingers to closed eyes. *Am I right?* Had she found a clue simply because she was looking for one? Were her connecting thoughts pointing to something more solid in the way of evidence ahead? She could almost hear an audible click as the piece slotted into place, though she knew there would have to be many more gathered into a frame before any sense could be made of the pattern beginning to form.

"He would win at all costs," Father Ignatius had called out after her. "I doubt it's a trait he would have grown out of."

Elinor sighed, at once deflated when she realized that the jigsaw piece she had just found might be nothing after all. From the information she had gathered thus far, Peregrine Gordon-Williams was an elitist snob, so any connection between a decorated peer of the realm and a south London family of Italian extraction known to abide on the wrong side of the law would be hard to imagine.

It was later, at home in Shacklehurst, as Elinor took the pistol from her shoulder bag and slipped it into a kitchen drawer rather than return it to the safety of the locked cupboard in the garage, that she thought about Father Ignatius. She wondered what he would have said had he known he was in the company of a woman who had broken several of the Ten Commandments. One in particular.

Thou Shalt Not Kill.

CHAPTER 16

August 1944

HITLER'S EUROPE INVADED

GREATEST MILITARY OPERATION IN HISTORY BEGINS

—*Times Examiner*, June 6, 1944

With each passing day, Elinor was surprised at her own survival, catching her breath when she emerged from sleep because every time she closed her eyes, she wondered if she would ever open them again. From the moment of arrival in Belgium, she had cycled from one town to another under the guise of a traveling representative selling cosmetics. Each time she was stopped and required to show papers to a German guard, she smiled and offered a lipstick or rouge, "For your girl at home." It had never failed; the papers were given a cursory glance and she was soon on her way—and not only to sell cosmetics, though she had become quite accomplished at the job. Each journey was to a place where she would oversee or assist in the organization of resistance to Belgium's German occupiers.

There were, however, days that felt almost normal, days when Elinor could go about her daily round, meet people, sit in a village square with a cup of coffee and return to her room feeling as if she belonged. And for Elinor belonging had been so elusive; a butterfly settling on a rose for just the briefest moment, leaving behind only a passing memory of color. She established regular stops as she went about the business of taking messages, passing instructions along a line of resistance operatives, most of whom would have been deemed "ordinary" before the war and would be again when war was done, if they survived. There was Berniss, who reminded her of her grandmother, a lady of a certain age who always had the kettle boiling when Elinor called, and who took and received messages with such a calm confidence that no German soldier would ever look at her twice. There were women with children, mothers with sons at the front, and the couple who ran a small grocery store in another village. Every single one of those precious contacts was a link in the chain they hoped in time could be drawn tight around Hitler's neck.

Among her favorite stops was a small coastal village, where she would visit Bruno and Gerda, their daughter Helaine and little Anique, their five-year-old granddaughter. Anique had never known her father; Helaine's husband had perished while fighting for his country when the German army invaded, the Nazis showing no respect for Belgium's neutrality.

Elinor laid out her sample lipsticks, rouge, powders and pencils on a cloth, ready to demonstrate how each could enhance a woman's beauty. They all knew it was important to go through the motions in case a German patrol arrived to conduct a spot check of houses in the neighborhood. Gerda had set a cup of tea next to her, and soon all three were seated at the table.

"Go along and play in your bedroom, Anique—we want to talk to Marianna."

"Can't I stay? Why does Grandpa always stay? He doesn't wear lipstick!"

Helaine sighed, ready to counter the willful child.

Elinor thought little Anique had a point, and leaned toward her. "Anique, Grandpa is here because Grandma likes his opinion, after all, he has to kiss her lips."

Anique frowned. "Yewww, that's not nice."

"Oh yes it is, young lady," said Bruno.

"Tell you what," said Elinor. "Let's choose one for you, then you can go to your bedroom and play."

"Will Grandpa want to kiss me?"

Bruno laughed. "Grandpa always wants to kiss you!"

"Right, let's see what we have here," said Elinor. "How about this pink—it's like peaches." She removed the top and rolled up the lipstick. "What do you think?"

Anique shook her head. "Red. I'd like red."

"Red it is—but I have five different reds." She tapped each lipstick until she found one she thought would appeal to Anique. "There, this one is called 'Scarlett O'Hara,' and it's new. What about it?" She opened the lipstick and drew a line across the inner mound of her thumb.

"Yes! Can you put it on for me?"

"Of course—and some powder on the nose, madam?"

The little girl giggled. "Yes!"

"What will I do with all these beautiful women around me?" said Bruno.

"Come on, pucker your lips like this, as if you were going to kiss a boy," said Elinor.

"Yewww," said Anique again, though she followed the instruction.

"Let's hope she still feels like that when she's sixteen," said Gerda.

Elinor applied the lipstick and gave it to Anique. "There, it's yours."

"Say thank you, Anique—and go to the bedroom," instructed Helaine.

As Anique left the kitchen and ran upstairs to the bedroom she shared with her mother, the mood became more serious.

"Will it be soon, Marianna?"

Elinor nodded. "Yes. Soon. I want you to pass these along—usual recipients, usual route. Destroy when they have read the instructions." She handed Helaine three buttons. "You know what to do."

Helaine nodded. "Papa and I will go as soon as you leave."

"We're ready, Marianna," said Gerda.

"It won't be long now."

As Elinor departed the house, she heard tapping coming from the upstairs window, followed by it being opened.

"Look at my doll, Marianna—she has lipstick."

"She's beautiful, Anique, and so are you!"

"Can I have a pink one next time?"

"Of course—watch out for me, I'll have it ready for you in a special little bag."

"Bye, Marianna."

"Bye, Anique—see you again soon!"

Elinor walked away smiling. She would see Anique only once more.

In person, Stephen Warren was an infrequent contact, though he exchanged messages with Elinor printed on silk in an ink invisible to the naked eye. Silk could be folded with ease, squashed into the most limited of spaces, often as small as the button on a jacket. It could be disposed of in an instant, and it left no residue in the way burned paper would leave its mark. For the most part, any male more mature than a young schoolboy or younger than an old man who had passed three score years and ten had been either rounded up and sent to a German work camp or shot. The deformed or incapacitated were not considered a threat, so on those occasions when Elinor met Warren face-to-face, he limped toward her, the caliper on his left leg testament to sickness and an inability to move with any speed. To the Nazi aggressor with an Aryan sensibility, an affliction of the body was a sign of a diseased mind, a malady that might be catching, so they kept a distance.

"It won't be long now, Marianna."

Elinor nodded. "I know. Everyone's ready. We're as covered as we would hope to be."

"The Germans were taken by surprise in Normandy—they fell for it and instead gathered their forces in Calais. It's a tried and tested plan."

Elinor nodded. "Luc, from the word along the line, it was still a bloodbath—more lost than could be accounted for."

"It could have been worse, Marianna."

She stared at the man before her. "I want to reconsider every aspect of the plan, and I'd like Anton, Nicholas, Mila and Louise present. They're all responsible for their part of the line and they're looking to us—to you—for leadership. And Blaz should be here too."

"Blaz?" Warren shook his head. "He only came out a few months ago."

"Luc, two months here is enough to put grey hairs on the head of a boy who hasn't yet grown the beard of a man. He's your radio operator, for heaven's sake—a vital cog in the wheel. And he's a million times better than Lise. The poor girl had a terrible outcome, but she put all of us at risk. She never had the temperament for this work and should never have been sent out. Just speaking the language was not enough to protect her."

"Li—sorry, Marianna—I'll talk to Blaz separately."

"He's an expert with the radio and has a distinctive fist. He's fast and his partner in London is never stymied, or left wondering what the heck he's tapping out." She took a deep breath. "But you've always had most contact with him, I suppose. You know him best."

"Yes, I do—and I know his background, and given *my* background, it's enough to give me reason for doubt."

"What did he do, then? Rob the Bank of England?"

Warren laughed. "No, Marianna, but suffice it to say, he's done time inside. Now then, let's go through the plan again, just you and me."

"And then we bring in the others."

"Alright. Then we'll bring in the others."

Following her initial landing in occupied Belgium, Elinor had returned to the London headquarters of the SOE twice—the first time picked up by a Lysander landing in a field; the second by fishing boat. In the midst of each short sojourn, she wanted nothing more than to return to Belgium following debriefings during which she pleaded for more arms, more support, and even more French lipsticks and powder, if it could possibly be arranged.

Despite the occupation, despite the horror of retribution following each act of sabotage—acts that often included assassination—Elinor found a strange comfort in being at home in the land where she had spent her early girlhood, where there were warm memories of family, of her father's presence, of Polo as a puppy. She realized that upon reflection she could not remember winter, as if everything that happened before 1914 was bathed in the warm glow of summer. Yet it was during one short stint in London that Elinor viewed a small mews flat in South Kensington and decided on the spot to buy it. The purchase was settled with speed, the money transferred from an account she had all but ignored for some years, and which had grown with inheritances from her deceased family. She had no idea if she would remain alive to return to her new home, but it soothed her to have a bolt-hole that was her own.

After concluding the meeting with a solicitor, she walked along the street in a daze, her buyer's remorse at odds with the staking of a claim in the future.

can't believe I bumped into you!" said Sophie, as they sat in a Kardomah coffee house, the entrance banked high with sandbags. "I'm not usually in London, and there you were, walking along just staring into space. I mean . . . Linni, are you listening? Linni?"

"Oh, sorry—I'm sorry, Sophie. I'm not usually here myself."

"I said your name twice, and you didn't turn around—and now you just keep looking at the door. Anyone would think you didn't know your name any . . . any . . . anymore." Sophie stared at her friend, then looked away. "Oh, Linni. I'm sorry—I should have guessed. It's only just dawned on me."

"It's alright, Sophie. Not to worry. Let's just drop it, shall we? And we should leave here before either of us says anything incriminating. I've to go to an important meeting anyway." She leaned toward her friend and whispered. "And let it be said, I guessed what you've been up to before the penny dropped about my job."

The women departed the coffee house and stood outside.

"Until the end of the war, then," said Sophie.

Elinor nodded. "Yes, until then. I'll be in touch."

"I know. When you're ready, you'll *eventually* be in touch." Sophie reached out and put her arms around her friend.

"You always were a big cuddler, weren't you, Soph?"

"Stay safe, Linni. I've lost too much to lose my best friend."

"Me too, Sophie. Me too. Now then, go back and play with your numbers so you can tell the navy where to find those damn U-boats."

Marianna—you seem miles away," said the man everyone in the group knew as Luc.

Elinor and Stephen Warren were of equal rank, though they would alternate leadership in meetings with agents and resistance lines. She was aware of Warren's tendency to lighten the atmosphere with a quip, one that sometimes undermined her, though she had become adept at deflecting his witticisms. Since their training days she had put his clowning down to a desire to be liked, to be seen as the one who kept spirits up when the chips were down. It was a characteristic she appreciated—some of the time.

"I beg your pardon. I was just running through the whole plan in my mind's eye, Luc." Elinor looked around the table at the two men and two women gathered in a farmhouse some five miles from the coast. She tapped the map. "And I wonder if we could reconsider every single move one more time—we must make sure there are no holes, nothing left to chance if at all possible."

"I agree," said Mila. "Marianna's right. We must leave nothing to chance."

"Go on then, Marianna," said Luc, folding his arms and grinning. "And in the spirit of double-checking, Marianna has already been back to the village square a million times, selling lipstick so she can walk everyone's allotted path to make absolutely sure we've considered all possible eventualities! She's even made a friend of a little girl who now has a more colorful choice of lipsticks than any grown woman I know!"

"What can I say, Luc?" said Elinor, smiling. "We all know the family has been more than helpful—and a stash of new lipsticks came in

with the last weapons drop, so I've been handing them out like sweets."
Elinor tapped the map. "Anyway, let's go over the plan, because as we
know, 'Le bon Dieu est dans le détail'—the good god is in the detail—
and you know me, I even check my shopping list a few times." She
waited for a brief flurry of nervous laughter to abate. Warren raised his
eyebrows in mock surprise that she had made a joke, smiling as she
continued. "We move into the fishing village here on Tuesday at 0600
hours—there is a beach to the west Luc has earmarked for landing craft
entering en masse, and that's where our friends will come in. Now, the
Germans have received 'intelligence' that the British and Canadians
are landing here, at this point." She moved her finger and tapped the
map to indicate a broad swathe of coastline several miles to the east.
"But we will have our people waiting to support the British and Canadians here." She pointed to the beach neighboring the village. Elinor
cast her gaze around the table to the gathered men and women.

"We're all with you," said Nicholas.

Elinor nodded. "Right. Initially, we'll position Anton and Mila with
groups one and two at strategic places around the square, as if we're preparing for market day, while Nick and Louise with groups three and four
will be in situ among the dunes just up from the beach. You've already
left handcarts and so on in the square, and you have people keeping an
eye on what's inside. With the market disguise, we can move around
and direct the Allies to a point behind the Germans here, so they can
be eliminated with as much ease as this sort of operation can expect,
allowing movement of more troops farther inland. We anticipate casualties, of course, but the plan is to terminate enough of the immediate
occupying army to allow for the eventual liberation of Belgium."

Luc laughed.

"What is it? What's wrong?"

"Marianna, really. Eliminate? Terminate? You sound like a bloody army manual. In short it boils down to the fact that we're going to take the Allied army along with us and attack the bloody Nazis in the rump—and we're in with a bloody good shot at success."

The four resistance operatives were silent, staring at Elinor, waiting for her response.

She took a deep breath. "There's one element we absolutely must remember above all else, Luc." She stared at Warren. "Civilians. People live in this village. Have we done all we can to make doubly sure the risk to their lives is minimized?"

Anton spoke up. "We've already facilitated the movement of a number of people from the village in small family groups, as if they're going away to visit relatives or friends, but it's difficult. Any significant departure of civilians from the area will alert the Germans to our plans. And we know there are some locals who may be sympathizers—there's the right-wing agitators in thrall to the Nazis, and they've been operating everywhere along this part of the coast."

"That doesn't mean they have active supporters though, Anton," said Louise. "I'm with Marianna—we must do all we can to keep the villagers safe."

"Our people will go to each house at a suitable moment before the landing and they will tell the families to remain inside," said Nicholas. "The Allies will move through the town as quickly as they can. That's the best we can do for civilians."

"Exactly, thank you, Nick," said Warren. "Let's not focus on a problem we don't have or can do nothing about, eh?" He shook his head. "I hate to say this, but you women always look beyond the plan to complicate the issue with more questions and minor concerns."

Elinor banged her fist on the table. "It's the laying out of the dead, Luc. We women lay out the dead, and we don't like the job—that's why we try to avoid it!"

———

There was little sleep to be had in the hours before the operation. People and arms were moved into position, and in the farmhouse, plans checked and rechecked. Anton, Nicholas, Mila and Louise would each lead one group of resistance volunteers. More armed men and women would be situated close to roads leading out of the village. Warren and Elinor, along with Blaz, the radio operator who had joined them in the farmhouse, would advance into place behind a cart close to the center of the square. So deep was her concentration that Elinor thought she could almost feel an armor forming, a shield beginning to wrap itself around their collective resistance. It was a casing formed of trained-in calm, along with the confidence that came from having a well-rehearsed plan and individual responsibilities repeated time and again. Modifications had been made for weather and any new intelligence regarding enemy movements. And yes, fear was part of the carapace—it was the key to survival, doubt becoming a final layer of protection to keep everyone alert, along with a smattering of optimism, but not too much. When they moved into position, Warren would be in the lead.

"Almost time," said Warren. "Blaz?"

The young man alongside him nodded, adjusted his headphones and tuned in to the BBC wireless service. He waited a moment or two, then smiled and removed his headphones, turning up the volume so everyone could hear the signal when it came. *Da-da-da-daaah. Da-da-da-daah.* It was the opening of Beethoven's Fifth Symphony; the composer's notes mirroring the series of dots and dashes that formed the Morse code for one very important letter: V, for Victory.

With silence and stealth Elinor and Warren, along with the four operatives and Blaz, left the farmhouse, each with their part memorized. Warren and Blaz proceeded in one direction, Elinor in another, where she met with other members of the resistance line for a final check. At 0700 hours on the dot, every volunteer involved in the quest was in position. Elinor moved on to rendezvous with Warren and Blaz.

The radio operator tuned in to a prearranged frequency and nodded. "They're on their way, sir. Union Jack and Maple Leaf flying."

"I hope that bit about the flags is a joke," whispered Elinor. She looked up, pointed toward a church tower. "Luc, do we have someone in position up there? I thought I saw—"

Warren looked up, shook his head and turned to face Elinor, lowering his voice to a whisper once more. "It's nothing, probably just a pigeon's shadow. Let's not get jumpy over a bird."

"But I—oh, you're probably right."

Elinor nodded, though Warren's constant rubbing of his hand across his forehead unsettled her. She could feel tension mounting already, as if every single member of the resistance line were ready for the unexpected, because they always had to be ready for the unplanned event. Their remit was to keep the local population safe, to direct the Allies inland before leading them up behind the Germans, who would have their heavy artillery facing the wrong direction.

0715 hours. Elinor rested a hand on Warren's arm and smiled in the hope that it would give him the confidence she felt was evaporating.

He smiled back. "Not long now." Leaning against a handcart, dressed in the garb of a simple market trader, Warren was afforded a view across the water to the horizon. "They should be here soon. In fact . . . yes, that looks like landing craft."

Elinor lifted her binoculars.

"Where? I'm looking hard, and I can't—"

The first volley hit a row of houses across the street to the left. Elinor covered her head with her hands and knelt to the ground behind the cart.

"What—"

"Stay down!" Warren hissed, kneeling beside her, with Blaz cowering next to him.

"They're here!" said Elinor. "The Germans know we're here."

Warren signaled group leaders to hold their fire and spread out their volunteers.

Heavy artillery and machine gun fire began to rain down upon the village. A few civilians came from their houses and ran toward neighboring homes, as if seeking comfort in numbers. The volunteers could not be held back, and returned fire toward Germans surrounding the village. Anton was down, then Mila and four of her group, as they moved in toward the square. Screams filled the air as more volunteers rushed forward, away from the square and in the direction of the enemy.

Elinor moved her weapon from her back, holding it ready. "Bastards!" She looked at Warren. "How the hell did this happen?"

"I don't bloody know." Warren turned to the radio operator, who was visibly shaking from his head to his fingers, "Blaz, find out now."

"Um, but sir—"

"Just do it!"

"Right, you three—" He pointed to several men and women from Louise's group who had moved into position several feet away, and indicated the side of a building. "Get over there ready to attack when they come through, because unless we have a boat, we're going to have to stand here and fight. They don't know our exact positions yet—they're firing all over the place." He pointed to others hiding behind carts, using hand signals to instruct them.

Elinor watched as more armed men and women moved across the square, heads down—yet again her attention was drawn to the bell tower and shadows that seemed to move around inside.

"Luc, I think—"

"Keep your bloody head down behind this cart, Linni, for god's sake!"

Then it happened; a hail of bullets cut down the moving resistance volunteers just as they reached the other side of the square.

"I knew it!" said Elinor. "German snipers in the church tower!"

She began to aim toward the tower, but was distracted by movement along the street.

"Oh my god! Oh no . . . oh no!"

The little girl, Anique, was running toward her.

"She must have seen me from a window," said Elinor. "She was watching all the time."

"Where's her bloody mother?" Warren hissed. "What's a child doing out? She'll give away our position."

Elinor began to move, but Warren pulled her down.

"No, Linni. Please, no. You're the best shot we've got—take her down now!"

"What?"

"I said do it—look around, she'll give away our position, and all the others who aren't dead already will be shot along with us."

"These Germans already know where we are."

"Take her down, stop her now!"

Elinor looked up at the bell tower and raised her rifle. "That's who I'm after."

"You fool! No . . . no . . ."

Elinor felt herself falling sideways. A sudden pain ricocheted into her skull like a dagger. She heard the retort of her gun, and in the next second, little Anique collapsed in the street. She tried to move, but she couldn't, nor could she utter a sound. Darkness spiraled in as her brain relinquished consciousness.

―――――

Elinor had no memory to draw upon. No recollection of anything at all as she began to open her eyes. She felt dizzy, a small room moving around her even though she was in bed. Bed? She fingered the smooth cotton sheet, and as she tried to focus, she could see only blurred movement through a film of white. She closed her eyes, trying not to stumble; she felt as if she were falling, even though she was not on her feet. A horizontal roll made her feel sick—was it real, or was she concussed? She lifted her hand to her mouth and began to retch. Every thought slowed to nothing. She could taste salt and retched again—and if she could vomit, it meant she was not dead, though she could be in hell.

Aware of a cloth being laid across her forehead, she tried to focus again, but instead she leaned forward, this time heaving bile into a bowl held at her chin by a nurse.

"Who are you? Where am I?" Elinor wiped her mouth with the back of her hand, and struggled to form words that echoed back at her as if she were speaking into a tin can.

"Do your best to settle down now, Captain White. We'll be docking in Ramsgate soon—you're almost home." It was a man's voice.

"Ramsgate? Am I on a boat?"

"A hospital ship. You sustained a nasty bang on the head when you fell."

"Fell? I don't think I fell. I think . . . I think . . . What happened to the little girl?"

"You fell, Captain White. You must have been dreaming about a little girl. Now then, Miles here is the best nurse on the ship—she will look after you. You'll be stretchered ashore. An ambulance is waiting to take you directly to hospital."

"I don't think I need . . ."

"Yes, you do. We've arranged for your immediate transfer to the Oxford military hospital for assessment and diagnosis, just to be on the safe side—they've excellent head people over there. It's actually St. Hugh's College, but now it's where we look at brain injuries. Won't keep you there for long because you'll be sent to a convalescent home to get well. Somewhere in the country for a nice rest. You've done your country proud. There's a medal in there for you, I daresay."

"Who are you?"

"Oh, that's not important. Right, I'd better be off."

And he was gone.

The nurse, a member of the Queen Alexandra Nursing Corps, handed Elinor two tablets and held a glass of water. "There, that'll help settle you. I'll be back soon enough to assist you with your uniform—we rustled up something for you because it looks better when you're transferred. Shipshape and Bristol fashion, as they say in the navy."

Elinor took the pills as instructed, allowing the nurse to hold the glass to her lips.

"I'll be back in a minute, Captain White."

Elinor nodded and leaned back on the pillow, watching the nurse leave. The narrow ship's door closed with a loud clunk. She ran her finger into the recess of her cheek and spat out the pills into her hand, then shoved them under the pillow.

Where was Steve Warren? Was he dead? How did she get on a ship? She raised her hand, clutching her forehead as if to massage her brain into action.

What had happened? What had come to pass after she killed a child? Oh, God in heaven, she had killed little Anique, the girl who loved lipstick. Why had Anique run from the house? Why hadn't her mother stopped her?

Elinor looked around the cabin, though at first it was hard to make her thoughts join one to the other. Then she realized what she was searching for. It was a tool. She wanted a knife, or anything a doctor would use that was sharp. Glass, broken into shards and pulled across the inside of her wrist would do the trick—but the nurse had removed the tumbler of water. She stood up and, holding on to a grab bar, opened each drawer and rummaged in a cupboard. She was a resourceful person, there must be something, anything she could use to do what needed to be done. It was what she deserved. The piper must be paid, she knew that, and she had been waiting for him for years. Fate was sprinting toward her, running along the decks, throwing open door after door in a quest to find Elinor De Witt, so she might as well get the job done herself. She was good at killing, it was her special talent; it would be easy to become her own target.

CHAPTER 17

1947

At home in Shacklehurst, Elinor could not settle. Was it time to stop pressing her old friend Steve Warren to help her protect a young couple and their child? A family who, to be honest, she was barely acquainted with, though she knew enough about them. When she reflected upon the speed with which she had acted out of sheer anger, it unsettled her. She had been at the mercy of an intense reaction running through every fiber of her being. There was nothing considered about her response—no thought, no weighing up of what might or might not happen, or the lack of power she had in a world of which she knew precious little—the librarian in Tunbridge Wells notwithstanding. The nearest she had come to black markets, the doping of horses and dogs, smash-and-grab raids, shoplifting, and anything else that occurred to the criminal mind was catching out the local butcher shafting his customers. But she knew all about secrecy and sleight of hand, so she had jumped into the fire with an idealistic belief that she could save Jim, Rose, and—most important—little Susie. Now she was stumped.

Yes, she knew the Mackie family was steeped in an underworld of rackets, a never-ending game of risk and chance passed from father to sons, with enviable profits and a strong balance sheet to feather a growing number of nests every single year. The war had been good for operators like the Mackies, and it seemed even Scotland Yard was picking its battles with organized crime. As Charlie Kettle said to her once in passing, "It's like any other game where the players are matched. You win some, you lose some."

In Belgium through two wars she had only ever lost one battle, and in this case, perhaps the best thing would be to step away and reconstitute her quiet life. It was a life she was grateful to have; so many had lost theirs. There were other ways she could be a good, caring neighbor to Jim, Rose and Susie. Especially Susie. She could leave the bigger Mackie problem to those who understood the nature of organized crime in a world where the darkness of war hadn't yet lifted.

Such thoughts came and went as the day passed, lingering on her lack of personal control and a visceral memory of the rush of fury she felt when she saw Rose and Susie outside the cottage where Jim's brothers were pushing him to return to his former life. It was a smoldering anger she could still feel burning away in her gut, and the only way she knew to keep it from flaring again was the physicality of working in her garden, pulling away weeds, time and again steeping her ungloved hands in the soil to ground the live, sparking wire she had become.

When dusk began to envelop the fields beyond the kitchen garden, the waning sun spread a mellow terra-cotta glow across the land, as if with nature's artistry a bucket of deep-orange wash had been thrown across the horizon. She scrubbed her hands at the kitchen sink before picking up her binoculars to scan the fence line on either side of the field, looking for movement along the perimeter of the woodland beyond. Nothing. She moved her attention to the path flanking the hedge to the right. Again, nothing. She put the binoculars away in the drawer where she had placed the Webley, and once again stared at the horizon.

A sudden knocking at the door startled her with its ferocity. It sounded as if the caller was banging with fists while calling out to her, screaming her name. A child was wailing.

"Miss White. Miss White. Are you there? Miss White. Please come. Please be there."

Elinor ran to the door, drew back the locks, as Rose Mackie put all her weight on the other side to gain entry faster. Clutching her screaming daughter, she burst into the house.

"Rose—what's the matter? Tell me."

Rose drew breath to speak but instead began to cough, her face flushed and her eyes reddened. Susie was crying, rivulets of tears and mucus rolling into her mouth. Elinor pulled a fresh handkerchief from her sleeve and wiped the child's face as her mother struggled to breathe, panic overwhelming her.

"Here, let me hold her for you," said Elinor, reaching for Susie, who accepted the open arms as if her own mother could never more be trusted. "Sit down, Rose. Take another deep breath. That's it. And another. Now talk to me. Tell me what's happened."

"They came again. His brothers. Two of them. Bobby and Sandy." She rested her hand on her chest. "I took Susie into the kitchen, popped her in the high chair while I put on the kettle so I could give them a cup of tea, then I heard all this yelling—only it was Jim doing the shouting, telling them they could take their . . . that they could take their effing plan and shove it. He was screaming at them that he was finished with their rotten jobs, and he was finished with the family altogether." Rose gasped to catch her breath. "I went in there thinking I could say something to settle him down—I'd never seen him like that, he's usually so calm—and there he was going for Sandy. And no one goes for Sandy if they want to stay alive." She took another deep breath. "He told me to run, so I grabbed Susie and came over to you . . . I didn't know where else to go."

Elinor's decision was instant. "Stay here." She settled Susie on her mother's lap. "Help yourself to anything you need. Just try to quiet yourself, Rose." She ran to the kitchen, took her old gardening jacket from a hook behind the door and put it on. She reached into the cutlery drawer for the semiautomatic pistol and shoved it into her pocket before returning to the sitting room. "Do not follow me. Is that clear?"

"But, Miss White—they're horrible men. Violent. You don't know what they're like."

"And they don't know what I'm like either, so the playing field is even. Now, stay here. Whatever you do, don't follow me, because I might not be able to protect Jim if I have to worry about you too."

Elinor left the house and ran down the road, slowing as she made her way in silence along the side of the Mackie's cottage. The dog was leashed to a tree and already barking, so any escalation of the creature's howling fury when Elinor reached the back of the dwelling would not herald the arrival of a stranger. The lights were on in the cottage. From a side window she could see Jim Mackie on the floor of the small, beamed sitting room. One man was leaning over him, pinning him down and then kicking him with feet clad in heavy workman's boots. The other man looked on, his back to the kitchen door, his arms folded while he gave orders and watched.

"Do we have to start all over again, Jimmy boy? Because the way you're going, you will be dead by the time we've finished."

Elinor moved toward the kitchen door at the rear of the house, opened it without discernable sound and stepped into the cottage. The curtains at windows facing the road had been drawn, so no one passing could witness what was happening inside. The man giving orders had his back to her, the other looking down at Jim Mackie, whose eyes were closed tight as he braced for the next blow, the next kick or punch. She had no choice but to make her entrance. Elinor stepped into the sitting room behind the man standing with folded arms. She lifted the gun, moved her forefinger from the barrel to the trigger and held the pistol to his neck.

"If you stir one muscle, one at all, I will kill you. Do not doubt me, because I have killed men far more powerful than you will ever be." She felt the man brace and pressed the weapon deeper into his flesh. "I said, do not doubt me. And above all, do not speak because there is nothing you can say that I have the patience to hear." She waited a second. "Good, we all know the name of the game. Now, you—thug with the boots—stand away from Mr. Mackie. Put your hands above your head where I can see them and stand by the door. Go no farther until I tell you. One error, and your brother—this one—will be dead before you've touched that gun strapped to your left ankle. As will you."

The man edged away from Jim Mackie and stepped toward the door, where he appeared about to turn.

"Do not look at me!" warned Elinor. "Remain absolutely still and do not move." She took a breath. "Jim, can you stand and walk?"

"Just about, miss—"

"That's enough—no need to say more unless I ask a question. Go to your brother by the door and remove his gun and the knife—I believe it's strapped to the other ankle. Then come back and take away this one's Luger—it's bound to be a Luger—from the holster underneath the left flap of his jacket. Oh, and please, sir, again, don't move because I'm awfully fast, though today I might be clumsy, miss your neck and go straight for your brain."

Jim followed Elinor's instructions.

"Good. Jim, walk quickly back through the kitchen and around to the front of the house. Check the motor car outside—you'll know where to find their armory. And start the engine for them, because they're leaving now, and I'm sure they want to be on their way back to Mickleham Street."

When Jim Mackie left the room, Elinor instructed the brother by the door to open it and emerge onto the front step and no farther, at which point she followed, her gun still fast against the neck of the one she suspected was a possible future patriarch of the Mackie tribe.

"So far, so good, gentlemen," said Elinor. "I must say, you're much easier to deal with than the Nazis. Now, I think we know what to do next."

Jim Mackie stepped away from the idling motor car as the brother who had kicked him in every part of his body and blackened his face with bruises slipped into the driver's seat. Elinor did not relinquish the pistol's pressure on the first brother's neck until he was seated.

"Your business is of no interest to me. But know this—if I see you on this road or anywhere near my friends again, I will hunt you down and I will end your sorry lives. Never let it enter your heads that I could not or would not keep my promise."

Elinor slammed the door and watched the Ford Pilot with its three-liter engine depart at speed, skidding around the corner and into the night.

"Miss White, I—"

She turned to Jim Mackie. "Jim, I know what you're going to say. You're about to warn me that they will be back, and when they get here, it will be team-handed, with as many men as they can muster. I also know they will have paid off any policeman who might try to stop them on the way for driving after dark. With that in mind, you must leave as soon as you can."

"But—but we've nowhere to go."

"I know—that's why I have a safe place for you."

"They'll find your house—they'll know."

"Of course they will. Come on—I daresay they will stop in the village to use the telephone kiosk, then wait until their cavalry arrives, so after they've made their call to arms, I would estimate we have two hours at the outside."

Now we're the ones driving after dark and breaking the law. Where are we going, Miss White?" Jim Mackie was next to Elinor in the passenger seat. In the back of the motor car, Susie was sleeping in her mother's arms. The scruffy dog—who, Elinor had discovered, was in fact named Scruff—leaned against Rose's shoulder.

"To the home of a friend of mine. She's expecting us—that's who I was placing a call to when we stopped in Flimwell."

"Does she live alone?"

"Yes, but the houses are close together, and she knows her neighbors."

"They'll find out who your friends are, Miss White."

Elinor laughed. "Not this one. Anyway, I'm sure they know all about me already, and then it might occur to them that I'm acquainted with a few people who are rather like me, people I can call upon in times of trouble."

Come in, come in—put your bag down anywhere. Jim, Rose and Susie, isn't it? And this must be Scruff. Welcome. I'm sure you'd like a nice hot bath and then go to bed." Sophie stood alongside the open door to her Georgian house on the outskirts of Burwash in Sussex. "But first let's feed you. I know time is getting on, but you'll sleep better after some hot soup—don't go to bed on an empty stomach, that's my motto.

It's chicken with vegetables—I hope you like it. And I'll put down some mashed bread and gravy for your dog—best I can do for her until tomorrow, I'm afraid."

"Thank you, Sophie," said Elinor, reaching out to embrace her friend.

"It's very kind of you, Mrs. Hunt. I don't know what to—" Jim Mackie might have appeared to blush, were his face not bathed in bruises now more livid and purple since embarking upon the journey.

"Young man, a friend of Elinor's is a friend of mine. Now then, let's get this dear little girl settled—I've put you in the guest room upstairs. It already has a cot in it. It's old-fashioned and well past its prime, but I found it in the attic, a leftover from my childhood. I kept it because you never know when something like that will come in handy for friends visiting with a small child." Sophie turned to Elinor. "Will you show Rose where the bathroom is while I put out the soup? Oh, and you'll find the first aid kit in the downstairs WC—handy for when I've done something silly to myself in the garden. There's some tincture to treat nasty bruises in the box."

The exhausted Mackie family said little beyond expressions of gratitude, and were in bed soon after eating, and—Elinor hoped—sleeping off the ordeal.

"You don't look so chipper yourself, Linni," said Sophie, as she handed Elinor a generous measure of brandy in a crystal snifter.

"I expected Jim's brothers to pay another visit, and I knew that when it came, it would be more violent than the first. It was lucky I was there to help out."

Sophie sipped her brandy and sat back in the armchair. "You told me a little on the telephone, but do you want to talk about it?"

Elinor shook her head. "It's a long story."

"Probably not that long—I think you just don't want to tell it." Sophie sighed, swirled her brandy in the balloon glass, sipped again and leaned forward.

Elinor braced herself.

"Linni, I've hardly seen you in three years—since 1944. This is only the second time you've been to my house. You came for a few days after the hospital discharged you, and then you retreated to the flat for a while until you moved down to Kent. I've been hoping for an invitation to your cottage since you sent me the address." She took another sip, set her glass on a side table and returned her attention to Elinor. "Look, neither of us wants to talk about what we did in the war—we avoided it like the plague when you were here before, and it's more than we dare do. But if you told me that nothing happened to break your heart, I know you would be lying. Everyone's heart was broken. David was already with the RAF when war was declared. He was so excited when he received the transfer to 617 Squadron. Because of my job, I know exactly where it happened and what he was doing. I can't stand it when I hear people talk about the Ruhr Dam and how thrilling it was that we destroyed part of the thing. So much for the 'we'—I lost my husband." She sighed and took another sip. "I know this much, Linni—there's something more to this story than just a local family you want to protect. The child is quite a charmer, isn't she?"

"Sophie, there is nothing to tell you, really. There are no big secrets, apart from the fact that you and I both have secrets, as you said. And as for the trio upstairs—yes, perhaps you've a point. I feel an affection for them. Jim was no saint in his early years, though coming from the Mackie family, it's hardly surprising, is it? But they are a lovely little unit, and—again, as you've said—we've seen so much heartbreak that I wanted to try to stop it touching Jim, Rose and Susie."

"Hmmm, alright. It's one of your weaker excuses, though I'll accept it because it's better than nothing. But here's the thing that bothers me." Sophie sighed, her gaze drawn across the room to a photograph on the wall of her late brother and sister. Elinor recognized the look—she had seen it one day in Kensington Gardens, when Sophie stared toward the place where her brother had trained in a royal park's make-believe trenches, a simulation that would be nothing like the real thing. "The part that bothers me, Elinor," Sophie continued, "is that these people you're getting mixed up with are killers. Even the police who are after them are killers. And I guessed long ago, Linni, that you also had to do your bit in that department—but if you put yourself up against that lot, there is going to be a very, very bad ending." She shrugged and reached out to take her friend's hand. "I just don't want the bad ending to be yours."

Elinor looked down into the brandy glass still held in her other hand. Tired and distracted in the moment, she began thinking how much the color and movement of liquid in the glass resembled the evening sunset across golden fields, a source of wonder in her world only minutes before a knock at the door changed everything. She lifted the glass to her lips, wincing and gripping Sophie's hand as she swallowed against the bite of brandy at her throat. "Sophie, I've already had one very bad ending—I'm trying hard not to have another."

Jim Mackie remained at the kitchen table after a breakfast prepared by Sophie and Elinor, who did their best to entertain with old stories of the terrible food endured at school, which they maintained had prepared them for the rationing that was to come when war broke out again. Soon, though, Sophie declared she had to prepare for several days of lectures at the university and "some other work" in London, during which time she would be staying at the flat she and her husband had bought before the war. The house in Burwash, she explained, had been her family home; she inherited it when her parents died.

"I'll be away for a night or two, but you must stay here. I'll show you and Rose where to find everything. I've let the gardener and my daily, Mrs. Moss, know that I have guests staying, so they won't be coming in this week."

"But Mrs. Hunt, Rose and me, we don't want you to go to all this trouble."

Elinor looked at the exhausted man, at his swollen face. "Jim, you have no other choice but to stay here. You cannot return to the cottage. I'm driving back to my house later this morning, so I will stop at the farm and explain to Mr. Wicks that you have been taken poorly after a fall, and you'll be returning to work in a few days. I will vouch for you."

"You don't know my family—it won't be over in a few days."

"One step at a time, Jim," counseled Elinor. "Just one step at a time."

Now they were alone, Sophie having repaired to her study while Rose carried Susie out into the garden to play.

"Miss White, I could see you know how to look after yourself, but really, you should stay away too. They'll come for you."

Elinor nodded. "Let me deal with it, Jim—and it's better sooner rather than later." She poured more tea for them both and pushed the sugar bowl toward Jim.

He shook his head. "I gave it up because it was easier than cutting down. I dunno, things are getting worse, not better, aren't they? What with the butter and meat ration being cut again, and the war's been over for two years. They say the bacon ration will be halved by this autumn. One thing about being a farmworker, you get an extra cheese ration." He gave a half-laugh. "Which is just as well, because Susie does like her cheese."

Elinor agreed about the ration situation, encouraging an easing of conversation to a point where she could ask a few more pertinent questions.

"You know, we went up to London on the train last October," said Jim. "I took a day off that was owing to me, so we thought we'd go to that exhibition the papers were going on about—it was called 'Britain Can Make It.' I thought it would be a bit of a tonic, you know, doing things other people do for a bit of fun. Then all we heard was people saying, "Britain can make it? It should be called 'Britain Can't Take It!'" The papers were full of it, and I started to wonder, you know, if perhaps the war wasn't worth winning. The countries that lost have come off rationing, and the likes of my so-called family up there in London are still making a fortune on the black market." He wiped the back of his hand across his eyes. "You know, all I ever wanted was to go straight."

"I know that, Jim."

"The war gave me a chance, and I came out of the army with a clean slate. My record was clean. I met Rose when I was stationed in London, and when we had Susie we knew it was time to get away from the Smoke, get away from where I was brought up." He leaned forward, elbows on the table. "You know, people think the world of my family in our part of London. They think the good old Mackies are keeping the streets clean of filth that the police don't care about or can't get rid of. But from London Bridge down to Greenwich, the boroughs south of the river are like a crime-infested swamp." Tears filled his eyes again. "And the swamp followed me and did this to my family, and all we wanted was quiet. Look, Miss White, I wasn't as pure as the driven snow growing up. But I knew what I was doing was bad, and let me tell you, being sent to a borstal was a big old lesson for me, and like a lot of others, the war was my ticket out."

"You've done well, Jim—I know people in the village like you and Rose very much, and of course everyone loves Susie."

"I hate my name, Miss White. I hate the Mackie family. Terrible thing to say, but I hate them."

"Forgiveness is the most difficult of journeys, Jim. Don't be hard on yourself." Elinor sipped tea that was now lukewarm.

"And you know how they get away with it?" Jim Mackie once again leaned forward, elbows on the table. "They pull strings as far up as the government, and they pull them hard."

"How do they do that, Jim? I mean, I can appreciate it's a way to control how things turn out, but how does a family like yours get into government?"

"I reckon you can guess, Miss White—after all, it's what goes on everywhere. It's why you had a place to bring us for a few days. It's why you know how to use that gun of yours. It's always down to who you know, and who that someone knows, and then they know another someone who knows a secret, and one secret leads to the next and before you know it, a piece of work like my dad has got the prime minister by the . . . well, you know what I mean."

"The prime minister?"

"Wouldn't surprise me. He pulls strings that go a long way, and don't let's even talk about the police."

Elinor pressed her lips together, her thoughts racing back over the past few weeks.

"Jim, does the name Peregrine Gordon-Williams ring any bells?"

He shook his head. "Not a name that I ever heard mentioned, but remember, I've been the black sheep of the family for a good while now, even before we came down here." He touched his face. "Well, I was out of the family until they needed me."

Elinor shrugged. "What about the police?"

"There's a lot of straight ones, but a good number of them are as bent as nine-bob notes." He lifted his left hand and rubbed his thumb against his two forefingers. "Money talks in all sorts of ways, and the Mackies will pay to make a profit."

"Yes, that's what I was afraid of," said Elinor.

"But remember what I said—it's what they know about the police that gives them power. If a copper is seeing someone who's not his wife, and one of my dad's people finds out about it—that's another one in the net, landed like a dopey fish. A copper might be found in a well, let's say a tricky position, and that sort of thing becomes knowledge for the family, and there's power again. They're like the sort of worm that works its way into a wooden house—one starts nibbling, and before you know it there's loads of them chomping away and the house falls down. See what I mean? That's how knowledge works, and my dad is a master of it." He shook his head, fatigue curving his shoulders forward, as if to protect his heart. "I was in the army, so I'm not silly—we all know what the intelligence bods do—but let me tell you, all this intelligence lark works on the other side of the law too." Jim Mackie stared at Elinor. "So, I reckon crime is like war, or war's a crime—sometimes I wonder which way the wind blows."

Elinor took a deep breath. There was more she wanted to know, and though she was tired and Jim seemed exhausted, he was in full flow, as if with every word he was cleansing darkness from his soul.

"Tell me about your aunt—about Elsie Finch."

Jim rolled his eyes and smiled. "You've asked about her before, haven't you? You know, I'm really fond of Auntie Elsie." He sat back in his chair, more relaxed. "She's had a lot to put up with, I reckon. My dad and his brothers watch out for her well enough, but they expect her to be the one to make sure my granddad is looked after. I always thought she had more going on upstairs than they gave her credit for. It was always 'Elsie do this' and 'Elsie do that,' and she did whatever the boys wanted of her. I saw the same thing happening to my cousins, the girls, that is."

"I think everyone must have been surprised when she married Abe Finch."

Jim inclined his head as he regarded Elinor. "You know about that as well? In fact, now I come to think about it, you know a lot about my aunt."

"Don't get angry, Jim," said Elinor. "I too have to know who's around me. I saw Rose crying outside your house when your brothers came the first time, so it made sense to find out a bit more about who your brothers were. I didn't know you very well then, and I probably don't know you well enough now, but I always looked forward to seeing Rose and Susie when I walked into the village. I didn't like what was happening to you."

"Sorry—I jumped there," said Jim. "I'm just edgy." He smiled. "I dunno if there's much more to tell you about my auntie. She has the same birthday as me—the fifth of May, so I suppose that's why she's sort of obsessed with the number five. Loves it. If she has a flutter on the horses, there has to be a five in there somewhere, and she's even more excited if the number is in the nag's name. When me and my brothers and cousins turned five, she would throw us parties with balloons, cake and jelly. She really went to town—especially on my birthday, it being hers as well. We put it down to the fact that she didn't have any nippers of her own." He shook his head and rubbed his eyes. "Anyway, she's got a few of her own little jobs going—it's just a bit of shoplifting, to be honest. My dad and my uncles let her do what she wants, as long as she doesn't bring home trouble and they don't have to worry about Grand-dad. As for poor old Uncle Abe—well, they sort of tolerated him if he kept away from their business. I don't think they were sorry when he died. In fact they were quite happy about it, because she had more time for Granddad. Abe might have been small-time as far as the brothers were concerned, but Aunt Elsie thought the world of him, and he loved her—you could see it in their eyes."

Elinor looked up at the clock. "I should leave now, Jim. And you must remain here until I let you know it's safer to return. I'll be in touch."

"Miss White—"

"Please—don't worry, Jim. I have a feeling that whatever your family needs you for might well cease to be of importance soon enough. I would imagine getting you back to drive a fast motor car is becoming too much trouble for them anyway."

"Drive a motor car?"

"Isn't that what you were sent down for in the first place? Driving a motor car away from the scene of a robbery?"

"Yeah, but there's plenty of blokes can do that."

"Then what is it? Can you tell me?"

"Miss White, I became an explosives expert in the army. I'm only used to being behind the wheel of a doddering old tractor now, but you never forget how to blow things up. That was what I learned first—I went through all the training before I was transferred to bomb disposal because I had such a steady touch. Being good at making and laying explosives makes you better and more careful at handling the detonators when you're looking at one of them big German bombs. And though I say it myself, I was the best of the bunch. Came sort of natural to me." He leaned forward. "My family wants me back because they're planning the biggest bank job in history. And the trouble is, since this last visit, I know all about it. That's why I lost my temper. Even if they get someone else, because of my training and my previous, I'll be the one the police finger when they do their investigating, and my brothers made it clear the family wouldn't lift a hand to save me. They told me I might as well stuff my pride and get on with it, and if I did, they'd put the coppers onto someone else who would take the fall—because the boys in blue always want a swift solution, and most of the time they don't care if they get the wrong bloke sent down."

Elinor did not rush her journey home to Shacklehurst. Before leaving Burwash, she placed a telephone call to Scotland Yard and left a message for Steve Warren to the effect that her neighbor—the one they had talked about—had received another visit from his brothers, and that she had sent them on their way.

"Does he know what this means?" asked Val.

"Yes, and you can tell him my neighbors are now staying with a friend of mine, so they're not at home. However—" Elinor ran the telephone cord through her fingers.

"However what, Miss White?"

"However, do let him know that I am expecting a visit from the family myself."

"Alrighty. All very cryptic, but I'm used to that. I'll give him the message as soon as he shows his face."

"Do you know when that might be?"

"You know DCI Warren, Miss White. That's like asking how long's a ray of sunshine. Mind you—I can tell you that just before he nipped out, I put through a call from his old mate, 'Sah Pereh,' so they could be lunching together, and that means he'll be gone for a while."

"Hmmm. Charlie and Bob not there to talk to?"

"No, they're out working."

"Thank you, Val. Much appreciated."

Approaching the house, Elinor took note of the black motor car parked just inside the turning to an adjacent field—not outside the house, though close enough for anyone to walk to her home.

"Well, it looks like I might have to deal with the man pulling the strings sooner rather than later." Elinor said the words aloud, and as she heard the echo of her own voice, she felt her hands begin to shake and a frisson of alarm run through her. "And his henchmen." Yet she smiled as another thought came to her.

Good, I could do with a dose of fear.

CHAPTER 18

Yes, they would be waiting for her. She suspected it would be John Mackie, Jim's father, accompanied by the brothers and perhaps another "associate" or two. She didn't think the Mackies would want to get their hands dirty taking out their anger on a woman, though there was that one big thug in the litter, the man who was bursting out of his Savile Row suit as if rationing had passed him by. If she didn't go back to the house, they would of course leave, though someone would stay—the man with the boots—and he would remain until she arrived home, at which point he would detain her, and it might well become brutal. The others would return. They would do whatever it was they had planned, her payback for getting involved in their private Mackie business. Perhaps they had a point.

But now, lingering by the fence, she knew she had time. Time to think, to reflect; and in that moment, she knew she had to stare memories in the face again. Not because they were deep inside, because they weren't—they jostled her every single day, lingering at the edge of everything she did, even on the good days. They were the memories that inspired her to act when she first saw Rose weeping, gripping her child while her husband was being beaten inside their home, the place where they should have been safe. Home is where everyone deserves to be safe.

Elinor clambered over the gate that led to a path through woodland at the edge of Denbury Forest, and continued until she reached a clearing. There she sat on the ground, her back against the trunk of an ancient tree. Even if someone passed, they would not know she was there; Elinor was always disguised. She had been trained to wear spring colors in spring, summer colors for warm sunny days, and she could walk through an autumn or winter forest and no one would see her move. She closed her eyes as sun filtered through the canopy overhead, and as if baring her chest for a blade to enter, she drew back the veil that kept 1944 at bay.

The doctor at the hospital in Oxford inspected the head wound, peering at her scalp and touching the flesh here and there with a disinfected swab while checking the stitches.

I could have used his scalpel, thought Elinor, as she stared at an array of instruments laid out on a tray. She flinched, feeling her skin move and the odd sharp pain. *I wouldn't have made such a mess of things if I'd found one of those—any one would have been the perfect tool.*

"Nasty fall, Captain White," said the doctor, placing the swab in a bowl and washing his hands at the sink before reaching for a clipboard with her hospital record. His name was Dr. Daniel Wright. She knew the nurses giggled about his name. She had heard speculation about how Dr. Wright might become some lucky girl's Mr. Right. "Now, tell me—what, exactly, did you hit your head on? I see you've been inoculated for tetanus." Wright looked up at her over the clipboard. "That's a godsend."

"I'm not sure, but I think it was a sort of metal part of a barrow, the rim around a wheel or the hub. And I didn't fall—I was pushed down."

"Hmmm, yes, I see. Major Warren reported that incoming fire from the enemy led you to take cover, which was when you fell."

"Did he tell you about the little girl?"

The doctor flicked through a couple of pages. "No. No, not seeing anything about a girl here." He looked up at her again.

Elinor nodded, tears forming at the corners of her eyes. "I . . . you see . . . I . . . um . . ."

Wright placed a hand on her arm, just above the thick white bandage around her left wrist. "Captain—Elinor—you really can't say anything to me. The fact that you were on the hospital ship at all has been treated with the utmost secrecy. I don't know any more than that, and I do not want to know."

Elinor nodded. "What happened to Major Warren?"

"Again, I don't know. I'm only a lowly doctor who will make a decision regarding your transfer."

"I don't need to go to a convalescent home."

"Captain White, I will agree that beyond the matter of healing from a very bad concussion, you will likely not require any occupational or neurological therapies. However, there is the other issue."

"What other issue?"

The doctor pulled up a chair and sat down so he was closer to Elinor. She wondered if he was old enough to be a doctor; he seemed so young. Wright was no more than a boy. Perhaps he was a student, or another sort of medic. He was in the army—she could see the uniform underneath the white coat—and his hair seemed to have been cut by a military barber. His round spectacles and pallor gave him the appearance of one who had never quite shrugged off a layer of schoolroom chalk dust.

"What other issue?" Elinor repeated.

"Captain White, you tried to kill yourself. You found a bottle in a cupboard on the ship, you smashed the top against the metal sink and you tried to slit your wrist." He turned his head to see if anyone passing might hear. "I am sure you are very good at what you do, and I am doubly sure that if you wanted to use a broken bottle against an enemy, he would be dead. But you are not dead, and that tells me something."

"And what might that be?" asked Elinor.

"It tells me that whatever happened to you, whatever ails you—at the end of the day, you really do want to live."

"No, I don't."

"I believe otherwise." He smiled and took her hand. "When I was a student, we had a professor who was a very odd sort. Always doling out stories from his vast medical experience. Here's what he told us one day: 'Just remember that as the doctor, you are really only there to distract the patient while time and nature do the work of healing.' So, Captain Elinor, allow time and nature to heal you. Give yourself another stab at life—oh dear, sorry about the pun." He smiled, pushing back the chair as he came to his feet, and picked up the clipboard. "Right, I'll get the nurse to come in and bathe that wound and dress it again."

"What about the convalescence?"

"I'm told it's to be a rather nice requisitioned stately home near the coast somewhere. Not one I know, but when I tell them you're ready to leave, your transportation will be arranged. I understand a motor car will come for you."

Elinor shook her head.

"I'm sure you'll be well cared for, Captain White," said the doctor. "I'll have a look at the wound again tomorrow."

Yes, it was all smoke and mirrors." Elinor stared up into shafts of sunlight beaming to the ground. "Smoke and mirrors."

She had known, as the kind doctor with schoolboy spectacles described the plan for her convalescence, that she would indeed be looked after. She would be fed and examined, and then she would be debriefed;

time and again required to repeat what had happened, an inquisition planned to reveal what she knew and whether she could be trusted. Above all, though, she understood it would be an assessment of her mental health, her ability to keep secrets and whether what she had seen and done would render her a liability. Later, as a nurse bathed the wound across the side of her head, she did her best to smile, to feign lightheartedness of character. She would take a leaf out of her dear Cecily's book. "The trouble with you, Ceci," their mother had once observed, following one of Cecily's outbursts, "is that you've always been a bit of a Sarah Bernhardt—you should have gone on the stage."

Convalescence would become Elinor's stage. The curtains would draw back, the interrogators would filter in from left and right, and she would impress them with her turn of phrase, her recall and her record of accomplishment in the guise of Marianna, a woman who sold lipsticks, powder and rouge door-to-door. This little episode with a broken bottle? Goodness, that was quite the whack she had sustained when she fell, wasn't it? And how did she fall? It must have been the shock of it all, the unexpected German attack, the child running in the street and her attempt to save lives by aiming at the sniper in the tower. Yes, she would fool them all. And one day, one day at some point in the future, there would be a next time, and she would be sure to end the pain, because when the next time came, she would find the perfect tool.

Well, that had been the plan.

Time to face the music," said Elinor. She came to her feet, brushed fallen leaves from her coat and began to walk toward her house, that generous gift of a grace-and-favor home for service to king and country, along with a medal. As if she needed another piece of metal on a ribbon.

She took a deep breath before slipping her key into the lock, and called out when the door was only two inches open.

"Hello! Mr. Mackie, sorry to keep you waiting! Just let me take my shoes off, and I'll join you." She heard movement behind the door, a pistol readied. "Look, I don't have a weapon, but I really would have appreciated it if you'd seen that little sign outside the door. You know, the one requesting callers to 'Please remove your shoes.' "

Jim's brother, the one with thinning hair, an ill-fitting suit and a Luger in his hand, pushed her toward the drawing room, where the man she assumed was John Mackie waited, seated in the Queen Anne armchair alongside the inglenook fireplace. Two younger men sat opposite him; one she recognized first because she had held a gun to his neck. He was cut from the same cloth as his father, with features marking him as a son of the Mackie family. The other startled her—she knew who he was, but tried not to show panic as she struggled to make the connection.

John Mackie wore a deep-navy-blue suit, a flourish of pale-aqua silk at the chest pocket, an exact match for a tie embellished with a pin in the shape of a small gold riding whip. His oiled jet-black hair was greying at the temples. He was relaxed, his elbows resting on the arms of the chair, his hands together, manicured fingers steepled.

"Miss Elinor White, isn't it? By the way—do you think you'll ever go back to De Witt?"

Elinor shrugged. "I might. It depends upon what the future might hold, and where I might find myself."

"Indeed it does." Mackie nodded toward his son. "Get off that chair and let the lady sit there—pull the other one over here for yourself."

With the favored son situated alongside his father—who had not offered an introduction to either man—John Mackie began.

"I think you know who this is." He pointed to the man who did not resemble his son, but who looked to be about Jim Mackie's age. He wore a suit of small houndstooth check, a crisp white shirt and black tie. His brown hair appeared to be going prematurely grey.

Elinor nodded. "I do. Yes."

"But I bet you don't know his real name."

"No, you're right. I don't."

"Before we get to our friend there—by the way, it's Michael Kemp, only we like to call him Mick—let me say a few things."

"Of course—after all, you're a guest in my house."

Mackie raised an eyebrow. The man who had pushed her into the room took a step forward, but Mackie wagged a finger at him.

Elinor did her best to temper her breathing. She was on thin ice. Again.

"Miss White—I suppose they don't call you 'Captain' anymore—anyway, Miss White, you have been a little thorn in my side. In fact, because you've drawn unwanted attention to my family, I have decided to abandon a business plan, a lovely idea that would have been very lucrative." He shook his head. "And I hate having to do that, especially as in this case I hoped getting stuck into the job would bring my youngest boy back into the fold. Yes, yes, I should have known I was on a fool's errand, but a father has to make the effort."

"It was probably a good decision," said Elinor.

"Shut your mouth, and don't speak until he tells you to speak!"

Elinor could feel the thug brother's breath as he leaned closer.

"Now then, you have also been keeping some sort of company with my sister," said Mackie. "Lovely girl, our Elsie, but you know—not exactly top drawer. In any case, we always like to know a bit more about anyone who shows an interest in our family. I'm sure you get my point, Miss White; after all, it seems you understand secrets."

Elinor said nothing, though she hoped that when the time came, the man with the Luger was an expert shot, and the end would be quick.

"Since the little—what shall we call it?" Mackie feigned thoughtfulness. "Yes, since the little intervention you staged yesterday—and by the way, we were all very impressed with your sleight of hand—I thought it would be a good idea to have this chat, so you could see that we're really on your side."

"I'm sorry—I don't understand," said Elinor. "How could you possibly be on my side?"

Mackie leaned forward. "Because you have absolutely no bleedin' idea what you are tinkering with. If you're going to go into the hives, then you should do your homework and put on the right overalls and one of them silly hats so you don't get stung. And before you say another word, Miss White—and let's face it, you are a bit of an interrupter, aren't you?—let me tell you this, love. If you want to lift the lid off a hive, start with Scotland Yard. The second hive is the other intelligence service, the one what's not so irregular as your SOE. See, I know a lot more than you might have thought, thanks to our Mick over there. There's people—and one in particular—in Whitehall who've got the sting that will finish you off if you keep poking around while they're about the business of making honey. But I can protect you from all that, if you leave us alone."

Elinor frowned, feeling herself become lightheaded.

"Son, get the lady a glass of water. And be careful—I've heard she's a bit of a dab hand with glass."

It was clear Mackie was in no rush. He settled deeper into the chair. Michael Kemp had hardly moved. When a glass of water was in Elinor's hands, Mackie continued.

"Right, now we've got that out of the way, let me tell you about Mick, and how we know this young man. Remind me, what was his name when you knew him?"

Elinor cleared her throat. "Blaz. And he was supposed to have kept it quiet."

"I'm sure he was," said John Mackie. "But we're like family to Mick here. And what sort of name is Blaz, anyway?"

"He was assigned a Belgian name for his work," said Elinor. "I think you already know that."

"No accounting for taste, is there? Anyway, young Mick is one of Jim's oldest mates—always round our house, he was, as a nipper. Clever too—well, anyone who can speak another language is clever in my book. I never did pick up much Italian from my dad. Mick's pop brought home a bride after the last war—which is why he can hold a conversation in Belgian and English, though I reckon the English is dodgy at times!"

There was laughter among the men, a few words bandied around about Cockney rhyming slang.

"Anyway," continued Mackie. "Mick and our Jim got themselves into a bit of bother with the boys in blue, and as you know they were sent down for it and thanks to old Hitler, both of them were pulled out again to serve in the war. Jim learned what you might call a trade—and so did our Mick here. He learned a lot of things that have been very useful to us." He smiled at Mick Kemp. "Mick, why don't you tell the lady about it—it's your story, after all."

Elinor turned to the man she had last seen clutching a headset to his ears in a small coastal village in Belgium, some three years earlier. "Yes, I think I'd like to know the story."

"Miss White, I just want you to know one thing first. I couldn't tell you what was going on, it was more than I—"

John Mackie interrupted him. "Mick, come on, start at the beginning, son. Don't dive into the middle and work both ways at once like my missus."

Kemp turned his attention back to Elinor. "I was recruited to serve in Belgium because I can speak the language. They knew my background, and they knew I wasn't squeaky clean, but as the boss said—"

"Which boss?" asked Elinor, moving her head away from the Luger that was still too close to her ear.

"The woman who interviewed me, who brought me in."

Elinor sighed. "Commander Clare Fields—was that her name?"

"Yes, that's her. Anyway, you know, I went through all the training, and then it turned out the radio lark was easy. I've always been interested in how things work, you know—electricity and anything with wires. They told me I was a natural."

"You were. I'll give you that," said Elinor. "You were the best I'd worked with."

"This is where it gets interesting," said John Mackie.

Elinor's mind began racing ahead. "Stephen Warren—we called him Luc then—you reported to him. What was he up to?"

"I'm nearly there, Miss White."

"Go on, son," said Mackie. "Take your time, and try not to let her hold you up every time she can't stop herself butting in."

Elinor stared at Jim Mackie's father, a man who she knew could be brutal yet appeared to be demonstrating an unexpected empathy.

Kemp cleared his throat. "I was sending special messages for him— for Luc. Not to the usual place, but to another . . . another unit." He stared at Elinor. "Look, I don't know exactly where they were, but it wasn't my usual partner—I think the messages went to another intelligence service. There was a different frequency."

"Was there a code name mentioned? Or a message recipient?" asked Elinor.

Kemp nodded. "Yes. It was 'Falcon.' Luc told me it was all about how we had to limit risks because there was fresh intelligence coming through, with new instructions . . . and you know, I was just the bloke with the radio."

"Falcon?"

"Yes, Miss White. That was the code."

The brother standing close to Elinor tapped her with the Luger. She turned, for the first time taking account of the scarring on his face, the residue of wounds a skilled American surgeon could not erase.

"Sorry," said Elinor. "Just tell the story, Mick."

Kemp fiddled with his tie, adjusting it and running his finger inside his collar. "Right, so what happened was that where we were, in that village—it wasn't the real landing place for our boys and the Canadians. We became the decoy because apparently the Germans had got wind of what was up, so the plans were changed at the last minute."

Elinor bit her lip to stop herself blurting out a stream of questions.

Kemp waited, then went on. "They had what they called 'casualty estimates,' but there was also a plan to get you, me and Warren out of there before the Germans really got stuck in. Our escape was to be by boat from along the coast. It looked like a fishing boat, but it was fast—we managed to get you over to it, then straight to the ship from there. It was all really bad."

There was silence in the room.

"I'm just trying to get this all straight," said Elinor.

"I know, Miss White. It's a lot."

Elinor saw tears well up in Kemp's eyes, but pressed him. "I just want to be clear. The plan—the original plan—was not the real plan, according to Luc."

"That's the measure of it."

"The real plan, the one that came from this other department in London, was the opposite, so the British and Canadian troops were actually landing along the coast, and the Germans were lining up at the back of us, behind all our people and the families living in the village. The Germans were there waiting for an influx of Allied troops, and were ready to render the village a battlefield. Is that right?"

"Yes."

"We were the eleventh-hour stool pigeons, the decoy, call it what you will. The prey."

"Yes." Kemp seemed to choke on the word. "I was following orders, Miss White. Luc was my guv'nor, after all. And we all had to trust one another, didn't we?"

Elinor looked up to the ceiling. She didn't want to meet Kemp's eyes and she didn't want to look at John Mackie. She took another deep breath and brought her attention back to Kemp.

"So, the Germans began the attack—it's seared into my mind, I'll never forget it. A sniper was up in the tower—I had seen him right from the moment we went into the village. The sniper began firing, then . . ."

Elinor put her hand to her chest as her words faltered, her heart inflamed as a deep melancholy rose up again. "Then the child—the little girl—ran out because she had seen me from a window or something. You know, I'd given her lipsticks, and she remembered. She had somehow seen me in the square and ran toward me. And I killed her. I shot that child and I killed her. I don't know what happened after I fainted, but—"

Elinor pressed her hands to her eyes.

"Miss White, what are you talking about?"

She looked up. "I killed that child. You were there. I saw her on the ground. I wanted to go to her, and then, then . . ."

Kemp's eyes were wide, his brow furrowed as he shook his head. "No, no, no—no, that's not what happened. It wasn't like that."

"What do you mean? I saw it with my own eyes."

"You didn't kill that little girl."

"Was it the sniper?"

"No." He glanced toward Mackie.

"Tell her, son. Go on. Tell her. Don't hold back."

"Luc—Warren—was telling you to take her down before she led them right to us—the sniper had an idea of where we were, but her running down the street was drawing attention. You wouldn't do it, and so you aimed for the sniper, but Warren grabbed your gun and he did it." He wiped his eyes. "He panicked and he shot the little girl. You were in a terrible state when you saw her in the square, and because you were about to run out there to her, he pushed you down again, and you hit your head on the iron hub sticking out of the wheel on that old cart." He took a deep breath. "Horrible wound, it was. Wide open and bleeding something horrible, so I'm not surprised you don't remember it all. But it stopped you running where the sniper would see you."

Elinor felt a strange silence descend upon the room. Though she was aware of the everyday sounds—a tractor in the field beyond, a wood saw in the distance, and even a motor car passing on the road outside— she felt as if she were either ascending into heaven or descending into hell, and she wasn't sure which. Kemp's racking sobs returned her to the moment.

"I didn't kill the little girl?" Elinor could not speak above a whisper. "It wasn't me?"

Kemp nodded.

"But he . . . Major Warren visited me in hospital. They sent me to a mental hospital because they said I needed psychiatric help. They—"

"We got you out of the village, Miss White, and you were bleeding badly from the head. Luc carried you all the way to the boat. It was all really terrible, terrifying—I didn't think we would ever get away. I've not been so frightened in my life. And I never knew what happened to you after we went on board that ship. I haven't seen Luc—Major Warren—since, and you were taken off somewhere. For all I knew, you were dead."

"Weren't you debriefed?"

"You mean, brought into a room and told it was all part of the plan, and it had to remain secret? That was the beginning and end of it, and then I was allowed to go home. Only I had no home to go to because the house had been bombed out and my mum and dad moved down to the country with my sister to stay with my aunt, and I just . . . I wasn't well myself." Kemp looked at John Mackie. "If you don't mind, Mr. Mackie . . . Miss White, I'm going to go out to your garden. I'll answer any more questions in a minute or two. I feel, you know, under the weather. Just need a bit of fresh air."

Elinor said nothing, her mind racing, memories surging forth, images clashing in her mind's eye. Images that had never been quelled by the electric shocks to her brain.

"Miss White," said John Mackie. "Miss White—can you hear me?"

"Sorry, yes. Yes, go on."

"Let me tell you what happened to Mick. He came home and couldn't settle, so I decided to help him out because I'm nobody's fool and it was obvious to me that the lad hadn't been in the proper army. You had it rough, but so did he, and he had no one to help. My business isn't aboveboard, but we don't deal in narcotics—we keep them off the street. Mick was starting to take pills, anything to stop the shaking and nightmares. I couldn't see him go down the drain, so I got him to tell me everything, and you know, in my business, his sort of story is money in the bank, and—"

"That's how you've got DCI Warren and a government minister who went by the name 'Falcon' under your thumb. You know the truth and its terrible consequences. And you know Warren killed a child, which in wartime is a crime, even if it's not on the books. You use that information to carry on your business without consequences."

"They're allowed a win every now and again, Miss White—after all, we like to be in a position to pull strings in high places, so we have to keep *our* stool pigeons nice and cozy."

"Isn't Kemp in danger? They could kill him."

"They could, but it wouldn't do them any good."

"I don't understand."

"I like to see a young man make something of himself, especially if he's a worker like our boys—and Mick Kemp is a worker. He's got a gift when it comes to anything with electrical sounds, that sort of thing, and you know, I reckon it's the future, and a man like me has to think ahead. The BBC started that television thing again after the war, and even though they've stopped it because we've got a fuel crisis, Mick reckons that next year, what with the Olympics, it'll be a bumper year. People will go out and buy a television set on the never-never, or a new radiogram, or a wireless, so I set him up in a little business. 'Kemp's Television and Wireless.' He's got his own shop in Peckham, sales and repairs, and he's doing very well for himself. And more to the point, he's got an in with an inventor friend at EMI, where they're fiddling around making this thing called a tape recorder."

"A what?"

"It records voices and it's called a reel-to-reel."

"This is all very interesting, Mr. Mackie, but about Mick—"

Mackie shrugged. "Have it your way—but I thought you'd like to know that Mick put it all on tape—or more to the point, Warren and the other bloke think he put it all on tape. So he's safe, because they reckon we have his voice telling the whole story. Personally, I'd rather he had it on a record—that's something I understand. But we keep them playing our game because we know your detective friend was working both sides of the intelligence racket—which means they ignore what we're doing most of the time. Warren was a plant from one secret section to another because the toff had him by the you-know-whats and probably told him it was all in the interests of the country." Mackie tapped the side of his nose. "Amazing what you can find out when you sniff around where these upper-class types went to school, don't you think? Knowledge is a wonderful thing, Miss White. It's what built our business from the day my dad stepped off the boat after working his way across to England on a merchant ship."

Elinor sat back and rubbed her head along the temple, hearing the whole story again as if she had one of those new-fangled recorders in her mind. "I wonder if . . . if Peregrine Gordon-Williams was playing another side too."

"Clever lady."

"The Nazis?"

"To be fair, Miss White, I reckon some of them had to be what they call double agents, but there again, it's in the past now, and I don't care who they fraternized with as long as I've got them under my thumb."

"Mr. Mackie, why have you told me all this? It's surely not in your interests to let me in on what's going on in your . . . in your line of work, though I . . . I—" Elinor held her hand to her chest and felt her voice catch. "I don't know what to say to you, because I've had to live believing I took the life of a child."

Mackie nodded to the man who had been standing next to Elinor since she had first been invited to take a seat in her own home. He turned to his other son—who had still not said a word.

"Bobby, go and get Mick. He's still feeling a bit rough, and we should take him home." He smiled at Elinor. "Tell Jim he can come back to that half-derelict shoebox down the road they call a house. We don't need him. That's what this is about. We won't ever call on him again.

My wife would like to see little Susie, but we won't push if he doesn't want to come."

"I suppose I'm in your debt now," said Elinor.

"I suppose you are, but I'm not in the business of giving jobs to ladies who know how to use a gun. But keep that in mind all the same—about the debt. Nice that Elsie has a friend, though—she doesn't get out much."

Elinor remained in the small drawing room as the men departed. The house was quiet again, still, the only sound coming from a pair of thrushes calling to each other in the tree outside. She stood up, went into the kitchen and opened a bottle of single-malt whisky. Pouring a good two fingers' worth into a glass, she drank the measure without pause and poured again, this time taking one sip at a time while standing at the sink and staring across the fields.

John Mackie had not become some sort of criminal saint overnight, but he wanted her to tell his son that he was off the hook. He had shone a light on the truth—though only time would reveal if any account would be presented to her for being in receipt of such a revelation. After all, there might be some honor in the thief, but she knew there was little in the way of a soul, despite any appearances to the contrary.

Elinor sighed. In one way her job was done—Jim, Rose and Susie were safe now. But . . . but . . . at the same time, another task had emerged, another account arising from Michael Kemp's story. She had questions about the proximity of the hospital ship, the sojourn in Oxford, her assessment and debriefing at that mansion in who knows where—another requisitioned stately home, this one very secret. Then there was yet another transfer. She remembered asking, "Where are you taking me now?" A man in uniform had leaned toward her. "It's to a place where we can help you, Miss White. You've had a very nasty wound, so we're going to get you the best treatment for it, make you feel better again, lift the melancholia."

Lift the melancholia?

The so-called lifting of her melancholia was a foul protocol that almost blew her brain out of her skull. "It will eliminate the pain in your mind," the faceless, nameless doctors had said. So Elinor had become a first-class patient, giving the right answers to questions and playing the game to get out, though she soon developed greater skill in poking pills into her cheek with her tongue and spitting them into the palm of her hand. She was released after a month, with the words of young Dr. Wright still fresh in her mind. *Let time and nature do the work of healing.*

Pressing a hand to her temple, she banished those memories from her mind as if taking photographs to a bonfire, until she was left with the one that would never fade. A child cut down by gunfire in a village square, her little white dress stained with blood, flapping in the breeze while her mother screamed, held back by her family. She remembered it all now.

Elinor White swallowed the remaining whisky in one more gulp and poured herself yet another. Then she howled and threw the glass at the wall.

"You bastard, Warren. You lying, murdering bastard!"

CHAPTER 19

Once more Elinor traveled by train to London. She could not take the Riley, because she would need her petrol and mileage allowance to collect Jim, Rose and Susie and bring them home to Shacklehurst on the morrow. She felt no anxiety during the journey, though she would admit to something of a headache.

A desk sergeant on duty recognized Elinor as she entered Scotland Yard, touching a finger to his helmet as he greeted her. "Morning, madam. Lovely day, isn't it? I don't think you're in luck today. DCI Warren's out on a call."

"Not to worry. Nothing urgent anyway—but is it alright if I go up? I just want a quick word with Val."

The policeman frowned, but acquiesced, allowing Elinor to continue on her way to the offices where DCI Stephen Warren and his crew were situated.

"Good morning, Val. How are you?"

"Morning to you, Miss White. They're all out at the moment, but I just had DCI Warren on the blower—he's on his way back in, but not staying long when he gets here."

"I'll wait in his office."

"He might be a little while—you never know with traffic. Would you like a cuppa?"

"Love one—thank you, Val."

"I could do with another too."

"Something up?"

"I'll say."

"What is it?"

"Big job been pulled off—I don't have the details yet. Anyway, you go in, and I'll bring you a cup of tea."

Elinor sipped the tea—thankfully hot and not too strong—and waited. She was seated on Warren's chair behind his desk, and after Val left her and closed the door, she slipped the Welrod pistol from her handbag and set it on the desk in front of her. It had been the agents' weapon of choice, known for being almost silent when discharged. She was deep in thought, holding her teacup and looking at the gun, when the door opened.

"Linni, look, I haven't the time—" Warren stared at the pistol.

"Sit down, Steve. Make yourself comfortable."

"What the—"

"Just sit down, would you?"

Warren pulled back the chair and slumped into it, loosening his tie. "I don't know what this is about, Linni, but I am not in the mood—"

"Neither am I, Steve, so I will get straight to the point." She lifted the pistol and pointed it at him, her right forefinger flanking the barrel. "Oh dear, now I've said that, I find myself unable to pinpoint exactly where I should start, but let me just dig in. A visitor to my house yesterday admonished a young man we both know for starting a story in the middle and working both ways at once. I now think that might be my best bet. Oh, it was a very interesting story, by the way. The young man sends his regards, though I will say, he looks a good deal older than when we knew him. The past three years haven't been kind to his nerves, but he's doing well for himself. Do you remember him? He's back to his real name now, though to us I suppose he will always be Blaz."

Elinor smiled, watching any remaining color drain from Steve Warren's face.

"Hmmm, thought you'd remember. Nice lad. Absolutely brilliant radio operator." She waved the pistol as if using it as a prop to emphasize her words. "You know, he's even better with this sort of—what would you call it? 'Sound' business? Oops, double meaning there. A sound business in the sound business!" Her laugh was deliberate, shallow. "Anyway, I know he has a very special recording of the whole story— you know, the tale of what really happened in September 1944. In that unimportant little Belgian village."

"Look, Linni, I can explain."

"No, Steve, you can't. There is nothing you can do to justify the killing of a child. There is nothing you can do to explain why you allowed me to think I had fired my gun at a five-year-old and taken her life. You told me I had to do what I had to do, and then you did it—you killed little Anique. You killed her, and you didn't have the guts to admit it."

"Don't you think I'm haunted too?"

"And we ended up smack in the middle of the real fight we had set up to happen a few miles along the coast, because you and your bloody falcon friend had other plans and brought them right to our door. You were the inside plant for another government intelligence service run by your old school chum. You undermined the SOE, with terrible consequences."

"I—"

"Oh, shut up. Nothing can ever put this right. I don't care if your old mate in Whitehall and his lot had a better plan than the one in motion—or should I say, the one that I and the others *thought* was in motion. And I don't care if he did his sums, and all those men and women who trusted us and put their lives at risk because they loved their country were just . . . what? A statistic? A casualty number? None of it makes sense, because you are a liar, a coward, a Judas and a murderer."

She pointed the pistol at him.

"You wouldn't dare."

"You're right. I wouldn't. Not here, not now and probably not ever— mind you, I might change my mind, and we both know you won't hear me coming. I want you to know that I can and will dare when I want, and I'm enjoying the look on your face." She rested the Welrod on the desk in front of her, stroking the barrel with her hand. "When you get home, Steve, stick your finger in an electrical socket and imagine what that feels like when the current runs into your head. They had no need to do it to me in that so-called convalescent home, and you were aware it was going on. I knew then that it was a warning, and I know even more now. You came to see me there, and just once more later to tell me about your bloody promotion. Did you think the treatment would eradicate all memories of what happened? Eh? Did you think I'd forget? I hate you, Steve. I hate the very ground you walk on."

"Linni, please, don't say—"

Elinor moved the gun to her lap as Bob Mills knocked and entered. "Sorry to disturb you, sir, and Miss White. Sir—there's more coming in. It's a bigger one than we thought, and we don't know who the heck is behind it."

"Alright, Bob. I'm coming."

"Charlie's waiting down at the front in the Humber. Bye, Miss White. Nice to see you." Mills left and closed the door.

"You'd better go, Steve. I won't lay eyes on you again—but I should let you know that our friend Blaz was in touch with his mate, you know, the one with the new-fangled recording machine. It turned out to be a very promising connection. I know you know about that machine—now, what did they call it? A tape recorder? Anyway, something like that. It was quite amazing, because I was able to record my whole story, just like Blaz. Beginning to end. Heaven knows how I'd be able to play it back, though I am sure someone would help me, in a push—someone like John Mackie." Elinor paused, lifting the Welrod and tapping it on the desk as if to emphasize her point. "Oh, and by the way, I didn't know you and Mr. Mackie were so pally, in touch all the time, and with that friend of yours. Peregrine Gordon-Williams. Falcon. It's been one surprise after another."

Warren scraped back his chair and stood by the door. "Linni, all that mattered to me was getting you out of Belgium alive. Getting you home. You were all that mattered—to me." He turned away and left the office.

Elinor remained still, staring at the closed door, until she took a deep breath and secured the Welrod in her shoulder bag.

They all seemed in a bit of a rush there, Val." Elinor had left the office, and was pulling on a pair of leather gloves as she chatted with the secretary. "Looked like 'all hands on deck'—so what is it? A bank job?"

Val widened her eyes. "A bank? No—" She leaned forward, ready to share a confidence, though there was no one remaining in the office. "There's more to it than one bank. It all started first thing this morning, and it was fast."

"What was fast? You're stringing it out, Val—I'm curious."

"Well, the first we heard was that a bank had been held up in

Sutton. Then another in Dorking, one more in Reigate, one in—where was it? Yes, Brighton, and then Eastbourne. The boys were just starting to move when a call came in about post offices, one after the other. Boom-boom-boom. Then the jewelers started calling in. And now it's the shops—the big ones. Liberty, Dickins and Jones, Fenwick, Harrods, Harvey Nichols, and—"

"Five big shops? Five banks?"

Val nodded, but held up one finger as she answered the telephone when it started to ring. She made notes, nodding as if the caller could see her, and then said, "Thank you very much—I'll let him know as soon as I can." She looked up at Elinor. "Well, blow me down."

"Val?"

"We're up to five post offices."

"Do they know who yet?"

She shook her head. "The word on the street is that all the usuals are spoken for. Everyone's mystified. Looks like a completely new lot— they're already calling them the 'Gang of Five'—though there must be at least ten of them! But you know the funny thing?"

"What's that?"

Val laughed. "I'm starting my new job at the BBC on Monday, so now I come to think about it, I don't care about telling you—but there are reports that it's all women. Even though they're dressed like men, witnesses have said they're a bit spry, light on their feet. Like women."

"Anyone hurt?"

She shook her head. "No one—and that makes a change."

"I look forward to reading about it in the evening papers. Good luck with the new job, Val."

Elinor did not smile as she departed Scotland Yard, though as she walked across the street to avoid activity outside, she could not help but whisper, "No one's under-esteemating you now, Elsie." She had no doubt that within hours Elsie Finch, née Mackie, would be in a Portuguese village or the French Riviera, perhaps Spain or even farther afield, raising a glass of champagne with her coterie of helpers, all young women who wanted something London wasn't offering. It wasn't the way she would have gone about getting even, but at least no one had died—which was more than she could say for her own work.

On the train home to Shacklehurst, Elinor felt a new fatigue envelop her. She had fought two wars and many skirmishes in between. Perhaps it was time to consider what might come next, though there was still one more person she wanted to call to account—if nothing else, for her own peace of mind. It would be an easy enough journey, as the destination was not too far from Burwash, where she would collect Jim, Rose and Susie from Sophie's house. She stopped at the telephone kiosk when she arrived in the village, where she placed a call to Sophie, asking her to let Jim know she would see them at noon the following day.

Glancing down at the address one more time, Elinor found the small fifteenth-century cottage on a narrow thoroughfare flanked by a mishmash of other dwellings from the fourteenth to nineteenth centuries. There was a pub on the corner, and if she had walked farther along toward the High Street, she would have passed two tea shops, four more pubs, a butcher, a baker and, thought Elinor, if the children's rhyme was anything to go by, probably a candlestick maker. She parked the motor car not far away from the neighboring Battle Abbey, named for the famous battle that had brought Norman invaders to England's shores, and close to a footpath that would take ramblers across a patchwork of farmland, forest and fields. It was a nice town, she thought; cozy, with enough visitors by train, bus or motor coach to distract attention from any locals who valued their privacy. She knocked on the door and waited.

"Coming!" a voice called out from inside the home.

Elinor heard footsteps approaching the door and two bolts being pulled back.

"Linni!"

"Don't look so surprised, Clare—I daresay you were expecting me. Oh, and you can put down the pistol in your other hand. I'm not armed."

"Nor should you be. Come in—your timing's good, the kettle's just boiled."

Elinor followed Clare Fields—the woman she had once known as Isabelle—into the kitchen, where she sat down at the table.

"Lovely house, Clare."

"Usual thing—only costs me a peppercorn rent until the day I die, thanks to the crown."

"I might have guessed you'd end up in a town named Battle."

"Yes, it is quite a lark. By the way, I'm brewing coffee. I am so sick of tea this and tea that." Fields seated herself opposite Elinor and poured strong black coffee. "They say a nice cup of tea pulled us through everything from the Boer War to the Blitz, but all I can taste now is weak and insipid Darjeeling-flavored hot water." She pushed a cup toward Elinor. "Though of course, there were those times with your mother and sister, in the first war, all sitting round the table. Another terrible time when I drank tea that tasted like dishwater in so many kitchens. Probably why I think of tea as the devil's brew."

"The Great War was a lifetime ago."

Fields stared at Elinor. "Funny, isn't it? You and I seem almost of a similar age now, though you've kept your features more than I have. I was only twenty-four when I first came to your house—about ten years older than you when I took you to the border."

"I'm not here to talk about how well either you or I have aged. Can we discuss what happened in 1944? What did you know, Clare? Be honest, could you have warned me?"

Fields shook her head. "Linni—I warned you as much as I could. I told you I didn't trust him, but I wasn't quite sure of myself. I explained how the SOE was viewed by other intelligence departments. They hated us, hated Churchill's support of us, and more than anything they detested the fact that we brought in skilled operatives wherever we could find them—even among the lower classes. That's what they called some of our people. Lower classes. Blaz was a case in point—a real Cockney lad from south of the river, but he knew his stuff; he had a solid fist for the codes, and we needed that kind of innate understanding. We didn't want to restrict ourselves to boys from upper-class families who thought they had an in by dint of their name, or were beholden to the old school tie." She gave a long exhale and stared at Elinor. "There was another reason I wanted you to keep a personal distance from Warren. It wouldn't have lasted, and—and he was in love with you, Linni. In truth, he still burns a torch for you. I knew I could trust you not to do anything stupid—beyond sharing his bed—but I couldn't trust him."

"I doubt . . ." Elinor faltered. "Yes, you're right. You could trust me, Clare. But . . . but did you know what was happening? Did you know about the last-minute change of plans?"

Fields shook her head. "No, and by the time I found out, we were on the back foot. I had the hospital ship diverted at great expense and risk."

"Expense—how?"

"I was sent lower down the pecking order. A few rungs, in fact, where there was less chance of me poking my nose into places where the boys didn't want it." She shrugged. "Affected my pension too."

"Did you know what was happening to me?"

"I hit a brick wall called Peregrine Gordon-Williams."

"But you knew about Anique, the little girl?"

Fields stared at Elinor. "In time I heard rumors. Reports implicating Warren came back to me, but as far as we knew, a local child was killed by a German sniper."

"You could have told me. I thought I'd killed her. You knew where to find me, just as I knew where to find you here. You owed it to me."

Fields sighed. "Owed? Oh, Linni. *Owed-owed-owed*. How we use that word—I owe you, you owe me. I asked people to do things, and they did them, but I don't ever remember forcing anyone to do anything. I might have come back a few times to that school to see if you'd change your mind about joining us at the SOE, but I never put you in shackles. Yes, your country owed you a debt of gratitude for wartime service that put you in danger—but tell that to the ATS girls who died at their posts while 'manning' ack-ack batteries. Tell that to the women blown up making bombs in munitions factories, or the other women who died doing exactly what you did, only they were caught and sent to Ravensbrück. Even if I told you, you wouldn't be able to imagine what happened to them." She shook her head. "I thought it best to let sleeping dogs lie, to just let everything go. And there was another reason."

"It had better be a good one."

Fields slammed her right hand down onto the wooden table, glaring at Elinor. "I was bloody tired too, Linni. Is that good enough for you? I was doing my best, and it wasn't always right, and I did it over two wars with everything in the middle—during which time I was in Berlin and Munich, and that wasn't a picnic either. So I was tired then, and I am tired now. I will probably still be tired in ten years' time. I didn't want to talk about the war, and unlike some of our brethren, I didn't want to have little reunion parties to natter about the good old days either, you know, those good old days when we went about the business of killing people. It was over, and I had a life to live. I didn't know if I would be long for this world, or if someone would come for me, but I had to give an ordinary life a chance. I suggest you do the same. Let it go, Linni. Let Warren go, let the service go. Let it all go, and you might find all manner of wonders opening up for you. It's worked for me."

"What do you mean?"

Fields smiled. "Nothing you'd expect. But nice and easy. A soft place to land."

"Clare?"

"I've been keeping company with the chairman of the local chess society. Very nice gentleman. Little bit older than me, but a good fellow all the same. And I like chess—it's a game of strategy."

"I—I came here to get answers," said Elinor.

Clare Fields reached for Elinor's hands and took them in her own. "Linni, you have as many answers as you need or are likely to get. Don't ask for more. I learned in the Great War that there are many battles to be fought, and one of the biggest is with the veils that come down around us—with all due respect to that American author, you know, Mr. Steinbeck, I call them the 'drapes of wrath.' They both hide the truth and shield us from the danger behind them. I couldn't see through all the veils, and neither can you—nor could Steve Warren, for that matter."

Elinor shrugged, shaking her head. " 'You win some, and you lose some,' to quote a policeman I know."

"And that's what it amounts to." Fields looked at the clock on the kitchen wall. "Oh dear, I'm sure you must be getting on your way, Linni. My gentleman friend is coming to call—we're going for a nice long walk followed by lunch at our local and a bit of cunning thrown in with a game of chess. I'm wallowing in a good dose of ordinary."

The women stood up at the same time, whereupon Fields placed a hand on Elinor's shoulder. "War is the moral failing, Linni, and one way or another we were all caught up in it. So let it go. Do all you can to put it behind you. If you don't, everything that went on in both those wars will destroy you—and you deserve a much better outcome."

"I don't want to feel like prey anymore, and I don't want to be a predator."

"The time has passed when you had to choose."

"A doctor once told me to let time and nature do the work of healing."

"That's all very well, but you've been late to start the clock. Find peace where you can, dear Linni. Get on with living—and find some joy, even if it is with an old codger from the chess society. Ordinary has its moments for people like us." She paused. "And Linni—when you knocked at the door, I wasn't holding any weapon. I won't have a gun in the house. Be rid of them. Put whatever comprises your armory into a sack and throw it in Denbury lake. No one who wants a peaceful, safe life needs a weapon. Only soldiers at war need guns, and we are not at war."

Elinor nodded. "You're right. I'll do it as soon as I get home."

The woman she had first known as Isabelle smiled. "Good. Come and see me again soon." They began to walk toward the door, and as Clare Fields stood on the threshold she smiled. "By the way, talking of doctors, we've a very nice new veterinary surgeon in town—I believe you may have crossed paths with him. He's moving down from London this week. Apparently he's had enough of it all up there and is looking forward to doing ordinary dog, cat and horse work. He's a widower—lost his wife in a motoring accident, and he's not an old codger, not like my chess partner. Anyway, just thought you'd like to know."

Given her parting information, Elinor drove away from Battle wondering how many threads of intelligence were still attached to the fabric of Clare Fields's life, despite her assurance to the contrary. But it was done now; she had no further need to continue the acquaintance and wondered if she would ever imagine a time when the two women could meet without her feeling Clare's hand on her young shoulders while the older woman instructed her in the skills required to become predator instead of prey.

Sophie stood on the doorstep ready to greet Elinor when she arrived at the house in Burwash.

"Good timing, Linni—bang on twelve!"

"I had to make one stop, but I didn't meet any traffic on the way over here."

"Important errand?"

Elinor reached for her friend.

"Oh, Linni, what is it? What's wrong?"

"Soph, will you come to stay with me soon, or may I come here again? I have some things I want to tell you, and not in a hurry. Things a best friend should know."

"And it's about time." Sophie gave a mischievous grin. "Will we get into trouble?"

"Only if you tell."

Sophie laughed. "I might have a few stories myself—perhaps these tales are better out in the open, but just between us. Come on—Jim, Rose and Susie are in the garden with that incorrigible scruffy hound."

Sophie led Elinor through the house, toward French windows opening out into the garden. "Jim's been raking leaves, and as you can see, little Susie is doing a grand job of taking them from the barrow and spreading them again to keep her poor dad in work."

Elinor waved as Sophie called out, "Look who's here to take you home!"

"Hello, Miss White. I just want to finish this job for Mrs. Hunt before we leave."

"Linneeee . . ." Susie threw a handful of leaves into the air and began to run toward Elinor, her arms wide.

Elinor scooped up the child, who wrapped her arms around Elinor's neck.

"Linneee, Linnee, Linnee," Susie squealed time and again.

"I'm so sorry, Miss White," said Rose as she walked toward them. "She picks up things so fast now, sweeping up every new word and saying it over and over again. We have to watch what we say in front of her—especially Jim, you know, if he bangs his finger with the hammer and says something he shouldn't. Susie heard Mrs. Hunt calling you 'Linni' and then again when she was on the phone to you, and now it's in her head, she won't stop. She's been asking all morning if Linni's coming. I'll make sure she knows better."

"It's alright, Rose. Really."

"Linnee—Linnee—Linnee," repeated Susie.

Elinor felt Susie playing with her hair as the little girl sang her name into a tune, the soft, rosy cheeks now pressed against her own. And though Elinor laughed, she lowered her head so her tears were hidden. The child in her arms was unlocking guilt that had imprisoned her for years; Susie Mackie was setting her free.

"Miss White," Jim called out while raking up more leaves, helped by Rose. "Wait until I tell you about Aunt Elsie. We heard some news on the wireless—about a big job pulled off yesterday. I don't know how she could have done it, but I've a funny feeling it was all down to Aunt Elsie."

Elinor smiled. "Well, you said she was a dark horse, Jim. Now then, let's get you all home." She turned to the little girl, who was running her hand across Elinor's damp cheek. "Ready to go home, Susie?"

The following morning Elinor rose early, wakened by shafts of sunlight shining through her bedroom window. Following a cup of strong black coffee made with freshly ground beans, she left the house, having denied herself the habit of first lifting her binoculars to study the woodland at the perimeter of the field beyond the back garden. She had no wish to indulge the need for constant surveillance of her surroundings any longer. Instead, she went straight to the garage and unlocked the door to her armory. Fields was right—the weapons held there served no purpose in a time of peace, and perhaps the intense vigilance she had become used to was indeed to her detriment. It was time to put an end to her wars. Fingering each firearm, she wavered over her hunting rifle. While it might be useful as a deterrent, it was not suited to self-defense—she had only ever fired it to provide food for herself. Should she keep it for that purpose, for bagging a pheasant or rabbit? Perhaps until rationing ended? She shook her head. No, it had to go. It all had to go.

Shoving the entire contents of her gun cupboard into a sack, Elinor tied it with string, heaved it up to balance across her shoulder, and left the garage to set off on the long walk across fields and through woodland until she reached the lake at the heart of Denbury Forest. She did not waver, denying herself any reflection upon the past and how she had taken life—and, to be fair, saved lives—across a span of two world wars. As she stood at the edge of the lake, Elinor White took a deep breath, and with every ounce of strength in her personal arsenal she drew back the sack with both hands and launched it into the water. She remained watching only for as long as it took the ripples to vanish, and as small waves lapped against the toes of her rubber boots, she smiled. The weight of war was beginning to lift from her shoulders. She turned and walked away from the lake, her thoughts amounting to very little as she ran her fingertips across the very fine point of the sharpened pencil she kept in her pocket.

Every war is a war against the child.

—Eglantyne Jebb, 1876–1928

Founder of Save the Children, 1919, Jebb drafted
the Declaration of the Rights of the Child, 1924

ACKNOWLEDGMENTS

The solitary process of writing a novel is at once daunting, creative, exciting, and often a source of great anxiety—and as soon as the early drafts are finished, it's time to take a deep breath, open the door, and let in a trusted advisor or two. First and foremost I am most grateful to my friend Lilly Golden, who offered sound editorial advice and wise professional counsel when she read the initial drafts of *The White Lady*. Those drafts were just the clay on the wheel, so thank you, Lilly, for respectfully directing me to the places where I needed to wield the scalpel with a steady hand or add more clay with care.

My gratitude, as always, to the stellar team at HarperCollins, including editor Sara Nelson, assistant editor Edie Astley, and marketing pros Tom Hopke and Heather Drucker. As someone who formerly worked in sales, I could never let publication day go by without thanking Josh Marwell, president of sales at HarperCollins, and his terrific team.

In the UK, many, many thanks, as always, to the wonderful Susie Dunlop and everyone at Allison and Busby Publishers—I've missed seeing you over these Covid years.

My thanks to artist and craftsman Andrew Davidson, who created the detailed wood engraving gracing the cover of *The White Lady*. Working to a tight deadline while suffering from Covid, Andrew never let us down. Many thanks, too, to the talented creative director, Archie

Ferguson, who pulled it all together, bringing the cover of *The White Lady* alive.

My literary agent and dear friend, Amy Rennert, was behind *The White Lady* from the moment I first shared my idea for a novel inspired by a mysterious woman I knew in childhood, a former wartime "operative" who later in my writerly imagination became Elinor White. Many thanks also to Jennifer Barth, former senior VP and executive editor at HarperCollins, who was equally enthused by the story and gave me the green light. I am ever grateful for the work of Katherine Beitner, formerly director of publicity at HarperCollins and a stalwart supporter of my writing.

This book is dedicated to my friend, writer Barbara Abercrombie, Distinguished Instructor on the UCLA Writers' Program, who died in 2022. I joined Barbara's nonfiction personal essay class some twenty years ago and over time observed Barbara's support for new writers working in any literary form, a gift that could not be underestimated. New and emerging writers are the lifeblood of storytelling, and crucial for publishers, booksellers, libraries, schools, and most importantly for readers, to broaden horizons and an understanding and appreciation of our diverse world while entertaining us through the written word. Barbara knew instinctively that those fresh voices remind us not to be afraid to try something different, and that exploring the limits of our creativity is inspiring far beyond the limits of our work.

ABOUT THE AUTHOR

JACQUELINE WINSPEAR is the author of the *New York Times* bestsellers *A Sunlit Weapon*, *The Consequences of Fear*, *The American Agent*, and *To Die but Once*, as well as thirteen other bestselling Maisie Dobbs novels and *The Care and Management of Lies*, a Dayton Literary Peace Prize finalist. Jacqueline has also published two nonfiction books, *What Would Maisie Do?* and a memoir, *This Time Next Year We'll Be Laughing*. Originally from the United Kingdom, she divides her time between California and the Pacific Northwest.

ORIGINS OF
THE WHITE LADY

Jacqueline Winspear

Where do stories come from? It's a question authors are asked time and again. Readers are curious about the inspiration behind a novel, or a given character, a scene, or perhaps a line of dialogue. What building blocks form the foundation of a story with many threads? If there's an obvious theme, readers are interested to know where it came from.

In truth, there is often more than one single answer. A scene taking place seventy years ago could have been inspired by a conversation the author overheard while doing the grocery shopping last week. A theme could be established with a single line read in a book the author has turned to during research. For my part, I have often thought that the initial work on a novel is rather like starting a fire. The kindling is set into the grate first, then the fuel added, but nothing will happen to start the blaze of story until a spark ignites inspiration, and flames begin to lick into the research, thoughts, feelings—and hopes—of the writer. The kindling for *The White Lady* was laid down during my childhood.

In my memoir, *This Time Next Year We'll Be Laughing* (Soho Press, 2020), I wrote about my newlywed parents leaving postwar London to get away from the bombsites, the lack of opportunity and in particular the scarcity of available housing wrought by war. So much of the housing stock in London had been decimated during those six years of bombing. Families had to move in together where they could, and most newlyweds started married life with one set of in-laws or the other. That was the only option for my parents, and they hated it. Moving to "the country" was their only option, though it was a choice that was tougher to endure than they had anticipated.

When I was a toddler, some six years following their departure from London, my parents decided to return to "the Smoke" (as London was known to her inhabitants) for a variety of reasons, not least the fact that, following an accident in which I was badly scalded, I had almost died because we were living so far from a hospital. But the London sojourn lasted only a matter of months, because my parents had become countryfolk through and through, and when the farmer my mother had worked for as a bookkeeper wanted her back because the accounts for all four farms had descended into a complete mess, my parents jumped at the opportunity to leave. A "tied" cottage went with my mother's farm job—housing tied to the land and work on a farm, as had been the way for centuries. My father secured work on another farm, and my parents were overjoyed on the day they moved away from London and into the small fifteenth century dwelling.

I was only three years of age, but I remember so much about living in that lovely cottage set at the edge of an expansive forest then owned by the "Crown" and now managed by Forestry England. I was fascinated by one neighbor in particular. Every day as I walked down to the farm with my mother (I would sit with my books and toys while my mother worked in the office), we would see a woman walking toward us along the road. She lived in a "grace and favor" home also set at the edge of the forest. Grace and favor homes are given as a sign of gratitude to a person who has served the monarch and the country; they are given leave to live in the property for the rest of their lives, often rent free. The woman always seemed to be "buttoned up" in her raincoat or jacket, and without fail wore a brimmed hat pulled down so you couldn't really see her eyes. Every time our paths crossed, my mother would greet her with a sunny "Good morning"—and in the early months of our life at the cottage, rarely was a reply forthcoming. In time the woman softened, and I remember the day she smiled at us, her eyes meeting mine. As we went on our way, my mother leaned down to me and whispered, "She's one of those women who parachuted into France, during the war." I think Mum realized I was far too young for the story when I asked, "What's a parachute?" But I never forgot the woman, even after we moved from the cottage a year or so later, when my father accepted a better job and we had to move to a house closer to his work.

As I grew up I wanted to know more about the women who worked in clandestine roles during the war, and I had a lot of questions about them. I think it was the idea of secrecy that sparked my curiosity—the fact that you not only had to keep a secret for a long time, but you had to live in secret with nothing but your wits to keep you safe. Even toward the end of WWII, films were already being made about the "spies" who had been sent to Europe to fight Hitler from within occupied territory, so a broad idea—if not the detail—of the work those brave men and women were engaged in was common knowledge. At one point my favorite childhood game—a game that other kids had little interest in playing—was to go down to the disused railway line close to our house and pretend we were spies escaping the German army. We would run through the tunnels and up alongside the verges, clambering through barbed wire fences and hiding behind the old bunkers where, years before, men working on the tracks would stop to rest or spend the night. If a light aircraft flew overhead, it added to the intrigue—they were after us! Everyone soon became bored with that game, except me—my imagination was working overtime!

The lady whose name I never knew became my kindling, along with another story—one that my mother recounted to me when I was a child, having heard it from her brother who had served with the Marines during the war. It was a heartrending story about a child caught in the crosshairs of battle. That story haunted me, and together with the experiences my mother recounted—about evacuation during the war, and later being caught in the bombings—cemented my feelings about how children, especially, suffer during a time of war.

As readers of my books know, the way in which the tentacles of conflict reach far beyond the dates recorded by historians has informed my storytelling. The kindling for *The White Lady* languished in a cold fireplace for a long time, until I began reading more about women working in intelligence and resistance during WWI—the Great War. During the years following WWI, women's roles were often whittled down to "temptress" (think Mata Hari), nurse, and "the girl left behind." Yet throughout Europe in WWI, not a field of endeavor was left untouched by a woman's hand, enabling men to be released for the battlefield. In Britain, the secret services would not have flourished without the work of women—from intelligence operatives to code-breakers, right down to the Girl Guides who ran messages between departments. Yet it was the covert involvement of girls and women in WWI Belgium that fascinated me.

When the Kaiser's army marched into Belgium and occupied the country, any men not already away in uniform were rounded up and taken away. Boys on the cusp of manhood and the elderly who looked as if they had enough fitness to fight were removed to either be slaughtered or sent to work camps. The women were not considered a threat. Oh, how wrong could the enemy be? Bankrolled by the British—who had a base in the Netherlands—La Dame Blanche—the White Lady network—was formed, taking its name from the legend that the fall of the Hohenzollern dynasty in Germany was heralded by a woman wearing white. In mythologies around the world and across millennia, women wearing white have been endowed with supernatural powers and strength.

Though Belgian men were most certainly involved in resistance work, women—from young girls to grandmothers—were recruited for all manner of tasks, including intelligence gathering, sabotage and even assassination. Their bravery knew no bounds. As I read more about La Dame Blanche (and interested readers might start with *Female Intelligence: Women and Intelligence in the First World War* by Dr. Tammy Proctor, professor of history at Utah State University), I kept wondering how it might feel to have been a girl in her early teens who was called upon to serve her country—and then approached again in womanhood to join the Belgian resistance as war ravaged Europe in WWII.

With my series featuring psychologist-investigator Maisie Dobbs, which comprises seventeen novels thus far, I have created the story arc of a woman from her pre–WWI girlhood, through the Great War, the Depression, the Spanish Civil War, and now to the Second World War. With the series, I wanted to explore how it might be for each of the cast of characters to live through a defining period of the twentieth century, anchoring them in the big and small events of their day. When I started thinking about *The White Lady*, I knew that within one novel I wanted to do something similar, and asked myself, "How would it be if a woman had been required to kill in two wars? And how would it be if I followed her journey from adolescence to womanhood, and then set her down amid the world of organized crime in postwar London?"

One of the worst winters on record heralded the start of 1947. Wartime organized crime was still rocketing, though the kingpins were finding it harder to make the same level of big money once Allied soldiers returned home. But they were helped by the fact that many guns came back to Britain with returning troops, and the American military, in particular, left plenty behind when their men sailed back to the USA. At the same time, homelessness was rife in Britain's cities, and in London the new prefab housing being constructed in a hurry to accommodate a war-weary citizenry would never meet demand. Most people agreed that postwar rationing, indeed postwar life on so many levels, was worse than when the bombs were dropping.

In her "grace and favor" home, Elinor White finds a fragile calm in the countryside, more than anything hoping to break free from her past. But she puts any chance of peace on the line when she is drawn into the brutal underworld her neighbors—a young couple, Jim and Rose Mackie, and their daughter, Susie—have left London to escape.

There is another part to this author's story. There was a point when I realized that to craft a story about a woman familiar with the use of firearms, I should probably know what it's like to hold a gun. It's something I'd never done before and will never do again. My first "lesson" was simply in handling the weapon safely—and it was a crucial lesson, because I realized how easy it would be to make a devastating error if it were a real handgun (and not one used with blanks for recreational target practice). The way people around me ducked when I held the weapon told me I would never be proficient in the handling of a gun. I was supposed to have a second lesson where I actually fired the handgun, just to feel what it was like—but for me one lesson was more than enough! Just fifteen minutes on the basic handling skills was more pressure than my emotions could stand. Handing back the gun with a sigh of relief, I decided my imagination had already brought me a long way on my journey as a storyteller—it would have to do the rest.